"Life's but a walking shadow, a poor player,
That struts and frets his hour upon the stage,
And then is heard no more."
WILLIAM SHAKESPEARE
Macbeth Act 5 scene 5

In the grimy litter-covered street, the skinny body of a young male, or what is left of him, lies sprawled on his back across the tarmac between two industrial-sized refuse bins, attracting a horde of hungry seagulls and crows; the skull has been crushed to a pulp and a fox has had a go at one of the arms. Soon, the authorities will turn up, alerted eventually by someone in the high-rise who won't give a name. The corpse will be scrutinised by police and then inserted into a black nylon bag, zipped up, labelled, and removed in an ambulance to the city's mortuary.

Two days later and a few miles away across the city, another body, this one a bloated older male who has lived a longer, more epicurean existence than the former corpse, is sprawled across the finest of Egyptian cotton sheets in a luxury hotel bedroom, inert and lifeless. The thick flesh is beginning to solidify and take on a yellow waxen hue.

Two deaths. Two days between them. Worlds apart.

THE DEADLY SHADOWS

Gordon Smart

RED DRAGON BOOKS

ISBN; 978-1-7391036-2-0

Second Publish in 2022 by Red Dragon Publishing LTD

1

Detective Inspector Shazia Khan was trying to concentrate on reading the post-mortem report on Sammy Scobie which had been emailed to her, but it was difficult with all the commotion that was going on both inside and outside her head. DCI Bill Cooper had just come into the office and, as it was his birthday, everyone, except Shazia, had gathered around him. He looked slightly uncomfortable away from the power base of his private office but was standing with a wide grin in the kitchen area, clearly revelling in the attention, particularly from some of the younger female officers whom he appeared only too eager to closely hug. She had always thought of him as slightly creepy and couldn't bear to be any longer in his company than was strictly necessary. The sooner she got through what had to be done today the sooner she would be able to get away, maybe not arriving home too late as was usually the case, and able to spend some precious time with her daughter.

The commotion inside her head was just as distracting. What went through someone's head when they were killing someone, she wondered? How did they justify it to themselves? Or did they not need to? Was it often just an action bred from the flight or fight instinct inside every human? But some killings were more calculated, involving planning and deception. She thought back to her university days, studying psychology and how she had once considered a postgraduate course in the subject, maybe going on to do a PhD. She could now have become a professor delivering a lecture on sociopaths instead of trying to find them. Her mind slipped down a rabbit warren following an entirely different career path in which she saw herself writing books and flying to overseas conferences to present papers on the criminal mind. Which would have been more satisfying? That or what she was doing now? She dismissed the reverie and forced herself to concentrate on what she was supposed to be reading.

Shazia was forty-five years old, divorced, and living in Lenzie on the outskirts of Glasgow with her sixteen-year-old daughter, Yasmeen, and her elderly parents. She was five foot four and, she liked to think, still reasonably attractive with dark shoulder-length hair. She was dressed in her customary dark trouser suit and crisp white blouse. She had worked in Glasgow CID all her career, was highly respected for her efficiency, but was also regarded as being rather unemotional, many of her male colleagues believing she lacked warmth. Shazia was aware of this attitude as one of her team, DC McLaughlin, had told her about it and it annoyed her. If only they knew what my emotions were really like, she thought. It's just that I don't bring them into the office. Unlike some of the men. She put it all down to sexism.

Shazia didn't think that she was being anti-social by not engaging in small talk with the others, it was just that work had to be done and she tried to shut out the noise of the chatter which bounced off the walls of this large open-plan office and focus on what she was reading. But she was finding that she had to constantly read and re-read the same sentences. The crime scene report which she had read the previous day had stated that there had been no sign of any mobile phone or laptop, but Forensics had managed to lift some fingerprints from inside the flat and these would be analysed to see if they produced a match with anyone on record.

She was halfway through the report when her phone rang; another body had been found, this time in a bedroom in the Moray Hotel in the city centre. She grabbed the keys to her black VW Golf and shouted to DS Joseph Boateng to come with her. He was on his way back to his desk with a coffee and a piece of cake. He started to ask what it was about but she was already out of the office and heading downstairs. He put down the coffee, stuffed the cake in his mouth, grabbed his jacket and took off in pursuit.

Outside, the sky was uniformly grey with sleet falling heavily. 'I can't believe I moved up here to this godforsaken place where the sun never shines. What fuckin' shitty weather. What's all this about anyway, ma'am?' asked Joseph, now seated in the passenger seat as Shazia accelerated into the busy traffic. The car's wipers batted to and fro furiously as sleet smothered the windscreen with icy sludge.

'A body in a hotel room. One of those boutique hotels in the city centre, apparently, the Moray. Don't know much more but the uniforms who attended reckon it doesn't look like natural causes.'

'Since when have uniform become pathologists?'

'Indeed. That's what I said when I got the call. It was a PC I know, young Ahmed Mahood, friend of the family. Knew I'd be interested. He just said it looked suspicious. And there was you thinking all you had to deal with was finding out who was responsible for throwing Sammy Scobie off his veranda? We are short-staffed as it is and all the other CID teams are busy with the three other murders, a bank robbery and the various shootings that have happened in the past few weeks, so I am afraid that we are *it* with both of these cases. Besides, it sounds interesting. A luxury hotel murder. How many of them do we get in a year? Hope you weren't planning to take leave any time soon?'

He grinned. 'Actually, I was going to speak to you about that, ma'am.'

Shazia gave Joseph a look that told him not to go any further.

'On the other hand, why would I want to be anywhere else when my job is so exciting?' He laughed and stared out of the window at the passing sights.

'That's more like it, Sergeant. Sorry you didn't get to enjoy the birthday cake!'

'I noticed you weren't congratulating him. I take it you didn't give him a card?'

'Put it this way. I wouldn't be first in line to give him the Heimlich Manoeuvre if he choked on his bloody cake.'

'Not a big fan of our DCI then?'

'What gives you that impression? Anyway, enough about him, how's the new house? Settled in? Enjoying living in the South Side? Or should I say, the new West End?'

'Well, that's what the estate agents call it. Yeah, it's fine.'

'Anyway, getting back to Sammy, the initial toxicology report shows that that he had high levels of cocaine and cannabis in his bloodstream. It also looked like he had definitely been having a struggle with someone at some point. He landed on his back but there were bruises on his face that looked like they could have come from punches. Don't suppose we've got any leads on who might have done the punching?'

'Well, the word on the street, or rather the word from the drug squad, is that our Sammy did quite a bit of business in drugs. As I'm new to the territory I thought you might want to point me in the right direction?'

'Maybe. First, tell me everything you know about him.'

Joseph Boateng, a new addition to Shazia's team, was thirty-five and six-foot-two in his stockinged soles, with short dark hair. He had been brought up on a south London estate where young men sometimes joined a gang and carried a knife as a survival strategy but Joseph had chosen a different path. His mother, whose husband had abandoned her shortly after Joseph was born, had encouraged him to work hard at school and he had intended to leave school to study history at university. He had become interested in history after he read a book about the slave trade, how immoral entrepreneurs used black lives as a commodity to make themselves profits and grow rich. For him, it represented one of the greatest crimes ever committed. But, instead, just after his eighteenth birthday he chose to apply to enter the police force. A policeman had visited his school when he was in the sixth form and given a careers talk about how the Met needed more diversity in its ranks in order to engage with local youth. He said that if they saw more black officers on the streets then maybe, just maybe, they would see that those representing law and order weren't just the white oppressors. He thought it was a ridiculously naïve idea to see himself as a role model, but the decision made him feel as if he was doing something more worthwhile than going to a university to immerse himself in dusty tomes. Young people in his community were being exploited by a new type of entrepreneur with no morals: gangsters and drug lords who consumed young lives as collateral in distributing their illegal wares around the capital and the rest of the country. He felt an urgent need to do something meaningful with his life to help young men like himself avoid that fate. At least, that was the theory. It didn't quite work out like that.

He had been going out with Angie since they were at school and they married in their mid-twenties. Even though she was now a nurse and he had a steady job, it seemed impossible to think that they could afford to buy anywhere to live in London, such were the astronomical prices for even the tiniest of flats, so they paid exorbitant rent for a one-bedroom flat in Croydon instead. Joseph had moved into CID by the time he was thirty but the job wasn't getting any easier. No matter what they did, violent crime in the capital escalated until it had become like a war zone. It didn't help that they were severely under-resourced due to government cuts. It was like trying to stop a sinking ship by baling out water with a teacup. Angie said it was the same in the NHS in London. Increasingly he and Angie felt that they needed a move out of London and he started to look for other posts. That led him to apply for a Detective Sergeant vacancy in Police Scotland's Glasgow HQ. Shazia's regular DCs, Michael McLaughlin and Joan Mitchell, had both applied for the post and Shazia had recommended each of them as highly suitable but the appointment was out of her hands. Joseph had evidently impressed the Detective Superintendent and Joseph and his wife bought a flat in Shawlands. Angie secured a post at the nearby Queen Elizabeth University Hospital.

Shazia and Joseph had visited the high-rise in Parkhill in the early hours of Sunday morning as soon as she had got the call. Outside, in the street, a team of forensic officers in white suits were already there, photographing the corpse and the surroundings, while uniformed officers tried to keep the curious locals from getting too close and contaminating the scene. The body was young and male, dressed in skinny black jeans, a black T-shirt and trainers. He was face down but Shazia could see the top of his head lying in a pool of blood which had spread out around him in a crimson puddle.

'Any CCTV working round here?' Shazia had asked one of the two uniformed officers standing at the entrance to the building.

'I'm afraid not ma'am. Out of order.' He shrugged his shoulders as if to say, what do you expect in a place like this?

'What floor did he fall from?' she asked.

'Eighteen, ma'am.'

Inside, the building smelled of stale vomit and urine and the walls were covered in graffiti, mostly gang-related.

There were two lifts, but only one was working. The odour inside the lift was even worse and Shazia held her breath for as long as she could as it made its slow, rattling ascent to the floor, although she consoled herself with the thought that at least one lift was working and they hadn't had to take the stairs. She looked at Joseph and saw that he was doing the same, even pinching his nose. He gave her a smile with clenched lips, but neither of them could hold their breath long enough to reach the floor and they exchanged grimaces until with great relief the lift doors opened and they stepped out onto the landing.

One of the flats had a line of blue and white tape tied across the front door with two bored-looking constables standing in front. 'Was it the pair of you who entered the flat?' asked Shazia?

'Yes ma'am,' said one of the officers. Shazia noticed that the front door had been forced open, the wood on the inside of the door-frame splintered.

'And was the door in this state or was that you?' she asked with a slight grin.

They laughed. 'No, ma'am,' said the other officer. 'We were first on the scene after the incident was called in and stayed by the body until another couple of officers arrived, then we came up here. It was just like this. All we did was peek inside to see if there was anyone there but it was empty. The SOCOs are in there now.'

'Who does the flat belong to?

'Sammy Scobie, ma'am. A neighbour has positively ID'd him as the body on the ground outside.'

The officers stood aside as they ducked under the tape, slipping latex gloves on their hands. The scenes of crime officers in their white suits were photographing and dusting everywhere. The place was an absolute tip. It could have been turned upside down by someone looking for money or drugs. Or it could have just been made to look like that, Shazia thought to herself. Then again, maybe this was just how he lived. Some drug paraphernalia lay scattered around a coffee table in the middle of the living room: torn up packets of cigarette papers, bits of tin foil and a few discarded small sealable plastic bags with traces of white powder stuck to the insides.

Was this the flat of a dealer or just a user, she thought? The place was sparsely furnished: a hi-fi system comprising a turntable, CD player, amp and speakers; a stack of vinyl LPs and CDs; a battered-looking acoustic guitar; a coffee table and two black leather sofas, both well-worn, scuffed and torn in places. The walls throughout had once been painted white but were now stained yellow; paint and plaster were peeling off in places and there were several large damp patches in the kitchen; the black mould on the bathroom's walls crawled over the ceiling like an invading army acquiring territory. Shazia didn't even want to look at the toilet. The place definitely wasn't viewing-ready for any prospective new tenants.

In the bedroom, a couple of posters were stuck to the walls with blue-tack: one was a black and white moody shot of James Dean and the other a team poster of Glasgow Rangers FC. There was a double bed and a chest of drawers, and a wardrobe with a meagre selection of clothes. If Scobie did make much money dealing, then he didn't have a lot to show for it, Shazia reflected. Maybe all of his earnings, whatever, they were, went up in smoke or up his nose? At the bottom of one of the drawers, under a pile of T-shirts she found a scrap of paper. It had a mobile number on it. She placed it carefully in a plastic bag and stuck it in her pocket.

The whole place stank and she felt sick. Maybe it was the pile of dirty clothes on the bedroom floor, she thought. Or the overflowing rubbish bin in the kitchen. Or the dampness everywhere. Or was it a combination of all three? There was no sign of a wallet or any money. So, it could be a robbery gone wrong, then, she thought. Gone badly wrong for the resident of the flat. Maybe whoever came in here was just after whatever stash of dope or money he had lying about but why throw him off the balcony? They took what they could carry, weren't interested in his guitar or hi-fi. Another part of her brain told her that this was exactly what she was supposed to think. Unless the unfortunate inhabitant had locked himself out, then in a fit of frustration and poverty hurled himself earthwards, forgetting to write a suicide note? Unlikely.

The door to the veranda was open and she stepped out, glad to get some fresh air into her lungs. She never understood the architectural madness which had insisted on having verandas on tower blocks in Glasgow. The south of France, yes, but Parkhill most definitely wasn't the Mediterranean. As if to emphasise the point, a bitterly cold wind blasted in her face and she shivered, partly from the cold and partly from the view. She had never liked heights. Here she was hundreds of feet up in the sky. A sense of vertigo hit her and she wondered if some mysterious force might pull her over the side, as it had Sammy. She steadied herself and took a deep breath.

'Are you alright?' enquired Joseph behind her.

She nodded at him and walked over to the edge and looked down. Scobie had either fallen or, more likely, was thrown, from here, eighteen storeys above street level. It was still dark but the ground was illuminated by streetlights. The people and cars below looked like miniature replicas, like figures in a model town she had visited somewhere on holiday with her parents when she had been a little girl. Where had that been? Torquay? Somewhere near there. Babbecombe, that was it. She was amazed that she could remember the name of the place. There had been models of houses, streets, all sorts of buildings. An entire town. A bit like Legoland in Windsor where she had once taken Yasmeen when she was small. But it was a little town that functioned. Without crime. Without people being hurled, or hurling themselves, off tower blocks. She wished, for an instant, that she was a tiny person who lived there.

2

'Bloody hell,' Shazia shouted as she swerved, going through a red light, narrowly avoiding a taxi driver who either didn't hear or see the siren and flashing blue lights behind the grille of the Golf, or chose to ignore them. Joseph had closed his eyes at that point and tensed himself ready for impact with the airbag in the collision, but when he opened them again, they had passed the obstacle and were heading onto the M74 motorway.

'Well?' said Shazia.

'Well, what?'

'Sammy!'

'Oh right, yes, well he is - or rather he was –a drug dealer in the scheme as we guessed. Twenty-eight years of age. Numerous convictions for drugs and motor theft. Last conviction was three years ago – eighteen months for possession of heroin with intent to supply. Bit of a hard upbringing, as is usually the case. Mother in and out of psychiatric hospitals. Took her own life. Sammy was taken into care early on, went through a succession of care homes and failed foster homes. His school history is a list of places he was excluded from, first on a temporary basis, then more permanently. That is, when he attended school in the first place. Mostly, he truanted. First picked up for shoplifting at twelve, then it's a list of convictions as long as your arm: housebreaking at fourteen, then holding up a shopkeeper with a knife when he was fifteen. He was sent to a Young Offender Institution then for two years which probably taught him more skills as, when he came out, he started stealing cars.'

'Sounds a familiar story,' said Shazia. 'Any thoughts on what brought about his sudden demise?'

'I guess he must have made some enemies. Unless he decided he had had enough of this cruel world and decided to top himself, which I wouldn't rule out. For all we know, that front door of his could have been like that for days, weeks. He might have locked himself out and broken in himself. It might not have been a break-in. On the other hand, would you just leave it open?'

'If you are going to top yourself, I don't suppose it matters if anyone steals your stuff after you're gone,' Shazia said.

'No. I suppose he could have ruffled a few feathers along the line and his punishment was going for a dive into the air. Maybe he was ripping off his supplier, who knows?'

Shazia nodded. 'He looked as if he had been given a good working over. Amongst my emails this morning was the name of who the mobile number belongs to that I found in Sammy's flat.'

'Yeah? Who is it?'

'Murray.'

'Murray? Paul Murray? I read about the case when I was down south. Abduction and rape. I'm aware that my predecessor, DS Armstrong, was providing Murray with inside information. Both behind bars now, aren't they?'

'Enough said about my former sergeant the better! But Paul Murray is still probably pulling the strings from inside Barlinnie, no doubt on an illegal mobile phone. Impossible to stop that kind of thing and drugs seem more plentiful inside than outside by all accounts. Instead of bringing stuff in through the traditional manner, that is up someone's jacksy, they are now using drones – isn't technology wonderful! But no, it's not Paul Murray, it's Greg, his younger brother. He has taken over the reins of the family business. He's expanding the empire, too, since Jim Kelly has decided to pack it in. I believe Kelly's thinking of heading for the Costa del Crime soon to get away from it all. He's probably got more friends out there than in Glasgow these days. Safer for him too to be out of the way. I notice that his house is up for sale, the High Chaparral they call it.

Would you buy it? I wouldn't. Nice view of Barlinnie and the M8 if you like that kind of thing but that place must have so many ghosts! And possibly a few bodies buried underneath the patio. Anyway, the Murray family are now free to spread their wings all over the city and it's likely it's their feathers that got ruffled, I'd say.'

Joseph was amazed at how fast and for how long Shazia could speak when she was on a roll. Eventually he got a chance to say something. 'So, Greg Murray is the man who is running the drugs scene in Glasgow then?'

'Well, on the north side of the city anyway, both east and west now. The problem with the Murray brothers has been that they have this reputation as untouchables. At first it was because they had all the right people in their pockets: councillors, local government officers, even some of those high up in our service, supposedly. Your predecessor was in Murray's pocket, of course, as you know. We only managed to get Paul Murray put away because he was careless and we finally got him for rape and bribing a policeman. The Murrays have the best accountants and a sharp lawyer to advise them on how to remain in the shadows, keep their money out of sight, and always keep a distance from those down the pecking order in the organisation who do the actual dirty work. If anyone gets caught it is always one of their underlings and they know to keep their mouths shut. And they don't stand still when it comes to moving their money around. As soon as one operation becomes suspicious, they shut it down and move on. Plus, they have various legitimate fronts. Greg Murray's are his fleet of taxis, Kelvin Cars, as well as several pubs and nightclubs.'

Joseph nodded. 'I was reading in the paper about some gangster in Aberdeen. His latest wheeze was to open a chain of so-called "Doggy Day-care" centres. Once it became obvious that the tanning salons were really more about laundering banknotes than giving the inhabitants of Aberdeen a tan, he apparently moved into the pet-care business. Guess he had to do something with the proceeds of his income from girls and drugs somewhere for it to look above board to the taxman. Though how do you explain a thousand pooches a week passing through your establishment without attracting suspicion? He didn't. He just got busted.'

Shazia said, 'Brace yourself, Sergeant I'm going through another set of red lights.'

Joseph closed his eyes and didn't open them until he felt they were clear of the junction. 'In Lewisham the drug barons ran their cash through the betting machines in the bookies, with dealers pumping money into electronic roulette games, putting £20 on red, £20 on black and £2 on zero. At odds of two to one, whether the ball lands on red or black, the punter only loses £2. If it lands on zero, he makes £72. So, the bookies maybe make about five or ten percent of what is being gambled. It's a small price to pay to convert illicit earnings into legal ones. Plus, the dealer who has made his money from selling drugs then has a receipt from the bookies for his apparent gambling winnings in case we stop and search him. Who says criminals are daft?'

'They do that here too. Car washes, nail bars, tanning salons, all sorts of fronts. It's a moveable feast. As soon as one thing gets shut down something else opens up. The difficulty is tying the businesses back to the gangsters who run them.'

'What's he like?' asked Joseph who was unfamiliar with the finer details of the Glasgow criminal fraternities' family trees.

'Greg Murray? Nutcase of the first order. Makes Paul look like Mary Poppins. Paul at least had a brain. He worked on manipulating people, threatening them with words. He got his thugs to carry out the nasty business. Greg likes to get down and dirty himself, allegedly with a baseball bat, or so I've heard. Unlike Paul, in his early days, he was caught and sent down a few times. But, now that he is in charge, he's learning to keep himself invisible. '

'Actually, I thought Mary Poppins was kind of scary.'

'Wait till you meet Greg. In fact, why don't you have a chat with him as soon as possible? Ask him why Sammy had his mobile number and if he knows anything about what happened to him? That will rattle his cage. See if he recalls turning Sammy into a human cannonball. I wouldn't put any money on a confession but it might just shake him up a bit. Here we are then.' She swerved the car suddenly and parked outside the hotel.

They had taken the M74 across the South Side, then joined the M8 and crossed over the Clyde via the Kingston Bridge to Charing Cross and headed along Argyle Street looking, futilely, for a place to park. The sleet had got heavier making it hard to see out of the windscreen even though the wipers batted from side to side as fast as they could, like tennis players engaged in a furious rally. In the end Shazia simply parked on the double yellow immediately outside the hotel's main entrance on Argyle Street, scribbling a note on a piece of paper identifying her unmarked car as 'On Police Business' and shoving it on top of the dashboard; though she knew from experience that this didn't guarantee she wouldn't be given a ticket by some over-zealous, disgruntled or myopic traffic warden. In any case, it would soon be invisible beneath the sleet covering the car.

The hotel was a handsome four-storey Victorian edifice built from red sandstone in the traditional Glasgow architectural style of the period with an ornate doorway decorated by lions' heads on either side. They entered through the revolving door and introduced themselves to the receptionist. The manager appeared a few minutes later, looking flustered and slightly agitated and, in a strong Dutch accent, introduced himself as Jan Van Dijk, saying how upsetting for everyone this was. He was in his forties, good-looking, tall, with blonde hair which was swept back and gelled. 'I just went into shock when I arrived here this morning and was told the news. This is awful for the hotel.'

'And for the victim's family,' said Shazia.'

'Yes, of course.' His expression was very serious.

'What is the victim's name?' Shazia asked him as he led them to the elevator.

'Charles Henderson,' said Van Dijk, looking at her meaningfully. Shazia recognised the name and it did seem familiar, but she couldn't quite place where she knew it from so simply nodded. 'He checked in just after five p.m. yesterday and was due to check out this morning. He had requested an alarm phone call at seven-thirty today but didn't answer it so Lenna, that's the assistant manager, asked Andreea, that's one of the chambermaids, to knock on his door. She knocked and there was no reply, so she went in and found him. He had a pillow over his face and wasn't responding. She came running down to reception. Lenna then went up to see what had happened and then phoned the emergency services.'

'We'll need to ask Lenna and the chambermaid to volunteer fingerprints so we can eliminate them both and we'll take formal statements from them both. I'd like to have a look at the body first.'

'Of course.'

'What CCTV do you have in operation here?'

'There are two cameras overlooking the car park at the rear and one here in the foyer which oversees reception and the entrance area, but we like our guests to enjoy a certain amount of privacy. This is a rather small but exclusive hotel, Inspector, and our guests prefer it to be discreet.'

Shazia looked at the camera. 'So, would you say that you put privacy over and above security?'

Van Dijk looked aghast at her comment. 'Certainly not! We have never had anything like this happen before. I can assure you that we take hotel security extremely seriously.'

Shazia ignored the comment. 'Tell me about ways in and out of the building.'

'As well as the front entrance, there are three emergency exits, at the rear out into the car park. There's also a service door near the kitchen. They are all alarmed of course, as are the windows on the ground floor. The front entrance is locked at midnight. Any guests who return later can ring and the night porter will admit them.'

'The stairs run down from the floors to the back of the hotel?'

'Yes. To the ground floor where there is a door leading out to the foyer beside the lift and a corridor running along the back where the emergency exits are.'

'OK. We'll need copies of all the CCTV footage from the last forty-eight hours. Was the victim staying here alone?'

'He certainly booked the room on his own, no one else was checked in with him, and he was alone when he was found this morning.'

'That's not to say he didn't invite any company at some point, is it?' asked Joseph, raising his eyebrows suggestively.

Van Dijk shrugged his shoulders. 'We are a very respectable hotel but if a guest wishes to invite company to his room we would not normally intervene. However, our staff are vigilant.'

'How many guests did you have staying here last night?' asked Shazia.

'There are twenty bedrooms in total: ten on the second floor and ten on the third floor. Fifteen were occupied last night, with a total of twenty-four guests, and there were five rooms vacant.'

'We'll speak to all of the guests. Make sure no one checks out.'

'I've already done that. As soon as Lenna phoned, we were told to do that. Some of the guests are very unhappy about that, Inspector. Could you speak to them please?'

'They will just have to wait. Who was working here during the night? You mentioned a night porter.'

'Yes, that is Callum Grant. He finished his shift at seven this morning but when I found out what had happened, I phoned him and asked him to come back in. He is now downstairs in my office.'

'That was very helpful, thanks. We will speak to him. Who else was working last night?'

'Anna was on reception until midnight, then Callum was on his own from then until Lenna started at six. The kitchen staff came in just after that and I came in at eight to be told there was a dead body in one of the rooms.'

'We'll need to speak to all the staff who were on duty yesterday and last night.'

'Yes, of course. I will phone them and ask them to come in right away.'

'OK. We'll see the body now then we'll speak to Callum.'

'Of course. Please follow me.'

They took the lift to the top floor and walked along the corridor. As they passed the rooms, some guests were hanging around the corridor and Shazia could see other guests waiting inside with bags packed and exasperated expressions. One tall man who looked very unhappy came out to speak to her. 'Can you tell me how much longer we have to wait here? I have to catch a plane to London.'

Shazia assessed him. He looked like a typical businessman from his appearance: an expensive suit, striped shirt and tie. Probably used to getting his own way, she thought. 'I'm afraid you will need to be patient, sir. This may take a while.' She turned away from him, hearing him utter several expletives as he slammed his bedroom door.

Two uniformed officers, both male, and a couple of paramedics, a male and a female, were standing outside the bedroom, chatting and laughing. Evidently one of the paramedics had just reached the punchline of a joke. As soon as they all saw Shazia and Joseph headed their way the laughter ceased and they assumed sober expressions. 'Morning, Inspector', said one of the constables.'

'Thanks for the call, PC Mahood. You haven't touched anything, have you?'

'No ma'am,' said Mahood. 'We had a look as soon as we got here but everything is exactly as it was. When I called it in as suspicious, I was told Forensics would be sent out. A SOCO team got here a while ago and are still in there now.'

Shazia looked at the paramedics. 'What state was the victim in when you found him?'

'I had to take the pillow from his face to see if he was breathing, then I checked the body for a pulse,' said the female paramedic, waving her hands like jazz hands and smiling to show blue latex gloves. She shook her head. 'There was nothing we could do.'

Shazia put on a similar pair of gloves and examined the bedroom door of the victim.

A SOCO came over to speak to her. 'The lock isn't broken, ma'am. No sign of it being forced. You can come in, we're more or less finished.'

Shazia turned to the hotel manager. 'Was the door fully closed and locked when the chambermaid entered the room?'

'Yes,' said Van Dijk. 'She said it was, anyway. She didn't suspect anything, that's why she got such a shock when she found him.'

'Would you know if there were any master keys missing?' Shazia asked.

'I'll be able to check at reception.'

Several masked, white-suited figures moved around the room, examining the scene and taking photographs, taking no notice of Shazia and Joseph. In the centre of the room was an enormous bed. Shazia stood and stared at the corpse lying on it. The body was naked apart from a pair of white boxer shorts. The duvet lay on the floor in a crumpled heap as if thrown off in the midst of a struggle. The victim's eyes, bulging like snooker balls, stared vacantly at the ceiling, and his mouth lay agape as if he was about to say something. He looked to be in his late fifties or so, though it was difficult to tell; in his present state he could easily be a decade older. Certainly not younger. The little hair that remained on his head was grey and thin, his face flabby and the torso large and overweight, the stomach bloated. Shazia imagined what had been going through the victim's head in those last few seconds of life as he flailed out at his attacker. Had he recognised who it was? Did he know why they were doing this?

Her eyes swept around the room. On the far side there was a window facing out onto Argyle Street. She went over and looked down at the street below. People were going about the ordinary business of life unaware of the gruesome scene of death up above them. She turned and looked at the room. On one wall there was a widescreen plasma TV above a dressing table on which she noticed the room's plastic keycard. There was a glass-topped coffee table with some glossy magazines, an empty wine bottle, a couple of wine glasses and an open laptop. On either side of the table sat a couple of matching leather armchairs. There was also a wardrobe with mirrored doors. The bathroom looked pristine. She had spotted a washbag with his shaving gear and toiletries.

One of the SOCOs came over to them holding up a small bag containing a used condom. 'We found this in the bin, ma'am. It'll get analysed for DNA. The pathologist is on the way.'

'So, he had company after all,' Shazia said. 'OK, so we've got a corpse, lying flat out in his bed who has had sex. Could it have been some sort of sex game gone wrong? Partial asphyxiation to heighten the orgasm? I've heard about that.'

Joseph grinned. 'Your knowledge astounds me, Inspector.'

'Wonder who his partner was? Reminds me of that scene in Psycho. Hotel murder. In the film it was the manager dressed up as his dead mother.'

'Except he's not in the shower,' said Joseph. 'But if that's the case, it narrows it down to any mother-fixated psychopaths who like to cross-dress that might have been staying in the hotel. I'll ask the manager for a list. Unless it was him of course, doing a Norman Bates impression.'

'We should check his office for old lady outfits. Ever since watching that film I've never liked the thought of being alone in a hotel room and taking a shower. OK, imagine this scene. The victim has already had penetrative sex, hence the condom. Then afterwards he's got partially dressed, then he's attacked. Why? By someone who gets off on murdering the person they have just had sex with?'

'Isn't that a bit Basic Instinct? Though I don't see any ice picks,' asked Joseph.

'I like your film knowledge, Sergeant. Maybe they were using cocaine too? Perhaps the sex wasn't good for her?

'Or him.'

'Indeed. We'll see what Forensics pick up.'

Shazia looked at the clothes that lay scattered around the room, some on the floor, others draped over chairs: suit trousers and jacket, a white shirt, a pair of black socks, and a pair of black brogues. They looked as if they had been hurriedly removed and unceremoniously discarded. A white hotel robe was slung over an armchair. On the bedside table she found a wallet and a mobile. She flicked open the wallet with a pen and her gloved fingertips, and looked at its contents. There were some credit and debit cards, all with C Henderson printed on them; there was also a driving licence with the name Charles Henderson, a return train ticket to Edinburgh and a hundred and sixty-five pounds in notes. One thing seemed clear: whatever the motive was for the killing, it wasn't robbery.

There was also a laptop bag on a chair and a black leather briefcase on the floor. Inside the briefcase were several folders, a notepad and a diary. She flicked through it: appointments and meetings were noted. For Monday 6th February it mentioned *Education Committee 10 am* then *Debating Chamber 2pm* and the *Moray Hotel 5pm.* For the following day, today, the entry was just *CoC.* There was nothing noted for the previous weekend. She looked back at the weeks before; it was all committee meetings and work-related items but for the 18th January she noticed something: *CF 7.30. The Balmoral.*

Inside the wardrobe, a coat had been hung on a hanger, along with a clean white shirt and a tie. Clean boxers and socks were neatly folded sitting on a shelf. There was a bag beside the wardrobe, a small black wheelie suitcase. It was empty. He'd been travelling light, just an overnight bag, she thought. Then she noticed something lying on the floor. It looked like an ID badge on a lanyard. It must have fallen out of the bag when he'd unpacked. She picked it up. It was a Holyrood Parliament ID badge in the name of Charles Henderson, Member of the Scottish Parliament. 'Shit. He's an MSP,' said Shazia.

'Fuck!' said Joseph, turning around and looking at the badge. 'We'll have Special Branch all over this.'

Shazia went out to the corridor and approached Van Dijk who was talking on his mobile. He finished the call abruptly. 'I've seen enough in here for the time being, take me on a tour of the building,' she said.

She followed him down the stairs, along the second floor, identical to the floor above then to the first floor.

A SOCO came along the corridor in their direction. 'I think you will want to see something in here, ma'am,' he said when he saw them. He took them back along to the end of the corridor and into a small meeting room. There was a round table in the middle of the room and half a dozen chairs around it. On the right-hand side of the room a window looked out to the side of the building, where there was a high wall about a metre away, dividing a lane from the hotel. It was an old-fashioned sash window, but with the glass divided into smaller panes, like most of the windows in the hotel, and the glass on one of the panes had been smashed, with broken glass littering the thick carpet. 'Looks like someone broke it and unlocked the window,' said the SOCO. 'We've been looking around the hotel for a point of entry. The windows on the ground floor are all alarmed but the rest of the hotel isn't. Whoever came in could have leapt onto the ledge from that wall. I can't see any footprints on the floor but he probably removed his shoes going in and out or cleaned up after himself. We used to be able to trace burglars from their shoe prints but they're getting wise to that. There might have been some on the window ledge but they would have been obliterated in this damn sleet.'

'Is this room normally locked?' asked Shazia, looking at Van Dijk.

He shook his head. 'No.'

'What rooms are on this floor?'

'There are no bedrooms on this floor. It's all meeting rooms. There's a larger room used for functions and conferences. On the ground floor there is a health suite with a Jacuzzi and beauty treatment rooms. Apart from that there is the restaurant of course as well as the kitchen.'

'OK,' said Shazia. 'We'll get the place thoroughly searched and take statements from the guests. I want to have a look around the ground floor then I think we'll speak to the night porter.'

After they had visited the ground floor, which appeared undisturbed with no signs of a break-in, they followed Van Dijk to the front of the building, passing behind reception and into an office full of filing cabinets, desks and computers. At the back of the room, a door led into the manager's office where a small man was seated in a chair, whom the manager introduced as Callum Grant, the night porter. As he looked at her, Shazia was aware of a strange look in the man's eyes, which she put down to the shocking circumstances and possibly lack of sleep.

'Callum, these officers want to speak to you. I'll leave you to it, Inspector.'

Shazia introduced herself and Joseph. Callum Grant was a small bald-headed man in his fifties with a goatee beard. He was wearing a blue puffa jacket, black jeans and trainers. 'I need to take a statement from you, Callum. Let's start with some basics. How long have you been the night porter here?'

'Five years.'

'When did your shift start last night?'

'At eleven. I'm on duty from then until seven. One of the duty managers starts at six.'

'And this morning I understand that was Lenna?'

He nodded. 'Yes.'

'So, last night, did anything unusual happen?'

He shook his head. 'The only thing was about midnight when someone phoned to complain about the guest next door having their TV on loudly. They said they couldn't get to sleep. I went up and asked them to turn it down. That's all.'

'And you didn't hear anything strange?'

Again, he shook his head. 'No. Nothing.'

'You didn't hear someone breaking a window upstairs, for example?'

Grant looked taken aback. 'Really? No. Where?'

'In the meeting room at the end of the corridor. You didn't see anything suspicious on the CCTV at the back of the building?'

He shook his head.

'Did any guests bring anyone back with them?'

'No.'

'Where were you during the night and what do you do during your shift?'

He pointed to the office behind reception. 'Out there or at the reception desk most of the time. I have various jobs to do. I'll let in any guests who arrive late. I'll tidy things up in the bar, empty the bins, make sure that the toilets are OK and so on. Sometimes a guest will want something brought to their room or need an early morning call. Things like that.'

'But there must be time where nothing much is happening? It must get a bit boring. Have you ever fallen asleep?'

'Certainly not,' he said, sounding deeply offended. 'I'll read a book for a bit, that's all.'

When Shazia got back to the bedroom, the pathologist, Dr Christine Marshall, had arrived and was busy dictating into her phone. She stopped and turned to Shazia. 'Oh, hello Inspector. I would have been here sooner, but we are short-staffed and I had to examine a young woman fished out of the Clyde this morning. Tragic. A student, poor thing. What are we doing to these young people? There's so much pressure on them. Is it the internet, all this social media? Anyway, what have we here?' She put her spectacles on and examined the corpse while Shazia and Joseph looked on.

'It's Charles Henderson, MSP,' said Shazia.

'Or, rather, he was an MSP,' said Joseph.

'Oh yes, I recognise him now. Well, it's difficult to say for sure but I'm noticing the bruising on his face and around his neck and shoulders. Looks like he was held down with some force, I'd say.'

'A pillow was found covering his face.'

'Well, he could have been suffocated. I won't know for certain until I've done the post-mortem.' Marshall carefully peered down the victim's throat. 'But that would be consistent with what I am seeing. Nothing down the throat as far as I can see.'

'Whoever did it, knew what they were about, eh?' said Joseph. Could it be just one person, you think, or two?' asked Joseph.

'Obviously easier with two but it depends what condition the victim was in or how resistant he was to begin with. And how strong the attacker is. Maybe the victim was intoxicated or drugged, too, which would make him weaker, less able to fight back.'

Shazia said, 'There was a used condom found. He had some company with him at some point last night. Maybe a prostitute. He checked in on his own and there was no one with him when he was found.'

Marshall's eyes opened wide. 'Really? Well, of course, he would be, wouldn't he? Kinky lot, aren't they? Always getting caught with porn on their computers or in flagrante in some dominatrix pad, aren't they?' she said

'Are they?' said Shazia.

'Well, I don't really know too much about that kind of thing, Inspector, living such a quiet kind of life in Newton Mearns,' said Marshall, raising her eyebrows and smiling. 'No doubt Forensics will see if there's anyone else's DNA on the victim and if it matches what's on the condom. Good luck finding who he was with, anyway. I'll send you my PM report ASAP.'

Shazia googled Henderson and discovered that he was married and lived in Perthshire. Then she made a series of phone calls. First, to Police HQ, asking for someone from the local police to visit Henderson's wife and break her the news about her husband and ask her to contact Glasgow Police HQ when she was able to come and formally identify his body. Then she phoned DCI Cooper to tell him about the murder and requested a team of uniformed officers to help with the process of interviewing all of the hotel guests. Lastly, she phoned Detective Constables Mitchell and McLaughlin to ask them to join her at the scene as soon as possible.

The rest of the morning was taken up with interviews while investigators continued to examine the hotel. The room adjacent to the room where the murder had happened had been vacant and the room on the other side had been occupied by an American couple who appeared to be in their seventies and hard of hearing. The room opposite was occupied by a Belgian couple in their forties. However, no one had heard anything suspicious during the night. No knocking on doors in the middle of the night, or shouting. The man in the room immediately below Henderson's bedroom, a businessman from London, who had retired early to bed, reported hearing a noise from the room above at some point in the night, but had put it down to an amorous couple being energetic in bed. He had no idea what time that was.

The assistant manager, Lenna Ivanova, was a tall young woman with light brown curly hair and large spectacles. She was Estonian and had only been working in the hotel for a few months, after qualifying in hospitality management in Tallinn. She looked completely distraught, shaken and nervous. Shazia tried to put her at her ease but she could hardly string sentences together, although her English was impeccable. She mostly nodded or shook her head in answer to questions, but she was able to confirm what Van Dijk had told her. She had come into the hotel at 5.45 a.m. and Grant had reported a quiet night apart from the disturbance of a TV. After the chambermaid came downstairs to report finding a guest unresponsive, she had gone to the bedroom and confirmed the situation. She then phoned the emergency services. She was also able to tell Shazia that there were no master keycards missing or any replacement keycards processed for Henderson's room.

The chambermaid, Andreea, was small and dark-haired. She was originally from Romania and her English wasn't great, but she was able to describe opening the room and finding the body. She confirmed that the door had been locked. She had tried knocking several times, then swiped her card in the slot and opened the door slightly, saying 'Hello' several times before opening the door wider and entering the room. When she found the body, she immediately ran downstairs to tell Ivanova.

Shazia and her team spent the rest of the day trying to piece together Henderson's movements from the previous day. They divided up the tasks between them. Mitchell phoned the MSP's office in Holyrood and found out from Henderson's PA that he had apparently been in meetings in Parliament all Monday, then travelled through to Glasgow by train. To find out what happened after that involved interviewing hotel staff. From the restaurant manager, Shazia discovered that apparently Henderson dined alone in the hotel and then had moved into the bar where he had several drinks. The barman, Miguel, noticed that at some point Henderson was joined by a young woman. 'A very attractive young woman, with long blonde hair,' said Miguel. 'She sounded East European.' Soon after that Henderson left the bar along with the young woman he was with. He had taken a bottle of wine and two glasses to his room with him. Anna, who had been on duty at reception, said that she had noticed Henderson going to the lift with a young woman. She said what had noticed most was their difference in ages. She described the young woman as pretty, with long blonde hair, of medium height and aged about nineteen or twenty. She couldn't remember seeing the couple again, or seeing the woman leave the hotel.

3

The Forsyth Apparel company boardroom was a bright airy space on the top floor of a modern office block in Glasgow's Central Business District. Along one side of the room were a series of floor to ceiling windows which looked out over the surrounding rooftops towards the river. The opposite wall was made of thick glass separating the room from the rest of the floor but leaving the room fully soundproof. The front and rear walls of the room were filled with photographs of models posing in the company's attire. Cameron Forsyth limped into the boardroom, placed himself in his customary position at the top of the table and poured himself a glass of water from the bottle of designer mineral water. He seemed to fill the space with his presence.

Forsyth was around six feet tall, broad-shouldered and barrel-chested, with a tanned complexion and a thatch of grey hair. The nips and tucks around the eyes, administered by a top plastic surgeon, were intended to make him appear younger than his fifty-nine years of age but, in reality, his face had an unblemished, artificial look. He growled to himself as he scanned the screen of his phone, placed it down on the table, then looked at the three men and three women who in effect managed his company; every one of them stared back at him with an expression of disquiet, not quite sure what to expect. They had been waiting for half an hour for him to arrive, so that the meeting could commence, and when Forsyth entered the room, the chatter had ceased instantly and the fiddling with mobiles terminated abruptly.

'OK, the sooner we get this fucking meeting started the sooner we can finish it, right?' Forsyth exclaimed in his characteristic bellow. No one dared point out that he was thirty minutes late for a meeting that he had called for twelve noon in an email the previous day, in which he had warned them to be punctual. He didn't expect an answer and followed this up with an instruction. 'Switch all your bloody phones off now! I want to concentrate on business,' he commanded, staring at his Financial Director, Robert Graham. 'Robert, what's the headlines on our finance figures?'

Graham, a tall thin man with a long face and thick spectacles, wearing a grey pin-stripe suit, looked at Forsyth. 'I have prepared a PowerPoint presentation, Mr Forsyth, if you will allow me to –'

'I don't have the fucking time to sit through a presentation,' Forsyth interrupted. 'Just give me the top line! Are we sitting pretty at the top of the tree or are we in deep shit?'

'Well, Mr Forsyth,' Graham began hesitantly, looking at a piece of paper in front of him. 'It's not quite as simple as that.'

'Make it simple then! And be damn quick about it,' barked Forsyth, taking another slug of water.

Graham took a deep breath. His face had taken on a florid hue.

'Well, man, get the fuck on with it!' barked Forsyth.

Graham didn't like to be the bringer of bad news and wasn't sure how Forsyth would take it. All eyes in the room were now focused on him and he realised he had better just say it and get it over with. 'It's not looking too good, I'm afraid, sir. I've analysed the stats and overall sales are down six per cent on the previous quarter and down eight percent on the same quarter last year. Footfall is down five per cent in the last month. Expenditure is also up, though this can largely be accounted for by the dividends paid to shareholders.' He looked up nervously at Forsyth who was staring at him with a look of intense hatred.

'Largely?' said Forsyth. Forsyth looked like a volcano about to explode. As the chairman and CEO, Forsyth held the majority of shares in the company and therefore a controlling stake. His company had been started by his father with half a dozen shops in the west of Scotland and had then grown into a major high street company with stores scattered across the British Isles. The parent company had its headquarters in Glasgow, but Forsyth also separately owned several large department stores in England, *Forsyth's*, which were run as an independent company from a London office. In the last ten years he had acquired several other similar businesses, along with their associated supply and distribution chains, and increasingly moved out of the high street and into out-of-town retail parks, expanding the range to include more of the growing market for sportswear and what was termed "athleisure"; the company name used the snappy *FA* for its online business. It had all been going well with the share price on the up and up. Up until now.

Over the past few months, however, stories had emerged in the media, beginning with a report on STV that had damaged the reputation of the company and which potentially lay behind the falling sales figures. There were tales of sweat-shops producing garments in Bangladesh and undercover reporters had exposed appalling working conditions in warehouses, revealing staff being treated more like prisoners than employees: workers subject to frequent and intrusive personal searches, staff forced to work long hours without breaks, employees being paid at below the minimum wage and being dismissed for complaining or for requesting improved conditions. As a result, the share price had also taken a severe hit in recent weeks.

'Eh, yes, largely,' said Graham.

'And your solution to this is what exactly?'

Graham looked flustered. 'I would have suggested rationalisation of the workforce, Mr Forsyth, but we have been doing that over the past year and each quarter profits have fallen. I think we need a different approach.'

'And what would that approach be?'

Graham was silent and shook his head.

'I don't want to hear what the problems are. I want fucking solutions. Does anyone have any better ideas?' Forsyth asked, looking around the table, drilling his blue eyes deep into each person's gaze.

After several painful seconds of silence, Emily Watson, the Human Resources Director, spoke up. She was an attractive blonde-haired woman in her mid-forties. 'You are, of course, entirely correct, Mr Forsyth. We have reduced the workforce to a level that is a minimum for any effective operation to succeed. The organisational restructuring has reduced the number of managers, salaries for all employees have been frozen, and working conditions have been revised to maximise productivity across the company, from warehouses and distribution to the remaining high street stores and out-of-town stores in retail parks. I think the problems are more with marketing. We are not making our brand as attractive as the competition.'

All eyes turned to look in the direction of the Marketing Director, Vincent Collingwood. 'What do you say to that, Vince? Bit of a broadside across your bows, eh?' said Forsyth, smiling and obviously enjoying the prospect of his chiefs locking horns with each other.

'I disagree. Although we have been criticised in the media over the past few months, I have launched a campaign to counter the allegations. I have worked tirelessly to promote the company's image and products in the best possible light. I don't think there is anything else we could have done. I do think the problem is with some of the products. People don't want to buy merchandise which they think is lacking in quality.'

'Then do something about it, for fuck's sake!' barked Forsyth, turning beetroot. 'Get it right. We are not Primark but we are not Armani either. We are selling quality clothes in the mid-price range, there has to be a market for that. As usual, I suppose it's me who has to come up with the fucking ideas. OK, here we go then! Write this down.'

All six grabbed a pen and sat poised over paper, blinking furiously and waiting for the starting gun like sprinters.

'We need to reduce costs further,' said Forsyth. We'll have a new share launch to raise capital. Robert, get to work on that. I can shed a few shares, if necessary, as long as I retain the largest share. Reduce the number of staff in the stores further. And Emily, institute a three percent pay cut across the company immediately, even if it means making everyone redundant and re-employing them on new contracts or with agency staff! I believe that most of our shop-floor staff are already on zero-hours contracts. Make that all of them! Let's go with the gig economy and see if we can avoid making them all employees at all, see if we can't just make them self-employed like these delivery guys pedalling like fuck with big fucking bags strapped to their backs to bring punters a fucking pizza. Alan, you're in charge of sales, identify the five worst performing stores and shut them down with immediate effect, laying off the workforce. The High Street is finished, business is moving online. OK we have a presence there but we need to grow it. I want that developed and expanded, it's the future of retail so Susan, get onto that with the IT team and see what can be done asap. Call it the Transformation Agenda or some bullshit phrase that sounds positive.' He turned to the Merchandising Director. 'Fiona, look at our suppliers and see if we can't source some lower-priced fucking sweatshops out there in Asia. I've heard Myanmar is now cheaper than Bangladesh, look into it! People will complain about human rights and the political situation there, but frankly I couldn't give a toss!

'I shouldn't really give a monkey's if we were to get rid of all the damn stores and go a hundred per cent online but I guess I'm just a sentimental bastard and can't help thinking about my old dad starting up his first shop. Vince, get the PR team to spin the story that we are becoming leaner and fitter to compete in the global marketplace. That always goes down well. Some bullshit along those lines. And change the marketing strategy so it works this time and I don't want to hear any more talk from you that is negative, otherwise you are out on your ear, do you understand?'

Forsyth stood up. 'Right, that's that sorted then. Send me reports on all of the above options and any other bright ideas any fucker has. I'm now off to this bloody Scottish Chamber of Commerce conference at the SECC to tell them how to fix the fucking economy.' With that, he went out, leaving those sitting around the table stunned and looking like an array of open-mouthed dummies in one of his store's windows.

4

The Scottish Chamber of Commerce conference was taking place at a time of economic turmoil in the disparate nations of the former United Kingdom. The newly independent Scotland, after some negotiation, had been able to retain membership of the European Union. The rest of the former UK, though, had voted in a referendum to leave the European Union.

This was the climate in which the business conference was taking place and which Cameron Forsyth was due to speak at. He had missed the earlier speeches, partly because he had other business to attend to, but also as he found these events extremely boring and tiresome. Why would he want to waste his time listening to what someone else thought? His only reason for attending was to vent his opinions and he was looking forward to doing so. There was nothing he loved more than a captive audience. He arrived ten minutes before he was due to go on stage. He could hear the government Finance Minister's high-pitched reedy voice on the loudspeakers claiming that the SNP government had a 'strong, clear vision for the country' and that 'despite fluctuations with the currency we as an independent nation are in a far better place than down south'. Typical, Forsyth thought, when things are bad just point to England and say look, at least you are not English! These nationalists really are so predictable.

The Holyrood election had produced a hung parliament. Eventually, after some horse-trading, a government had been formed, comprising a coalition of the Scottish National Party and the Scottish Greens. This had, however, held for only six months after breaking down in bitter disagreements over taxation policy and distinct policy differences. There was a sudden slump in oil prices, plummeting from $120 to $35 a barrel and, as the economy stumbled, the SNP wanted to freeze income tax and institute cuts in public spending, while the Greens were demanding a redistribution of wealth through increased taxation, including the introduction of a higher top-rate for higher earners as well as greater investment in infrastructure to revive the economy. Consequently, the coalition fell apart. The SNP were now effectively operating as a minority government and were increasingly dependent on the support of the Scottish Conservatives as they were the only ones who backed its tax changes. The Greens and the Scottish Labour Party were now a united opposition and were calling for a snap election to bring about stability and were said to be in secret discussions about forming a progressive alliance.

The minister, James Stewart, continued his speech in his thin whiny voice. 'We are attracting record levels of investment. We are building a record number of homes. Exports are at an all-time record level,' he announced proudly. 'But we cannot be complacent. We will, of course, consult with a broad range of stakeholders before any decisions are taken on the future economic strategy. And that, of course, must involve yourselves as Scotland's leaders of enterprise.

'When the nation achieved independence, we successfully negotiated EU membership and we must continue to strive to improve that union so that it benefits our country. There are some who question whether it is right to remain part of the European Union. They will say that we would be better off outside it as England, Wales and Northern Ireland have opted to do. I say, remember the disastrous two world wars in Europe in the last century. We owe it to our children and grandchildren to make sure that our future is a prosperous and peaceful one. Membership of the EU brings us many advantages, including free trade with our neighbours on the continent which has helped build a flourishing business sector. Free movement of people allows our industries to recruit the skilled workers from across

Europe that our country needs. One thing is certain: our future lies in being integrated with the European Union. That may even mean joining the euro at some stage, if the conditions are suitable. We should not shy away from a debate on that. If it is in our country's best interests, then it would be foolish to continue to tie ourselves to sterling. After a lengthy debate, you will recall that we decided to retain the pound when we separated from the United Kingdom, but times change and we have seen the value of the currency in freefall since the decision down south to leave the EU, so we may have to think again. That is for the future. But, as I have said, we have opted to be a part of the European Union and we should not need to think about that just because those in Westminster have chosen a different path. It is in our country's best interests to have a voice within the EU, influencing its policies and direction, something which those down south will no longer be able to do. Our country is stronger in Europe, not outside it, and Europe is stronger with Scotland inside it.'

The minister left the platform to a light sprinkling of applause, but by no means an enthusiastic reception. He was not a great speaker, lacked gravitas, and somehow everything he said sounded too heavily scripted. The economic facts were that inflation was rising and the Bank of England had raised interest rates as a result. Borrowing, therefore, was costly. The economy was in a far less healthy state than he had portrayed it.

Cameron Forsyth was a staunch Tory and a major donor to the party. In contrast to the minister, he saw the European Union as nothing but a liberal experiment intent on strangling free markets with its interminable regulations on workers' rights and health and safety. Through his London-based company he had donated £4 million to the campaign to leave the EU as well as millions to the No campaign in the Scottish independence referendum. His speech was going to be very different in tone from that of the previous speaker. He crossed the platform swiftly and approached the microphone, his limp apparent yet clearly not hindering him. Indeed, he seemed to exude energy as he began his address to the audience, waving his hands in the air. 'You have heard the minister telling you that all is rosy in the country with record this and record that, but as people in the real world of business we know that is not the case. We know what is really happening. Businesses are closing every day. It is impossible to keep up with repayments on loans. This government is not on the side of business.'

There was applause from the crowd, which he soaked up. It wasn't just the words that were different: Forsyth's voice was bold and confident, that of a natural orator, sure of his own superior wisdom, something which his critics would say was the result of his privileged background and private education.

Forsyth continued. 'The minister wants to debate the currency. What he means by that is that he really wants us to join the euro, but is scared to say so. Well, does it make sense to cut ourselves off from our nearest and dearest trading partner? And by that, I mean England, not Belgium! I say no. Joining the euro would be a disaster. Think about having to change money every time you go to Newcastle, Manchester or Birmingham for the day! No, we must never do that. We have rising unemployment in this country. Why? We have record levels of immigration because of free movement inside the EU! Where is the sense in that? What is the SNP doing about that? Nothing! I say, we need Scottish jobs for Scottish workers! We may have lost the union with England, but our links with London served this country well for three hundred years. The union built the wealth that this great city of Glasgow is founded on. Glasgow was the second city of the empire. The union provided prosperity and industry which produced jobs, something which we need more than ever. Something which those who propose we replace our Queen with a president forget!'

There was laughter in the hall, as he expected, and he paused. 'Of course, I believe that eventually the solution will be for us to have another referendum and reject this nationalist experiment that we have had for the past two years. The stark truth is that we cannot afford to be independent and we must eventually re-think independence. It is clear that separation from the rest of Britain does not make sense. But I am a realist and I know that day is not now. Now, I say, we need to hold our nerve. The pound will be strong again. And the euro will fall, I predict, catastrophically. There will be another Greece just around the corner. Then we will see who is talking up the euro! Once a deal between London and Brussels has been sorted out, I believe that the pound will be stronger than ever. I say let's keep the pound and not even consider thinking again about that. In contrast to the minister, I say it is time for Scotland to debate remaining in the EU. With its directives on this and its directives on that it is suffocating the entrepreneurs of this country. Let's start asking the question, if the rest of Britain has left the EU, why should we stay in? Do we really want to have customs checks at the English border? Does it make sense for us to be part of a union based in Brussels when we could have a better relationship with our closest partner just down the M74?

'But my other message to the government in Holyrood today is simple. Remember business. The business people of Scotland create jobs. Without jobs, where are we as a nation? Where are we as people? There is a slogan in George Square which says People Make Glasgow. Well, I say, business makes people. Business gives people much more than their livelihood, it creates confidence, develops skills and builds communities of individuals. The climate for people starting a business at this moment in time is appalling. That needs to change. I say to the government, ask us what you can do for the businessmen and businesswomen of Scotland! Then do it!'

It was noticeable that the applause was louder than that for the government minister. Flashes from the cameras positioned below the stage exploded, lighting up the stage. Forsyth's comments about the euro and the EU had found sympathy amongst delegates in the hall. Many on the right of the Scottish Conservative Party agreed with his stance on Europe, although the current leader did not. There were in fact rumours that she was thinking of quitting Scottish politics. She was keen on a broadcasting career, it was known, and it was not thought that she would be able to resist the lure of chairing her own current affairs chat show on a major television channel. Forsyth was articulate, charismatic, and the media loved him. He stood on the platform waving to the crowd, smiling and shaking hands with the Chamber's director, then limped off stage in triumph, noticing that almost all of those around him were staring at their phones and exchanging concerned looks. He took out his own mobile and glanced at the news on the screen. There was a Reuters' report of the suspicious death of an MSP, as yet unnamed.

5

'Finally, how does Shakespeare view the act of taking a life?' asked Stephen Christie, standing at the lectern facing the eager faces of undergraduates in the hall. He was coming to the end of his lecture on Shakespeare's attitude to morality and couldn't wait to get there. He felt terrible, but stuck to the task of trying to say something that made sense. 'In what circumstances can it be justified, and what are the consequences for those involved? Shakespeare, remember, was fundamentally an Elizabethan and Jacobean dramatist but, unlike some of the other playwrights of his time, he didn't present straightforward issues. He preferred to pose questions, deal in ambiguities, construct moral dilemmas, or, you might say, create fifty shades of grey.' There was some giggling in the audience at this reference to the soft-porn novel. 'Shakespeare explores what the right action is. In a society which was moving from medieval to modern, he was concerned with the individual and what was legally or morally the right thing to do. Consider first what happens in a play which focuses on the legal situation. Measure for Measure has been described as a Problem Play. What does that mean? It has a problem that is not easily solved, full of dilemmas and ambiguities. Isabella, with her zealous religious principles as a novice nun, accepts that Angelo took the right decision in condemning her brother to death for fornication, as this was the penalty sanctioned by law and her brother had broken the law by his own action. But, of course, Angelo is a hypocrite as he himself wants to fornicate with Isabella. Incidentally, Isabella also goes on to say that she was responsible for tempting Angelo when he demanded the price of showing mercy to her brother was for her to sleep with him. Would we agree with that suggestion today? Of course not, but remember it was a deeply patriarchal society then. Unlike our modern entirely unsexist society today!' The audience of undergraduates laughed. They enjoyed Stephen Christie's lectures. He was renowned as being entertaining, idiosyncratic, iconoclastic even. He was also young, handsome and charming, which endeared him to the largely female class who had opted for the Shakespeare module as part of their course in English Literature. He wore wire-rimmed spectacles, had thick jet-black curly hair, and a thick black beard to match.

He heard the tower bell chime the quarter hour and realised he had better hurry up and get to the conclusion of this lecture. It was warm in the hall and he was sweating profusely. 'What about deliberately murdering someone? In Macbeth, Macbeth's mind is a seething mass of conflicting emotions. He doesn't know whether to act on his urges to kill Duncan or not. Can murdering the king be justified? he asks himself, but he can't see how it possibly can be. It is his wife, Lady Macbeth, who persuades him by mocking him, questioning his manhood in fact. Something that we west of Scotland males take great exception to, by the way!' A flurry of laughter echoed around the lecture hall. 'Macbeth descends into paranoia after the murder. His innermost fears plague him, and after his wife's suicide he sees no point in living any more. His motive for killing Duncan had been his ambition and, although Shakespeare is saying that we cannot approve of that, he turns Macbeth into a tragic hero whom we sympathise with, tricked and manipulated by the witches and, to an extent, by his own wife. Although we may resent the misogyny today!' Christie smiled as his audience laughed.

'But what about revenge? Is it an honourable motive? What about the greatest tragic hero of them all, Hamlet? It's more complicated. Claudius has killed the king, Hamlet's father, also because of ambition, and Hamlet seeks to kill him out of revenge. We sympathise, but in the end, he achieves it at a terrible cost to himself and those whom he loves. Was it all worth it, we ask ourselves?

'In each of these examples, Shakespeare is saying taking a life is never quite an unambiguous issue. It could be right and legally sanctioned, but hypocritical, or it could be illegal but nevertheless some form of natural justice. But before we commit to it, we had better be sure about what the consequences will be, both legally, and for our conscience.'

Christie gave a slight wave to his audience. The lecture had not been one of his best, in fact it was probably one of his worst. At one point he had lost his entire train of thought. It didn't help that he hadn't had any notes and was winging it. The events of the last twenty-four hours had infected his thoughts and the notion of conscience was battering at his brain. It had been rambling and disconnected but at least he had got through it without collapsing, as several times during it he had wondered if he could stay on his feet. He had a quick look around the hall but couldn't spot Chloe. Just as he thought: she would have gone home to spend the day in bed, feeling even worse than he was. After each of them had been interviewed by the police, they had taken a taxi to the university where Chloe immediately rushed to the toilet and he just managed to reach the lecture theatre in time for his two o' clock lecture. He gave a slight smile then departed the stage, where a trio of attractive female students had already gathered to speak to him.

Twenty minutes later, Christie was back in his room, a pile of student essays lying on his desk in front of him waiting to be marked, but he couldn't face them. He had a headache coming on. He removed his spectacles and rubbed his eyes. His hangover was coming back to attack him. He'd numbed it earlier by taking a handful of paracetamol and ibuprofen when it had felt like someone splitting his skull with a sledgehammer but he could feel it returning, this time coming back to assault his head with a pneumatic drill. Instead, he took out his phone and checked to see if there were any messages or missed calls from during the lecture when he had it switched off. None. Surely if anything had happened, they would let him know?

His mother's condition had sharply deteriorated in the last few weeks and she had been admitted to a hospice for palliative care. She would not recover but he had refused to accept it. Until yesterday. She had developed breast cancer and had undergone chemo and radio-therapy, but had then been diagnosed with terminal cancer of the liver. He thought about their last conversation a few days ago. Despite being heavily dosed with morphine, she had suddenly seemed lucid; it was as if she realised that her time in the world was coming to an end and this moment was precious. Some part of her brain had retrieved its ability to remember and communicate clearly, if only temporarily. He wasn't sure whether to believe half of the stuff she had told him then or not but, in the end, he had been convinced. The secret of who his father was had been finally revealed to him after she had kept it from him for thirty years. She had even shown him a photograph which she kept in her handbag, taken many years ago of the two of them together, his mother and father. She said that the married man who was his father had rejected her after she fell pregnant and she had been so hurt that she had wanted nothing to do with him ever again. For her, and for him, she had said, it was best this way, to carry on as if the man had never had existed. But she realised now that she did not have long to live and that it was probably important that Stephen now know who he was.

He had said very little. He had long ago given up expecting ever to know anything about his biological father. When he had been young and had questioned her about who his father was, she had always said it was a man she had spent one night with and never saw again. A sailor she met in a dance hall. She didn't even know his first name, she said. But he knew now that that had been a lie. His whole life had been built on a lie and he questioned who he really was. And questioned who she was. He was angry with her

47

for keeping it from him all these years. Now, after that last conversation, she had weakened. When he visited her in the hospice the following day, she didn't seem to know who he was, her brain befuddled by morphine.

He decided that he couldn't possibly concentrate on any more work today. He was supposed to be taking a seminar at four o'clock, but he could feel the headache beginning to squeeze his temples in a vice-like grip. He would ask a colleague to cover for him, saying he was sick, which was true. He had done the same for others so there wouldn't be a problem. He would even take the marking home with him. Perhaps he would feel better later and do it then. He might take it up to the hospice and do it at her bedside. It would give him something else to think about. He picked up the phone and dialled Jeremy's number. He had a room further along the corridor, but he couldn't face walking along there and seeing him in person. Jeremy said he could cover the seminar but he didn't sound too happy about it. Christie stuffed the pile of essays into his briefcase, switched off the lights and locked his office door.

He walked across the Glasgow University quadrangle towards the University Avenue exit. The sleet had turned into a fine drizzle and the sky was dark and leaden. It was making his headache worse. As soon as he got back to his flat, he would have a couple more paracetamol and lie down. That should make it better. He was almost at the junction with Byres Road when his mobile rang.

When he got back home to the Hyndland flat he was surprised to see his wife, Juliet, there. He had expected her to be at work but then he remembered that she was working from home that day. Her long blonde hair was tied back in a ponytail, emphasising her cheekbones and slender neck. She worked for an insurance firm in Edinburgh and faced a daily commute by train that was long and tedious, but every Tuesday she was able to work from home. He'd forgotten that this was a Tuesday. His brain felt as if a fog had descended on it.

'I didn't expect to see you, honey,' she said as he opened the door and came in. She came over and kissed him. 'What's wrong?' she asked seeing the pale, drained look on his face.

'She's gone.'

'I'm so sorry.' Juliet hugged him and held him tightly. When she released him, she looked into his eyes. 'I didn't know if you would go to work today after staying the night there. You couldn't have got much sleep; you must be exhausted!'

Christie didn't know what to say. He hadn't thought this through properly. What the hell was wrong with him? His thoughts went into a jumble. 'Yes, actually I've got a splitting headache. I think I'll go and lie down.'

'You do that. I'll bring you some tea.'

He went through to the bedroom and lay down, staring at the ceiling. The previous twenty-four hours now seemed like a dream. It had all started when he recognised that man on the train yesterday, the man he now knew was his father. The man who had neglected his mother and him all his life. His blood had boiled over and he had had to do something about it.

6

When Shazia got back outside the hotel, she saw with dismay that a parking ticket had been attached to her car's windscreen, nailed down with the windscreen wipers. As she had anticipated, the sleet had made her note invisible, though maybe the zealous warden would have ignored it anyway and still issued a ticket just to be a pain. She tore it off and stuffed it into her pocket. Perhaps she could claim it under expenses, she thought. She returned to the station and switched on her computer, keen to find out more about the victim.

Joseph had returned along with her and was sitting at the adjacent desk in the open-plan office. Only senior officers from the rank of Chief Inspector upwards were given the luxury of individual offices, the majority of the building resembling a call centre, though at least it wasn't hot-desking. Each officer was allocated their own space with a computer. Some officers decorated their space with photographs. Shazia's had several photos of Yasmeen. Joseph's desk was littered with files, documents and papers. He put down his phone and turned to speak to her. 'Just told Mr Murray that I would like to speak to him. I said it's about the death of Sammy Scobie.'

'What did he say?'

'First, he said, who? Then when I told him I would explain when I saw him, he asked if he needed his lawyer with him. I said, "That's up to you. I just want to ask a few questions." He said he was at home at the moment but would be going out later. I told him I would be right over.'

Shazia raised her eyebrows. 'Take Joan with you. Murray will definitely have his solicitor there. Did he give you the address?'

'Yes, on some estate in Bearsden. Academy Park.'

'Oh yes. You should see it. Millionaires' Row, more like. Smallest house is a five-bedroom with triple garages. Good luck!'

Joseph headed over to speak to DC Mitchell and the two of them then left the office. As she waited for her computer to load up, Shazia made herself a coffee in her *World's Best Mum* mug that Yasmeen had bought her for Christmas.

As she was making it, DCI Cooper appeared, hovering beside her. 'Having a nice birthday?' she asked, trying to sound as if she cared.

He smiled. 'The cake was a nice touch. But I feel old. I'll be hanging up my boots soon, eh?'

Shazia hated this small talk with Cooper and couldn't wait to just get back to her desk. 'How would you like to give me an update?' It wasn't really a question, more a command, she thought as she followed him down the corridor clutching her mug. His tall angular frame raced ahead with long strides. 'Close the door and take a seat,' he said. She closed the door and sat down on the chair. A document caught his eye and he picked it up. It had a post-it note attached to the front and he flicked through it. She took a sip of coffee and waited for him to speak. His grey hair was thinner now than the last time she had noticed and she could see that a bald patch was appearing in the centre of his head. He resembled a bird, she thought, some kind of wading bird. A heron. It wasn't just the long stork-like legs but the pointed nose was like a beak and the sharp chin jutted out. He was skin and bone, very little flesh. He finished reading what had distracted him, putting the document that had been left on his desk aside.

'Eh, sorry about that. I'll deal with that later. This Henderson murder then. You said you got tipped off?'

'Yes, sir. PC Mahood, friend of the family.'

'Tell me what we know and what your thinking is so far?'

'The victim, as you already know, was Charles Henderson MSP, sir. He had been attacked in his hotel bedroom. There's no sign of forced entry to the bedroom so they may have used the old trick of claiming they were room service or hotel management to gain entry, then overpowered him. Henderson appears to have been smothered with a pillow. Death looked pretty quick but we will see what the post-mortem shows us. No guests heard anything suspicious, nor did the night porter. At some point Henderson went to his room with a young woman he met in the bar and there are signs that they had sex; she is possibly a sex worker. We'll examine the CCTV evidence and also see what Forensics can come up with.'

Cooper nodded. 'That's good, Shazia. I've already had the Assistant Chief Constable asking me about the case. It's a shitstorm. Obviously, the murder of an MSP is high profile to put it mildly, and the media will be all over us like fucking hyenas. We've had Special Branch clamouring to take over but the Super is keeping them at bay for the moment. We will need to keep those above us in the picture, otherwise all sorts of rumours will spread so we'll organise a press conference as soon as possible.'

'Yes, sir.'

'Keep me informed promptly of any developments, though, eh? Before you make any public statements or any arrests. I don't want to hear it first on the TV news.'

'Yes, sir.'

'By the way, how is the Samuel Scobie investigation going? Any leads?'

'No leads, sir. The usual wall of silence, I'm afraid. Traced a mobile number found in his flat to our friend Greg Murray and DC Boateng has gone out to question him about it.'

'I'm afraid it's likely to be yet another unsolved case. It's the gangsters sorting things out themselves. Don't spend too much time on it, use the resources you've got to find

Henderson's killer. That will be all.' He returned to the document he had looked at previously. She resisted the urge to tell him that all lives mattered equally and she was as determined to find Sammy Scobie's killer as much as Charles Henderson's.

7

When she got back to her desk, Shazia searched for information about Charles Henderson on the internet. When that hotel manager had said his name, it hadn't registered immediately with her that he had meant that particular Charles Henderson but, of course, she now recalled who he was. She realised that she had lost interest in politics and didn't pay much attention to what was going on in the Scottish Parliament. Maybe instead of watching TV box sets in the little spare time which she had, she should read more of the newspaper or watch the news? When she did have time to herself, she just wanted to switch off and escape, not read or hear about atrocities that had happened somewhere in the world. That was all the news seemed to consist of and she had enough of that in her daily job.

She found Henderson's Wikipedia entry. He sounded like a typical Tory, she thought: privately educated at a top Scottish independent school, Fettes, then onto Edinburgh University where he was president of the debating society and gained a law degree; a successful legal career then, finally, a move into politics, first as a councillor then an MSP. He was married to Valerie Farquharson, a former banker and now journalist, who was the daughter of the Duke of Abernethy. They lived in the Perthshire countryside and had two grown-up children.

Yes, she knew of Valerie Farquharson. Occasionally on a Sunday, Shazia scanned the papers that her father brought home from the shop and had read Farquharson's column from time to time. It was full of reactionary opinions; she was anti-abortion, anti-feminist and anti-political correctness. There was more than a whiff of racism about her views too, Shazia thought. In one column that she remembered reading, Farquharson had indulged in a rant about why most of those working in the hospitality industry in Scotland were from outside Scotland. She hadn't explicitly said it but her message was clear: let's stop these foreigners taking all the jobs, in fact let's stop them coming here at all. Farquharson had called for better vocational training for Scottish youngsters, to produce a workforce that would work in the country's hotels and restaurants. In principle, there was nothing wrong with saying let's train our young people for those jobs, Shazia had thought when she read it. Her daughter Yasmeen might be suited to a job in hospitality. Academically, Yasmeen was struggling with mainstream school, and university was a non-starter. Shazia was all in favour of training young people for jobs. But the trouble was the inference that somehow there were outsiders taking the jobs. She didn't agree with that, didn't like the xenophobic tone. As someone whose own parents had been immigrants into Scotland from the Asian sub-continent, this kind of thing irked her.

She remembered that Valerie Farquharson had begun the column by describing her experience of staying in a hotel in the Highlands and noticing that not one, "NOT ONE", as she had written it, "of the staff had been from the British Isles. And", she said, "some of them could barely speak English!" The article had nauseated her and now she was going to have to go and speak to this woman. She would have to present a face that didn't reveal her true feelings towards her. But she was good at that. After all, who knew how she really felt? And hadn't she just convinced Cooper that she was interested in his birthday?

Why had Henderson been killed, she thought? Was it something to do with his personal life? Or was it political? Had he made an enemy? Or was it an act of passion? Was the woman he had been with a prostitute or his mistress? She spent the next hour reading everything she could about him, speeches he had made, and his rise through the Scottish Conservatives. She looked to see his social media presence. He had a Linked In account as well as Twitter and Facebook.

They presented an image of a respectable, family man: the truth was that he was most likely a serial shagger of sex workers and she knew that men who used prostitutes didn't just do it once. Of course, maybe the woman hadn't been a prostitute. But, if not, what had happened to her? Where was she?

She found a number for Farquharson and phoned her now, offering her condolences and arranging to visit her tomorrow. She did sound upset. Of course, she was. Her husband had just died. Shazia wondered if she should share the news of her husband's infidelity when she saw her. Yes, she would have to, it was crucial to the investigation to know if the deceased's wife knew anything about her husband's life outside their marriage. Maybe she already knew what he was like and wouldn't be surprised. You could never tell from the outside what a marriage was really like. Her own one, for example. To her friends and relatives, she and her husband had been a picture of happiness. They didn't see the suppurating ulcer under the skin until it eventually exploded when her husband had left her and taken up with a younger model.

Shazia had had enough for the day and switched off her computer. At least now there was her mother's cooking to look forward to. Better than a ready-meal from Marks and Spencer. Yasmeen would have been collected from school. Less things to have to worry about. Though she would always worry about Yasmeen in one way or another. Then there was Omar. She sent him a text saying she would give him a phone later on. Hopefully they could see each other at the weekend. He would have finished his shift at the hospital by now. He was a consultant, specialising in orthopaedics. She had met him after trying to meet someone through an online dating agency, something she thought she would never have done but after she was attacked at her home last year, when someone had appeared in her garden with a knife and tried to stab her, most likely a thug hired by Paul

Murray, she had felt alone and vulnerable. Having her parents now living with her had helped but it also made her feel like a child again having them in the house. She was proud of her independence and wasn't looking for a man to protect her; after all she had fought off her attacker that time. But she wanted someone to share her thoughts and feelings with and talk about things she couldn't share with her parents.

Not to mention sexual desire. It had been a long time since she had been with a man, not since her acrimonious divorce in fact. So, she had bravely put herself out there on the internet marketplace, not really thinking that she would find anyone. At first, she felt embarrassed about the whole thing and it felt a little grubby; the whole operation was an exercise in marketing yourself. Wasn't that what the whole internet had become, she thought? Coming up with words to sound desirable, taking a selfie that didn't look unnatural, selecting the correct clothes, pose and expression – it all seemed wrong and distasteful. She had felt like a prostitute, and the memory of that feeling made her think about the woman that Henderson had been with. Those thoughts again. Who was she?

For several months Shazia had exchanged messages with strangers online. She almost packed the whole thing in after receiving several sleazy requests for *more revealing* pictures or being asked about what her underwear was like, or from some weirdo who seemed fixated on her shoes. Then there were those who sounded promising but turned out to be less so in person. She went on dates with some men she would gladly never meet again, men who, the instant she set eyes on, she knew weren't for her, but morally felt obliged to talk to for an hour before lying that she would be in touch. Some obviously expected sex on the first date, inviting her back to their place or suggesting a hotel, a sure sign that they were already married. Nearly all were older than she was by a good few years. Some of them were even older than her father and all were older than they had claimed to be in their online profiles on the site. The photos they had posted must have been taken many years earlier and flattered them so much that in real life they were unrecognisable now from their past selves. Hair had gone grey or disappeared entirely. One, who had struggled into the café with a walking stick, began the encounter by asking her, 'Do you have all your own hair and teeth?'

So many of them only wanted to talk about themselves and didn't seem at all interested in what she thought of anything. They wanted to impress her with their knowledge, it seemed, but their knowledge was mainly of things she wasn't interested in, like sport or cars. She was bored of experiencing mansplaining at first hand and was about to abandon the entire thing when she had met Omar. Ironically, she hadn't met him on the dating site at all but got talking to him at the gym one night and he asked her out. She was speechless at first but then agreed. He was handsome and looked younger than his fifty-five years, with dark hair beginning to go grey and a neatly-trimmed beard. But it was his eyes that captivated her: they seemed to drill into her being and unlike most men she had dated he actually listened to her and seemed genuinely interested in her opinions. Their first date was for a coffee in Princes Square and she couldn't believe how differently she felt afterwards. He was charming. They talked for hours non-stop and she had to control her emotions afterwards. Like her, he was divorced. His two children, two boys, were in their twenties. One was studying medicine in Dundee; the other had just qualified as a doctor and was working in Australia.

If he hadn't replied after their first date she would have felt so low. But that didn't happen. He messaged her the very next day and suggested a meal at the weekend. From there on it progressed until he invited her back to his place after they had been for a curry at Mother India. He had a large flat in the Merchant City and she agreed, stepping into the taxi, her heart fluttering, part of her telling her this was a mistake, the other part telling that part of her brain to shut up. As soon as they were in the flat, they launched themselves at each other hungrily, tearing off clothes as they made their way to the bedroom. Omar was a gentle and patient lover, unlike Shazia's previous husband, and the sex was the best she had, in her limited experience, ever had.

'It's my surgeon's fingers,' he told her. She laughed. She liked that about him most of all. He made her laugh and have fun again. It was like being a teenager. She lost count of how many times they made love that night but she left very early the next morning and rushed home in a taxi, also feeling like a teenager doing the walk of shame as she went up to her front door as dawn was breaking. She hadn't wanted Yasmeen to be up and about in the morning and notice that her mum wasn't there. How would she explain that?

When she got home from work, she found the house in uproar. Yasmeen was screaming and had been hitting herself repeatedly, something she had always done occasionally. Shazia's mother was trying to calm her granddaughter down but it wasn't until Shazia arrived that Yasmeen felt able to talk about what had upset her. Apparently, there had been a meeting at school for pupils going on the forthcoming trip to Barcelona, and the teacher in charge had asked them all to agree on who they wanted to share a bedroom with. Yasmeen had asked several other girls, but all of them had said that they were sharing with someone else, even though she knew that some hadn't already got a partner. She couldn't understand why none of the girls wanted to share with her and she had then burst into tears in front of everyone. In the end the teacher said that as it had proved too difficult for everyone to find a partner to room-share with, they would draw lots and assign room-mates randomly. Yasmeen told her that all of the girls had been unhappy with this and now blamed her for them not being able to share with who they wanted.

Shazia spent dinner time trying to console her daughter. To distract her, she went out to the garden and fetched Hermione, Yasmeen's rabbit, and brought the little bunny into the house. The sight of the bundle of black and white fur hopping around the kitchen soon took Yasmeen's mind off her woes. Finally, after cuddling and stroking the rabbit for a while, Yasmeen appeared to calm down and finally went upstairs to read her favourite Harry Potter book and get ready for bed. Shazia finally had a chance to talk to her mum and dad.

Her dad looked exhausted, struggling to keep his eyes open as he tried to watch TV. His eyes looked glazed and milky and there were large bags under them. Since his illness he had been increasingly tired and she wondered how much longer he would be able to continue working, but he refused to concede that anything had changed and still got up early to open up the shop at seven every morning and work there until three each afternoon. Her sister, Nazia, who worked part-time in the shop, had told her he had been increasingly irascible and bad-tempered with some of the staff, something that was very much out of character. Shazia thought that this was probably because he was physically struggling to cope with the demands of the job, though he would never admit as much.

'How was the shop today, dad?' she asked as they sat round the kitchen table drinking decaf tea once Yasmeen was upstairs and the dishes were loaded into the dishwasher. Classic FM played in the background. She recognised Vivaldi's Four Seasons.

'That bloody boy, Iqbal! I don't know why I hired him. Would you believe how many times I had to tell him to break up the cardboard boxes in the back room and take them out to the recycling bin? Does he do it? No. Every time I look at him, he is on his bloody mobile phone.'

'Dad, don't you think you should be taking things a bit easier? You're not as young as you used to be, you know.'

'There's nothing wrong with me, it's these lazy young scamps.'

She knew it was pointless even trying to persuade him to cut back his hours, even though he had suffered a serious stroke. He would probably keep working until they carried him out in a wooden box. Her mother sat knitting, occasionally looking up and shaking her head: she knew how stubborn the old man was. She had lived with him for over fifty years and was used to his intransigence. People were like leopards, Shazia thought: they can't change their spots. Also, who knew what would happen if her dad decided to stop working? He might be equally bad-mooded in the house with all of them! That would be even worse. He probably wouldn't know what to do with himself if he retired. He had no hobbies, other than complaining about council services, if you could call that a hobby. The number of unfilled potholes on the roads and the inconsistency of the refuse collections were his favourite topics, if anyone cared to listen. He was constantly filling in the council's complaints forms online and then complaining that they didn't get back to him. Even if they did respond he would still mumble and groan about them to himself.

So, it had been a relief at last to view an hour of TV on her own at the end of the day after her mother and father went to bed, watching Bake Off on catch-up, then off to bed to read a chapter of Ian Rankin's latest Rebus novel. Rebus had now retired but he seemed to be enjoying it and was a calmer figure. He didn't appear to have any hobbies but was pretty much full-time occupied helping out his former colleagues in their investigations. Maybe that's the secret, she thought. Stop working full-time but still have some kind of advisory role. Would that work for dad, she wondered, as she started to feel drowsy and sleep beckoned? He could be on hand, more of a back-seat role. Would he accept that? Probably not but maybe there was something in it, she wondered, as she felt herself getting drowsy.

8

The next morning Shazia was pleased that Yasmeen seemed to have forgotten everything from the day before and was her usual self again. But she knew that she would worry about her, nevertheless, wondering if the slightest thing might trigger a reaction in her daughter and if she would get a phone call from the school asking her to take her home. It wouldn't be the first time that had happened. Her mum was normally able to go but she always felt guilty if she wasn't the one to go to the school. The anticipation of a phone call would be at the back of her mind all day.

Once she arrived in the office, she assembled her team in a meeting room. They were seated around the table facing her: Joseph, McLaughlin and Mitchell. DC Michael McLaughlin was thirty-six years of age, five foot ten with cropped dark hair, and liked to keep himself fit, though since he had been seriously injured in a shooting the previous year he no longer worked out in the gym so much and drove to work, rather than cycled, and as a result he had put on a bit of weight. He lived in a one-bedroom tenement flat in the South Side with his wife, Catriona, who was expecting their first child; they were looking to move to somewhere with a garden in the spring. He was wearing a dark blue suit and a white shirt with a blue and white striped tie. Shazia thought it was so good to see him looking well again. He had had to take a lengthy period off on sick leave after being wounded. He was the most extrovert member of the team, sharing a joke or a funny story to cheer them all up when things seemed to be going nowhere or getting them down, though, since the shooting, Shazia had noticed that he was sometimes more subdued and serious. Today, when he had breezed into the room that morning with a cake that Catriona had baked, he tried to pretend that he had made it, but no one was fooled. When everyone laughed and Mitchell said, 'Aye, that will be right!' he added, 'No, you're right, I'm fucking hopeless in the kitchen. I don't even know how to turn on the washing machine. But see when that wee baby arrives, I'll be changing nappies. For one thing, if I didn't Cat would kill me!' Mitchell sighed. As much as she liked McLaughlin, and he had saved her life in the past, he was a bit of a troglodyte in the equality stakes.

DC Joan Mitchell was thirty-four years of age, five foot six with bright red hair which she had recently had cut short. She lived with her partner, Grace, in a flat in Dennistoun. Shazia knew that Grace was some sort of artist but she wasn't too sure exactly what it was that she painted, sculpted or whatever. She thought she must ask her some time but there never seemed time to discuss personal matters. Shazia hoped that Mitchell didn't think she wasn't interested in her but at the same time didn't want to sound too nosy. Mitchell was keen to share her research into the victim with the others, most of which Shazia was already aware of.

'Henderson was fifty-eight, married with two adult children, lived in Strathtay and had been an MSP for Perthshire West for ten years. He has been prominent in the debate about the future of the head of state, along with the rest of his fellow Scottish Conservative MSPs, and he has several written newspaper articles on that issue and other political issues. Also active on Twitter and Facebook too.'

Since Scotland had voted for independence there had been a debate as to who the head of state should be and, after the Holyrood parliamentary election which produced a coalition between the Scottish National Party and the Scottish Greens, parliament had debated whether to hold a referendum on whether Scotland should retain the monarch or choose to have an elected head of state. Opinion was divided. Monarchists still had the support of the Scottish Tories and other unionists while the Scottish Greens were in favour of choosing an elected figure. The SNP, the Scottish Labour Party and the Scottish Liberal Democrats were divided on the issue and in the end the government had decided to kick the question into the long grass and delay having a referendum.

'What did he think about that?' asked Shazia.

'What?'

'Keeping the monarchy.'

'He was in favour of it, but he has gone along with the idea of a referendum on the issue.' She glanced at her notebook. 'Yes. Oh, and Henderson's widow is Valerie Farquharson, the journalist.'

'Yes,' said Shazia, nodding her head. 'I know that. I spoke to her yesterday. We're seeing her today.'

'She used to work for an investment bank as a hedge fund manager and had quite a successful career, rising to the top, then gave it up to write a column for a newspaper. She's very opinionated and always criticising the "loony left" as she calls it. She's scathing about political correctness and that kind of thing. The kind of person who makes my blood boil, actually!'

'If he was an MSP for Perthshire West and lives in Strathtay, what was he doing in Glasgow on Monday evening, do we know?' asked Joseph.

McLaughlin answered. 'I know about this. I phoned his office in Holyrood and spoke to his secretary. He was due to attend a conference with business leaders at the SEC yesterday. Apparently, he was to deliver a speech and the organisers were confused when he didn't turn up. His secretary said he asked her to book him into a hotel instead of travelling through from Edinburgh on the day. He apparently said it would be more convenient to stay near the conference venue as he was due to speak in the morning.'

'More convenient for shagging, more like it,' said Mitchell. They all laughed.

'Edinburgh? Did he have a flat there then?' asked Shazia.

'Yes,' said McLaughlin. 'His secretary said he usually stayed there during the week. On weekends he was back at his house in the wilds of Perthshire.'

'I hope he wasn't putting the flat on expenses. As a taxpayer, I don't like the idea of these politicians paying out for hotel rooms and flats all over the place!'

'They aren't allowed to do that anymore. By all accounts the flat in Edinburgh was worth a packet. I got the address. It's in the New Town. Sounds pretty swish.'

'Well, we're going to have to search it. We've got keys that were found in Henderson's room. Presumably some of them are for the Edinburgh flat. OK everybody, thanks, here's the plan. We all spent a lot of time at the hotel yesterday and with your information we are beginning to get a picture of the victim. We've arranged to speak to his wife today and Joseph and I will go up to Strathtay to see her this afternoon, but we need to find out what else he did that evening. We know that he met a woman in the hotel. We need to find out who she was. We also need someone to go through to Holyrood at some point and do a bit of digging into how he got on with people through there and what they thought of him, and find out if there is anything anyone knows about him there that could be helpful. As far as evidence from the scene goes, we should get some results from Forensics soon but I know the lab is really busy and short-staffed. Anyway, we now have the CCTV pictures from the hotel for the duration of Henderson's stay. The hotel emailed them to me and I have put them into the secure shared area. Michael, I want you to look through them and see what they tell us. Do we see Henderson? Who is he

66

with? When? Someone was in the victim's room that night or that morning. How did he or she get in there? There may be a clue on the CCTV. The post-mortem is being carried out today and I will let you know the results as soon as I have them.'

Shazia wondered about this man, Henderson, and what he had been up to in the hotel that night. Was he seeing some long-standing mistress or was it a casual encounter, someone he had picked up in the hotel, such as a call-girl from one of the city's many escort agencies? She knew that these, like most of the nightclubs and casinos, were under the umbrella of the various organised crime syndicates which, despite pressure from the authorities, managed to evade prosecution. These cartels, usually family affairs, had reigned in Glasgow since the 1930s, often feuding with each other and managing to stay afloat by bribing officials in high office in the council or even within the police service. It was common knowledge that freemasonry membership was at work as part of this. That was one club she wasn't likely to be invited to join any time soon, she thought. Exposure of corruption in the force was rare but it had happened a few times in Shazia's time in service, the last time being less than a year ago and in Shazia's own team. A short time later, McLaughlin leaned over from his desk and said, 'Ma'am, I think you better come over and look at this.'

McLaughlin had clearly been busy scrutinising the CCTV images from the hotel. Shazia pulled up a chair and sat beside him. He clicked on a file on his monitor to enlarge it. 'The footage from the cameras at the rear doesn't reveal anything. The cameras above the service entrance look both ways over the back of the building and the car park, but unfortunately the coverage doesn't extend to the sides so there's a bit of a blind spot where the intruder got in through that first-floor window. But this is the recording from the foyer.' There was a timer at the bottom of the screen showing 23:05. 'OK, here is Henderson walking past the

67

desk. You will notice that he is not alone.' Shazia recognised the bulky figure of Henderson even from the grainy black and white pictures on the CCTV camera. He was swaying as he came past reception, facing the camera, one arm draped around a young woman. She had long blonde hair and was wearing a short white dress, thigh-high black boots, black gloves, and what looked like a white fur jacket with a large handbag slung over one arm. Unfortunately, though, her face was turned away from the camera so it was impossible to see what she looked like.

'She certainly looks like a working girl, doesn't she? So, then I fast-forwarded through the next hour or so and here we are.' McLaughlin dragged the cursor along the bottom of the screen until the timer read 00:11. 'The same woman appears passing reception in the opposite direction, alone this time and heading for the exit. Again, she is looking away from the camera. She knows it's there. Doesn't want to be seen.'

This, undoubtedly, was a breakthrough in the case, just what was needed. Shazia nodded her head enthusiastically and smiled. 'That's great stuff, Michael. So, he meets up with a young woman. That confirms what the hotel staff told us. And she is with him for just over an hour. Confirms the prostitute theory, as we thought. See if anyone on the vice squad has any idea who she is, even though we can't see her face.'

Joseph had been listening to the exchange. 'We should contact the escort agencies and find out if any of them had a girl booked to go to the Moray Hotel on Monday evening. The barman thought she might be East European from what he heard of her accent.'

'Isn't the hotel's front door locked at midnight? Wouldn't that mean someone had to let her out?' said Shazia.

'I phoned the hotel and asked about that,' said McLaughlin. 'Apparently, there's a button on the wall that releases the lock for a door at the side of the revolving doors. You can press the button to open the door to go out; you just can't get in that way when the door is locked.'

'No point seeing if there are prints on that door button, as she was wearing gloves. Her fingerprints will be in the bedroom, though.'

'Unless she kept her gloves on while they had sex,' said Joseph, smiling.

'That's a bit kinky, isn't it?' Shazia laughed and returned to her desk feeling enthused with this seeming progress in the case, checking her emails to see if anything had come through from Forensics. There was nothing yet. She sighed and turned to Joseph. 'By the way, how did you get on yesterday with the younger Murray brother?'

'I don't know whether he was speechless because I was the first black officer with a south London accent he had ever encountered, or he is always like that, but it was a regular brick wall. His solicitor, Malcolm King, was there of course, as you predicted, to guide him through what to say, or rather what not to say. Says he didn't know Scobie of course, never heard of him. Didn't have a clue how he had his phone number.'

'Of course. Alibi?'

'At home with the missus, naturally, all that night. Love's young dream, those two. Joan interviewed her while I spoke to him. Miraculously word for word, same story as Greg. Wonders will never cease! After that I went back to Parkhill with a few uniforms and sounded out the neighbours in the tower block once more. Naturally no one saw or heard a thing. Sammy must have had a lot of deaf and blind neighbours!'

'Get used to it. This is bloody Glasgow.'

Joseph then told her what else had happened when he had met Murray. The gangster had made Joseph an offer at the end of the interview when King had left the room and he and Joseph were left alone. 'Are you open to a business proposition?' asked Murray. Murray produced a bulging roll of fifty-pound notes from his pocket and placed it on the table between him and Joseph. 'That's yours. Just for starters. To make sure that you always dae yer best to keep my name out of anything you investigate, if you catch my drift?'

Joseph had looked at the cash. Then he stared at Murray. 'I don't take bribes. Put your money away.'

'Is that right? Squeaky clean, are you?' said Murray, snatching the money back and smiling. 'If ye change yer mind let me know.'

After he finished relating the encounter, Shazia smiled. 'That's the Murrays for you. Of course, he made sure there were no witnesses so he will deny it. He really is a chancer!'

Suddenly Mitchell exclaimed: 'Wait till you hear this! I just had a word with the head of police security in Holyrood to see if there had been any concerns regarding Henderson's security there. He said there was an incident outside the parliament a few weeks ago. As Henderson was leaving the building, there was some kind of altercation between him and someone else. The Holyrood police intervened and apprehended the man and tried to calm things down.'

'Really?' said Shazia.

'Yes. I asked what it was about. Seemed to concern a woman who worked there, Lorna Galbraith. It turned out that the man, whose name is Peter Boyle, is the boyfriend of this woman. Security told me to speak to HR so I did. They told me that there had also been a sexual harassment case brought against Henderson by Galbraith who, until recently, was employed in his office. A disciplinary investigation by the Parliamentary Standards Office was launched.'

'Interesting. I'm starting to go off this guy Henderson. OK, we need to speak to this Peter Boyle.'

'Anyway, although they didn't charge him, they did record his details, address and place of work,' said Mitchell. 'And what is really interesting is that he works in the Moray Hotel.'

9

Shona Williamson was interviewing the al-Abdallah family, whose home had been petrol-bombed the previous night. She was listening as the daughter told the story of the attack and its aftermath. Shona had got their whereabouts from the Scottish Refugee Council. The family were asylum seekers from Syria, who had been living in a block of flats in Springburn. The flats were three storeys and the al-Abdallahs, husband, wife and their four children, lived on the top floor. At some point during the night, they had been woken by one of the children shouting and the beeping of a smoke alarm, and discovered that the kitchen was thick with smoke and flames. They had managed to escape, raising the alarm by banging on their neighbours' doors. The fire had then spread through the flat and they watched the flames lick the roof of the building from the street below with their evacuated neighbours.

The fire service had arrived within minutes and swiftly extinguished the fire, but their home was gutted and they had lost nearly all of their possessions, some of which they had carried with them all the way from Syria, as they hadn't had time to gather anything together before they fled the burning building. The flat had been badly damaged from the smoke and the water used to put out the fire so they had been temporarily re-housed by the housing association as an emergency in a high-rise flat nearby. The parents had little English so Shona communicated with their daughter, Amira, a brown-eyed girl of fifteen, with an expression of quiet dignity. Amira told her the story of the fire in amazingly almost fluent English, despite the fact that she had to learn it from scratch since arriving in the country twelve months before.

Shona learned that the family had fled from Syria and travelled through Turkey and across the Mediterranean in an over-filled dingy to a Greek island, then to a camp just outside Athens. From there they became one of the fortunate families to be selected to be re-homed in Scotland under the Scottish Government's refugee scheme. 'Things had been fine until the fire,' Amira said. 'We have lost everything before. There is hatred all over the world. But we must not live in fear. Love is stronger than hate.' She flashed Shona a beautiful smile.

Shona hoped so too; she felt deeply moved by the family's resilience in the wake of such terror and their refusal to be cowed by hatred. She gave Amira a hug and wished her all the best. The photographer from the paper took a group photograph of the family. Despite all that they had been through, they looked proud and defiant.

After she had met the family, Shona paid a visit to see what remained of the al-Abdallah's fire-damaged flat. Police and a TV crew were standing outside. The windows looked like blackened eyes, empty and foreboding. Above the windows, the smoke had blackened the outside of the building but the roof was undamaged and workmen were waiting to be allowed in to clear out the flat. Police incident tape prevented her from going inside and the door was boarded up. A solitary uniformed police office stood outside. He told her that no one had reported seeing anything suspicious leading up to the fire, but it appeared that the kitchen window had been broken and the flat petrol-bombed. There was no CCTV camera in the vicinity, he said, with a sigh.

The front door of the flat opened onto an open passageway. Beside the front door on the wall she could see that someone had spray-painted IMMIGRANTS OUT! SCOTTISH ACTION NOW. She asked the photographer who was with her to make sure he took a photograph of the graffiti.

Shona drove back to the Gazette's offices and typed up her report on the attack on the al-Abdallahs. She knew that Scottish Action was a secretive far-right group dedicated to opposing immigration. It had claimed several attacks on refugees in the past few months. Since the bombing of the Buchanan Street Underground Station in Glasgow the year before by a 'lone wolf' Islamist terrorist pledging allegiance to so-called Islamic State, there had been an upsurge in hate crimes against Muslims and refugees in the city. She suspected that it wasn't necessarily the case that more people were committing these crimes but that the small minority of racists were exploiting the situation and trying to whip up resentment against immigrants. Perhaps, she thought, that by attacking refugees they believed they would produce a backlash which would in turn lead to more popular support for opposition to immigrants. William Paterson, the Orange Order member who had attempted to assassinate the Scottish Greens' MSP Aileen Buchan, had claimed to be a member of Scottish Action. The group occasionally issued statements on obscure internet sites saying that what they termed "direct action" had become the only way to draw attention to the "liberal immigration policies of the government which were bringing the country to its knees". On every occasion that a refugee family had been attacked in Scotland in recent months, the group had claimed responsibility. A right-wing political organisation called Britain United blamed the attacks on the SNP government for their immigration policy and lambasted the European Union's policy of freedom of movement across the EU. 'We need to take back control of our borders,' they proclaimed, a sentiment echoed in sections of the more right-wing mainstream media.

Shona concluded her article on the attack on the al-Abdallah family by highlighting the Scottish Action graffiti outside the burnt-out flat, listing the history of similar attacks and quoting a government spokesman as saying the action was 'disgusting and abhorrent'.

10

Shazia phoned the Moray Hotel to find out if Peter Boyle was on shift and, when it was confirmed that he was, she told the manager she would be straight over to see him. She asked Joseph to come with her before they headed to Strathtay. This time she found the hotel car park at the rear of the building by driving down a side street and into a lane. As she locked the car, she looked around. The back of the hotel looked out over the small parking area. She spotted the service door with the CCTV cameras situated outside it and a line of large bins nearby. She observed that on both sides of the building, lanes ran down towards the Broomielaw and the river. It looked like they interconnected with other lanes which crossed them, creating a maze of routes which someone could easily have used to approach or escape from the hotel undetected.

Jan Van Dijk, the hotel manager, had arranged for her to use his office to speak to Boyle. Van Dijk confirmed that Boyle had not been working on the Monday night before Boyle appeared from the kitchen wearing his chef's uniform, black and white checked trousers and white jacket. He was in his early twenties with cropped red hair, a gold earring and a neatly-trimmed ginger beard. He was about five foot nine and had a bit of a swagger as he walked in to the manager's office, but Shazia thought that his face also had a trace of anxiety as he sat down. Shazia said, 'Peter, we are investigating a murder that happened in this hotel.'

Boyle nodded. 'Everyone knows about it. What's it got to do with me?'

'The reason we need to speak to you is the connection between you and the victim.'

Boyle remained silent.

'Your girlfriend, Lorna, worked for the deceased.'

'Yes, that's right. So what?'

'You knew he was staying here?'

'I was on the phone to Lorna and she said that this guy who she had worked for had been killed in the hotel. I knew about the murder, of course, but I didn't put two and two together until she told me he was the guy who had been pestering her.'

'You knew about the sexual harassment allegation she made against him.'

'I knew that some creep had been bothering her. But I didn't even know his name. She pointed him out to me once, that's all.'

'And you confronted him outside the parliament building?'

Boyle was looking increasingly agitated. He was fidgeting with his fingers, twisting a silver ring with a skull on his right hand round and round. His eyes seemed to have grown larger, the pupils dilating, sweat appearing on his forehead. 'I was meeting Lorna after work and she pointed him out. I just told him he was a pervert. He called over some security guy and the cops got involved. That was all that happened. He said I threatened him; that was a load of crap.'

'Did you know he was staying in the hotel on Monday?'

Boyle shook his head. 'No, I told you, I didn't know until Lorna told me after he'd been killed. How would I? I work in the kitchens; we don't know anything about who is staying here.'

'Someone else who works here might have told you he was here. Where were you on Monday night?'

'It was one of my nights off. I was with Lorna. She came through from Edinburgh for the night. We went to the pictures and then back to my flat.'

'What film did you see?' asked Joseph.

'Eh? What was it called again? House of Evil, that was it. A horror. Lorna loves those. She's a bit of a Goth.'

'Where was that?'

'Cineworld. In the city centre.'

'Do you still have the tickets?'

He shook his head and smiled. 'Who keeps cinema tickets? And I paid cash so I don't even have a credit card receipt.'

'Then you went home?' said Shazia.

'Yes.'

'And the next day?'

'Well, she lives in Edinburgh. We only see each other about once a week. I don't get many days off. We just see each other whenever we can. We spent the day in bed.' He smiled. A faint blush crept over his cheeks.

'So, you spent all night and the next day together?'

'That's right. Until about three o' clock in the afternoon, then she left and got the train back to Edinburgh. I had to go into work for five.'

'You didn't come back to the hotel at any point on Monday night or Tuesday morning?' asked Shazia.

'No, why would I do that?'

Shazia and Joseph went for some food after the meeting with Boyle. Joseph suggested a pub nearby. The pub had once been a bank and inside it was immense, a monument to capitalism at the height of the British Empire, and despite having been given an obvious makeover by modern stylists, it retained many of its original Victorian features, such an elaborate frieze of decorative plasterwork on the ceiling. The most impressive feature was its hemispheric glassed cupola, from which at some point, no doubt, a glittering chandelier would have hung.

Joseph ordered a fresh orange for himself and a sparkling mineral water for Shazia. She had ordered vegetarian lasagne and he had fish and chips and it arrived within minutes. 'This is good,' she said. 'There are some rough pubs in the centre of town. Believe me, this is sophisticated for the city centre. There's still plenty of the old Glasgow to be found in some of the watering holes. I've been in plenty looking for suspects. And you don't want to go near them. Might meet a few of the worthies we are used to crossing swords with.' She took a forkful of lasagne and quenched it with water. It was burning hot. 'What did you make of our friend Boyle? He seemed a bit shifty to me and I don't know how much to believe his story. Wouldn't Lorna have told him the name of the guy who pestered her?'

'Yes,' said Joseph. 'Not much of an alibi. In bed with your girlfriend all night. I've never known alibi to work as a defence. Obviously, they'll want to stick up for each other if they planned to kill Henderson. He could have broken in, knowing the hotel as he does, talked his way into the bedroom, maybe even pinched a key or got a friend on reception to give him one. Maybe they made a mistake when they said there were no keys missing. He's definitely got to be in the frame. I thought he was lying, too.'

Shazia nodded as she sipped her mineral water, waiting for the meal to cool down before having another mouthful. 'Well, he has the motive. Henderson harassed his girlfriend. I don't believe for a second either that she didn't tell him the name of the man she worked for and who had molested her.'

'Aye, that doesn't sound right? And he would be furious. Any guy would.'

'But furious enough to kill?'

'That's the sixty-four-thousand-dollar question, isn't it?'

''I think there's enough grounds for suspicion to search his flat. We'll get a search warrant. Anyway, this looks like I can eat it now. We've got a long drive ahead of us.'

After they left the A9, Shazia followed the road along the River Tay, passing rolling fields with grazing sheep and horses, neatly forested hills, and even the occasional castle. The weather had deteriorated as they had driven out of Glasgow and north into the countryside. The road passed a distillery and then branched off uphill towards the village of Strathtay. As they approached the village they ran into a snowstorm, a sudden blizzard sweeping down from the surrounding hills. Shazia noticed the outside temperature gauge on her dashboard falling suddenly.

'Scenery's a bit different from Parkhill, eh?' she grinned, grasping the steering wheel tightly as she swung around another tight bend. 'Very posh isn't it. You won't find too many used syringes lying around here.'

'No but, probably plenty of cocaine being shoved up noses, I bet!' Joseph wasn't used to being in the passenger seat and was still feeling anxious after the near miss the other day. He had stretched his long legs out and tried to relax by taking deep breaths but it wasn't working. He felt like a coiled spring. She liked to drive fast. At one point she took a corner at speed and narrowly avoided a tractor that suddenly pulled out from a field onto the road.

Shazia could sense his anxiety. 'Soon be there don't worry. Satnav says it's only another couple of miles.'

Joseph laughed. 'I looked up some of Ms Farquharson's columns. She doesn't strike me as a big friend of the BAME community. Wait till she gets a look at us two appearing on her doorstep! She'll probably have a heart attack.'

The Farquharson-Henderson family home was an imposing grey Victorian mansion on the edge of the village, set in extensive grounds. Remote-controlled gates swung open to allow them in once Shazia had announced who she was into the intercom. The front garden was long and wide with carefully cultivated flower beds. A white Range Rover with a personalised number-plate identifying it as belonging to Valerie sat outside, but there was enough room to park a couple of double-decker buses. A tower in the Scottish baronial style rose above the main entrance, giving the overall impression of a castle.

Valerie Farquharson came out to meet them accompanied by two golden retrievers as they pulled up on the gravelled driveway. She was an attractive woman in her mid-fifties, with a sweep of dyed blonde hair, and was wearing a green waterproof Barbour jacket. It was unzipped and beneath it was a tartan shirt above red corduroy trousers. Her face was heavy with make-up and Shazia wondered if she always wore so much or was this to cover up any signs of grief?

As Joseph had predicted, her face was a mixture of incredulity and exasperation as she struggled to retain an impassive expression on greeting the two police officers. After the introductions, she took them into the house, passing through an oak-panelled hall and then into a large room filled with antiques and oil paintings which she announced rather grandly to be the 'drawing room'. The room had a timber floor with an oak-lined bay window which looked out over the front gardens; a fireplace housed a log fire, in front of which a leather sofa and several armchairs were set around a highly-polished mahogany coffee table.

'Please have a seat,' said Farquharson. Would you like some tea or coffee?' Her voice had an accent that betrayed no hint of being Scottish yet didn't sound English either. It did sound familiar though. Shazia wondered where she had heard that tone before as she and Joseph sat down side by side on the sofa.

'No thank you, Ms Farquharson. I would like to once again offer our sincere condolences.' Shazia realised how artificial these words sounded. 'We realise that this is a very difficult time for you and do not wish to intrude on you more than is necessary. Can I ask you how you are coping after what has happened? Are you getting enough support?' Shazia was never sure how a deceased's partner would be. Would they be too grief-stricken and upset to talk, shocked and staring at visitors with eyes like fish? Or doped up with some strong sedative or other? Valerie Farquharson appeared to be none of these. She exuded calmness, her expression blank. Maybe she was on heavy tranquillisers, but Shazia doubted it. She had the feeling that this was the type of person who believed in the stiff-upper-lip mentality of the upper classes. Show no weakness to the enemy. Were they the enemy?

Farquharson sat down on the armchair opposite them, smiled and said, 'Thank you so much for asking. Yes, my son and daughter have been very good. I am lucky to have such a wonderful family.' The politeness was slightly strained as if she was putting on an act. She didn't want them here, poking their noses in, asking questions, but she would give a good impression that she did.

'Can you tell me about your children?' said Shazia.

'Of course.' Farquharson's mouth suggested a slight smile and she walked across the room and picked up a silver-framed photograph. A tall handsome fair-haired young man in a kilt stood beside a pretty young woman with long blonde hair in a flowery summer dress. 'Though they are not really children now, they're both grown up. Euan is twenty-six and works in IT in Edinburgh for a big pensions company. He's doing very well and intent on making pots of money. He certainly likes spending it! He just bought himself a Porsche, his pride and joy. He lives in Morningside with his girlfriend in a sweet little flat. He came through and took me to Glasgow last night to identify Charles's body. I couldn't have done that on my own. He brought me back and stayed the night, actually, but he had to go into the office early this morning. Amanda is twenty and reading PPE at Oxford. Brasenose College. She wanted to come up straight away but I told her to wait until the weekend, so she will come up on Friday night. No need to miss classes, I told her. We Skyped last night, though. She is devastated, poor girl. She was very close to her father. We all were, naturally, but there was a special bond between the two of them, you know, father and daughter. Euan is more like me. A bit hard-nosed, stoical: we just get on with whatever life throws at us. She's more sensitive but also a political animal, wants to be a politician like her father, only, would you believe it, she is a nationalist.' Farquharson laughed. 'An actual nationalist in the family, can you believe it! She and Charles have had some debates around the supper table, I can tell you! Where did we go wrong, I ask you? Do you have any children, Inspector?'

Shazia instantly found herself lost for words. She couldn't help comparing her autistic daughter with these high-achieving young people. Yasmeen would never manage to attend a university, let alone Oxbridge, and a career in IT or politics was out of the question. What would the future hold for her, she wondered? Yasmeen could not sense how others were feeling, couldn't look them in the eyes, and had great difficulty forming any kinds of friendships. She needed order around her and her life to be run in a fixed pattern or she panicked. She couldn't cope with change or unexpected events. Socially she was awkward and far removed from these precocious young adults. Yet, she could apply herself to a task with amazing attention to detail and produce beautifully intricate pieces of artwork and designs. Shazia felt such love and affection for her daughter that she could never honestly envy anyone else's children. The thought of losing Yasmeen terrified her more than anything. When she had found out that she had been self-harming, the idea that Yasmeen could be taken away from her became overpowering, and Shazia began to sleep badly. She gathered her thoughts together. 'Yes, I have a daughter. They make life worth living, don't they!'

'Absolutely,' said Farquharson, smiling politely.

'Could you give me contact details for your son and daughter as we'll need to speak to them in case your husband had mentioned anything to them, or they know anything that is useful.'

'Of course.' She stood up, opened a drawer from a bureau and scribbled something down on a notepad with a fountain pen, tore off the sheet and handed it to Shazia. 'That's their mobile numbers. I've also given you Euan's address in case you wish to visit him in person in Edinburgh. I didn't imagine you would travel down to Oxford to see Amanda, but she will be here at the weekend as I said.'

'Thanks, that is very helpful. If you wouldn't mind, I would like to just ask you some questions about your husband to try to get a clearer picture of his life. I am sure that you understand that we need to find out why someone would want to kill him.'

Valerie Farquharson took out a cloth handkerchief and dabbed her eyes, smudging her mascara, and shook her head. 'Of course. I don't understand who would want to do such a terrible thing to Charles. Underneath that tough political exterior, he was really such a gentle soul.'

Shazia tried to reconcile this description of the man with the one she had seen on the YouTube clips she had looked at since his murder, in which he was often aggressively attacking his political opponents, whether in a TV studio or in the Holyrood debating chamber, seemingly revelling in the cut and thrust of political combat. However, she smiled and nodded at the grieving widow. 'Yes. I know you must be terribly shocked. When did you last speak to him?'

'On Monday evening. About six or so when he phoned.'

'How did he sound?'

'Fine. Just the same as usual.'

'Did Charles ever speak about anyone or anything that he was worried about? Or about anyone who had threatened him?'

'I don't know how much you know, Inspector, about the life of a politician, but there is constant abuse and criticism. And I don't just mean the speeches made by his political opponents in parliament. All this commentary online. He hated that as I am sure all politicians do. There were some awful messages on Twitter, on Facebook. Vile, nasty stuff, full of vitriol. Real hatred. I told him to ignore it but I don't think he could.'

Shazia remembered reading one of this woman's newspaper columns in which she attacked certain public figures because of their views and opinions. There didn't seem much difference from what she was describing and the comments which ordinary members of the public made on the internet. Her columns were just as public in fact and just as abusive, often personal attacks on someone she took a dislike to.

Joseph said, 'Yes, we will have a look at his social media accounts to see what is there. As you say, it's not uncommon for people in the public eye to receive abuse these days. Most of the time it doesn't lead to anything, it's just idiots, but it can be offensive and we have a team working full time on cyber abuse. Did he speak of any actual death threats or anything like that?'

Farquharson shook her head. 'No, nothing like that, as far as I am aware. It's so easy now, though, isn't it? With a smartphone and an app, in a couple of seconds you've told someone they deserve to be raped or to die. It's shocking. Something ought to be done about it by the companies running these platforms, or the government. There needs to be some sort of filter to prevent abuse, surely?'

Shazia nodded. 'I don't use social media, partly because of that.'

Farquharson looked at her as if she was an extinct species, someone from the previous century. 'Really? Well, I am afraid that I do. It's so handy to keep in touch with what family and friends are up to. And for work, too, Twitter is vital in my job. Charles said it was essential. It was how he kept in touch with people and what they were thinking. It is only a minority who abuse it of course, but they don't deserve to be able to use it.'

'Apart from some messages on social media,' said Shazia, 'was there anything else that Charles was worried about?'

Farquharson paused and thought about this. 'He didn't seem to be himself recently. He was spending a lot of time in his study when he came home. I would hardly see him. Normally at weekends we would go out and walk the dogs together. He said he had too much to do and locked himself away. I don't know what that was about. I tried asking him but he wouldn't tell me. He just said, "It's the usual boring political stuff," whenever I asked.'

'We'll need to have a look in his study if that is alright?'

'Yes, of course. He carried his laptop with him. I expect you found it.'

'Yes, we have it. Do you know if he was going to meet anyone on Monday night in Glasgow?'

'No, he didn't say.'

'I am sorry to pry into personal matters but did you know about the grievance that was taken out against him by someone in his office?'

She nodded. 'Yes, that troublesome Galbraith girl. He told me all about it. Apparently, she was all over him like a rash from the first day she got the job. Proper little minx, I think she was. No doubt she thought she could latch onto him and make some money, saw him as, what do they call them, a "Sugar Daddy"? Of course, he told her he wasn't interested but didn't report it. She then claimed *he* had harassed her! In fact, it was the other way round! Little bitch!'

Joseph said, 'Was that the only time anything like that had ever happened?'

Farquharson's face went pale and she shook a little. It was as if she had turned in on herself and was viewing a memory lodged deep within her mind.

Shazia said, 'Is there anything else that you think we ought to know, Valerie?'

'About thirty years ago, we had not long been married in fact, Charles had an affair. It was that old cliché; he fell for his secretary. He was a young solicitor then, building up his practice when we lived in Edinburgh. She was another type like that Lorna Galbraith girl. Wore short skirts all the time. Always showing off her legs. I mean, some of these girls lead men on, don't they?'

Joseph asked, 'So what happened?'

'When I found out about the affair, I told him to end it, find her another job elsewhere. That's what happened.'

'Where did she go?'

'I have no idea. We never spoke about it again. I haven't told anyone about it until this minute. It was all gone and forgotten as far as I am concerned until you asked me that question.'

'What was the woman's name?'

Farquharson drew a deep breath, closed her eyes and said, 'Let me think now, what was her name? Fiona something. Ah yes, Christie. Her name was Fiona Christie.'

'I don't suppose you know where she is now?' asked Shazia.

Farquharson shook her head. 'No idea. It was a long time ago, Inspector.'

Joseph wrote the name down in his notebook and said, 'And as far as you know, Charles didn't have any other affairs or complaints against him until the allegation by Ms Galbraith?'

'No. certainly not. I would have known. Charles had one lapse and put it behind him. Everything he stood for, personally and politically, was about supporting family values, the same as I am. The family was paramount to him.

He would never have touched that girl in his office, I am sure of it.'

Shazia hesitated. What she was about to say was going to contradict everything that Farquharson had just claimed about her husband. But she had to know. 'I know this will come as a shock to you, Valerie, but it will have to come out at some stage. We suspect that your husband spent some time with a woman, possibly a sex worker, on the night that he died.'

Farquharson's hands instantly went to her face, pinching her cheeks. She looked stunned and was silent for a second. 'No! Oh my God! It gets worse. A prostitute? That can't be true, there must be some mistake, surely.'

'I can't tell you any more, Valerie, but we have evidence that points in that direction.'

'He must have been put up to this by someone. It must have been a trap. A honey trap, isn't that what they call it? Surely it's some kind of a set-up?'

Joseph said, 'We can't rule out that as a possibility of course but I wanted to make you aware of the circumstances that we know about.'

Farquharson took some time to compose herself, coming to terms with what the police officers had just told her. Then she said in a faltering voice, 'Thank you for coming to see me and being so frank but I don't think that I have been very helpful to you. If that is all, Inspector, I think I would like to lie down now. This has all been a terrible shock.'

Shazia suddenly remembered who Farquharson's voice reminded her of. It was her old headteacher from her schooldays at an independent girls' school in the South Side of Glasgow. She remembered the headteacher's name, Miss Neil. Shazia had hated attending that school, with its dismal dark brown blazers, but her father had insisted that she and her sister went there rather than go to the local authority's comprehensive. He believed that in paying for a private education he was guaranteeing educational success for his daughters. It was certainly a hothouse learning environment designed to pursue academic success above anything else. Preparation to pass exams was the goal and not just to pass, the expectation was that you had to achieve 'A' passes, the highest possible grade, in all of your subjects.

She remembered Miss Neil's assemblies, in which she lectured the girls to avoid all distractions. It was the same cut-glass posh accent as Valerie Farquharson's. There was certainly no trace of the west of Scotland in it, in fact nothing Scottish about it at all. Miss Neil had emphasised how they must focus on study and nothing else. Otherwise they would regret not having worked hard enough. Shazia had known several schoolfriends who had ended up having nervous breakdowns after suffering in silence, whether from personal issues they could not discuss openly, or from the remorseless academic pressure which made them feel that anything less than straight 'A's was going to brand them a failure. One girl had even tried to commit suicide.

'I'm sorry to ask you this, but can you tell me where you were on Monday night?' Shazia asked.

'I was here. And before you ask, yes, I was alone. So, I suppose I have no alibi if I had wanted to kill my husband, if that is what you are thinking, Inspector. We didn't have a perfect marriage, but who does?'

'Thank you. It's just procedure. I am sure you want the investigation to be absolutely thorough.'

'Of course.'

'If it's alright, we would like to have a look in Mr Henderson's study now, just in case there is anything which might help us in the investigation.'

'Of course, I'll show you where it is.'

She led them back into the hall and up an oak-panelled staircase to the first floor. Henderson's study consisted of a gloomy room at the end of a corridor. A small window allowed some light, but it looked out to the back garden where a large chestnut tree stood, its bare branches like spindly arms reaching out towards the house. The desk was littered with papers. There were a few family photographs on the desk and photographs of the children from when they were much younger. One photograph showed the boy pushing a wheelbarrow with the girl inside it, laughing.

'I will leave you to it,' said Farquharson, retreating from the room and closing the door.

Shazia sat down at the desk and looked through the drawers. In amongst a pile of receipts, she found a restaurant bill for £262.35 from the Number One, The Balmoral in Edinburgh on Wednesday 18th January. This could be the item in his diary, meeting CF. She placed it carefully into an evidence bag.

Joseph concentrated on looking through a filing cabinet. 'There's a folder here marked Finance. Looks like Henderson had taken out a large mortgage to buy the property in Edinburgh. Not only did he buy a flat, he bought the entire townhouse it is in and was letting out the ground floor. There are copies of bank and credit card statements; might be useful to have these.'

'Definitely, we'll take that. Otherwise, not much else here. We'll get his office in Holyrood checked out too. But I can't see anything else significant here.'

After looking through the rest of the papers on his desk, Shazia and Joseph went back downstairs and found Valerie Farquharson lying on the sofa with an ice-pack on her head.

'Just a migraine,' she said.

'Stay where you are,' said Shazia. 'We'll show ourselves out. Just one more thing you might be able to help us with, though. In a diary we found in his briefcase there is a mention of a dinner appointment a few weeks ago with someone with the initials CF. You wouldn't happen to know who that is, would you?'

'Yes, that would be Cameron, that's his oldest friend, he was his best man at our wedding. They were at school together at Fettes in Edinburgh. Cameron lives in Helensburgh now.'

'What is Cameron's last name?'

'Cameron Forsyth. The businessman. I'm sure you will have heard of him.'

'Oh yes, of course, he owns a chain of clothes stores, doesn't he?'

'Yes. He and Charles go way back. They were very close. Charles is his oldest friend. I'm sorry, Inspector, I don't think I've helped you very much.' She wiped a tear from her cheek. Her mascara had made little black lines from her eyes, like rivers, down her cheek.

They drove away from the Farquharson-Henderson home both wondering if they had dropped a stone of reality into this rural pond, sending waves out in all directions across the pastoral landscape. It certainly didn't seem to disturb the sheep, though: they carried on chewing the grass and didn't even look up when Shazia's Volkswagen sped past.

Joseph got a number for Cameron Forsyth's office. His PA told him he was away on business in London but would be back in Glasgow on Thursday. He told her to ask him to get in touch with the police, leaving numbers for himself and Shazia.

Forsyth phoned Shazia back almost straight away and Shazia put him on speakerphone but it wasn't a good signal, probably because they were driving through the Scottish countryside and she expected to be cut off at any moment. From the background noise of traffic, it sounded as if he was in a busy street somewhere. 'Can I speak to you when I am back in Scotland later tomorrow?' he said. 'I will give you a ring when I arrive.'

Shazia didn't think it was worth trying to have an interview with him over the phone and it wasn't a clear enough line to continue the conversation at the moment anyway. 'OK, see you then.'

'Do you think,' said Joseph, 'that she knew her husband was a philanderer?'

'That's a fancy word for it,' said Shazia. 'You mean a shagger?'

'For a woman of your background, Inspector, you do have a surprising grasp of basic vocabulary.'

'I didn't used to swear or use words like that, Sergeant. But sometimes, especially for some men, they are entirely appropriate! In this case, yes, I think Valerie Farquharson knew very well what her husband got up to on his nights away. The question is, did it bother her. And if it did, did it bother her enough to have him killed?'

'Interesting thought. Maybe she isn't so morally upright herself.'

On the drive back from Strathtay she dialled her mum's mobile on the hands-free set in the car and told her that she didn't know when she would be home, just to have dinner without her and ask Yasmeen to get ready for bed. Her mother wasn't surprised. It was more of a surprise these days when Shazia was able to come home and eat with the rest of the family.

11

'I now have the PM report on Charles Henderson,' said Shazia, looking at Joseph and McLaughlin. 'As expected, the cause of death was asphyxiation, consistent with suffocation from a pillow being held over the mouth and nose and pressure exerted on the trachea. There were a number of bruises to the face, throat, arms and shoulders, which indicate he was held down with extreme force. Time of death is put at between midnight and four a.m. Initial toxicology results show a high amount of alcohol in the bloodstream as well as ketamine.'

'Ketamine?' said Joseph.

'Yes,' said Shazia. They were all thinking the same thing, she knew. 'His drink could have been spiked but, equally, he may have taken it knowingly. We're still waiting on a report from Forensics and I'll let you know as soon as I have it.'

McLaughlin said, 'OK. Picture this. Henderson is asleep. Someone knocks at his door in the middle of the night and wakes him up. Perhaps they say they are from the hotel. Confused and disorientated from the drugs and the alcohol, he gets up and opens the door. Then, they suddenly attack him, forcing him back onto the bed, and suffocate him.'

'It's possible', said Shazia. 'Or the woman he had sex with lets the killer into the room, whoever broke in through that window.'

Shazia then related her conversations she had had with Henderson's son and daughter the previous evening. 'I phoned his son Euan last night but didn't get anything much from him. He said he had been away skiing for a week. I told him that someone would arrange to see him so I asked Joan to go through to Edinburgh today and take a statement from him. She has also arranged to interview Lorna Galbraith, the woman who was his assistant, and she'll have a look at Henderson's flat. I spoke to the daughter, Amanda. She told me her father seemed happy when she spoke to him at the weekend. "His normal self", she said. So, nothing really helpful there from either of them, I'm afraid.'

She emailed the officer in charge of the team which specialised in prostitution and asked for the description of the woman seen in the hotel with Henderson to be shared with some of the sex workers whom the team knew. This produced a positive result when, a few hours later, she got word that one of the sex workers thought she knew who the young woman was. The sex worker, Emma, had met her at a hotel one night in December when they had both been booked for a threesome with a man in another hotel. Emma mostly worked freelance, but had done some work for other agencies in the past, which was when she had met the girl who she thought might be her. She said she was called Natalia and that she was from somewhere in Eastern Europe. Emma said Natalia was working for Discreet Escorts at the time, one of the city's escort agencies. She shared the information with the others and phoned the Discreet agency number and spoke to the agency's manager, David Robertson, who told her that none of the girls on their books had been booked for any appointment in the Moray Hotel that evening and he knew of no one called Natalia. Joseph reported that, disappointingly, the agency's website didn't reveal anyone called Natalia.

But McLaughlin then announced he had found something significant. 'I've been looking at the records from Henderson's mobile phone and found something interesting,' said McLaughlin. 'He probably booked an escort on Thursday 2nd February. There is a call to a mobile number just after three that afternoon which is the contact number on the website of this escort agency, Discreet Escorts. It belongs to the manager, David Robertson.'

'Excellent! We'll bring him in. Anything else significant on the phone?' asked Shazia.

'Other than that, there's some calls to his wife and his secretary on the Monday. I also checked his social media accounts. He received a few abusive messages including at least one death threat claiming he has insulted Islam, which I'm trying to trace. There're also people attacking him as being too right wing and others saying he's too left wing. Bit of a confusing mess actually. There's a lot of angry people out there who get off on raging at someone. The internet history on his laptop also shows that as well as the inevitable porn sites, he visited an online gambling site quite a lot.'

Joseph said, 'That explains something else. I looked through those bank statements we picked up from Henderson's house yesterday. He took out a mortgage for one and a half million for the townhouse in the New Town which he purchased a few years ago and then converted. There's also a lot of money flowing in and out regularly. Mostly out. He certainly went through a lot of cash. His savings accounts seem to have taken quite a hit. At one time he had several hundred thousand stashed away, but the balance has fallen a lot in the last few years. The guy had quite a large credit card debt, too.'

Shazia sent McLaughlin and a team of uniformed officers, armed with a search warrant, to the Discreet Escort office, a sleazy room above a bookmaker's in Possil, to bring the manager in for questioning. McLaughlin was glad to get out of the office but he was aware of pain in his shoulder. It had never been quite the same since the shooting and he realised that it might hamper him if the raid led to a situation where he had to try to restrain someone or even defend himself. The shooting itself had made him wary and cautious in such situations; unlike how, previously, when he faced them with confidence. He even sometimes now wondered if his future lay in the police force at all. The injury, and being about to become a father, along with disappointment in being unsuccessful in applying for the post of Detective Sergeant, had made him consider whether in fact he should think about another career, a less dangerous one. However, the surprise raid on the escort agency's office didn't result in any physical confrontation, merely a tirade of verbal abuse by the manager. While there, an officer accessed the office computer and discovered files listing names and addresses of the various brothels where young women were being kept, along with details of the women themselves, including a photograph and details of a "Natalia from Latvia", but whose real name was listed as Katarina Marková from Slovakia. She was pictured in her underwear, lying on a sofa in front of a red backcloth. McLaughlin guessed that the image had previously been used on the website as an advert but it had since been removed along with the name "Natalia". He took a photo of her face with his phone and stopped off at the hotel on his way back to HQ. The barman wasn't on duty but the receptionist, Anna, who had been on duty, looked closely at the photo on his phone and confirmed that this was the woman she had seen with Henderson that night.

When McLaughlin returned to HQ, he summarised what he had discovered. 'Her real name is Katarina Marková and there is an address together with the names and addresses of all of the other girls on the agency's books, many of whom appear to be of Eastern European origin.' Shazia picked up the phone and immediately passed the information onto the Public Protection team in the force which specialised in human trafficking. Several raids took place that day around the city, resulting in twenty-five women between the ages of sixteen and twenty-three being held under suspicion of being victims of human trafficking. Katarina was one of those brought in.

*

When she had heard them breaking down the door and crashing into the flat, Katarina had to remind herself that she was not still living in the slums she had grown up, where they were regularly raided by angry men on some pretext or other. It wasn't often the authorities or the police, though, who usually steered well clear of the ghettoes, leaving them to be preyed on by criminal gangs. She had been glad to have the opportunity to escape from Slovakia along with her friend Dominika.

The two of them had been on their way home from school one summer's day near the end of term and had just got off the school bus when they were approached by a handsome man in his early thirties, looking for directions. The two girls, both blonde and attractive, were eighteen and dreamed of going to college or university when they left school that year but knew that the financial realities of how to afford such a step meant such a dream was impossible. They lived in the same overcrowded block of flats, each sharing a cramped bedroom with their younger siblings. Their parents would rely on them to earn some money but where was there work to be found? The best they could hope for was to find work in Bratislava or another city, but the competition for jobs meant that their chances of success were slim.

The man, Matej, was tall and good-looking, with slicked-back black hair. He was smartly dressed in a well-cut blue suit, white linen shirt and highly-polished black shoes. He was clean-shaven and sounded educated and friendly: the epitome of a respectable businessman, very unlike the gangster types that tended to hang about the area, who invariably wore black leather jackets and jeans and had sour, unshaven faces. Matej had approached them asking for direction, got talking to them, then invited them to join him for a coffee. The two girls immediately accepted. What harm could there be sitting down at a pavement café for a coffee?

Matej told them stories of his life in Bratislava, making it sound a million miles from their own humdrum existence in this sleepy provincial town. He said he worked for an employment agency and was on his way to interview someone who had applied for a job as an engineer, but he was a bit too early so was going for a coffee to pass the time, and how lovely it was to meet two such attractive young women who had helped him to find the address he was looking for.

Matej described the places he liked to eat and drink in the capital city and showed them some photographs of his apartment on his smartphone. It looked fantastic, full of designer furnishings and with a balcony overlooking the rooftops. The girls were captivated. He then showed them some photographs of exclusive hotels and restaurants in Scotland where he said there were ample opportunities for working and building a career in hospitality. Plus, he said, the cities there were better than in Eastern Europe, better even than Bratislava. There were nightclubs where you could dance all night to top DJs. He asked them how good their English was, and he said it sounded good enough for them to be taken on. He even spoke about the possibility of gaining qualifications in the industry and the potential for promotion.

The girls were attracted to the idea but had some reservations. They weren't sure exactly where Scotland was though Matej said it was near England. What if they didn't like it there? Matej reassured them. Not only would the agency pay for their travel to Scotland and their accommodation, they could have free return tickets whenever they chose to come back and they could terminate their contracts when they wanted. There was no obligation to stay for any set period. They could try it for a while if they liked, and they would be able to save enough money to then put themselves through college or university. It sounded like all their dreams had come true.

The pay he spoke about was about ten or twenty times what it was possible to earn in Slovakia and they would be able to send back a decent amount to their families but it was a big step. They said they would have to speak to their parents. Matej said he understood and was happy to speak to them too and they could have time to think about it, but he needed to know by the following week, otherwise the places that the agency would be offering would be gone. There were lots of other towns and villages with girls like them who were desperate to find work, he said.

Matej gave them his phone number and they watched him get in his black Mercedes and drive off. They felt stunned and overcome with excitement and rushed home to tell their families. A month later, passports for them having been sorted out with Matej's help, they found themselves on a bus heading west through Europe towards Scotland. Eight months on, the door of her Glasgow flat was smashed in.

'Why didn't you open the door?' the policeman asked.

Katarina looked back blankly at him and said nothing. The officer then realised that she couldn't open the door even if she had wanted to. The inhabitants of the flat, apart from an older woman, were prisoners. She and Dominika were led out of the flat and down the stairs and into a police van, along with the two other Slovakian girls who shared the flat and the older Slovakian woman who, the police suspected, acted as their keeper in this brothel and makeshift prison. She felt numb. The dream had long ago turned into a nightmare. Surely it couldn't get any worse?

12

Katarina was now seated in Interview Room 1 on the first floor of police HQ, shaking and looking pale and terrified in a thin short-sleeved black T-shirt. Joseph switched on the recorder and a red light came on the machine. As with all interviews, the session would be filmed. Shazia described who was present. A duty lawyer sat in on the interview to represent Katarina but, as it was ascertained that her English was sufficiently good and that she understood them, it was decided that an interpreter was unnecessary. Shazia was relieved; it would have meant a further delay in proceedings while they found one, and she was keen to move fast with the interview. Once they got past the details about her name and where she came from and when and how she came to be in Glasgow, Shazia told her that her circumstances amounted to being a victim of illegal human trafficking, but they needed to question her in relation to a serious offence. Shazia asked about who she worked for in Glasgow and Katarina at first looked like she would be unwilling to speak. Shazia then made it clear that she was being considered as a suspect in a murder investigation and that if she was at all involved, then her cooperation would result in a shorter sentence. She explained that Katarina had been identified as being with the victim that night in the hotel. Katarina looked shocked, sobbing for a few minutes, and Shazia was on the verge of accepting that they would get nothing from her when the young woman started speaking.

'I not know his name,' she said. 'I come to Glasgow with my friend and we are taken to flat by man. He say he has to have our passports but he not give them back.'

Shazia said, 'What was this man like? Was he Scottish? Slovakian?'

Katarina's lips were pursed and she stared hard at the floor. Evidently, she was not going to reveal anything about her captors. She just shook her head slightly.

'How did you end up in the Moray Hotel on Monday night?' said Joseph.

She shrugged her shoulders 'Man pick me up in his car and bring me to hotel. I was told to meet man in bar.'

'What kind of car was it?' asked Shazia.

'What make? What colour?' asked Joseph.

'I don't know.'

Shazia nodded. 'What happened when you arrived at the hotel?'

'Man sit at table in bar on his own. I go over to his table, we have drink then go to room.'

'What happened in the hotel room?'

'We go to bed. We have sex. I tell him to use condom. I carry condom in handbag.'

Shazia looked into her eyes: 'He was alive when you left him then? You didn't kill him?'

She shook her head. 'No. No. No. I not kill man. He alive when I go.' She started to cry again. Her body shook. 'No. Please believe me. I only there to sleep with man. Why would I him kill?'

'How long did you stay in the room with him?' asked Shazia.

'One hour he pay for.'

'How much did he pay for this hour?'

'Two hundred and fifty. Cash.'

'Is that the usual amount?'

She looked embarrassed and suddenly appeared to be the young teenage girl that she really was. 'Depends what they want. Straight sex. With condom. One hour is two hundred and fifty.'

'So, he had straight sex?'

She nodded.

'Had you ever seen him before?'

'No.'

'Did you use any drugs in the room?'

She shook her head.

'Did you bring ketamine with you and give it to your client?'

Again, she shook her head.

'Did you spike his drink?'

'No.'

'You need to tell us the truth, Katarina.'

She remained silent.

'Did you let anyone into the room when you left?'

She shook her head.

'Please answer. For the record.'

'No.'

'You let someone else in who killed him, didn't you?'

'No.'

'What happened after you left the room? How did you get back to your flat?'

'Man pick me up in car and take me back to flat.'

'What happened to the money? Did you keep it?'

'No. Man take it all.'

'OK. We will need a description of the man who held you in the flat and brought you to the hotel.'

Katarina looked anxious. She shook her head. 'No. I cannot.' This clearly was something that she was not going to divulge.

'Katarina, we will provide you with protection as someone who has been trafficked. Plus, we are investigating a murder and you may, at the very least, have been an accessory to this, and I don't feel that you are telling us everything we need to know. Maybe you have been threatened or someone has made you afraid that if you cooperate with the police something bad will happen. You will receive medical attention, but we require to take your fingerprints and a DNA sample. Do you understand?' She nodded.

One they were out of the room, Shazia said, 'Let's grab a coffee and take stock of where we are.' They sat down at her desk with McLaughlin.

Shazia said, 'So Henderson arranged to have a prostitute delivered to his hotel. Katarina gets picked for the job. Possibly she killed him, or she helped someone to. The only mobile phone found in her flat belongs to the older woman. We'll see what contacts are on it and hopefully get a lead to this man but it may be that it all was done through the agency. The young women didn't have any phones, no doubt so they couldn't contact their homes. But the important thing is, we need to find out who this man was who took her to the hotel. She was probably dropped and picked up somewhere not far from the hotel so Michael, have a look at CCTV in the streets around the hotel and see if you can pick up any sign of her being dropped off, maybe even a registration number. We might get an image of the driver if we're lucky. Also, find out who owns the flat she was living in.'

'Yes, ma'am.'

'Do you think maybe she had a hand in it?' asked Joseph. 'Even killed him?'

'Undoubtedly, she is involved in some way, but in this job, as you know, you have to keep an open mind. She could be innocent or a liar, but I get the feeling that she is just scared out of her wits and with a bit of time she might crack, if she has got anything to do with it. She will have been told that her family will be killed if she grasses but let's get her to look at the mugshots in the database anyway. Maybe she will start to be a bit more co-operative and then we'll really be getting somewhere. Get in touch with the Protected Persons Unit. Make sure she is taken somewhere safe where an eye can be kept on her. She doesn't have a passport so she shouldn't be able to flee the country. It's in her own best interests that she doesn't go walkabout. Try and get that explained to her and maybe, once we have made more progress, she will tell us what she knows.'

Joseph nodded and said, 'Let's say that she knew there was someone going to come in after her so she lets the person into the room, easily done. Maybe she didn't know what he was going to do. What I'd like to know is why?'

'Henderson was targeted by someone with a grievance of some sort. He rubbed somebody up the wrong way big time! We'll find out, Joseph, don't worry.'

'I admire your optimism, ma'am.'

'It's not optimism. It's experience. Somebody always slips up somewhere. They will have made a mistake along the line at some point, believe me.'

The manager of the escort agency, David Robertson, was a small, overweight man in his early forties. He wore thick spectacles and had an unpleasant, sweaty odour. Joseph thought that his face resembled a flounder, with his thick lips and flabby cheeks. The hair that he had left on his head was in the style of the comb-over to attempt to disguise the encroaching baldness, and the disparity between this repulsive specimen and the glamorous girls whose photos adorned his company's website was striking.

Robertson vehemently denied knowing anything about how the girls came to Scotland. He said that the girls volunteered to register with his agency and were not, technically, employees. His lawyer, a middle-aged woman called Frances Donaldson, repeatedly intervened on Robertson's behalf, arguing that her client was an innocent businessman running a legitimate business.

'A man called Charles Henderson made a call to the number listed for your agency, which is your mobile number, last Thursday about three to book an escort, didn't he?' said Joseph.

'Did he? I cannae remember.' He claimed to know nothing about any booking of Katarina and had got confused when the police had phoned and asked about Natalia as he knew her as Katarina. No, he didn't know why her photo was not on the website but, yes, she occasionally did some work with them, but not on that night. 'She must have been freelancing,' he suggested.

'Who owns the agency?' asked Shazia.

'I do,' said Robertson.

Shazia was not convinced by his answer.

The young women found in flats being used as brothels would be interviewed as witnesses and Robertson was remanded in custody, held on suspicion of being involved in human trafficking.

13

Shazia was thinking about Katarina as she went over her notes for the press conference at noon. Katarina reminded her of the Russian model, Olga Yevdokimova. They both had the same long blonde hair and sparkling blue eyes, though Katarina did not quite have the same beauty or figure that made the Russian such a sought-after international model. She had finally interviewed the Russian model a year ago, six months after the killing of the Glasgow politician, Colin Chisholm, in what had turned out to be a failed SVR plot to recruit him to work for the Russian state. Yevdokimova had been having an affair with Chisholm and she had then disappeared after his death.

Shazia had travelled to Berlin in October to ask Yevdokimova what she knew about the killing, but she had got nothing out of her during the interview in a Berlin police station. The Russian had been perfectly pleasant, charming even, but it had been like having a conversation with a robot programmed to give certain answers as she sat there feeding biscuits to her white Chihuahua perched on her lap. Yevdokimova had claimed that the first she had heard about Chisholm's death had been from TV when she was in Spain. Her relationship with Chisholm had been brief, she said, and they broke up by mutual agreement. It was, she claimed, just a coincidence that she knew the Russian oligarch Boris Morozov and had simply gone on holiday on his yacht. It was later suspected that Morozov's sons had murdered Chisholm on the instructions of their father. Yevdokimova denied any suggestions that she was implicated in blackmail or murder and insisted that she knew nothing about the tape leaked to the press that had exposed Chisholm's drug-taking and corruption. There was nothing else Shazia could do. There was no evidence against her and so Shazia had to leave it at that, though she was convinced most of what she had been told had been a pack of lies. Shazia wasn't convinced of her innocence: there was something deeply disturbing about the Russian model. Was Katarina similar in her ability to deceive?

At the press conference, held in the large conference room on the ground floor of Police Scotland's Glasgow HQ, Shazia waited while Detective Superintendent Hamilton provided the media with what was known about the murder so far. She was seated between Hamilton and DCI Cooper behind a table, looking out at the sea of journalists' faces. Press reports for the past two days had covered the mere basics, splashing the news of an MSP's murder over the front pages, but there had been widespread speculation and rumour across social media and the internet. Less than a year ago a local politician had been murdered in a case involving foreign powers and alleged links to the criminal underworld. Was this something similar, or was it purely personal, the media wanted to know?

Hamilton presented the facts about the case in terms of confirming the name of the victim and the location and approximate time of the crime. 'Mr Henderson was brutally murdered, sometime during the night of sixth to seventh February, when he was staying overnight in the Moray Hotel in Glasgow. His body was discovered by a member of the hotel staff. The investigation is ongoing and we are still looking for more information and appeal for anyone with information to come forward. DCI Cooper will be overseeing the investigation which is being led by the senior investigating officer, Detective Inspector Khan of the Major Crime Unit. DI Khan will now update you on the investigation so far and answer any questions.'

Shazia was able to announce that they had made some progress with the investigation and had detained two individuals in connection with the case but couldn't give any more details at this stage. When it came time for questions, there was a forest of hands. Was it true that the victim was found almost naked in his bed? That he had been smothered with a pillow? Shazia realised that either the chambermaid or the assistant manager had probably blabbed about it and probably everyone who worked in the hotel now knew the story. In an age of social media when it was impossible to be discreet about anything, she had learned to accept that not much remained secret anymore.

'Do you have any idea what the motive could be?' Shona Williamson of the Glasgow Gazette asked.

'We are keeping an open mind,' she said.

'Could the killer still be at large then, even though you have people in custody?' asked George Guthrie of the Scottish Courier.

DCI Cooper decided to terminate the conference abruptly. 'As has been indicated, the investigation is ongoing. Thank you for your all questions but I must end this conference now. I am sure you will appreciate that the priority is to put all our time and resources into the enquiry. We will continue to keep you updated on developments with the case.'

Shazia left the room and hurried back to her office with the questions ringing in her ears.

14

DC Mitchell, accompanied by a uniformed officer, Jill Fraser, called in to see Euan Henderson, Charles Henderson's son. They had arranged to see him in his Morningside flat before he went to work. It was located in a leafy street with a white Porsche parked outside. Everything in the flat looked expensive: the furnishings, the rugs, the paintings, even the paint on the walls. Mitchell spoke to him while PC Fraser spoke to his girlfriend, Fiona Sutherland, a slim, dark-haired woman. 'It's a nightmare,' he said. He was unable to offer any explanation as to why his father might have been killed. 'I don't understand it. Dad never harmed anyone. Why would anyone want to kill him?' In answer to where he had been on Monday night, he said they were in Switzerland on a week's skiing holiday and only got back on Tuesday to learn of his father's death. 'I went to see mum immediately and took her through to Glasgow in the evening to identify the body.'

'When did you last speak to your father?' asked Mitchell.

'Eh, the weekend before we went skiing. Fiona and I went up to Strathtay and had Sunday lunch.'

'How did he seem?'

He shrugged. 'Just the same as always.'

'He didn't tell you anything was troubling him?'

Henderson shook his head. 'No.' He looked genuinely sad and distraught.

PC Fraser told Mitchell that his girlfriend, Sutherland, a trainee solicitor with a bob of dark brown hair, had confirmed that they had both been away skiing in St Moritz since the previous Tuesday.

Mitchell had managed to get hold of Galbraith on her mobile the previous day when she had called the Holyrood HR office. The woman she had spoken to was at first reluctant to give her a contact number for Galbraith, but when Mitchell stressed that it was in relation to the death of Charles Henderson, she said she would ask Galbraith to phone her. Galbraith had then phoned Mitchell later that evening. She sounded anxious, informing Mitchell that she was presently on sick leave. Mitchell asked her if she wanted to have a lawyer with her when they met, but Galbraith said no. Mitchell told her she could choose the location; they could meet in a police station or anywhere she wanted. Finally, Galbraith agreed and told Mitchell where to meet. The location Galbraith had chosen was a grungy café, dimly lit, the walls littered with posters for upcoming gigs and events. The furniture was best described as shabby chic: worn leather sofas and scratched coffee tables, with low-key acoustic music in the background. The welcome from the young woman behind the counter was warm. It was quiet, just a few student-types gathered in one counter looking hungover and an earnest young man on one couch reading a thick novel. How very bohemian, thought Mitchell.

She didn't really know what she expected Galbraith to be like, but it wasn't anything like the young Goth-like woman who introduced herself. She had blue hair, black torn jeans, a gold nose piercing, a black leather biker jacket and bright red lipstick which accentuated the pale white skin on her face. She didn't look like someone who had been the assistant to a Conservative MSP and worked in the Scottish Parliament.

She bought Galbraith a fruit juice. 'Thanks for agreeing to meet us,' said Mitchell. 'Interesting place you chose to meet!'

Galbraith shrugged her shoulders. 'This is handy for me, though. It's not far from where I stay.' The young woman had a distinctive east coast accent.

'Where's that?' asked Mitchell.

'I share a flat in Bread Street with a couple of friends just round the corner from the Pubic Triangle!' She laughed.

Mitchell laughed too. 'Oh yes, I've heard about that place. Where all the strip clubs are. It must be a bit dodgy living round there, eh?'

'No, it's OK. You get used to it! There's a few weirdos sometimes, but I can look after myself. I've done martial arts, ken.'

'Is that right?'

'Aye. Anyway, so you want to talk to me about Henderson, is that right?'

'Yes. Obviously it's a murder investigation and we are at an early stage so we are looking for anything that might shed light on why it happened. I've got some questions and PC Fraser will just make a few notes, OK?'

'Aye, no bother. Crack on!'

Fraser took out her notebook and a pen. 'What was your job when you worked for Henderson?' asked Mitchell.

'I was an admin assistant. I did mostly clerical work, like typing up anything he dictated, drafting letters from him to constituents, and the odd bit of research. That kind of thing. I worked for his PA really but it was in his office so I suppose he was really the boss.'

'How long did you work for him at Holyrood?'

'Only twelve weeks. I was there to replace someone else.'

'What do you mean?'

'Well, no one spoke about it, but after I blew the whistle on him people came up to me and said the same thing had been happening to the woman who did the job before me, but she had never raised a formal complaint. She just left, apparently.'

'That's interesting. I'll get her details from Holyrood. Tell me about Henderson. What was he like?'

Galbraith laughed. 'Total sleaze-ball. Two-sided, too. He could be all pleasant and charming, like. That was the public persona. People said, though, that if you worked for him and you slipped up, he'd soon let you know.'

'Did that happen to you?'

'No. I made sure I didn't slip up. He was disgusting, though. A fat pervert! Always leaning into me. Making it look like an accident when he brushed up against my tits as he went past me or stood at my desk looking down my blouse. I didn't dress like this in the office, of course. He had a reputation as a bit of a pervert, that was well known. But I had to work in his office and he would look at you all the time as if he was mentally undressing you. At first, I would catch him just staring at me. I felt uncomfortable. Then he started saying things. He would tell me he liked how my sweater showed off my figure. As you can see, I'm not exactly small breasted, but why should I hide it? He told me I had good legs and should wear shorter skirts more often. Then one day…' She stopped and breathed heavily. Tears sprung from her eyes. Mitchell passed her a handkerchief.

'It's alright, take your time,' said Mitchell.

Galbraith continued. 'We were alone in his office. I realised that he was standing behind me looking over my shoulder. When I turned round, he was in front of the door facing my back. The sick bastard had his prick out and was masturbating.'

'Jesus! What did you do?'

'I was terrified. He said he wanted me to suck him off. There was no way out of the room as he was blocking the exit but I screamed "Let me out!", pushed past him and flew out of the door. That was when I had enough and I reported him.'

'When was this?'

'A couple of months ago.'

'What happened?'

'I went to see the parliament's chief clerk. I was transferred to another section immediately, supporting one of the committees. There was an investigation into it, but of course he denied it. He had made sure there were no witnesses. It was his word against mine. The thing is, I've heard that the woman I replaced, the one who left, the same thing had happened to her. She's probably accepted some generous pay-off with a confidentiality clause and found another job somewhere else. Makes you want to puke!'

'How did you feel about that?'

'Fucking angry. Things like that shouldn't happen. Now I am the one on sick leave. I had to go to the doctor as I can't sleep. He's put me on sleeping tablets and Valium. Now I feel like a zombie all day. He turned me into a fucking junkie!'

'When did you go off sick?'

'Since Monday. I just couldn't face going in there anymore.'

'Why didn't you go to the police when the incident happened?'

'I should have but I didn't. I just thought no one would believe me, there were no witnesses anyway, what was the point? And it would probably be the end of my career. I did think of telling my story to the papers and getting a load of money for it, but I couldn't stand the idea of my face being plastered all over the front page of some newspaper. And I'd probably never get hired again.'

'You should have reported it to the police. That's the only way to stop these men. Otherwise they just keep doing the same thing. Over and over again, to other women.'

'I know. No point now, though. He's dead!'

'How do you feel about that?' asked Mitchell.

'I can't say I am sorry, to tell you the truth. Someone must have hated him even more than me, though.'

'How did he get on with other MSPs?'

'He was quite popular. God know why!'

'You don't strike me as a natural Tory. How come you ended up working for them?'

'It was a job. I'm interested in politics, but not actually a member of any party. I have a degree in economics.'

'Were there any MSPs he was close to you that you know of?'

She nodded. 'Angus McLennan. They were good friends. I often saw them together. Though the rumour is that McLennan is shagging Henderson's wife.'

'Really?'

'As I say, it's just a rumour. Holyrood is like that, though. Nothing is kept secret for long.'

'Thanks. I need to ask you about your whereabouts the night he was murdered. We have already spoken to your boyfriend, Peter, as you probably know. Can you confirm where you were on Monday night?'

'At the cinema in Glasgow with Peter. Then I stayed at his flat. You can ask him. He had the night off. So, I went through to Glasgow and stayed the night through there.'

'How did you two meet?'

'Oh, at a club in Glasgow. He knows a friend of mine, Amy, who I went to school with. She works with him in his kitchen.'

'There was an incident outside the parliament building involving Peter and Charles wasn't there? Can you tell us about it?'

She looked surprised that the police knew about that and there was a moment's hesitation before she spoke. 'Eh, that's right. It was a couple of weeks ago. Peter had the day off and came through to Edinburgh. He'd been in the pub drinking all afternoon and was waiting outside the building for me. I came out, and Charles came out about the same time as me, and I pointed him out to Peter. I shouldn't have. Peter went over and just started saying things to him. I didn't even hear what he said but next thing I know Peter is grabbed by security. They took him back inside. Eventually they let him go. That's it. It was a storm in a teacup! Peter didn't do anything, like.'

After Galbraith left, Mitchell phoned the parliament building and asked if she could speak to Angus McLennan

MSP, thinking as they were in Edinburgh and Shazia had asked them to dig up what they could from Holyrood, maybe they could have a word with him before the weekend. She was asked what it was in connection with and she said that she was following a line of enquiry related to the death of Charles Henderson MSP. She was put on hold. Then transferred. Twice. She had to repeat her name and rank several times. Classical music played down the phone. Very loudly. She had to hold the handset a foot away from her ear to stop it deafening her. It was something vaguely Scottish, she thought, though she couldn't remember what it was called. She found the sound mildly irritating. The wait was irritating too. When someone eventually came on the line, she told her that McLennan wasn't available. She left her number and asked if he would contact her. She then asked to be transferred to HR and spoke to someone about the assistant who Galbraith had talked about. She was given a number for a woman called Alison Stevens.

Mitchell phoned the number and a woman answered. She was very suspicious. 'How did you get this number?' she asked. Mitchell explained. 'How do I really know that you are the police? There's all sorts of phone scams, people pretending they are the police to get bank details.'

'We are not interested in bank details, Alison,' said Mitchell. 'I'd like to speak to you about Charles Henderson. I understand that you made a complaint about him, is that correct?' Stevens didn't answer. 'Hello, are you still there?' asked Mitchell.

'Yes, I'm here. But I can't speak to you about Mr Henderson. I signed a confidentiality clause.'

'But, as you will be aware, Mr Henderson is no longer alive. I'm sure that doesn't apply anymore.'

'I'd rather not discuss the matter.'

'I'm sorry, but this is part of a murder investigation, Alison. We need to speak to you. I'm in Edinburgh at the moment. Can I call in to see you later?'

Stevens reluctantly agreed, gave her address and Mitchell arranged to see her at home that evening. First, though, she and Fraser would visit Henderson's flat.

The flat was in the New Town in an elegant square. There was a neat garden in the middle of the square, surrounded by an iron fence. Mitchell located the property and parked outside. She took out the set of keys which Shazia had given her and after trying several ones, she opened the door into the vestibule, a large space with black and white tiles on the floor and red walls. She remembered that Henderson had occupied the first floor. Before going upstairs, she knocked on the door of the ground floor flat. There was no answer at first. She tried again. She didn't expect anyone to answer but eventually a woman in her early thirties came to the door. She had dark hair in a ponytail and was carrying a baby in her arms. 'Sorry, I was in the middle of changing her,' she said. When they introduced themselves as police officers, they were invited in and found themselves sitting on a sofa opposite the young woman. She introduced herself as Isabel Fernandes. She said that she and her husband were from Brazil. Her husband was a lecturer in Zoology currently seconded to Edinburgh University. They had been living in the flat for the last six months. No, she didn't know Mr Henderson very well, but exchanged pleasantries with him if they met. All financial details regarding payment of rent were done through an agency.

Her husband arrived home while they were talking. He was tall with a beard and, like his wife, dark-haired. He introduced himself as Joao. Also, like his wife, there was little he could tell them about Charles Henderson. He had only met him a few times. They were both shocked by the news of Henderson's death.

'Did Mr Henderson have many visitors?' asked Mitchell. The couple exchanged a furtive glance. What's wrong, she wondered? Were there shouting matches upstairs with visitors, slammed doors, scenes on the staircase or in the hall?

'There were young women,' said Joao. 'Late at night.'

'I see,' said Mitchell. Anybody else?'

'His son,' said Isabel. 'He was here yesterday, in fact. I met him at the front door.'

The flat upstairs was very tidy. Too tidy, perhaps? What had Euan Henderson been doing here, she thought? She looked around. It was expensively decorated. Henderson obviously hadn't scrimped on furnishings. Not for him, finding things in flea markets. Everything looked new and top of the range, including the kitchen, which looked as if it had never been put to use. He probably lived on takeaways, Mitchell thought. Mitchell hadn't been sure what to expect. If it had been burgled, she would have called in a SOCO team, but everything appeared normal as far as she could tell. She and PC Fraser spent an hour searching through the flat for anything significant but came away empty-handed.

When they met Alison Stevens at her house on the outskirts of Edinburgh, it was a similar story. Stevens was a small mousy woman with dark brown hair cut in a bob and thin lips. She wore thick glasses. With her flat chest and unflattering figure, generally she was a complete contrast to Galbraith. Evidently Henderson had not been fussy who he molested. Mitchell thought back to the time she was followed home from school when she was fifteen. She had taken a short cut through a park and was aware of someone behind her but had been too afraid to turn around. Suddenly she realised that there was no one else about and quickened her pace. Before she knew it, she had been grabbed from behind and dragged into bushes. She started to scream but a hand was firmly placed over her mouth. The attacker was still behind her and the fact that she couldn't see his face made the situation all the more terrifying. She felt his other hand up her skirt and then she lashed out with her elbow and heard a crunch as it collided with his mouth. 'Fuck,' he had shouted but the impact had loosened his hold on her and she broke free. She ran and ran until she was home. Her parents took her to the police station to report the assault but she was unable to describe him and the investigation hit the buffers even before it had started. There had been no other witnesses and so the attacker was never found. Mitchell had been confused about her sexuality at the time, aware that she felt an attraction to girls more than boys. The incident reinforced these feelings and she lost trust in males for a long time. The other consequence of the incident was to interest Mitchell in the police. Although the investigation into her assault came to nothing, she was intrigued by the female detective she met, her questioning techniques, and the whole procedure of investigating a crime, which would lead her towards deciding later on her future career.

Stevens appeared very nervous and clearly didn't want to talk about Henderson but after sitting down with some tea, she relaxed and opened up. Henderson had made several lewd comments to her and had once touched her inappropriately, she said. She had not complained but, instead, decided to leave her job in Holyrood. She had then been offered money by a solicitor working for Henderson on the condition that she sign a non-disclosure agreement, which she had done as she was struggling financially at the time. She said that she had not spoken to anyone else about the matter and was at home alone on the Monday night. No, she didn't know anyone who might want to kill Henderson but, frankly, she couldn't care less that he was dead.

15

While Joseph fiddled with his phone in the car seat beside her and she drove through the countryside, Shazia found her thoughts turning to Yasmeen and wondering what future lay ahead of her. Yasmeen was now sixteen and coping better than she had been for a long time, but she still had outbursts and tantrums. She had never found it easy to make friends and there had been some problems with bullying online, but Shazia had spoken to the school and it had been sorted out.

At home Yasmeen still spent most of the time on her own and rarely saw any friends but this didn't seem to trouble her. There had been a review held in school a few weeks previously which Shazia had attended with the deputy head, Yasmeen's Guidance teacher, and the educational psychologist in attendance. The parent and the 'professionals' met first then Yasmeen joined them for the second half.

At the start of the meeting, the deputy head spoke about a recent incident in school. Yasmeen had been upset as she said all the other girls were refusing to speak to her and had told her Guidance teacher, who had investigated and discovered that a girl had claimed that Yasmeen had told her she didn't like her new haircut, saying that she had looked better the way she had it before. The girl had become upset and told her friends and they had all then ignored Yasmeen.

Shazia knew that this kind of thing was common with children and young people on the autistic spectrum and it was the type of remark which she knew Yasmeen was likely to make as she didn't realise how her words could affect others' feelings, and wouldn't think of observing the kind of social codes that prevented most people from blurting out what they thought for fear of upsetting someone else. There was some discussion about how the school could support Yasmeen to become more aware of how words can impact on others and ways in which this could be reinforced at home, using social stories with illustrations.

Shazia liked the attitude and approach of the professionals and felt able to relax, feeling that she was able to trust them. She shared with the others that since her parents had sold their house and moved in with her and Yasmeen, looking after her daughter had become slightly easier to manage. She didn't have to juggle care for Yasmeen, shuttling her between her parents' house and her sister's. Her father still worked in the shop some of the time, but her mother was at home constantly. As a result, the shopping and housework was done, and Yasmeen was taken to school and collected, and things were mostly OK, although there could still sometimes be the odd occasion when things didn't go according to plan as far as Yasmeen was concerned and she became upset.

Being the mother of a child with autism had never been easy, especially as a single parent; that and trying to have a career in a demanding job as a police detective. She knew she relied on her parents and couldn't have coped without them but it did feel claustrophobic actually always having them in the house and there was little time when it was just her and Yasmeen alone together.

The Henderson investigation was taking up most of their time but she didn't want to neglect trying to find some leads on who killed Sammy Scobie. So they were heading for a housing scheme on the outskirts of Clydebank to speak to Sammy Scobie's maternal grandparents. Social Work had alerted her to the fact that they were the closest surviving family members Sammy had contact with when he had been in the care of the local authority, and it was they who formally identified his body.

The grandparents' home was in a nondescript street on the edge of the council estate, a procession of uniformly bland pebble-dashed apartment blocks built sometime in the 1950s. Their flat was on the ground floor and Scobie's grandmother, Angela, holding onto her walking stick with fierce determination, greeted Shazia and Joseph warmly at the door and led them into the living room where Bill, her husband got up from his chair to shake their hands with one hand while his other clutched a can of lager. The contrast between the elderly couple could not have been clearer; Angela stick-like thin with permed white hair, bird-like in her delicate features, while Bill was a large bear-like man, grey haired and unshaven. Angela had tea and chocolate biscuits ready for the expected visitors in the living room and they sat down to talk.

The decor in the room was a mishmash of colours and patterns, and the place was cluttered with ornaments. The three-piece suite looked worn, as did the carpet, but the place was clean, unlike, Shazia remembered, their grandson's flat in Parkhill had been. She noticed a photograph of a smiling young girl aged about five years old in school uniform on a sideboard, along with a similar one of a boy around the same age: Primary One photos of Sammy and his mum in more innocent days, preserved for eternity, or at least until the grandparents shuffled off.

Bill said little, mainly because he seemed to have some sort of breathing difficulties, coughing and puffing on an asthma inhaler in between taking swigs of his beer, but Angela, it seemed, could talk for Scotland, clearly enjoying the company and relating tales of Sammy's mother, Liz, and how she had been 'a star' at primary school until she had got in with 'a bad crowd' at secondary school and 'wandered off the straight and narrow' and moved away to the big city. It was a neat euphemism for the woman's downward spiral into alcoholism, prostitution and mental illness. As far as Sammy was concerned, what she could tell them was sketchier. Neither of them had been in good enough health to care for the boy when he was little and 'Liz gave him up to the care of the social services' or, more accurately, Shazia knew, social work had forcibly removed him from his mother under child protection jurisdiction.

Shazia was interested to know if the grandparents had had any more recent contact with Sammy. 'Aye, he kept in touch fae time to time,' Angela said.

'Aye, when he wis skint an' lookin' fur a bung,' wheezed Bill.

'He was a good lad,' said Angela. 'But, like his mum, he was easily led astray. They drugs are a menace!' she said, starting to shed a tear. 'Ma heart broke when I saw his poor wee body lying on that trolley, so it did. I thought, if only we had brought him up, maybe he wouldnae huv ended up like that.'

Bill shook his head. 'Naw, he wus jist like his mither. They both hud a wild streak in them, it wouldnae huv mattered whit we hud done.'

Angela gave him a scathing look. 'Wonder where they goat that fae?'

'Did he ever mention any friends?' asked Joseph.

'He talked about a pal, Tommy, the last time he came here. He said he and Tommy had been up the toon the night before and he had a hangover. I gave him some Alka Seltzer.' She gave a slight grin.

'When was that?'

'A couple of weeks ago.'

'Did he mention anyone he was afraid of?'

'No, I don't remember him saying anything about anyone he was scared of. He was an easy-going lad, nae harm in him. It's a tragedy whit happened tae him, so it is. Him an' his poor mither. Whit happened, dae ye think, hen?'

'We're still investigating,' said Shazia. 'We don't know yet.' She didn't want to tell her that forensics analysis from the crime scene had turned up nothing. The prints found in the flat belonged to Scobie or his regular drug clients on the estate, all of whom, except one, had been identified; their previous prints were on record. They had been interviewed and had provided alibis for the night of the murder which, although not ruling them out as suspects, without any other evidence made their guilt impossible to prove. There was, however, one set of unidentified prints which didn't match anything on the police database, and Shazia was keen to identify this person. However, the grandparents weren't able to furnish them with any more information on the mysterious Tommy.

Shazia also hadn't been able to trace any phone that he had used as he most likely used a pay-as-you-go one without any contract or registration recorded, and it had probably been taken by whoever had been in his flat that night. He didn't appear to use any social media and, in the absence of finding any devices, they had no internet history to search. In short, they had no clues to give them any leads as to what led to their grandson's death. They had hit the proverbial brick wall.

They didn't find out much else from the visit and were about to set off back to Glasgow, but as they were leaving Shazia's phone rang. It was Cameron Forsyth. He said he was driving from the airport and was currently on the way home, offering to come to the police station tomorrow if she wished. But Shazia told him they could meet him at home now as they were not too far away. The sooner they talked to him the better. He said he would be home in half an hour and gave her his address. Joseph looked it up on his smartphone and found a picture and information about it as she drove in the direction of Helensburgh. 'It's about as impressive as Valerie Farquharson's place. Designed, according to Wikipedia, by William Leiper, who it says here was the architect who designed, amongst other things, the Templeton Carpet Factory. He seemed to have lived in Helensburgh. Heard of him?'

'I haven't heard of Leiper but the Templeton factory building I have. It's beside Glasgow Green. Looks like a Venetian palace. I think it's a pub or something now.'

'Well, this looks like quite a building too. Part of the Gothic revival, it says here. Another substantial Victorian pile. It was built in the nineteenth century for a shipping magnate, apparently.'

'Makes a change from the damp-ridden high-rises or the grotty bedsits we usually find ourselves in, I suppose.'

'It was always said that these men got rich through trading tobacco or tea or cotton. What's never usually added is that all this only was possible because of slavery. Of course, it was slaves who worked in all those plantations, and the merchants who shipped back those cargoes had shipped thousands of folks from West Africa to the plantations of the Caribbean or the Deep South. Then the ships carried tobacco or whatever back to Britain and then filled up the ships with merchandise to sell to Africans or exchange them for slaves. And so it went on. Until slavery was abolished. Mind you, the slave owners were handsomely compensated. They got millions in today's money.'

'You really are a history buff, aren't you?'

'My parents came from Ghana and I've been back there a few times to visit relatives. I've sometimes thought my family were the lucky ones. We were left behind. Most folk on those boats didn't survive the voyage.'

'There's still slavery these days, too. Look at Katarina's story.'

'That's true. There will always be some people who see an opportunity to make a fast buck regardless of what the cost is to other humans. I saw a film on the news the other night. These poor bastards off the Libyan coast. Smuggling gangs are packing them into inflatables that can barely float. They're packed in there like sardines with no life-jackets or anything. These poor bastards are running away from a miserable existence, or from terrorism or war, and what happens? They pay a fortune, probably all they have in the world after selling everything they have and travelling for hundreds of miles, then get taken advantage of by ruthless criminals and sent out to sea to die. Or they make it ashore and end up on the streets. What kind of shit world do we live in, eh?'

'Or if they get housed somewhere, they have their house fire-bombed by crazy racists like that refugee family in Glasgow the other day,' said Shazia. 'Crime never goes away. There are always some who will make money from human misery. My family weren't always doing well either. My father came to this country from a village in Pakistan with nothing. He knew someone in Glasgow who found him work as a bus driver. Eventually he made enough money to take over running a shop. But he told me how tough it was for Asians in those days. When I was younger, I couldn't believe some of his stories. Then it got tough again for us. After the bombing in Buchanan Street last year my daughter was too scared to go to school. She was being sent messages on the internet telling her she was a terrorist and why didn't she go and live in the Middle East. Thank God all of that has died down, but it had an effect on her. She'll never forget it. Anyway, now we've thoroughly depressed ourselves with the state of the world!'

'Wonder what Cameron Forsyth will be like?' said Joseph. 'Don't suppose anyone in his family was ever a bus driver?'

'Probably never even been on a bus,' said Shazia.

16

In Helensburgh, they navigated the grid of wide streets uphill from the centre which divided its grand houses, their little strips of manicured grass running down the front in place of a common pavement, as if declaring that nothing common belonged here. Shazia stopped the car outside the gates to Forsyth's imposing house. It was another gated property and so they had to wait for the gates to be electronically opened. The snow had stopped but there was a strong wind and a fine drizzle. The house was downhill from the Hill House, Charles Rennie Mackintosh's masterpiece, its modernism fused with Scottish baronial to create a unique style. Forsyth's house, by contrast, was more traditional: a large three-storey Victorian villa with large well-tended gardens. A dark blue Bentley was parked on the driveway, along with a silver Mercedes E-Class cabriolet. A pretty young woman with blonde hair in a ponytail opened the door, introducing herself as Helga. 'Mr Forsyth is expecting you', said Helga in impeccable English with just a trace of a Scandinavian accent. 'I am the au pair. He is just taking a call in his study and asked me to show you into the dining room.' She led the way across the hall and they followed her into a large room, at the centre of which was a long dining table which could easily accommodate at least a dozen guests.

A few moments later, Forsyth entered the room. Shazia noticed the limp in his right leg. It was slight but it affected his movement, the right leg falling somewhat behind the left when he walked. He was wearing a pale blue striped shirt and dark trousers. 'I am sorry. That was New York on the phone. And, honestly, Americans, they are hard work! You must be Inspector Khan,' he said coming over to shake her hand.

'Yes,' said Shazia. 'This is Detective Sergeant Boateng.' Forsyth shook Joseph's hand.

'Of course. Please sit down. That will be all, Helga, thank you.' He nodded at the au pair, who smiled and closed the door. Forsyth watched her walk out of the room, seeming to appreciate the way she moved with a lascivious smile. 'Fantastic young girl. Don't know what we would do without her. Adele certainly couldn't run her business anyway, that's for sure.'

'Quite a place you've got here, Mr Forsyth,' said Shazia.

'It's how I met my wife, actually. I bought this place eight years ago. After the divorce from my first marriage. Bit of an investment when I floated the company and came into some cash. Anyway, the place was a wreck. It needed a complete makeover, you know. So, I saw this feature in a magazine about this young interior designer from Paris who was making waves in London. I thought, "That's the girl for me!" and it was. Not just for the house, too.' He laughed loudly. 'Love at first sight. Or should I say lust? No, better not, eh? Bloody political correctness police will do me, what? Shit, sorry, didn't mean to insult you folks. I talk too much, don't know when to be quiet, that's my problem. Shut up, Cameron!' He made a sign as if to zip his mouth.

Shazia stared at him, momentarily lost for words. As they sat around the highly polished dining table, Shazia was now aware of the fabrics and furnishings in the room: it could have come straight out of a colour supplement or interior design magazine. In fact, it probably had featured in several. 'As you know, Mr Forsyth, we are investigating the death of Charles Henderson. I understand you were a close friend of his?'

'Call me Cameron, by the way. Yes, old friends, we go way back to school days in fact. Bloody awful what happened to him. Poor Charles. It's terribly sad. I can't believe anyone would want to kill him.'

Joseph asked, 'When did you last see Charles?'

'Eh, sometime last month, actually. We had dinner together.'

'How did that come about?' asked Shazia.

'We have dinner every so often. I was going to be in Edinburgh that day for some meetings so we agreed a while ago to chew the fat over some food.'

'How did it go?'

'It was good to catch up. He told me he was due to address the Chamber of Commerce conference and I told him I had been asked to speak too. Of course, I said yes, even though I was flying down to London later that afternoon. I'm not known for hiding my light under a bloody bushel! I never miss an opportunity to sound off, that's me.' He laughed.

'How was he when you saw him?' asked Shazia.

'Charles? Just his usual self! Full of mischief.'

'What kind of mischief?'

'Oh, you know what politicians are like. Always scheming. He reckoned we could get the Nationalists to reduce corporation tax, said they were moving to the right. I told him he was living in cloud cuckoo land if he thought that. Just because we are keeping the SNP government afloat doesn't mean they will dance to anyone else's tune, let alone the Scottish Conservatives. He said it was all about striking a deal.'

'I take it you didn't always agree with each other then?'

'Agree? No, but we always agreed to disagree if you know what I mean? Healthy exchange of views and all that! Oh, but we agreed on more things than we disagreed on. Got to keep the bloody nationalists and socialists at bay, what! Us Tories need to stick together!'

'What did you talk about?'

Forsyth laughed. 'Oh, you know. This and that. Politics, mainly. We had our usual lively and robust conversation. We say what we think to each other. Or, rather, we did. He probably had a bit too much grape juice, that night! I was sober as I was driving home, but he just had to stagger back to his flat.'

'Did he say anything when you last met him? Was he worried about anything?'

Forsyth shook his head. 'No. No, I don't think so.'

'He didn't mention any threats he had received or anything like that?'

Forsyth shook his head. 'No, not at all. What happened to Charles is an absolute outrage. I would be looking at some of these Islamist extremist groups, though. I served Queen and country with pride until a fucking Taliban bullet, if you'll excuse my language, Inspector, turned me into a cripple. Ended my life in the regiment too, of course, and everything I lived for. That was my life until one of those Islamist nutters took a pot-shot at me when we were on patrol in Helmand. They were the enemy out there then, but there's an enemy within now. These people will stop at nothing to subvert our democracy. You should get in touch with Special Branch.'

Shazia grimaced and said, 'Thanks for the advice but if you don't mind sir, leave me to do my job and I'll leave you to do yours.'

'I take it that you are a Muslim, Inspector?'

'What has that got to do with it?'

'It's about time that the Muslim leaders took a stand and decried the extremists. You will know that the imams do nothing to counter them, some of them are even encouraging it.'

Shazia had to fight to control herself up against this rabid Islamophobia. 'Mr Forsyth, may I remind you that we are investigating a murder and there is nothing, so far, to link it to any Islamists, as far as I am aware.'

But Forsyth didn't appear to have listened. 'I don't want to cause offence to your religion, Inspector, but in my opinion these Muslim fundamentalists won't stop until they have conquered the world. They're still living in the Middle Ages. Mark my words!'

This time Shazia decided to ignore his remark. 'One more thing, sir. Standard question for all those who were close to him. What were your movements on Monday night?'

Forsyth looked taken aback at the question. 'Eh? Oh, I worked late at the office.'

'So, you went straight home after that then.'

He paused. 'Eh, no, actually.'

'Where did you go?'

'Does it matter?'

'Yes. We do need to know your whereabouts that night.'

'Look, it's just this is a bit personal. Actually, I had dinner with a friend and stayed the night at her flat.'

'Who was the friend?'

Forsyth took a deep breath and exhaled slowly. 'Oh, I might as well tell you. I've nothing to hide. I'd rather keep her out of it, though, if you don't mind.'

'Actually, we do mind.'

'It was my PA, Jennifer Gibson.'

Shazia wrote the name down in her notebook. 'Where does she live?'

'Glasgow Harbour. I can give you the flat number if you want.'

'Yes, we'll need that, thank you.' Shazia wrote the details into her notebook. 'So, you had dinner together and went to her flat in Glasgow Harbour. When did you get there?'

He paused. 'Just after ten, I suppose, something like that. Jennifer drove. I'd left my car in the office car park overnight, you see, and had some wine with the meal. I never drink and drive, officer.'

'I see. Are you in the habit of spending the night with Jennifer?'

Forsyth again looked sheepish, but nodded. 'Yes. I suppose you could call her my mistress if you wanted to be all dramatic about it, though that does sound like something from a period-piece when I put it like that doesn't it? Listen, there's no need for Adele to know about any of this is there?'

'That will be for us to decide, sir. What about your wife? What did you tell her about where you were that night?'

'Actually, she was in Paris for a few days visiting her family. She actually flew back on Tuesday.'

'How long have you been in a relationship with Jennifer?' asked Boating.

'Eh, about two years, I suppose.'

'Do you know of anyone who would want to kill Mr Henderson?' Shazia asked.

Forsyth shook his head. 'I haven't a clue. As I said, most likely some fundamentalist crackpots. Charles could be annoying at times, like most politicians. Stubborn as hell. Mind you, I'm probably the same. But kill him? It just doesn't make sense. Probably some nutcase who thinks he can change the world by killing us off. I could be next! I just hope you catch the bastards first! Let me know if there is anything else I can help you with, officers.'

On their way back into Glasgow, McLaughlin called to tell them about his search through city centre CCTV. 'A camera on Hope Street at 22: 53 that evening shows a private hire cab, a red Skoda, stopping and a woman similar to Katarina getting out. It picks her up again at the same spot at 00:16. The registration shows it belongs to a Robert Jackson. He's got previous for violence. I sent a couple of officers round to the property the DVLA have for the car as a registered address. It's a top-floor flat in Whiteinch but there's no response.'

Shazia said, 'OK. Good work. Now that we have picked up Katarina, he will no doubt know we are looking for him and have gone to ground. Get a search warrant, force an entry and see what there is to be found there. Also, contact Border Control here and down south in case he's thinking of skipping the country. Ask them to issue alerts at ports and airports.'

Jennifer Gibson lived in a penthouse apartment on the top floor of the Glasgow Harbour complex, a waterfront development, with a magnificent view over the Clyde and beyond from its panoramic windows. In better weather you could sit on its balcony and sun yourself, but Shazia thought that if you tried that at the moment you were in danger of frostbite or being blown into the river. Gibson invited the detectives into her living room and they took a seat on a pristine white leather sofa. In fact, everything was either black or white. The white carpet was thick and soft and several large modernist canvases hung on the walls. There was no point in wondering how a PA could manage to afford such an apartment as the answer was obvious. Shazia was sure that Forsyth would also have phoned Gibson the second that they had left his house and so she hadn't looked at all surprised when they appeared.

She was a stunningly beautiful blonde, tall and slim, in her late twenties and clearly with an expensive wardrobe, judging from the designer black Chanel dress she was wearing. Her long shiny red fingernails flashed as she shook their hands and she smelled strongly of an expensive scent. The television on the wall was showing a news channel displaying an image of the Moray Hotel on the screen. A reporter stood outside doing a piece to camera. Gibson picked up a remote control, pointed it at the screen and muted the sound. Shazia noticed a tattoo of a butterfly on the inside of her left wrist.

She confirmed Forsyth's account. 'Yes, I was with Cameron all night. We had dinner in the Rogano and came back here.'

'And he stayed the night here with you?'

'Yes. I gave him a lift into the office in the morning.'

'How do you know he didn't leave your flat while you were asleep?'

'I am a very light sleeper. Besides, we didn't do a lot of sleeping!' she said with a smile.

17

Jamie McEwan was nursing a pint as he waited in the pub for Shona. He was thinking how that morning he lay in bed and watched her naked body rise from the bed. She was small, with long dark hair which fell down her back, and he admired her petite rear as she disappeared into the ensuite bathroom. He thought how amazed his friend Fergus would have been by the longevity of his relationship with her. Fergus had always predicted how each girlfriend he found wouldn't last longer than a few weeks: a serial monogamist, he called him, and mostly he was right. But not this time. They hadn't been together for long before Fergus had been killed, after being caught up in a Russian plot that took him to Spain and ended with bullets to his head. And it had all started with Fergus meeting a Russian model, Olga Yevdokimova, here in the Ubiquitous Chip. He reminded himself how lucky he was to be alive and living with a beautiful woman. Then he saw Shona coming into the bar.

'Here's to us and to Fergus! Wherever you are!' said Jamie.

'Fergus!' echoed Shona, clinking glasses. 'I'll never forget that day I drove him out to spy at Paul Murray's mansion in Mugdock. I was sure he was going to get shot. I have to confess I wasn't going to go hang about if the shooting had started. I may write about it but I am a coward when it comes to violence.'

'Unfortunately, neither of us was around him when the shooting did start, in Spain. He always liked to do things his own way. Still, that exclusive story he managed to get changed history. If he hadn't written about how the Russians had compromised Schmidt, we would have had a crazy megalomaniac reactionary president in the United States who was also doing the Russian president's job for him, with all that that meant. Goodbye to the Ukraine and the Baltic states for a start. Maybe even starting a war with North Korea! Who knows?'

'You're right. I read today that Schmidt is considered to be so extreme in his right-wing views that even senior figures in the Republican Party think his ideas go too far. The problem is that he has a following amongst white rural voters who believe the lies he is putting out about immigrants being rapists and murderers.'

Jamie nodded. 'There are definite echoes of fascism about him. He vows to have another stab at the presidency and he may well succeed next time. But I don't think Fergus would be so happy with how politics here are turning out though, would he? He thought that if the Scottish Greens could get into coalition in government, they would manage to pull the SNP in a more left-wing direction. Instead, the opposite has now happened. We've got the SNP being propped up by Tories and getting pulled rightwards.'

'That's because there are still enough old-guard SNP Tartan Tories in the guise of being nationalists,' said Shona. 'The SNP were never going to last long as a progressive force once we had achieved independence. They had enough success at the last election, still riding that wave of support on the back of winning the referendum, but now they are beginning to split.'

Jamie said, 'We actually need another election to sort things out, but we won't get one unless there's a wave of defections or a lot more MSPs get killed off. Speaking of which, did you learn anything interesting at the press conference?'

Shona sipped at her champagne. 'They didn't say much other than they have two in custody. It's amazing how much staff in the hotel know, though. I've heard he had a prostitute in his room the night he died. She is one of the ones in custody. An East European by all accounts. Apparently, there was a raid on a property in the South Side and she was picked up there with other young women who'd been trafficked here and forced into selling their bodies. There's been several other raids too and an arrest of an escort agency manager. I guess he is the other one connected to the case. We're covering it all in tomorrow's paper.'

'Isn't it typical that the guys who preach so-called moral superiority and family values, like Henderson, are the ones who are funding the exploitation of young women and taking pleasure in it themselves? He was married to that bigot of a journalist of course, who is always banging on about how we need family values in society. What's her name? Valerie Farquharson.'

'Yeah, Henderson always had a reputation as a bit of a lecher, though. A member of his staff in Holyrood apparently made an allegation of sexual harassment against him a while ago. Not for the first time, I hear. I've tried to get the inside story on that but no one will talk to me about it. That's how Holyrood works. They close ranks and shut up shop!'

Jamie sat back in his chair and scratched his head. 'So, who killed him then? The prostitute he was with? Why would she do that?'

Shona yawned and poured the last few drops of champagne into their glasses. 'Maybe he didn't pay up? Or, maybe she had nothing to do with it? Anyway, drink up and let's head home. I've had a long day and it is catching up with me.'

Their flat had belonged to Jamie since he was a young lawyer fifteen years before. It was part of a conversion in Botanic Crescent, a Victorian terrace overlooking the River Kelvin in the West End of Glasgow. The rain had stopped and the walk up Byres Road and Queen Margaret Drive had taken fifteen minutes, and the fresh air had revived Shona and she wrapped her arms around Jamie as they stood in the centre of the living room, kissing.

'How about a nightcap?' said Jamie. He picked up a bottle of Laphroaig from a shelf and poured two fingers into a couple of glasses.

Shona selected a CD. The music echoed around the living room as they sank into the sofa. Jamie said, 'Nice choice. Jeff Buckley.' He took a sip of whisky and relished the sweet burning sensation as it slid down his throat.

'I fell in love with this record the first time you played me it,' Shona said.

'I know. That was when I knew I loved you. If you'd hated it, you were out the door!' He laughed.

Shona threw him backwards on the sofa. 'Liar! You just wanted to get me into your bed whatever music I liked.'

'True. Hey, watch out, you'll spill the drink!'

She knocked back her drink and leaned in and kissed him. My life is perfect, thought Jamie as he put his glass down and pulled her close. In the months to come, he would look back at this moment as a time of innocence before their world was turned upside down.

18

Shazia came into the station that day feeling exhausted. Thoughts of the murders of Scobie and Henderson had preoccupied her all night and she felt as if she had barely slept. Whenever she did manage to fall asleep, images of throttled faces and brains spilling out onto the road seemed to jolt her awake.

She was looking forward to having some time off at the weekend if she could. Her ex-husband, Yasmeen's father, Farooq, was going to spend the day with his daughter on Saturday and she consoled herself with the thought of having some time to herself, then immediately felt guilty about it. Since their divorce, he rarely saw his daughter. He had another wife and children now and lots of excuses not to see her but Shazia had insisted that he didn't change his mind. He was going to collect Yasmeen in the morning and take her out for the day. It would be good for Yasmeen to spend some time with her father, she believed, even if he was an absolute shit in her eyes. He had abandoned them when Yasmeen was small, just when her daughter's behaviour was becoming erratic, and he had taken up with a young woman instead. Shazia had been furious at the time. Now she just thought what an arsehole he was and wondered what she had ever seen in him.

As she sat down and scanned her emails, she saw that the results from Forensics were in. One thing in particular caught her eye and she turned to the Henderson case file, examining the statements from the hotel guests. Just then her phone rang. It was DCI Bill Cooper. He wanted to see her in his office. Right away.

'Give me an update on the Henderson investigation,' said Cooper. He was seated in one of the armchairs in a corner of his office, reserved for informal discussions. There was a low coffee table between them and she was seated in an identical chair. His eyes seemed to repeatedly glance towards her body, making her feel uncomfortable. Or was it just her imagination?

Cooper listened intently to what she had to say about the investigation. She told him the post-mortem results and what they had found out so far about Katarina Marková and what DC Mitchell had found out from Lorna Galbraith. Mitchell had phoned her last night to update her on what Henderson's former assistant had told her. Cooper sat back in his chair and crossed his arms over his broad chest. She could tell there was something bothering him. 'I've just had the Deputy Chief Constable on the phone,' he said. 'He says that one of your officers was on the phone to Holyrood yesterday, trying to speak to an MSP. DC Mitchell. Is that the case?'

Mitchell hadn't told her about trying to get hold of any MSP but she wouldn't let Cooper know this. 'Henderson was close to another MSP in his party, Angus McLennan. Who's rumoured to be on intimate terms with Valerie Farquharson. We need to speak to him and some other MSPs and see if there is anything that they can tell us about Henderson's death. There may be important information that they can disclose which will be helpful to the investigation.'

His leaned forward and stared at her. 'There are protocols for this, as you should know. I don't want any of you going storming in there. And the Chief Constable wouldn't be impressed either if your team went blundering about the corridors of Holyrood. So, tread very carefully.'

'Yes, sir.'

'There is a standard procedure for this sort of thing. Your officer did not follow that and I expect you to speak to her about it. Do I make myself clear?'

'Yes, sir. It's my fault, sir. I asked her to get in touch with other MSPs.'

'Well, we have already made it apparent that we want anyone who has any information useful to the investigation to contact us, and the politicians are very aware of that. The last thing I want is to be bloody reprimanded for officers stamping around Holyrood with their size nines by letting you loose in that place. Maybe we should see if any of them wish to talk to us first.'

'With respect, sir, it's essential that we talk to his fellow politicians. They may know something vital to the case.'

He paused. 'Alright, I will speak to the Detective Superintendent and we'll inform the parliamentary office that your officers will need to speak to the victim's colleagues. But I want this handled with tact. The last thing I want is a complaint. If you can't handle this case, Inspector, I will take over as chief investigating officer myself. Thank you, that is all.' Cooper stood up and went back to his desk and turned his attention to his computer and Shazia knew that the meeting was at an end.

When Shazia returned to the office, she took Mitchell aside. 'Joan, you shouldn't have tried to speak to any of Henderson's fellow MSPs in the way that you did yesterday; there's been a complaint. But don't worry about it. You should have told me. I know you were only trying to move the investigation on quickly and that I said you were to do it; but there is a procedure we have to follow.'

'Sorry boss,' said Mitchell.

'Anyway, that's the matter dealt with, let's get on.'

Shazia gathered the team together in an incident room.

'Well?' asked Joseph. 'What did Cooper want?'

'What he wanted was for us to sit back and wait for the MSPs to come to us,' said Shazia.

'That's ridiculous!' said Mitchell.

'I agree. I told him so,' said Shazia. 'But we have to remember that we are dealing with politicians here, a very sensitive breed of humans, apparently, and we are going to have to be extremely careful how we approach this. DCI Cooper clearly doesn't want us to upset anyone but, if we do, then I will take responsibility for it. These MSPs aren't a protected species! Joseph, I want you and Joan to arrange to speak to the other Tory MSPs as soon as you can, but go through the correct channels. Try and get something sorted out for the start of next week. Michael, have you traced that death threat you found?'

'Yes and no. It's anonymous. Basically, Islamist propaganda. Seems that Henderson made a few anti-Muslim remarks in in some speeches after the Buchanan Street bombing, then he got that death threat a couple of months later. The account it came from has been shut down by the social media company and they tell me it was a fake account. Whoever was responsible can't be traced.'

'What about who owns the flat in Govanhill where Katarina was living, are we any further forward with that?'

'It's a housing association,' said McLaughlin. 'The tenant is supposed to be a Polish family, but nobody in the block has ever seen or heard of them. Sounds like a scam. They get the tenancy with fake documents, housing association gets the rent paid, asks no questions. Meanwhile a knocking shop is set up and we can't trace who is behind it. The girls claim to know no real names of the chancers running the show and the older woman who was in the flat, Sofia Kovacová, isn't cooperating. But amongst the contacts on her phone was David Robertson from the escort agency, and she had frequent contact with him from what we can see.'

'What about the mugshots in the database? Did Katarina pick anyone out?'

'No. I reckon she is only willing to cooperate up to a point. She seems scared. Probably thinking she doesn't want to find herself accused of being a grass and facing the consequences of that. Guess it's the same in Slovakia as in Scotland. If they don't get you, they will get your family.'

Shazia nodded. 'We'll keep her under protection as a vulnerable witness but I'm convinced she is holding something back. Did anything turn up in Jackson's flat?'

'No. The place was spotless,' said McLaughlin.

'Still no sign of him?'

'I've alerted all units to be on the lookout for his vehicle.'

'OK. Anyway, we now have the report from Forensics for the hotel room,' said Shazia. 'No traces of ketamine in the wine glasses, though they could have been rinsed out by the killer, of course. No fingerprints around the broken window on the first floor, but they did find some prints in the room belonging to someone else. Once it was run through the database up popped the name of Stephen Christie.'

'Stephen Christie? Who's he?' said Joseph.

'I checked the list of those who were staying at the hotel. Christie was staying on the floor below Henderson that night. He didn't mention anything about being in Henderson's room in his statement when he was interviewed in the hotel on Tuesday morning. Funny that! He was in the system as he was convicted of possessing cannabis eleven years ago when he was a student. I tried to think of a link to Henderson and, of course, the name Christie rang an obvious bell. Fiona Christie. The woman who Henderson had an affair with thirty years ago. We'll bring him in and see how he explains himself.'

19

Earlier in the day, Stephen Christie had been contemplating his mother's funeral arrangements. In her instructions, he knew that she had decided to leave her body to the university for medical research so, strictly speaking, there was to be no actual funeral as such, but he wanted there to be something, a memorial service or just a gathering. She was strongly atheistic in her views so it would have to be a humanist service, if service was the right word. He didn't know. Probably nothing needed to be done right away anyway. It could wait a few weeks.

He was glad. As the only child of the deceased the responsibility fell on him. As it was, he just had to notify the university and complete a form requesting they pick up her body. That was it. His mother had already signed and authorised everything else. Asking the university to take his mother's corpse felt odd. He would have to go into work there, passing by the building where they kept the cadavers for sweaty, nervous medical students to dissect. The thought was macabre and made him feel physically sick.

He told the university he would be taking time off for bereavement leave. His head of department sounded sympathetic and told him to take as much time as he needed. Juliet also couldn't do enough to try to console him, which should have made him feel guilty. It should have but it didn't. She had gone to work, so he was alone in the flat with time to reflect on what had happened.

Henderson's death was the major news, of course, and he had spent the morning reading the reports on the internet. But, for him, the interest wasn't for political or prurient reasons; it was personal. Speculation and rumours in the media about the death of Henderson were, of course, widespread, and there was no shortage of commentators offering their opinions of the man's life. He was variously described as a devoted family man, a misogynist with a penchant for prostitutes and gambling, an ambitious and ruthless politician, a compassionate conservative, and a conceited, vain inheritor of class privilege. Take your pick.

Believe what you want, thought Stephen. Maybe he was all of these at the same time. People have layers, like onions, he thought. Does anyone ever truly know what another person is really like? We project the image to the world that we want others to see, to believe in. But is that what the person is really like? Never, he thought. Even if it isn't fake, it is only a part of a person. What secrets do they keep to themselves? We are all actors of some sort.

Christie had his own secrets. One of them concerned what happened that night in the hotel. It opened up a part of him that he hadn't even known had existed. He didn't feel remotely guilty, though. He had long ago decided that guilt was an unnecessary emotion. What was the point of guilt or regret? Once you had done something there was no point punishing yourself for doing it, was there? You had freely chosen to commit the act, therefore you had to accept it; whether it was morally right or wrong was a different matter, and anyway wasn't morality somewhat arbitrary?

Two of his favourite writers were Dostoevsky and Camus. In 'The Brothers Karamazov', Ivan was the brother he most admired. Dmitri was foolish, pulled this way and that by his passions, his sensuality, his balls. Alyosha was too good, the angelic brother who always said and did the right thing. Boring. No, it had to be Ivan. He was the deep thinker, questioning everything. Society. Religion. Morality. Everything is allowed, he said. But Ivan, like Raskolnikov in Crime and Punishment, in the end is tortured by his conscience. Dostoevsky, essentially a religious and spiritual writer, had wanted to show that you couldn't act independently from a moral code. But Camus took it a stage further. You could. That was the difference. Camus had shown that we could break free from social bonds that held us. In fact, we needed to, Christie told himself, to be truly free beings.

Christie wanted to be like that. He told himself not to feel any guilt about Monday night and all that had happened. He had chosen not to visit his mother on Monday evening. Even if he had visited her, she wouldn't have known, lying there unconscious, he told himself. Throughout his life, until her illness, they had been very close. As a single mother she had sometimes struggled to make ends meet, but he had never gone without. She had earned enough to raise him and made sure that he apply himself to school work, encouraged him to attend university, supported him until he graduated. He had been fortunate also to gain a scholarship for a Masters and to be accepted onto a funded PhD course. Finally, the university offered him a permanent post. He had married Juliet three years ago, after going out since they were undergraduates together. Juliet had asked about his father, of course, and he had told her the story he had been told, which he now knew wasn't true. Then, when he had finally found out the truth, he hadn't shared it with her. He wasn't sure why.

Chloe was a student in Christie's Shakespeare class and a member of his tutorial group. She was stunningly attractive, with long wavy chestnut hair and a fabulous slim figure giving her what he thought of as Pre-Raphaelite looks. In his mind, she could have been one of Dante Gabriel Rossetti's models and he increasingly found himself staring at her during the tutorials, noticing that she returned his stares with smiles. One day she had stayed behind after the rest of the class had left the room and asked him if he would read some poems she had written and tell her what he thought of them. He took the folder she held out to him as her eyes pierced his, making him feel like a fish caught on a line. She smiled. 'Thanks. Please let me know what you think of them,' she said.

He opened the folder later that night after Juliet had gone to bed and he was alone in the room he used as a study. Inside it, along with the poems, was a note with the words '*I think you're sexy xxx*' and her mobile number. He thought he should immediately throw it away, but instead he folded it and put it in his wallet. He read through the poems. They were mostly mediocre imagist poems of little literary merit. The note, however, stirred him and he couldn't stop thinking about her. He even took out his phone and wondered about sending her a text, starting to write one before erasing it.

On the train back from a one-day conference in Edinburgh that Monday afternoon, he had a call on his mobile from the hospice telling him that his mother had slipped into a coma and was fading fast and unlikely to survive the night. He knew what he should do but something in him urged him to do the opposite. The idea of seeing Chloe came to him and he succumbed to a fantasy of slowly undressing her. A line of William Blake's came to him, about how it was better to murder an infant in its cradle than nurse unacted desires. He felt full of unacted desires. Suddenly, he couldn't bear the thought of the bedside vigil with his mother lying unconscious beside him. He wanted to feel alive, not be surrounded by death. He wanted to taste her lips and feel drunk in her embraces.

Without thinking, almost as an automatic reflex, he pulled out the piece of paper with Chloe's number which he had stuck in his wallet. He must have subconsciously thought that he would make use of it in this way some day. He sent her a text asking if she was free that evening. She answered almost immediately, saying she was. He phoned Juliet saying he would be spending the night at the hospice and he would see her tomorrow. She said she was thinking about him.

At that precise moment, Christie had looked up from his phone and noticed a man sitting on the other side of the carriage. He wasn't sure it was him at first but he Googled him on his phone and then was certain. From Queen Street station he followed him down Buchanan Street and westwards along Argyle Street and saw him enter a hotel. As if pulled by some inexorable force, Christie felt himself being drawn into the hotel, stand behind the man at reception, and check into a double room for one night.

He sent Chloe another text arranging to meet her in Sarti's in Renfield Street. When she appeared, she looked stunning, wearing a tight-fitting red dress which emphasised her curves, and his mind filled with desire to take her in his arms. At first, she seemed a little nervous and unsure. Christie realised he would have to steady his own emotions or he might scare her off. He had already had a few drinks and made sure he refilled her glass with wine frequently, though, and soon she looked more relaxed. She told him about her flatmates and about how wild they were. She said that she was normally more of an introvert, preferring to stay in and read books or write while they went out clubbing. After dinner he took her back to the hotel and they went into the hotel bar for more drinks. That's when he noticed him there, sitting at a table alone.

Christie had drunk more than he should have, mainly to steady his nerves. He had had a couple of cocktails in the hotel bar before he went to the restaurant to meet Chloe, then they had drunk champagne with dinner and now were sharing a bottle of wine.

'Do you know him?' Chloe asked.

'Who?'

She nodded in the direction of a table on the other side of the bar. 'That man over there. You keep staring at him.'

'Do I? Sorry. I thought I recognised him. Eh, no, no idea who he is.'

A moment later Chloe said she had to use the bathroom. Suddenly he was alone in the bar with him. There were no other guests around. This was his chance. He stood up and walked over to his table.

Henderson looked up from the phone that he was intently studying, aware that a figure was hovering over him. 'Can I help you?' he said, confused as to why this stranger, who was clearly heavily inebriated, was standing over him in an almost menacing way.

'Do you know who I am?' Christie said, slurring his words and trying hard to remain stable on his feet.

'Should I?'

'You knew my mother.'

'I don't think so. Now if you wouldn't mind, I don't really feel like having a conversation with strangers. Especially drunk ones.'

'She wasn't a stranger to you,' he slurred.

The older man began to feel unnerved. He shook his head and looked back down at his phone, deciding that it was probably best to ignore this character and he would go away. If he didn't, then he could probably summon the barman for help.

'Her name was Fiona Christie. You knew her well enough thirty years ago.'

Henderson blanched and looked up at the young man's face. Yes, now he could see the resemblance to his former secretary. God, this man must be...No, surely not. It can't be.

'I thought you would want to know that she told me about you and how you treated her. I'm the son you never wanted and now she is dying. You bastard!'

Henderson was shocked, confused, and also afraid. 'Listen, I'm sorry. Very sorry to hear about your mother. I don't know what she said but I would be happy to put the record straight. If you are staying here then I suggest we meet in the morning. Perhaps I could see you at breakfast in the restaurant and we could talk then. I think you've maybe had a little too much to drink, don't you? If that's not suitable, get in touch and we'll meet and have a chat.' He fished into his jacket and brought out a business card and handed it to him.

Christie noticed another card lying on the table. It was one the hotel issued their guests with, identifying the room number so they could order drinks at the bar. Room 15 it said. Christie felt his head beginning to spin and realised he needed to sit down. He turned around and could see Chloe returning to their table. 'I'll be seeing you,' he said pointing a finger accusingly at Henderson.

'I really am sorry about your mother,' said Henderson, but Christie had already turned his back and headed back across the bar.

'Did you know that man, then?' Chloe asked.

'No. It was a mistake,' he said, refilling her glass. Christie saw a young woman with blonde hair enter the bar and go over to Henderson's table. They exchanged a few words, then he saw them get up to leave together. A woman young enough to be his granddaughter. Rage boiled up in him. He clearly hadn't changed since he was cheating on his wife with his mother all those years ago. At the same time, he was aware that he was copying his biological father's behaviour. Here he was, also cheating on Juliet, so maybe there was something in his genes. He had just wanted to experience something that was the opposite of going to that hospice, holding a hand that was soon going to be taken by death. He wanted to feel alive and lose himself in her young tender body.

And he soon did. It felt wonderful to forget about pain or suffering or sadness when they made love. Soon Chloe fell asleep but he was wide awake. Reality came back and hit him like a hammer. He guessed Henderson would still be awake. He couldn't wait until the morning or to arrange another meeting. He would go and talk to him now and have it out. He got up and dressed quickly and slipped out of the room, closing the door silently.

Stephen Christie was now seated in an interview room in police headquarters, his mind a blur, feeling as if his life had become a scene in a movie. His eyes looked hollow. He had been brought to the police station by two police officers who had appeared at his front door. He was in the flat on his own, his wife out somewhere with friends for a drink. When he got to the police station, he had immediately requested legal representation and had accepted a duty solicitor, Jamie McEwan, of McEwan and Sellars. Then he had been cautioned by a couple of detectives. It felt exactly like cop shows on TV or film. The lead detective, a female, had spoken the names of everyone in the room and the date and time while the interview was being recorded. The female detective, who introduced herself as Detective Inspector Shazia Khan, had asked him if the statement he had given to police was true. Christie hadn't answered. Instead, he looked at Jamie. 'You see, Stephen, your fingerprints were found in Charles Henderson's hotel room. How do you explain that?'

'I was in the hotel bar with a friend.' Christie said. 'I spotted Mr Henderson and went over to speak to him. I'd probably had a bit too much to drink, but I wouldn't describe it as an altercation.'

'What did you say to him?' asked Shazia.

'I told him who I was, that I was his son.'

Shazia nodded. 'His son? Go on.'

'Yes. I had only recently discovered this. It was the first time I had seen him in the flesh. When my mother told me his name, just recently, I Googled it and, of course, saw that he was an MSP. She told me that she had worked for him a long time ago when he was a solicitor. When I saw him in the hotel, I went over to him and told him who I was and that my mother was now dying. I wanted to see his face when he heard that.'

'And you just happened to be staying in the same hotel as him?'

'Yes.'

'Bit of a coincidence, isn't it?' asked Joseph.

'I suppose so,' said Christie, remembering how he had followed the MSP all the way from the station to the hotel.

'Why were you staying in the hotel, anyway? You live in Glasgow.'

Christie stared back at Shazia as if pondering how to reply. Eventually he muttered. 'It's private.'

Shazia shook her head. 'Actually no, Stephen. This is a murder investigation. But we'll come back to that. What was his reaction when you told him who you were?'

'Totally shocked. He didn't believe me at first, but when I said her name and he looked at my face he realised it was true. He told me to get in touch another time. He gave me his business card. I've still got it somewhere.'

'So how come your prints were in his room?'

'I couldn't sleep that night. I kept thinking about what I wanted to say to him, so I got up and went to his room and knocked on the door.'

'How did you know his room number?'

Christie hesitated. If he told them he had noticed it on his room card that would sound suspicious. 'He told me his room number when he asked me to come and see him in the morning, but I couldn't wait until then.'

Christie thought back to what happened. He had knocked and knocked and eventually Henderson had answered the door. He looked drowsy, confused, didn't seem to know who Christie was. He told him to go away and started to close the door. Christie had barged in and looked around. He was surprised the young woman wasn't there. He was feeling full of rage. All those years of his mother struggling to bring him up with little money, and there he was, this rich Tory bastard! He hadn't acknowledged his son, hadn't offered any assistance. He had made all this money and lived a luxury lifestyle while they struggled, and his mother was now dying.

Christie paused and took a sip of water. His face was red and he was sweating.

'What time was this?' asked Joseph.

'About half past twelve, I think.'

'Go on, what happened.'

'He let me in. Then we talked. He told me he was sorry for what had happened with my mum. He said he wasn't proud of it. He said that he had wanted her to have the baby and said he would support her. He blamed his wife, saying she made him choose to either tell my mum to have an abortion or she would leave him and have his reputation ruined. She said she would drag him through the courts as an adulterer and his political career would be finished. He said he was a local councillor then and had political ambitions. He claimed he gave my mother money and told her to have an abortion. He said she quit her job and moved away from Edinburgh and he never heard from her again. He had assumed that she had had the abortion until that night when I confronted him.'

Shazia nodded. 'How long did you stay?'

Christie looked as if he was trying to remember something from the distant past, not an event from a few days ago. 'Eh, not long. Maybe half an hour. He said he was tired. I don't really know.'

'What was he wearing when he answered the door?' asked Shazia.

'Wearing?'

'Yes. Was he dressed? Naked? What did he have on?'

He hesitated. 'Erm…boxers, I think. When I got in the room he put on a robe.'

Shazia looked at some papers on the desk. 'Hmm. So, you were with Chloe Sinclair in the hotel. Who's she?'

Christie looked down at his shoes. 'Does she have to be involved?'

'Stephen, a man died that night. This man, who you say was your father. You were with him shortly before he died. We need to know who you were with.'

'She's a friend.'

'Your girlfriend?'

Christie stared at a poster on the wall about reporting crime, with a phone number and a website. He nodded.

'I understand from your statement that you are a university lecturer. How do you know Chloe?'

Christie looked embarrassed. 'She's one of my students.'

'Are you married, Stephen?' Shazia asked.

'Yes.'

'And does your wife know about Chloe?'

Christie shook his head. 'No. She thinks I was staying at the hospice that night. My mother was very ill. Dying, in fact. She died that night. I told Juliet, that's my wife, that I stayed there with her.'

'We will need to speak to her.'

'She doesn't know anything about it though.'

Shazia ignored this. 'How did you explain being out of the room in the night?'

'I don't think Chloe noticed I wasn't there. She was asleep. She was quite drunk.'

'So, you lied to us when you gave your statement, and you are telling us that you have lied to two women in your life, Stephen, about what happened that night. Are you lying now?'

'No. It's the truth, I tell you.'

'Why did you lie when you gave your statement in the hotel?'

'I don't know. I was scared. I heard someone say there had been a murder and mention the room number. I realised it was Henderson's room. I panicked, I guess. I didn't want you to know I had been in there.'

Joseph folded his arms and glared at Christie. 'It's quite a coincidence, isn't it?' he said. 'You just happen to be staying the night in the same hotel as the man who was your biological father, that you haven't known all your life. You've only just found out he is your father, then you see him, then he is murdered. You had a fight with him, didn't you, you were drunk and in a rage. You killed him.'

'No. That isn't true. I didn't kill him.'

'You found out which room he was in and you killed him when you went to his room. This story you have just told us about how you talked is all lies, isn't it?'

'My client has given you a statement, freely,' said Jamie. 'You should not be subjecting him to pressure to try to change it.'

'Listen, can I phone my wife?' asked Christie.

'No.'

'I'm telling you I had nothing to do with it.'

Shazia looked at Joseph and nodded her head towards the door, and they got up and left the room. 'Let's leave him to stew for a bit,' she said. 'He's not telling us everything. Tell him we are detaining him for twenty-four hours on suspicion of murder and we'll get a warrant and search his house and see if anything turns up there.'

20

Juliet Wilson had arrived home to find her husband gone. She tried ringing his mobile but got no answer. She was puzzled. She had been out for drinks with friends and got home just after ten, expecting to see Stephen. He hadn't texted her to say he was going out. She would have been surprised as his mood since Tuesday had been morose. It was not surprising, she thought. He had just lost his mother. He wasn't able to go to work and she didn't think he would feel like going out socialising on a Friday night. She was going to cancel going out with her friends but Stephen had insisted, saying he wouldn't be much company.

She was speechless when she answered the door just before midnight and saw several police officers there. A policeman who introduced himself as Detective Sergeant Boateng explained that he had a search warrant and he brought in a team of officers. When the sergeant took her aside and told her that Christie was being detained as part of a murder investigation, she told him that he couldn't have had anything to do with it as he was at his mother's bedside all that night and they could check with the hospice, but Joseph informed her that her husband had admitted staying in a hotel and this had been confirmed.

'That can't be true,' she said.

Joseph shook his head. 'I am afraid I cannot give you any more information, Mrs Christie but it is the truth. He stayed in the hotel that night.'

'The lying shit!' she said. 'And it's not Mrs Christie. I've never used that name and I never will. I'm Juliet Wilson.' She sat on a stool in the kitchen as the team conducted their search.

'Did Stephen ever talk to you about his biological father?' asked Joseph.

She shook her head. 'He said he didn't know who he was. A seaman, he thought.'

'What clothes was Stephen wearing when he came home on Tuesday, Juliet?'

'Let me get them.' She handed over a bundle of clothing containing black leather gloves, a pair of black corduroy trousers, a light blue shirt, a grey jumper, and a black padded waterproof jacket. A police officer placed them into plastic bags.

'What about shoes?'

'He usually wears his brown brogues during the week. They're in the porch.'

An officer bagged the shoes. Once the flat was empty again, she poured herself a large glass of white wine and sat down on the sofa in the living room. The phone rang. It was her husband. 'I'm at the police station. I'm sorry. I'll explain.'

'You told me you were at your dying mother's bedside all night! Now a policeman comes here and tells me you stayed in a hotel. What the hell is going on, Stephen?'

'I'll explain.'

'You've said that already. A hotel! You were with some woman that night, weren't you? Who was she?'

'It didn't mean anything. Let me explain.'

She didn't want to hear any more. 'This is the end, Stephen. Fuck off and don't call me again. I don't want to hear from you.' She knew exactly what he had been up to. Shagging some little tart, probably a student, the bastard! She disconnected the call. Tears flooded out and she was angry at herself for letting him make her weep. How could she have been so stupid? He probably had been having lots of affairs. He had just got caught this time. Not for the first time either. Well, this would be the last time. They were finished. She didn't want to live with someone she couldn't trust. And she wasn't moving out either, that was certain. He would have to find somewhere else to live. If they let him out. Maybe he did kill someone after all and would go to prison for life anyway. The way she was feeling right now, she wouldn't care. She had thought she knew him. That was the worst part. All those years that you spend with someone, thinking you know what they are like. Then something happens and you realise you don't. It makes you feel stupid. She was annoyed at herself for being taken in by him. Never again, she told herself.

She gulped back the wine. It felt sharp and stung her throat but she didn't mind. She enjoyed the sting. She poured another glass. Once she finished packing up his things and putting them in bin bags in the hall for him to collect, she would pour herself some more. As she threw clothes into a bin bag, not bothering to fold anything, she felt better. Yes, she told herself, a new start. That's what's needed. A new start.

It was late. Shazia looked at the others in the room. She outlined everything that they knew about the case so far. A dead body in a locked room. A broken window. A prostitute, Katarina Marková, who had been hired to sleep with the victim. Stephen Christie, the illegitimate son of Henderson who had been in the bedroom. A young woman who worked with the victim, whose boyfriend worked in the hotel. 'Well, from what Christie says, at least we know that Katarina isn't the killer. Any other thoughts?' she said.

Mitchell nodded and said, 'Christie did it. He goes to Henderson's room, flies into a rage, and loses the plot. He's drunk and he kills him.'

Shazia said, 'Christie says Henderson put on a robe. But he wasn't wearing one when he was found dead. Of course, he could be lying.'

'He's definitely not telling us the full story,' said Joseph.

'He could have killed him the second the door was shut,' said Mitchell. 'Or, let's say they talk, but things quickly get heated. Christie forces Henderson onto the bed and smothers him in a moment of madness.'

'What about the broken window?' asked Shazia.

'He makes it look like a break-in,' said Mitchell. 'He returns to his room, puts on a pair of gloves, goes down to the first floor, undoes the catch on the window, steps out onto the ledge, then breaks the glass.'

'How would he do that?'

'Maybe with his phone or something like that? The room he stayed in will have been cleaned, but it's worth asking Forensics to examine it and see if there's any trace of glass. There might even be shreds of broken glass on his clothing, for example.'

'Not much chance of finding anything by now, as you say, but we will get the room looked at just in case,' said Shazia. We'll keep him in the cells overnight anyway. OK folks, it's late, let's all go home and get some sleep.'

21

When he had finally got home late on Friday night, after spending several hours with Stephen Christie, Jamie told Shona that he had picked up a voicemail message from his old friend, Aileen Buchan, asking Shona to contact her. She hadn't contacted her through the newspaper so had phoned him as she wanted it to be kept confidential. Aileen, Jamie and Fergus Mulrein had been friends at university and she was now an MSP for the Scottish Greens. When she had been wounded by a right-wing extremist at a husting meeting in the City Halls, her attacker had claimed to be acting on behalf of Scottish Action, but it was never clear whether the attack was the work of a lone, mentally unstable individual or a planned coordinated attempted political assassination by an organised group.

Shona called Aileen's number on Saturday morning. 'I don't want to speak about it over the phone,' Aileen said. 'Can you come through to Edinburgh. How about today?' Shona wondered if Aileen was being a bit paranoid being so cautious in her approach but put this down to anxiety, which she no doubt experienced after being the victim of such a serious assault.

She took the train through to Waverley, then walked to a pub on Rose Street where they had arranged to meet. It was windy and raining heavily and Shona was soaked by the time she got there, cursing the fact that she had neglected to bring an umbrella. She ordered a white wine and took a seat at a corner table, hanging her sopping wet denim jacket over the chair. Her feet, in her Converse trainers, felt soggy. The

MSP arrived shortly afterwards, a small figure with her long red hair tied back in a ponytail, carrying a backpack, a brolly and wearing a cagoule and a pair of Doc Martens. Shona, recognising her immediately, waved Aileen over. 'Lovely to meet you. Doesn't rain here as much as in the west, but when it does you know about it,' she said with a grin as she gave Shona a friendly hug, then removed her coat. Underneath, she was wearing a purple jumper and skinny jeans. Shona asked her what she would like to drink and then went to the bar and returned with a large glass of white wine the same as her own.

'Great to meet you, said Shona, raising her glass in a toast. 'It's not every day I get to have a one-to-one with a politician!'

'Likewise,' said Aileen. 'I read your piece in the Gazette on the attack on those refugees. Appalling, after all that those people have suffered.'

'I know. Makes me ashamed to be Scottish. But they were amazing. So resilient.'

Aileen nodded, took a drink of wine and smiled at Shona, appraising her. 'So, you're the one that at last has tamed Jamie. Despite all appearances he used to be a wild one and said he never wanted to settle down.'

Shona wasn't sure how to take this. 'Not sure there's been any taming involved.'

'You're right.' She slapped herself on the forehead. 'Wrong word. Who doesn't want to go a bit wild sometimes? I must be getting too boring and staid. It's what Holyrood does to you. It all gets a bit serious and I have no time for any social life anymore.'

Shona smiled and nodded. 'That's OK. Must be interesting at times, though?'

Aileen considered this, pursing her thin lips, then nodded very slowly. 'Eh, ye...es, sort of. Fucking frustrating actually. It's better not being in coalition though. Certainly not with the SNP.' She took a large drink of her wine.

159

'Why's that?'

Aileen shook her head in reply. 'Well, they just looked on us for votes to get through their policies. Talk about an unequal partnership! Every time we tried to get one of ours through, forget it. Yes, they talked the talk but did they walk the walk? No. Look at how they backtracked on agreeing to support a referendum on the head of state. They would let us have the debates, but would they support us? No way. Plus, look at where they are taking the country? It's neoliberalism all over again. No, we need to build a real progressive alliance and I think we can. But they've got the Tories propping them up now, so another election is a long way off. But listen, I hear that you were also a friend of Fergus's, is that right?'

'Yes, he helped me with the Colin Chisholm story. It was really all his work and so sad how things turned out for him.'

'Yes, poor Fergus. I loved him dearly. We all miss him. I know he would have wanted me to help you with your investigation. As I said, I read your report on those refugees who were fire-bombed. How much do you know about Scottish Action who, I guess, were responsible, seeing the graffiti that was there?' Aileen had made a name for herself as a well-known opponent of the far right and had made several speeches in parliament condemning the actions of right-wing extremist groups, including Scottish Action.

'It's difficult to find out who they really are.' said Shona. 'There's a wall of silence around them. A reporter I worked with tried to find out about them a year or so ago but they put the frighteners on him. I think that's what led him to quit Glasgow. I know that they are far-right extremists, in particular anti-Muslim.'

'Yes. I know the reporter you mean, Alex Mancini. Nice guy. I met him during the referendum campaign. He managed to uncover some good stuff about their local fund-raising in Glasgow. They are rumoured to have some links

160

to the Orange Order and are fiercely opposed to independence, of course, not to mention the whole idea of consigning the monarchy in Scotland to history. Their strategy is to use violence and terror to undermine immigration and intimidate their opponents. You may know that Scottish Action is also closely allied to unionist paramilitary groups in England and Northern Ireland. Like them, they are a proscribed group. They share common goals, like opposing republicanism, and their long-term objective is to unite Scotland with England again as a United Kingdom. Like the groups in England and Northern Ireland, they are also racist, anti-immigrant and homophobic. You're right to say Scottish Action are incredibly secretive. They are not really interested in democracy, though you probably know that the far-right political group, Britain United, is rumoured to be their mouthpiece. They are neo- Nazis, basically.'

'I guess I know most of what you have told me already, but I assume you have something else?'

Aileen lowered her voice and produced an envelope from her bag. 'Yes. Someone sent me some information. It arrived in an anonymous email so I have no idea who sent it, but it looks entirely genuine so I suppose it's been hacked or leaked. I've copied it for you,' she said handing Shona the envelope.

'What is this?'

'There's a memory stick in there revealing how Britain United, and probably Scottish Action, is being funded. Up to now no one knew where Britain United's money came from, all we knew was they seemed to have plenty of it. As well as their glossy magazines, they are bombarding the internet with social media advertising, disseminating fake news, organising demonstrations and so on, playing the race card, trying to say that we are being – as they delicately put it in their language – "swamped" by an influx of people from Eastern Europe and African

161

refugees and economic migrants. All of it completely untrue of course. In fact, as a country, we actually need to increase our net migration. Anyway, all of this activity costs money. A lot of money. Internet advertising doesn't come cheap. Certainly not on the scale that they are operating on. I have long wondered who is paying for all of it and now I know at least where some of it is coming from.' She pointed at the envelope. 'In here is a copy of a series of confidential documents from a law firm based in the British Virgin Islands, Atlantic Legal. I've kept a copy for myself. There's no doubt at all about its authenticity. Have a look at it and I am sure you will want to follow it up. It has details about someone who has contributed a lot of money to a source close to Britain United, Cameron Forsyth.'

'Cameron Forsyth? The Tory businessman? Why would he be donating to a far-right group? Would he really want to back a bunch of extremists?'

'Maybe you should ask him? What is not so well known is that he has overseas investments in tax havens as you will see from these papers. I don't think he will want that to come out, never mind his links to terrorists.'

Shona thanked Aileen for the information and, after chatting for a bit longer, she hurried back towards Glasgow, thinking that if she managed to get a start on analysing what was on the memory stick, she might manage to pull a story together for Monday's paper. When she got back home, Jamie was out somewhere, so she had peace and quiet to focus on the job at hand. She realised that the documents on the stick were copies of legal contracts on Atlantic Legal headed paper as well as copies of emails from a company called Paradise Investments to and from the law firm. As Aileen had said, Atlantic Legal was a law firm registered in the British Virgin Islands, and the papers showed that Paradise Investments was a company also registered there. As the British Virgin Islands was essentially a tax haven, it enjoyed laws which prevented the disclosure of the ownership of companies registered there, so it was not usually possible to know who owned them. But these documents revealed that Paradise Investments was in fact owned by Cameron Forsyth.

From the documents, she saw that money was regularly being paid out from Paradise Investments via Atlantic Legal to a Scottish company called Mercat Partners. Paradise Investments had transferred £500,000 in the last financial year to this company. It was registered at an address in West George Street, Glasgow which, Shona soon discovered with a quick web search, turned out to be simply a mailbox, just a registered address with no actual staff, contact details or premises. Another web search revealed that Mercat Partners was registered in Glasgow as a Scottish Limited Partnership, an SLP. This meant that there were no responsible officers publicly named or identified in any way that were connected to the company. She was aware that these partnerships did not have to reveal who owned them. In other words, it was a shell company.

She knew that these SLPs were well known as vehicles for laundering illegal money, money that often had its source in organised crime or in former Soviet Union states such as Azerbaijan. Billions of pounds were being syphoned off to benefit the ruling elites of these countries through the purchase of luxury goods, cars, houses, private school fees and private healthcare. Finance was also used to grease the palms of politicians throughout Europe to make them friendlier towards these regimes and influence national and international policy towards them. It wasn't known as the Global Laundromat for nothing, she thought, conjuring up an image of a never-ending row of washing machines filled with cash in various denominations.

Shona couldn't believe the sums which were going through the accounts of Forsyth's tax haven company, Paradise Investments. Millions had been paid into the company from accounts in banks in various countries around the world: Cyprus, the Cayman Islands, Estonia, Malta, and Singapore. Where was all this money coming from? she wondered. The sources behind the accounts weren't revealed, though. A payment of just over a million Canadian dollars had been paid out to a company registered in Toronto called International Data Research. Shona had heard about this innocuous-sounding outfit and knew that what they did was actually rather sinister. They managed to obtain personal data from the major players on the internet, including the main social media platforms, and use this to target political advertising at individuals through covert psychological profiling obtained from harvesting millions of users' information without actual consent. They passed it on to groups which set up fake accounts and used 'bots' to bombard users with messages, including messaging internet users with fake news and scare stories about immigrants. There had also been a payment made from Paradise Investments to Forsyth's English company, CF Capital, for £4 million at the time of the EU referendum, coincidentally the same sum which his company had given to the campaign to leave the EU.

The emails also revealed that the individuals responsible for Mercat Partners were Andrew Campbell, the general partner, and Cameron Forsyth, the limited partner, something that was not public knowledge. She did an online search for Campbell. Campbell was the leader of Britain United. He had been convicted five years previously for an attack on a mosque for which Scottish Action had claimed responsibility, and had been given an eighteen-month sentence. It didn't take long for her to find some recent examples of the poisonous rantings that Campbell had spouted on social media. There was vile abuse of Muslims and immigrants, blaming them for the Buchanan Street bombing, for pressure on housing, schools, welfare, and the health service. Some politicians and public figures were vilified, in particular Scottish Greens and anyone considered to be left-wing, but members of the SNP government were also accused of being complicit, standing by and doing nothing while the number of asylum seekers and immigrants in Scotland swelled.

The fact that Forsyth was now revealed to be covertly funding a right-wing extremist showed him to be operating well outside of the mainstream of politics at the very least. He was, in effect, potentially colluding in direct acts of terrorism by being linked to someone like Campbell.

22

Shazia spent an hour interviewing Chloe Sinclair, Christie's girlfriend. She looked very young, almost a schoolgirl, and Shazia felt a sickening distaste for the predatory university lecturer who had seduced her into spending the night with him. Sinclair's statement only confirmed what Christie had said: she had been drunk, they had sex, she had fallen asleep and wasn't aware of him exiting and entering the room during the night. When the call from Forensics came, though, it was disappointing. They were short-staffed and wouldn't manage to analyse anything until Monday. Even if they couldn't charge Christie at the moment, she wouldn't rush to release him. Let him sweat a little, she thought.

When her mobile rang, she wondered if it was Forensics again. Maybe they had found more evidence after all, but it was something else entirely. 'DI Khan here…Yes…What happened? …You have him in custody?... I'll be right over.'

Robert Jackson's vehicle had been spotted on Maryhill Road that morning by a patrol car which indicated for him to stop. He didn't stop and they followed him in pursuit until he took a corner at top speed and his vehicle ended up upside down in a field on the back road between Summerston and Balmore Road. Shazia called Joseph, who said he would like to come in and sit in on the interview.

A while later, Jackson sat in the interview room, legs outstretched and looking bored. He was a powerfully-built man in his mid-forties with a shaved head, a thick tattooed neck and a scar down his right cheek. He was wearing a black T-shirt, the muscles on his biceps bulging as if they had been inflated. He clearly either spent most of his leisure time at the gym, pumping weights, or was on steroids. Or both. Tattoos covered his neck and arms in a mosaic of intricate designs including birds of prey, daggers, and even what looked like an AK47 submachine gun. He had a bloodied bandage on his head, no doubt from injuries sustained in the crash, and an arm in a sling. Beside him sat his lawyer.

Shazia placed a folder on the table. 'First of all, Robert, why didn't you stop when the police car signalled for you to pull over?'

Jackson shrugged.

'Maybe something to do with the bag of drugs we found inside? We'll come to that later. Robert, we wish to ask you some questions in connection with the events of 6th and 7th February and about the death of Charles Henderson. Firstly, can you tell me your whereabouts on the evening and night of Monday 6th February, in particular from 9:00 p.m. onwards?'

'No comment,' said Jackson.

'Robert, we have images of a suspect getting out of your car caught on CCTV in the city centre that evening. So, either you were driving it or someone else was. Was it you who was driving the car?'

Jackson remained silent.

'You are a taxi driver, is that correct?'

'Aye, I'm a taxi driver.'

'Who do you work for?'

'I'm self-employed.'

'But you take work from Kelvin Cars, don't you? Their cards were found in your car.'

He shrugged. 'Sometimes, I dae jobs for them amongst others, aye.'

'Kelvin Cars is owned by Greg Murray. Do you know him?'

Jackson shook his head. 'No.'

'Were you working on the night of Monday 6th February?'

'Maybe. I cannae mind.'

'Try harder.'

'OK. I might have been.'

'Did you drop off a passenger in Hope Street in the city centre that evening?'

'I cannae remember.'

'Do you know Katarina Marková, a Slovakian national?'

Jackson stared at the ceiling and said nothing.

'We are conducting a murder enquiry. If you remain silent, that could be interpreted as being non-cooperative and might lead people to think you have something to hide.'

David Semple, the solicitor representing Jackson, a stocky, bald man in his fifties with a face like a bulldog and a temper to match, said belligerently, 'My client has the right to remain silent. As you know, he is not required to answer any of your questions.'

Shazia ignored the interruption. 'Katarina Marková was working as an escort in the Moray Hotel on Monday evening. We will be showing Katarina your photograph and asking her if she knows you. What do you think she will say? Her details were discovered in a file in the escort agency's computer and she has been positively identified by two independent witnesses as being seen with Charles Henderson the night he died. How do you know her?'

Jackson just shook his head. 'No comment.'

'You do know her, don't you?'

Jackson shook his head.

Shazia said, 'Do you know anything about the death of Charles Henderson in the Moray hotel on the night of 6th to 7th February?'

Jackson shrugged again. 'I don't know anything about any murder. OK?'

Shazia opened the folder and spread out several photographs of Henderson's corpse on the table. 'Not a pretty sight, is it? He was suffocated with a pillow, held down with extreme force.'

Jackson raised his voice. 'I've fuckin' tell't ye, I know fuck all. I'm a taxi driver, that's all!'

'You knew Katarina had an appointment with Mr Henderson the night that he died, didn't you?'

'No comment.'

'Where were you the rest of that night after you took Katarina to the hotel?'

Jackson looked at Semple and the lawyer nodded. Evidently, they had discussed this and agreed that Jackson should make a statement. 'Look. I pick people up. I just take them to where they want to go and bring them back. That's all. If it's a girl meeting somebody, I don't know anything about what happens between them.'

'Does anyone else drive your cab?'

'No.'

'Let's assume that it was you who took the passenger and dropped her off. How was the booking made?'

He shook his head. 'I don't know. I can't remember.'

'And you picked her up again later, didn't you?'

'I've told you. I can't remember.'

'The escort agency booked you to take her to the hotel and back again to her flat. Your number was called by the agency boss, David Robertson. Except that's not all is it, Robert? You get the money that she makes sleeping with the client. You were her pimp and her gaoler, providing her and the other girls with everything they needed – food, toiletries and, probably, drugs to keep them compliant. You have keys to her flat, don't you?'

Jackson's mouth twisted into a kind of smile as he shook his head, his lip curling into a sneer. 'No comment.'

'We'll see if any of the keys on your keyring match the lock on her flat. You supply drugs as well, don't you?'

'No comment.'

'What about that large stash of cocaine you had in the glove compartment of your car?'

'No comment.'

'Did you supply ketamine for Henderson that night in the hotel as well?'

'No comment.'

'We also suspect that you were involved in trafficking and forcing Katarina and other girls to work as a prostitute. Not just her but more than twenty other girls.'

Jackson shook his head.

'Maybe you do other work for some people too. Like murder?'

'I don't know what the fuck you are talking about!' Jackson's face had turned beetroot. It was easy to imagine how frightening this man could be, thought Shazia.

'My client has made it clear that he has nothing to do with the death of Mr Henderson,' said Semple.

'Bit of a coincidence, though, isn't it? That you drive a hooker to a rendezvous with someone who ends up dead, you having previous for violence?'

'No comment.'

'OK. So, what did you do after you finished working that night?' asked Shazia.

'I went to my girlfriend's flat, stayed the night there. Is that a crime?'

'What's her name?'

'Nicky. Nicola.'

'Surname?'

'Murdoch.'

'Where does she live?'

'Knightswood.'

'Is that where you have been hiding out?'

'I huvnae been hiding. We went away for a few days, that's aw. And why the hell have you searched ma flat while I was away? What right did you have to dae that?'

Shazia ignored his questions. 'Where did you go?'

'To a hotel up north, if ye really want to know.'

'We'll need to know exactly where you went and we'll check that out. We'll also need Nicola's contact details from you. Then, maybe once you have time to think about things, you will be more forthcoming in your answers, In the meantime, we are detaining you in custody for being in possession of an illegal substance with intent to supply Do you have anything to say?'

Jackson shook his head.

Joseph received a strange message later that day. A phone call had come in to the switchboard from a public phone box in the city centre. The caller wouldn't give a name but left a message for the officer investigating Sammy Scobie's murder, the 'big black cockney guy,' as the caller described him. The mysterious caller said he had some information about Scobie. The switchboard operator told Joseph the voice was male and said he could meet him tonight at nine o' clock at the Nelson monument on Glasgow Green, but he had to come alone.

Joseph parked near Glasgow Green and sauntered into the park. He looked up. Dark clouds were moving fast; at least it was dry for the time being, but it was freezing. The wind seemed to cut right through him and he shivered. He walked past the People's Palace. Inside the building behind him there were a few lights that were clearly left on as a security measure, but everywhere else was plunged into darkness. There was a bench near the monument but he preferred to keep moving around, stamping his feet to keep warm. He checked his watch. Just coming up for nine. He looked around. The place seemed deserted. Maybe this guy wouldn't turn up. The location was a mugger's paradise. Why the hell had he agreed to meet someone here alone, he thought? The whole thing could be a trap. He wondered if he was shivering from the cold or from fear, and thought back to one night on an estate in Lewisham when he had confronted a knife-wielding teenager who had struck out at him and stabbed him in the arm. He cursed his own stupidity and took out his phone, pretending to be engaged in reading something, while all the time scanning his surroundings surreptitiously.

Suddenly a voice whispered in his ear, 'You found it alright then?' He hadn't been aware of anyone approaching. He turned to his left. The figure seemed to have appeared out of nowhere. He couldn't actually see the person's face but he was much smaller than Joseph, maybe about five-seven in height. He was wearing a black hoodie with the hood covering his head and some kind of scarf covering his face apart from his eyes.

'Yes,' said Joseph. 'No problem. Now can we cut the mystery? What's this about?'

'I can't give you my name. I don't generally trust the Glasgow police. They'll fit you up as soon as look at you. But you're new here so I'm taking a chance on you. I heard you were asking around Sammy's neighbours if they knew anything.'

Joseph felt flattered yet suspicious at the same time. 'What is it you want to tell me?'

'As I said, I heard you were knocking on the neighbours' doors asking about Sammy. Sammy was my pal,' said the stranger. 'He wasn't an angel, I know that. But he didn't deserve to die.'

'So, do you know something about his death? Who was responsible?'

'I don't want to get involved. That's why I wanted to meet you here. This is far from my usual stamping ground, do you understand?'

'Yes, but without knowing more how can I be sure what you are telling me is reliable?'

'You can't. But I think it's important that you know something about Sammy. You probably know already that he made a wee bit of dosh dealing. You don't need to be

Sherlock fucking Holmes to work that one out, though Sammy never made any money that he didn't blow right away.'

'What, on drugs?'

'Yeah, he had a bit of a coke problem, but he was trying to straighten himself out and get off the gear. Like I said, I was Sammy's friend. Probably his only friend. He told me things but, like I said, I can't get involved.'

Joseph remembered what Scobie's grandparents had said, about a friend called Tommy. 'What's your name?' he asked. 'Is it Tommy?'

The man took a step back and Joseph wondered if he had said the wrong thing and scared him off, but there was a sound of voices behind him and Joseph realised that was what had startled him.

'Never mind my name,' he said, starting to move away. The important thing is Sammy was meeting someone called Jack the night he died.'

'Jack? Who is Jack?'

The voices were getting nearer and Joseph saw the young man looking past him.

'Jack is –'

There was the sound of footsteps behind them. 'What's going on here?' said a voice.

'Just find Jack and you'll find Sammy's killer,' said the man, sprinting towards the boundary of the green and disappearing into the darkness.

'Hey you, come back here,' shouted a voice.

Joseph turned around. Two uniformed officers were walking towards him. Joseph put his hand into his jacket and produced his warrant card and waved it at the officers. 'Sorry, sir. We thought you were in some danger,' said one of the officers. 'Should we go after him?'

Joseph cursed. 'No, It's fine. Leave it.' Whatever else the young man was going to tell him was lost. But at least he had a name. Jack. Who the hell was Jack?

23

Greg Murray was apoplectic with rage. He was sitting at his desk, staring into space and vaping on an e-cigarette which sent out clouds of steam from his mouth and nostrils, making him resemble a dragon in its cave. Even his balding pate seemed to have taken on a patina of anger, veins pulsing furiously below the surface of the skin. He stroked his neatly-trimmed grey goatee beard in frustration. His office was situated on the top floor of a building in Bath Street which housed a nightclub in the basement and a pub on the ground floor, all owned by him and his brother. Since he had heard that Robert Jackson had been arrested, he was furious and sweating. 'That prick better not grass me up. I'll fucking rip his tongue out and stick it up his arse!' he bellowed.

Iain Thompson hadn't seen his boss that angry in a long time, and that was saying something as Murray was regularly losing his temper at something or someone. As his right-hand man in charge of security at his premises, Thompson was often called on to deal with the matter. He was an intimidating figure, not particularly tall, but broad-shouldered and muscular, his bullet-like head closely shaved. 'Don't worry, boss. He'll keep his mouth shut, he knows the score,' said Thompson.

'Aye, well if he disnae, he knows whit will happen! While you were off shagging your girlfriend in Gran Canaria for a fortnight, the guys I've got working for me have been worse than useless and the shit has hit the fan. Tell that arsehole, Robertson, I want to see him pronto. He fucked up big time. He better have a good explanation.'

Robertson appeared in Murray's office half an hour later. He had appeared in court on Friday morning and pleaded not guilty to the trafficking charge and, after intervention pleas from his lawyer, he had been released on bail. When he entered Murray's office he was unnerved by how calm and pleasant Murray was towards him, which made him even more nervous than if he had been shouted at.

'Close the door and have a seat, Davy. How are you?' Murray smiled and raised a hand pointing to the chair on the other side of the desk from where he sat. Robertson closed the door and sat down shaking, his legs suddenly feeling like straws. He had never been alone with Murray before. There was always someone else there when they met, often Thompson who had met him at the front door and who had escorted him upstairs to Murray's office, but had then been told to go. He could feel a stream of perspiration running down his back underneath his shirt. 'I'm fine, boss. Thanks for bailing me out, by the way I owe you big time!'

Murray inhaled a lungful of vapour and blew it into Robertson's face. 'Aye, we'll come to that, don't worry, I huvnae forgot. By the way, officially I didnae bail ye oot so don't go blabbing that tae any cunt. The money was paid by somebody else through legal channels unconnected tae me, OK? I'm not daft. Anyway, Davy, there's a wee matter I wanted to talk to you about. One of our employees has managed to get himself into a wee bit of bother with the local constabulary and I am wondering how that happened? Maybe he has been a bit careless. Don't worry, I'll sort that out.'

Robertson nodded. 'Aye. I heard about that, boss.'

'Did ye now? OK, well here's the thing. Part of the problem is that it all stems from a certain young lady being ID'd by the fuzz. Are ye following me, Davy?'

'Aye, boss.'

Suddenly Murray stood up, brandishing a metal baseball bat which he had produced from under his desk. He wasn't particularly tall but made up for it in bulk. Unlike his elder brother, who had the physique of a ferret, the younger Murray brother more closely resembled an ox: squat and sturdy, a muscular frame with flab around his neck and middle, his belly particularly pushing out through the waistband. He swung the bat casually, looking down menacingly, his smile now removed and replaced with a mad grin instead. When he spoke, his voice had changed, too, no longer a calm tone but one of boiling rage. 'I want to know how the fuck you let those bastards take away files, not only finding this Slovakian bitch, but every other bit of Eastern European fanny we have hidden away across this city. As a result, every flat has been raided and we no longer have a viable business and I'm jist waiting on the polis arriving at ma door to ask me whit the fuck I huv tae dae wi' it!'

Every molecule of Robertson's frame had turned to jelly. He thought that if Murray swung the bat at his head he would simply be splashed across the walls of the office like strawberry jam. He tried to open his mouth to say something, but couldn't. He wasn't even very sure what he would say even if he managed to produce an utterance.

'Talk me through whit the fuck happened, Davy!' Murray ordered.

Robertson took a deep breath. His throat felt like sandpaper. It was hard to swallow. Eventually, he mumbled, 'I took that girl's profile aff the site on Sunday, like you told me to. I told them we didnae huv anyone called Natalia when they phoned. But then they just appeared with a search warrant, boss.'

Murray laughed and nodded several times. 'Aye, they had a search warrant. Of course they had a fucking search warrant! They had already phoned you and asked for information about wan o' the girls so it wisnae rocket science to know that they would come calling with a search warrant. Whit the fuck were you thinking of?'

'I dunno. I just didn't think, boss.'

'Jesus, why do I have fucking dimwits working for me?' He paced around the room swinging the bat then suddenly brought it down with a crash onto the desk in front of Robertson, making a dent in its wooden surface and turning the river of sweat running down Robertson's back into a cascade. 'Anybody wi' half a brain could work that one out. What I want to know is why didn't you delete the files that had the stuff about those girls we've brought into the country from the computer after the polis got in touch wi' you the first time? You could have saved them on a memory stick and given them tae somebody to stash then we wouldnae be in this fuckin' mess.'

'I don't know, boss. Sorry, boss.'

Murray shook his head and stared out of the window, his back to Robertson. There was silence in the room. Robertson fidgeted in his seat, not sure what was going to happen next. 'I'm sorry, boss,' he said.

Murray had made sure that in setting up the agency there was nothing to link his name to the business. The company and the rental of the office space were entirely in Robertson's name and the income was paid into an account that had no connection to Murray but from which payments found their way to him via several other accounts overseas. His accountant had assured him that the financial threads were indecipherable, lost in a maze of limited partnership companies and offshore banks which also, conveniently, ensured that most of the proceeds from the enterprise and the drug money which was fed through the accounts were invisible to the tax authorities.

'Damn right you're sorry.' Murray quickly turned and smashed the bat into Robertson's right knee.

'Fuckin' hell. Jesus Christ!' shrieked Robertson. The pain was excruciating and Robertson fell from the seat onto the floor, instinctively on the other side of his body as he

177

clutched at his knee which felt as if it had been splintered into a thousand pieces.

'Now get up on your feet and fuck off back to Possil and make sure you never screw up again or else this will connect with your heid next time. Understand?'

'Yes boss,' Robertson managed to stammer. He thought it would be impossible to stand, never mind walk, but realised that he had no choice. He was being given a chance to get out alive and better take it, he thought. He pushed down on the chair with his left hand and managed to lift himself up onto his left leg. The room seemed to swim around him and he thought he might faint, but managed to push that thought out of his head and steady himself. He saw that Murray had already gone back to his chair at his desk and he turned and headed towards the door, dragging his limp leg behind him, afraid that at any moment he might feel the bat crashing down on his skull.

Murray summoned Thompson back into the room. 'I've got eejits working for me who don't know their arses from their elbows and the whole fucking business is in danger of going down the pan. Ma trouble is I'm too kind-hearted to the fuckers!' He laughed. Thompson didn't recognise the description of his friend, whom he regarded as having as much empathy as Joseph Goebbels.

'We'll wind up Discreet Escorts and replace it with a new business under a new name with someone reliable in charge but unconnected to me. Phone King and get him to sort out the paperwork so we can have a new agency up and running pronto. There's plenty of girls out there looking for work in this city.'

'Yes boss.'

'And get Andy to help you dispose of that useless fuckin' cretin that was just up here. I don't want to see or hear of him again.'

'OK. I've just been speaking to him, boss. It looks like Cammy has a job for the two of us next week. I might have to take some time off.'

'Nae problem, Iain. Just remember. Keep ma name out of it if it goes pear-shaped!'

'Of course, boss.'

24

Shazia was enjoying a long soak in the bath, something she couldn't remember having done for ages. She closed her eyes and felt her muscles relax. From downstairs she could hear Yasmeen singing along with a pop song on the radio, and the noise of pots and pans from the kitchen as her mum cooked lunch. The previous day, after finally getting Robert Jackson into custody, she had managed to come home and have some time to herself. Yasmeen was out with her father so Shazia made the most of the rare opportunity to have the house to herself, as her parents had gone out shopping. She was supposed to see Omar in the evening but by the time it came to go out, she felt too tired and let him know. He didn't disguise his disappointment, but she just wasn't in the mood. Today, she thought, it would be good to do something nice with Yasmeen. Maybe eventually take her to see that film, or just watch a movie together on TV. But the tranquillity of her leisurely bath was suddenly disturbed by her mobile ringing. She picked it up off the bathroom floor but it slid through her soapy fingers and she had to get out of the bath to get it and was standing naked when she managed to answer it. It was a sergeant in Maryhill Police Station. He told her they had recovered a body found in the canal with a gunshot wound to the skull. It was someone he thought she would be interested in.

She drove over to Maryhill and was there within the hour. The location was at the Maryhill Locks, just off Skaethorn Road, only fifty yards from Maryhill Road but ideal for dumping a body in the middle of the night. It was a dismal scene. The sky above was leaden grey with the gasworks towering in the distance like a metal skeleton. You could drive off the road into a space behind a high wall and easily deposit a body into the canal without anyone seeing you from the road; there were no houses or any other buildings overlooking the site never mind any CCTV cameras. The entrance from the road had been cordoned off with police tape, and uniformed officers were dotted around the perimeter of the crime scene.

She walked over to where the body was. It had been taken out of the water and laid on a plastic sheet under a small white tent. A SOCO, watching the pathologist at work, turned to Shazia when she entered the tent. 'He had ID on him, a driving licence, which identified him as David Robertson.'

She nodded. 'Yes, that's him alright,' she said. 'He was out on bail on a case I'm investigating. That's why Maryhill contacted me. They saw that I was listed in the system as the arresting officer.'

The rain pattered off the roof in a constant drum. She could clearly see the exit wound which had smashed open his forehead. His face was covered in bruises. The pathologist, Christine Marshall, turned the body over. The entry wound was smaller at the back of the skull. She said, 'Well, Shazia, it looks like this is going to be another interesting day. No rest for the wicked. Unless you're this poor bastard!'

'Any idea of time of death?' Shazia asked.

'I'd say, sometime last night or in the early hours of the morning. Looks like he has been roughed up a bit too. Cause of death would appear straightforward, though.' She pointed to the bullet hole.

Shazia went over to speak to one of the uniformed officers who had stationed themselves on the towpath. 'Any witnesses?'

The officer shook his head. 'Not so far. Jogger called it in about seven. Spotted the body floating face down.'

The SOCO team were combing the area looking for evidence. 'Found anything?' she asked. The officer in charge shook his head. 'We fished him out of the water over there. No bullet found so far, or much in the way of blood. He's probably been shot somewhere else then brought here and dumped.'

There was no sign of the weapon. It could be lying at the bottom of the canal and divers would have a search, but it could be anywhere. Most likely, kept somewhere to be used again. In any event, even if they found it, linking it to a suspect would be difficult. She could guarantee there would be no prints on it. Illegal firearms were abundant and easy to get hold of in Glasgow's underworld; there were some pubs where you could order one along with your pint, it was said.

No witnesses, no bullet, no weapon. But she had a fair idea who was behind it.

25

The tall figure of Alex Mancini stretched out his long legs on a seat in Melbourne's Tullamarine Airport departure lounge, switched on his phone, and scanned the websites of the Scottish newspapers to find out what awaited him at his final destination. There was some coverage of the death of the Tory MSP and deputy leader, Charles Henderson, in an apparent murder, and there was much salacious speculation about his involvement with prostitutes and even rumours of connections to organised crime, mirroring the case of Colin Chisholm a year earlier.

In other news, there had been a rally organised by a far-right group, Britain United, in Glasgow's George Square. The rally had been organised to protest against immigration and the numbers of refugees and asylum seekers taking refuge in Scotland. There had been only a few hundred right-wingers who had turned out to support it but they had provoked plenty of anger, with chants and slogans intended to cause outrage, and a counter demonstration by the Scottish Anti-Fascist League had drawn thousands more supporters. The left-wing counter-demonstrators had succeeded in drowning out a speech by one of the rally organisers and confrontation had mostly been avoided as police had managed to keep the groups apart until near the end of the rally, when a far-right demonstrator broke through the police ranks and attacked the counter-demonstrators, slashing at them with a knife. Several people were seriously injured, one seriously; the casualties had been taken to hospital but, fortunately, there were no fatalities. The unknown assailant, who had been wearing a mask, had escaped; police had launched a manhunt across the city for him.

Alex had tried to keep up with the Scottish news all the time he had been in Australia. It was simple these days as even local news was so accessible instantly from anywhere in the world. That was one good thing about the internet, he thought, though he knew, equally there were plenty of bad things too: the ability of those with malice in mind to exploit the vulnerable or to spread lies and abuse others. The technology, itself, of course was not to blame; it was the dark side of human beings that was responsible. It would have been the same at the time of the invention of the printing press, he mused.

He had been especially keeping an eye on the political situation. Things looked precarious for the SNP government as they were increasingly unpopular and fragile: a budget had been produced which people were labelling as the start of further austerity. The government in Edinburgh suddenly faced some stark choices and had chosen to implement cuts to public services which, for many of their own supporters, were tantamount to the kinds of austerity policies that former UK Tory administration had inflicted and which had contributed to the Scottish electorate's decision to finally back independence.

Support for the SNP was receding as badly as the Prime Minister's hair, he thought; their partners in the coalition, the Scottish Greens, had abandoned them and the resurgent Scottish Labour Party had meanwhile been transformed into a left-wing alternative with policies advocating re-nationalisation of public services. Under the leadership of their dynamic new leader, Kelly McFarlane, they were being tipped to replace the SNP in the next government if a snap election was called. McFarlane was in her early thirties and been an SNP member until the independence referendum, though she was always on the left wing of the party. After the referendum she had switched to the Scottish Labour Party and had quickly established herself as a rising star, so much so that two years later, after what some in the Scottish Labour Party thought a disappointing result in the election, she stood in the leadership contest and, to the amazement of most commentators, ran a blistering radical campaign and won. She had called for nothing less than a programme of renationalisation, investment in public services and the transformation of Scotland into a democratic socialist state. As the government tightened the belt on public spending, McFarlane's vision was becoming increasingly popular to the electorate, according to the latest opinion polls.

Scotland was going through the painful process of establishing itself as an independent nation and he had felt increasingly excluded from it, being thousands of miles away. That was another reason to return, he thought, though he felt torn. Life in Australia had worked out well. Why throw that away just to go back? But there was one strong reason.

The turning point had come on a Sunday morning several weeks before, when he had observed a scene that made up his mind to go back to Scotland. He was going to have to leave Australia anyway as his visa was about to run out after being in the country for twelve months, and he had considered where he might go next. Maybe South America, he thought. Then, early that morning, he had watched a female wallaby munching the kangaroo grass just about twenty metres from his bedroom window when a young joey appeared from inside its pouch. It gave a little hop and moved to a juicy patch and munched, emulating its mother. He stared out of his bedroom window at the scene and snapped a few shots on his camera, thinking it was a lovely way to start the day. The father wallaby then made an appearance and he loved seeing the three of them enjoying the fruits of the garden in their domestic bliss. Then they seemed to sense something which made them nervous and suddenly they were gone.

His thoughts turned to his daughter, Emily: she would now be nearly ten, getting bigger, growing up and forgetting who her dad was. He had kept an eye on his ex-partner's Facebook page, where she occasionally posted photos, and he found himself unexpectedly wiping away tears, noticing how she was growing up. He phoned occasionally and managed to speak to Emily but the longer he was away the stranger it became. He could feel the distance between them growing. Something inside him exerted a force that he couldn't control. The decision was made there and then. He couldn't believe how he would fall for such a sentimental scene. It was like something out of fucking Bambi but it hit him where it hurt, like a punch to the guts.

He decided he could hand in his notice at the pub where he worked, as he only needed to give a week's notice and he had enough in his savings account to buy a plane ticket with a good bit left over. He wasn't sure if he would stay in Scotland, though. He'd got used to the weather and the lifestyle all felt very laid-back and comfortable. In the mornings, when the sun rose, it cast plenty of shade amongst the trees and dappled light over the small copse of trees surrounding the bungalow. He still felt amazed by the beauty of the landscape and its flora and fauna. It was isolation that he had craved and he had certainly discovered it here. The little settlement in Victoria was pretty remote, in the Outback. The house itself had three acres of land surrounding it. He felt lucky, very lucky, all the more so when he turned away from gazing at the wallabies and got back into bed and cuddled into Suzanne's soft warm body. She groaned, turned round, and opened her eyes.

'Good morning,' he said.

'G'day,' she said. She had come to the district from Melbourne twelve years before, following a bloke who had long disappeared back to the city.

He kissed her on the forehead, then on the neck, moving down her body. She gave a moan and reached out and put her arms around his neck and soon they were making love in long languorous motions. Afterwards, he brought her orange juice and coffee and they lay in bed. 'I love weekends,' he said. 'Wouldn't it be nice not to have to work? Every day would be like a weekend.'

She twisted his nose. 'Then it wouldn't be lovely,' she said. 'But, unless I win the lotto, it's not going to happen, lover boy.'

She taught maths at the local secondary school and as soon as he had started working in the pub, he had noticed her coming in and got chatting to her. They became friendly. Then, somehow, after she had had a few drinks one Friday evening she invited him to come back for a night cap when he finished his shift. He didn't say no and it became more than a nightcap and they became more than friends. He had been living in a grotty room in a shared house in the town, with two other blokes who never did any cleaning or washing up, and Suzanne had refused to darken its door so he had ended up moving in with her in April. She had a house, rented from a farmer, which she had shared with her previous partner until they split up and he moved back to Melbourne. The rent was cheap and she could easily have afforded the rent herself but his moving in made financial and practical sense. He didn't earn a lot from the bar job, but it was cash in hand.

Suzanne was older than he was by more than ten years; she would be forty-five in a couple of months, but he found her body still youthful and sexy: she was small and slim with blonde shoulder-length hair, a turned-up nose and freckles. The two of them contrasted strongly: he was tall, six foot two with light brown hair and a thick brown beard which he had grown since he had left Scotland. He hesitated before telling her his decision. 'I need to go back to Scotland and see my daughter before she forgets who I am. I'm sorry.' He felt shit telling her that. But he knew he had to go home.

'No you aren't, you Pommy bastard.'

He heard his name being called over the loudspeakers. 'Would passenger Mancini travelling to

Dubai on Emirates flight 1789 proceed to Gate 21.' He must have missed the call that the gate was open, he had been so absorbed in reading the news and thinking about going home. He got up and headed for the gate. This was it. He was about to get on the flight to Glasgow, and find himself somewhere he hadn't been for more than a year. Part of him wanted to turn round and head back to the farm cottage, back to Suzanne; the other part told him he had to see his daughter, and that was the part that won.

By the end of Sunday afternoon, Shona had completed her research and drafted her article. She revealed Forsyth as one of the partners behind Mercat Partners and his funding of International Data Research. She disclosed details of his offshore company based in the Caribbean and raised the issue of tax avoidance. She asked where Forsyth's money was really coming from at a time when there was speculation in the financial press about how his companies were struggling. Finally, she drew links to Scottish Action and referred to the attack on the Farah family in Springburn and the Scottish Action graffiti outside their burned-out flat. Then she emailed a copy to her editor after giving him the heads-up over the phone.

He rang back a while later, after clearly seeking some legal advice, and told her they could not publish any possibility of a link between Forsyth and Scottish Action. She reluctantly accepted the legal position. She had no choice. Nevertheless, the article would make it clear that there was a financial trail from Forsyth to Campbell, an individual associated with Britain United, an organisation which, at the very least, had voiced its support for Scottish Action. All that she needed to do was to contact Forsyth and tell him what she had and that it was going into the newspaper, anyway, and ask him if he wished to make a comment.

She couldn't get through to Forsyth so she left a voicemail for him, telling him that there was going to be a newspaper article about his business published on Monday and she wanted to speak to him. Forsyth's lawyer phoned back later and she told him about the story. He said he would speak to Forsyth. When he called back again, he said that Mr Forsyth rejected all suggestions that he condoned or supported extremism, violence or racism, and refuted the suggestion that there was any financial connection between Mr Forsyth's companies and any right-wing groups. 'Mr Forsyth's investments are dealt with by an independent team of financial advisers and Mr Forsyth does not interfere in their decisions,' he said. 'All financial transactions are, as far as Mr Forsyth believes, fully compliant with local tax regulations and the law.' No one from Atlantic Legal or Paradise Investments was available for comment. Andrew Campbell, likewise, did not reply to her request for him to get in touch with her. Finally, just before nine o' clock, she sent the final copy to the editor for publication and poured herself a large glass of wine and awaited the shitstorm she knew the story would produce.

26

Yasmeen had been in quite a state on Sunday night and it had been very difficult to know what the cause was. She was shouting and hysterical for several hours, repeatedly hitting herself with her fists on the face, and had to be restrained by Shazia and her mother, pinning her arms to her sides and holding her tightly until she calmed down. Every now and again she would have episodes like that and it was difficult to know what triggered it. Sometimes they had to give her some medication to sedate her. Eventually she fell asleep having exhausted herself.

As Shazia left for work, she decided to phone the school later anyway and speak to her Guidance teacher to find out how Yasmeen was and whether there could have been anything happening at school recently which could have been a source of distress to her. It may well have had nothing to do with school, though, it could just be a sign of Yasmeen's overall frustration. It was likely that as she got older she was growing more aware of how different she was from her peers, who were now becoming young women and interested in all the things adolescent girls were interested in, such as boys. It was difficult to know what went on inside Yasmeen's head or know what her understanding of the world was like, but in many ways she appeared much younger than her biological age. She had always loved drawing pictures of unicorns and mythical creatures, for which she had an amazing aptitude, and was obsessed with Harry Potter. But she had, oddly, also recently become fixated on the characters in the world of WWE, the superstars of professional wrestling. She spent her pocket money on WWE magazines and had discovered videos of wrestling matches on YouTube. In a notepad she drew pictures of her wrestling heroes. Shazia wondered if the hormones surging through Yasmeen's body somehow accounted for her sudden interest in the muscular forms of the male and female WWE wrestlers with their exaggerated physiques.

Shazia tried to focus on work, on the two investigations, as she drove to the station. It wasn't uncommon to have several investigations on the go at one time, in fact it was the norm as cuts to the police budget meant that there were fewer detectives. Could Christie really have murdered his biological father? Who broke into the hotel? What about the boyfriend of the parliamentary assistant, the chef, Boyle? Could the pair of them have acted together? No, that was ridiculous, they didn't even know each other. Then there was the prostitute, Katarina Marková. Surely it was too much of a coincidence that she had slept with Henderson the night he died. Could Christie or Boyle have a connection with her? Then there was Robert Jackson, definitely an underworld character if ever there was one. Shazia had found out that he had a criminal record, including convictions for assault and for possession of Class A drugs with intent to supply. He drove a taxi for one of Murray's companies. It was like a ball of wool which had become tangled and she couldn't untangle it to make it make sense. There was something missing.

There was also the Scobie murder. He belonged to the opposite end of the social spectrum from Henderson, with his country estate and flashy cars. Scobie was one of life's unfortunates; he probably never had much of a chance whereas Henderson had been gifted everything that money and class could bestow in terms of education and upbringing. Scobie had been killed most likely because he owed money. Probably to someone like Murray, whose phone number he kept in a drawer – he must have been given it at some point as someone who could give him work to do. Now David Robertson was dead and she suspected Murray was also somehow involved there too.

The station was like a nest of busy insects with a constant drone of activity. Officers scuttled back and forth and there was an incessant noise as phones rang, voices were raised and doors opened and closed. When Shazia arrived in the office, Joseph was already at his desk. He looked up from his computer when she came in. 'Good morning,' he said. 'Did you manage to unwind after all the excitement yesterday? I couldn't believe it when you phoned to tell me about Robertson.'

'I was supposed to see Omar last night but I cancelled. Don't think he was too pleased. He'll probably chuck me soon. How about you?'

'We discovered a new place in Strathbungo last night. Apparently, according to the owner, Strathbungo is now the latest hot-spot in Glasgow! Who knew, eh? Anyway, delicious food. You should try it. I'll text you the details.'

'Thanks. First off, for your information, I grew up near there, in Pollokshields. I've always known it's a great area. Don't believe all this hot-spot mullarkey. Last year it was supposed to be Finnieston. Hipster capital of Glasgow they are calling it. I know Strathbungo. I haven't always lived in boring old Lenzie, you know. Anyway, yes, thanks for the tip. If Omar ever speaks to me again, I'll suggest we go there.'

'Hey, turns out Angie knows Omar. Guess they both work in the same hospital, but that place is enormous, I didn't think their paths would cross.'

'Is that right? Small world, isn't it? Just as well I'm not protective of my own privacy. Glasgow is like a bloody village.'

'What do you mean? You don't even have a Facebook account, of course you are protective of your privacy! Unlike the rest of us, who open ourselves up to the world.'

'When would I find the time to put anything on it? And what would I say? Oh yes, had a great curry at Mother India. Again. Who wants to read that?'

'You'd be surprised. I love posting stuff on Instagram. I snapped a pic of my dessert in the restaurant and had it posted before I had taken a bite of it! I had ten *likes* before we even had coffee. I've got a couple of hundred followers, you know. I could even quit policing and become an internet foodie influencer!'

Shazia laughed. 'That is just mad! I don't even know what that means, I must be getting old.'

'No, it's what everyone does these days. Just not you! Fancy a coffee? I promise I won't photograph you drinking it.'

'Yes, please. Make it a strong one.'

She started up her computer. When Joseph returned with two mugs of coffee, he told her about meeting the mysterious figure on Glasgow Green on Saturday night. 'I've been searching through the records for someone called Jack who might have a connection to Scobie,' he said. 'By the way, have you seen the news, about our friend Forsyth?'

'No, why?'

'Check out the Gazette website.'

She looked it up on the internet and saw that Cameron Forsyth was alleged to be involved in some sort of money laundering operation with links to extreme right-wing politics. Her immediate thought was: did this have anything to do with the Henderson murder? After she read the article, she realised that she had better go and see DCI Cooper and update him on developments. As soon as she got to his office, she explained about the arrest of Robert Jackson on Saturday and the discovery of Robertson's body yesterday. 'It was definitely a professional hit.'

'Who do you think is responsible?' he asked.

'I don't know. But I think it's got to be linked to the case. Robertson knew Katarina had been booked by Henderson and he could have been a link to the killer. Whoever is behind this may have thought he was a weak link, didn't want to take any chances, in case he tried to plea bargain his way out of it.'

'He was charged with human trafficking, though. He could have just been killed to prevent him talking about that. He might not know anything about the murder.'

Shazia nodded. 'I wouldn't be surprised if our friend Greg Murray is really behind the escort agency.'

'Find me some evidence. Otherwise, we'd be wasting our time bringing him and his damned lawyer in.' He peppered her with questions about the case, to which she batted back responses like a tennis player being hit with a series of fierce shots. *Who are the chief suspects? What evidence is there to link any of the possible suspects to the killing? Who have you spoken to? What have Forensics come up with? What about this Islamist who sent the death threat? Who is he?* He seemed agitated and slightly anxious. Probably he was getting more pressure from above about the case, she thought.

'Jackson has to be a suspect,' said Cooper.

Shazia nodded. 'His girlfriend is his alibi for the night of the murder but he definitely knew Katarina. One of the keys found on him fits the door of her flat. We'll get uniforms to search his place today.'

'OK, good, but this guy Christie also interests me,' said Cooper. 'He was in Henderson's room that night and has a clear motive for killing him. He is one of the last people we think was with the victim. The break-in could be a distraction of his to send us in another direction, away from him. Have you done a thorough search of his home, his office in the university, to see if there is anything linking him to the supposed break-in, like shards of glass on his clothing?'

'We've done all that, sir. We didn't have enough to hold him. There has been an exhaustive search of his home and his office in the university. There was nothing. So far, it's all really circumstantial.'

'What about this girlfriend of his, the student he was with that night? What does she say happened?'

'I spoke to her on Saturday, sir. She seems to have had a lot to drink that night and says she blacked out in the hotel room. She doesn't remember him leaving the room or coming back again. Of course, she could be lying. She says she remembers him speaking to someone in the bar the night before, whom she now realises was Henderson, but that's all. She says that Christie appeared normal the next morning. Hungover, that's all. As she was.'

Cooper was chewing the end of a ballpoint pen while she spoke. He put it down on his desk. 'Do you want me to put some pressure on him? See if I can break him down?'

'I am perfectly capable of putting on pressure myself, sir.'

'I didn't mean to offend you, Inspector.'

'No offence taken, sir. But I don't think we can charge Christie. Not at this stage. I haven't eliminated him from the investigation, though. He is still a suspect.'

'I don't want this investigation dragging on, Inspector. We need to make more progress. I've just had the Assistant Chief Constable on the phone asking what's happening. We are under real pressure to get a result quickly. I've got a lot on my plate, but as I told you before, I'll happily take over the investigation.'

'That won't be necessary, sir.'

''Well, we'll see what you can turn up in the next few days, eh?'

Shazia returned to her desk. She didn't know much about Cooper's personal life other than there was a Mrs Cooper and a grown-up son. He never spoke about them and today was no exception. There was something about the

195

man that repelled her, though. She remembered an incident a couple of years ago. She had been alone with him in the lift when he had pressed himself up against her and she had felt his elbow touch her breasts. She hadn't said anything to anyone about it. Cooper would have said that any contact had been accidental. But now, thinking about Henderson's assistant and thinking about all the other women who had been sexually harassed at their work, she knew that she should have said something. However, it would have been career suicide.

She opened her emails. Someone she had worked with was looking for a reference for a post. A thirty-one-year-old male had been stabbed outside a pub in Easterhouse and she was asked to look into it. There never seemed enough time to get on top of the work. Shazia sighed. Some days she loved her job; other days it depressed her. Even if they managed to clear up these two murder cases, the flow of crime kept on coming. All they did was slow down the flow for a bit until it rose up again, destroying everything in its path, like lava from an erupting volcano.

27

Shona walked into the morning editorial meeting to be met with a round of applause from the rest of the news team, causing her to blush furiously. Her editor, Robin Smith, a hardened veteran of the Glasgow newspaper scene with a face that rarely smiled, even broke into an unheard-of grin and nodded his head, his long grey locks falling over his similarly grey bearded face. She had never seen him so animated.

'Well, I think we can truly say that piece of yours, Shona, has shaken up the political establishment more than anything I have seen since you exposed the secret life of Colin Chisholm,' said Smith. 'Did you hear the Tory MSPs on Good Morning Scotland this morning trying to distance themselves from Forsyth?'

'Thanks,' said Shona, feeling slightly overwhelmed by the adulation.

'I don't want you to stop. See what else you can dig up on him and these groups he's linked to. I know you won't disclose your source but whoever you got that data from must surely be able to come up with some more dirt on him.'

'I'll see what I can do,' she said.

'Good stuff,' said Smith. 'OK, everyone, lots of stories to cover today. There is a rumour flying around about a young assistant who worked for Henderson. Apparently, she alleged that he sexually harassed her. Fiona, can you track her down and get a comment from her? With photographs. Simon, see if there is any other sleaze below the surface in Holyrood. Fire in an FOI asking for the number of sexual harassment allegations over the past five years and see if you can get any staff to speak about it. This is a scandal just waiting to be exposed. Tip of the iceberg stuff. Liz, get in touch with the researcher for the government minister, Craig Maxwell. There are rumours flying about that he was seen trying to feel her up at the party conference in Perth. Try to get some photographs of this sleazeball, check out his social media, and see if you can track down some of his exes to get a kiss n' tell.'

Liz nodded. 'I know the type. Probably a serial offender. The kind who likes to use the political equivalent of the casting couch.'

'And oh yes, here's another thing,' added Smith. 'Andrew, there's a school janitor who was caught in the shower with a sixteen-year-old pupil – and he wasn't auditioning her as a cleaner! Doorstep him and get a quote. OK, guys, keep up the good work!'

Alex got off the airport bus at Buchanan Bus Station. He felt stiff from the long flight from Melbourne, even if he had been able to stretch his long legs in Dubai when he had to change flights. He wished he had been able to afford to fly business class, but had had to contend with economy and its lack of legroom. At least the entertainment on the flight had been OK and he'd watched The Big Lebowski for the umpteenth time, then, unable to sleep, turned to reading the latest Jo Nesbo thriller. Good old Harry Hole, he thought, grumpy but funny at the same time. He phoned his parents to tell them he was back in Scotland and would see them soon. As if to welcome him back to Glasgow, it had started raining, which made him laugh. He bought a copy of the Gazette, zipped up his jacket and sat down under cover on a bench in the bus station to wait for the rain to stop. The lead story had caught his eye. It was an exclusive revealing how the far-right organisation, Britain United, was being funded. He noted with interest the name of the reporter and smiled. She's done well, he thought. The headline read:

EXCLUSIVE: FORSYTH TAX HAVEN MONEY LINKED TO FAR-RIGHT GROUP
Report by Shona Williamson

Links between a top Scottish businessman and the extreme right in Scotland can today be revealed by the Glasgow Gazette with the release of documents which show that a top Scottish businessman has been using an overseas tax haven to avoid tax and to secretly finance a company with links to a controversial right-wing group. The funding sources are revealed in a confidential document obtained from law firm Atlantic Legal, based in the British Virgin Islands, which has been leaked to the Glasgow Gazette.

The papers reveal that the owner of the Forsyth Apparel clothing chain, Cameron Forsyth, has been funding a shell company, Mercat Partners, a Scottish Limited Partnership registered in Glasgow. The company's purpose is obscure and it is not known what its income is used for, but the documents show that the person named as being responsible for managing the company is Andrew Campbell, with Forsyth acting as a limited partner. Campbell is the leader of the far-right political group Britain United, who have voiced support for the outlawed terrorist organisation Scottish Action. He was convicted of an attempted arson attack on a mosque five years ago, for which the terrorist group claimed responsibility.

The papers show that Paradise Investments, a secretive company based in the British Virgin Islands in the Caribbean, an overseas tax haven, is owned by Cameron Forsyth. In the last year £500,000 was transferred from Paradise Investments into Mercat Partners. Well-known Scottish business leader Cameron Forsyth, owner and chairman of the Forsyth Apparel chain of clothing stores, is also a prominent supporter and funder of the Scottish Conservatives. The documents also show that over the past few years, Paradise Investments have received several large payments amounting to millions of pounds from banks around the world, including one in in Cyprus and another in the Cayman Islands, both suspected as being centres for money laundering. Paradise Investments also transferred £4

199

million to Capital PLC, Cameron Forsyth's English company which runs a chain of department stores, Forsyth's. Capital PLC made a donation of the same sum to the Leave campaign during the EU referendum. This raises the question of what was the true source for Mr Forsyth's donations. In addition, the complex financial arrangements involving offshore companies mean that there is now a question mark over whether Forsyth has been involved in tax evasion.

There is no suggestion that Mr Forsyth knowingly has been funding Scottish Action but the revelation that he is connected to someone involved with the far-right group, Britain United, will come as a major embarrassment to the businessman. Scottish Action have claimed responsibility in the past for attacks on mosques, immigrants and asylum seekers, which have increased since the bombing of the Buchanan Street underground station in Glasgow last year. Britain United have praised attacks on immigrants and asylum seekers and its members have been jailed for hate crimes. In addition, last year an individual claiming to be a member of the Scottish Action was convicted for an attempted assassination of Scottish Green party MSP Aileen Buchan. The papers also show that a million Canadian dollars went from Paradise Investments to International Data Research, a Canadian company which helps organisations to target internet users with advertising, often for political purposes.

A spokesman for Mr Forsyth denied any financial connections between Mr Forsyth and extremists, saying 'Mr Forsyth's investments and financial transactions are, as far as Mr Forsyth believes, fully compliant with tax regulations and the law. Mr Forsyth believes that these scurrilous lies have been concocted by his political opponents in order to smear him. He is considering legal action.' Neither Andrew Campbell nor anyone from Atlantic Legal or Paradise Investments responded to requests for comment.

Full article on pages 2 and 3.

It was all too familiar. Alex had come close to finding out about Scottish Action's leadership when he had been a tabloid reporter investigating them undercover, frequenting some of the more fervently loyalist pubs. He claimed that he had grown up in Dundee and was now looking for work here as a security guard, that he had been working in Iraq as a security guard for a few years, and said he was sickened by all the privileges these refugees were getting when there were Scots who needed help, finding a receptive audience for what he had to say. He was helped by him having inherited his mother's Scottish features, being pale-skinned. If he had resembled his father with his olive skin and his curly black hair, he might have raised more suspicions. As it was, if they had found out that he came from a family of fish and chip shop-owning Scots-Italians in Dumfries, he knew he would have ended up at the bottom of the Clyde wearing concrete wellies. His father had met his mother when they were at school, fallen in love and married, and still ran the chip shop.

Alex been had been gathering some interesting leads on Scottish Action when one night he was bluntly made aware that there were suspicions about him. In a pub car park, at the end of a baseball bat wielded by a gang of loyalists demanding answers. 'Your name isn't Ross Young, is it? Who the fuck are you?' they demanded, punctuating each word with a punch to his kidneys. His fake ID in that name didn't appear to satisfy them. 'You're always asking too many fucking questions,' one of them said. He had told them nothing despite getting severely beaten up and having two broken ribs that night. But the writing was on the wall. They were onto him and it was only a matter of time before he was exposed as being Alex Mancini, reporter for the Scottish Courier, instead of Ross Young from Dundee. He printed the story but even he knew it was insubstantial, anecdotal. He hadn't been able to name any of the leadership, but he had managed to secretly film a meeting in a loyalist social club where there was fund-raising for Scottish Action and anti-Islamic speeches, naming several figures in the organisation who had claimed they were members of Scottish Action.

Then the death threats started. Messages on social media, graffiti on his front door and his car fire-bombed. He knew the next thing would be a gunshot in the back of the head on his way home one night. He just couldn't stand the pressure of it all. He couldn't sleep and he started suffering from the constant sense of being followed. Everywhere he went he was looking over his shoulder. He and Paula had parted company years ago and he had never managed to sustain any other long-term relationship with anyone since. The only thing stopping him was his daughter, Emily. She was seven. He knew he would miss her terribly but surely he could keep in touch with her. He just had to get away. His flat was rented and he didn't have much in the way of possessions anyway.

One night he phoned Paula, Emily and his parents and sent his editor an email and jumped on a London train heading south, away from Glasgow, away from Scotland, to start a new life. He ended up in Melbourne, a beautiful city where he spent a few weeks and would have loved to have stayed longer. But it was too busy. He lived in perpetual fear of being recognised and attacked. He might end up at the bottom of the Yarra River instead of the Clyde. Australia also had its issues, of course. Plenty of racism, too, that was for sure and the Melbourne gangsters had a reputation for violence second to none anywhere else. So, he got on a bus and headed out north by northwest to the interior, feeling like Cary Grant, far enough from the madding crowd, where he could feel safer. And he had been.

The fact, though, was that now he was back in Scotland and he suddenly realised, reading the article, how unsafe he was, and wondered if he had made a mistake. Had he really naively thought that when the country had voted for independence it would transform the country into a brave new world in which there would be happiness and prosperity for all, that sectarianism and violence would cease? It had been such an exciting moment at the time. Once the result was declared that September night, thousands had poured into George Square and the city became a sea of revelling independence supporters. Saltires were waved, there was hugging and kissing and, of course, something which Glasgow had always excelled at and had world status in, excessive drinking. It had been one wild party which went on all through the night. The police had even turned a blind eye to the open-air drinking in breach of the Glasgow bye-laws prohibiting the consumption of alcohol on the streets. There had been a few minor incidents that night when some unionists waving their Union Jack flags, frustrated and disappointed by the result, had attacked some of the independence supporters, but they were so heavily outnumbered that they quickly retreated and evaporated into the darkness. The night had belonged to independence and the hopes and dreams and aspirations of its supporters.

Scotland woke up to one hell of a hangover, as if it was all the previous New Year's Days rolled into one. Except people had to go to work the next day. Not that anyone did much work. TVs and computers in every office were tuned to the rolling news. What would happen now, everyone wanted to know? There was a sudden dawning realisation of what had occurred. What they had done? *"Fuck, did that really happen?"* was the collective response followed by: *"Shit, ma heed hurts!"* Then began the long period of intensive negotiation between the politicians of Holyrood and Westminster, which eventually resulted in agreements and the formal declaration of independence. More wild celebrations and parties followed that day and through the night. He knew that to transform a country

203

would be a long and a frustrating and, at times, painful process. There was still poverty and division. There were still the same inequalities in society. But he had had some faint hopes that the new minority SNP government, in coalition with the Scottish Greens, might bring about a fairer society, but his hopes, like those of so many of his compatriots had quickly crumbled.

After he had read the full article, he felt several conflicting emotions: excitement and pride in what Shona had managed to uncover, along with a certain worry and concern for her safety. He knew that these people were dangerous foes and by exposing them she could be putting herself at risk. Alongside those feelings he felt guilt: Shona was a friend, a fellow journalist he'd worked with at the Gazette years before, whom he trusted. She had thought at the time that he had wanted to take their relationship further, but she had been going out with someone at the time and didn't want to complicate things. Even after he moved to the Courier they had kept in touch. But he hadn't kept in touch with her after he'd moved away. He had wanted to start a new life. The reason was fear: he had felt seriously in danger. Yes, he trusted Shona but he didn't trust everyone on the newspapers, he wasn't naive enough to think that. The right-wing zealots and the gangsters had their sources inside newspapers as they had everywhere else, including the council, the police, and probably even the government.

His life had clearly been in danger so he had escaped to a remote part of the world and lain low,but events had moved on in the last year and he was glad to be back in Scotland and especially looking forward to seeing Emily. He had effectively disappeared and no doubt some people maybe even thought he was dead. He wandered through the city centre feeling like a ghost that had come back to haunt its previous life and checked into a budget hotel and lay down on the bed. He should really try to get some shut-eye, he thought, but his mind was racing like an express train and he knew that sleep was as likely as Scotland winning the next World Cup.

Shona couldn't believe it when she answered her phone and the speaker said he was Alex Mancini. 'Listen Alex, I'm busy right now but come round to the flat tonight. I'll introduce you to Jamie. You'll like him. You can have something to eat and tell me what you've been up to. I can't wait to hear it.' After she gave him her address and told him she'd see him later he lay back and stared at the ceiling. Those far-right bastards made me leave here once, he thought. I'm not going to let them do it twice.

28

'I've been looking into Jackson and there's a link to Sammy Scobie,' said Joseph.

'Scobie?' said Shazia.

'Yes. That's the good news. Turns out that the two of them were in Barlinnie at the same time. Staff there remember the two of them actually shared a cell. And Jackson's nickname is Jack. That's who that guy I met on the Green was on about. Jack. Short for Jackson. Of course! But those unidentified prints found in the flat don't match Jackson's, otherwise we would have been onto him before now.'

'Most likely he was gloved up.'

'Jackson must have been supplying Scobie's drugs and they had some sort of falling out.'

Shazia nodded. 'Scobie gets killed. Then Henderson. Jackson has a link to both. Coincidence? Hardly likely, but what's the connection? Jackson could have given Scobie Murray's number when he got out of prison. It's too much of a coincidence that Henderson dies after sleeping with a prostitute driven there by a convicted hard man and drug dealer. Let's have another word with Katarina. We need her to positively ID Jackson as her pimp anyway.'

Katarina was sitting in an interview room with her lawyer present when Shazia and Joseph entered the room. Shazia thought Katarina looked much worse than she had the last time she had seen her. She hardly resembled the glamorous photo of her which had been in the escort agency's files and now just looked sick, lost and confused. Her eyes were sunken, she appeared to have lost weight, and she was shaking constantly. She was clearly suffering: sweaty, trembling, constantly fidgeting, scratching herself and tugging at her hair. She had been living under supervision in a location which the Protected Persons Unit considered a safe environment for her but Shazia wondered if she was living in fear of being attacked or worse, permanently silenced for anything she knew and could present in court about those involved in trafficking, Jackson included. Although Jackson was being detained, she would know that he had powerful friends who would be prepared to do anything to keep her quiet, maybe even threaten her family back in Slovakia. She had, after all, been entrapped and subjected to horrific acts, forced into sexual slavery after innocently believing that she was furthering her future prospects. Now she was psychologically damaged, she would never be the same again.

Shazia enquired how she was and offered her a drink. She asked for a Coke. She sipped it from the can as Shazia showed her a mugshot of Jackson. 'Is this the man who took you to the hotel?'

Katarina looked blankly at the photograph then stared into space, saying nothing.

'We know this is the driver of the car the night you met Henderson. What can you tell us about him?'

Again, she just stared into space.

Shazia said, 'Katarina, we know that it was Robert Jackson who was your pimp and brought you to the hotel.'

Her lawyer, Anne Wright, a middle-aged woman with dyed blonde hair and glasses said, 'Inspector, my client is the victim of trafficking and abuse. She is frightened.'

'I understand what you are saying, Ms Wright. She may have been threatened or forced to do something against her will, but I am trying to establish what she knows about a murder.'

Katarina suddenly spoke. 'I just want to go home. I don't know anything about man's death. Believe me.' She then muttered something in Slovakian to herself and burst into tears.

'Just take your time,' said Shazia. 'We can help you. You can trust us. But we need you to tell us the truth of what happened that night.'

There was a lengthy pause then Katarina began to talk. 'I am told that if I help police then my family will suffer. Man say they have contacts in Slovakia. They say they will kill them. All I want is to go back home to Slovakia.'

Shazia nodded. It was what she expected to hear. It wasn't good to hear, but at least Katarina was now talking. 'I understand your fears. But you may have been a willing accessory to a homicide and if we find that out then you will be charged with murder.' Shazia went on to explain that at some stage in the future she would also be asked to act as a witness in a prosecution of those accused of trafficking. Katarina seemed to have retreated into herself and was looking anxious and withdrawn. To Ms Wright, Shazia said, 'I have reason to believe that Katarina is, at the very least, an important witness to the events of that night. I understand her concerns for her family, though. If she is willing to cooperate with us, we can contact the authorities in Slovakia and ask for protection for them. If she has been forced to do something against her will, and she is willing to fully cooperate, there is a chance that any charges against her could be dropped, as her circumstances as a victim will be taken into account. But, if not, then she may be seen as an accomplice in murder. We will leave you for a while to discuss this.' She turned to Katarina. 'Katarina, when the truth comes out and it's found that you have lied to us, it will be much worse for you.' Shazia and Joseph left the room.

Once outside, Joseph said, 'I don't think we'll get anything out of her. She's too scared of what will happen to her family. I don't think she thinks much of any protection they might get from the Slovak police.'

'Let's see,' said Shazia. 'I don't think she wants to face a lengthy prison sentence.'

Half an hour later, Wright signalled that the detectives should return to the room. Either the fight had gone out of her or she had been persuaded to cooperate by her solicitor. In any case, she was ready to make a confession. She explained that she had been told by Jackson that he needed her to do something for him that night. She was warned that if she didn't, one of her family in Slovakia would be killed. He told her to avoid the camera on going into and leaving the hotel lobby. She was to find Henderson's keycard when she was in his room and, when she was about to leave, to put her gloves on, then pick it up. When she got back out to the car, she was to give it to him. She said she had no idea why he had wanted the key. She didn't know anything about a plan to murder someone.

Shazia held out a photo of Jackson. 'Is this the man you gave the key to, the man who drove you there?'

She nodded. Shazia then asked her to answer aloud. 'Yes,' she said, again breaking down into tears which came flooding out of her as if a dam had burst. She was shaking uncontrollably. When she calmed down, Katarina started to talk about what she had been through. 'He make me take drug. Then he have sex with me. Soon men come to the flat to have sex. Some days twenty men come. Some nights I am taken to hotels. I am given pills. They make me sleepy.'

'What about the ketamine? Did you spike his drink?'

'Yes. I am told to mix powder in his drink when he not looking and make sure he drink it. I put it in his wine when he in bathroom.' She started to cry. 'I am sorry. I not know people want to kill him. I was afraid.'

As Katarina was led out of the room, weeping, by a female uniformed officer, she looked as if at any moment she might collapse. After they had left the interview room, Shazia looked at Joseph. 'Poor girl. I can't imagine what horrors she has been through. Her young life ruined by men. It makes me sick. She would have had no idea what she was getting involved in.'

Joseph nodded. 'Here's how I picture it. After Jackson had been given the keycard for Henderson's room by Katarina, he took her back to her flat and then drove to his girlfriend's in Knightswood. Later, he went back into the city centre, maybe not using his own car, either by taxi or someone gave him a lift, and headed for the hotel. We should check the taxis for that night, though I don't think he would be stupid enough to use one we could find out about. He broke in through the unalarmed window, making sure to leave no finger or footprints, then made his way up to the top floor, slipped into Henderson's room using the keycard, and killed him while he was sleeping, knowing that the ketamine would have made him drowsy. Then made his escape.'

It would be difficult to prove that Jackson actually had carried out the killing, though, thought Shazia. 'But there's no forensic evidence linking him to being inside the hotel,' she said. 'We need something else, even though his girlfriend as his alibi is flimsy.' Katarina's confession of drugging him, stealing the keycard and giving it to Jackson was a big step forward, but the motive was still unclear. There was also the connection to Scobie. Had Jackson murdered both? 'Let's head back out to the Parkhill estate and flash the mugshot of Jackson around. Get hold of Joan and Michael and ask them to meet us there.'

The four detectives spent hours along with a team of uniformed officers going door-to-door with Jackson's photograph. She was ready to accept that it was going to be a waste of time when she thought they were onto something. On the sixth floor of the tower block next to Scobie's, an elderly man, Hugh McPherson, had stared at the photograph for several seconds, then looked Shazia in the eye. 'Never seen him before.'

'Are you sure?'

'Sorry, I can't help you,' he said, closing the door.

Shazia could tell he was lying.

She and Joseph then made their way over to Barlinnie where Jackson was being held on remand. Every time she visited the place, Shazia was overwhelmed by its bleakness. Some of it had been modernised but the building still exuded all the charm of a Victorian penal institution. The grey towering stone exterior gave it the look of a castle, a medieval fortress. Entering it, Shazia felt as if time slipped away and she felt unsure even what day, month or year it was. God knows what it was like for its inhabitants. They were taken through a maze of brightly-lit corridors to an interview room, where Robert Jackson sat with his legs extended and his arms crossed, staring at the blank white wall. 'We now have information linking you to Samuel Scobie, who was found dead in the early hours of fifth February. What was your relationship with him?' asked Joseph.

Jackson didn't say a word this time but he looked surprised. His solicitor, David Semple, sitting beside him, also looked stunned and turned and gave Jackson a sharp look. Shazia interpreted their body language as signifying that this matter had not been discussed and wasn't expected to be raised. Seemingly, it was all new to Semple.

'We believe you were supplying Scobie with drugs and it was you who threw Sammy off his veranda that night.'

'I don't know who the fuck you're talking about,' said Jackson.

'I thought you might say that,' said Joseph. 'Let me refresh your memory. You shared a cell with him here in Barlinnie, Robert, or should I call you Jack?'

Jackson smiled. 'I shared cells wi' lots of folk. I cannae remember them all.'

'This is what he looked like after he hit the ground from his tower block.' He placed a photograph on the table, a picture of Scobie lying on the ground in a pool of blood, his skull crushed. 'Look at it. What did he do to deserve that?'

Jackson shook his head. 'I wouldnae know.'

'Can you tell us where you were on the night of Saturday 4th February and early hours of 5th February?' asked Shazia.

'At my girlfriend's flat in Knightswood. All night.'

Shazia nodded her head. 'How convenient. Seems she is very useful at providing you with an alibi every time there is a murder. I don't believe you. I reckon you visited Sammy that night. I think you killed him.'

Jackson smiled and thought back to that night. 'You can think all you like, Inspector. It disnae make it happen.' There had been a man out walking his dog, passing by the entrance to Scobie's tower block when Jackson had emerged and headed towards his car. Jackson saw the man looking at him and had gone over and grabbed him by the throat. 'I wisnae here, understand! You didnae see nothing, right?' The passer-by understood the inherent threat in the rhetorical question alright and communicated his assent with a nervous nod as Jackson released his hold on his neck. 'Because if you make as much as a peep about seeing me or this car to the cops, you are dead.' Jackson was confident he had frightened the man into silence.

'Maybe you can also explain the money found in your girlfriend's flat?' asked Joseph. Jackson looked surprised. 'Yes, we've just had the place searched and guess what we found under one of the floorboards? That's right. Twenty grand. Was that for killing Scobie or killing Henderson? Or is it money you'd made from selling cocaine, because we found more of that too in her flat?' Jackson stared at the bare white walls of the room in stony silence as if he wasn't interested in anything being said.

'Go fuck yourself!' said Jackson.

'Maybe your girlfriend will have more to say now that she's also in custody. Worried she might grass you in?'

Jackson remained silent.

'That tanning salon she manages. It's owned by Greg Murray.'

'Is it?'

'So, you do a bit of taxi work for Murray as well as sell drugs and she runs one of his salons. There wouldn't be a bit of money laundering going on there, would there?'

'I huvnae a clue what you're on about.'

'Who asked you to kill Charles Henderson?'

'No comment.'

'Was it Greg Murray?'

'No comment.'

'Did you persuade Katarina Marková to steal a keycard to Henderson's room?'

'No.'

'She says you did. She has identified you and said you told her to spike his drink and steal the key to his room.'

'She's a fucking liar.'

'Sergeant, this is pointless,' said Semple. 'I would like some time to speak with my client alone.' After Semple had been allowed to confer with his client for ten minutes, he came to speak to Shazia. 'My client is prepared to make a statement.' When the recording apparatus was switched back on, Jackson began a short speech, the gist of which was that he admitted that he and Scobie had known each other in Barlinnie prison as they had shared a cell, but that he had not been in contact with Scobie since then.

'Here's what I think,' said Joseph, shaking his head. 'You came to see Sammy Scobie the night he died. Maybe he owed you money, maybe he was ripping you off, diluting the gear you sold him? Whatever, you went prepared, wore gloves so you didn't leave any prints, and attacked him in his flat, throwing him off the veranda. You took his phone and his laptop to make it look like a burglary.'

Semple repeated that his client denied any involvement in the deaths of Scobie or Henderson.

'Why would she lie, Robert?' asked Shazia.

Jackson smiled. 'You really want to know? Because she wanted a relationship, that's why. Aye, I shagged her. But she wanted more. She wisnae happy. Took the cream puff! So that's why she wants to get back at me. The whore is lying her fucking heid aff.'

'Have you heard of Stockholm Syndrome?' asked Shazia.

'What are you on about?' said Jackson.

'It's when captives develop a psychological attachment to their captors. It's born out of survival and not to be mistaken for real affection. What you actually did was commit rape.'

'Bullshit!'

When Jackson had been taken back to his cell, Shazia said, 'I'm sure Jackson's involved in both deaths and they are somehow linked. Robertson must have known something about it too, but unfortunately now he is dead. And I don't think we've seen the last of the bodies in this case.'

29

Stephen Christie was alone in Chloe Sinclair's West End flat, which she shared with another two students. They had all gone out early that day to attend lectures. He poked around the room and found a small stash of weed in a wooden box. He and Chloe had smoked some together the previous evening. He rolled himself a joint with a small amount, opened the window, and leaned out to smoke, contemplating what had become of his life. He had been told by the university to take so-called 'garden leave' in an email from the faculty head. She had told him that the Principal took the view that it was better for him to stay away from students for the time being and an internal investigation was being launched against him with potential disciplinary measures if he was found to have breached the staff-student protocol. Christie cursed his fate. There was only one way that his employer could have found out about his relationship with Chloe: Juliet. His wife must have contacted the university, maybe even emailing the Principal himself to accuse him. Christie recalled their argument a couple of years ago when she had seen him going into a pub with a young woman. She was a post-grad student, Vanessa, who had asked for his advice on applying for PhD funding.

'You were wanting to fuck her, weren't you?' Juliet told him when he got home in the middle of the night, drunk.

'Correction,' he replied through a drunken haze, 'I did fuck her!'

'Well, if you fuck her again, or any other of your students, we are finished, do you get it?'

They had stopped having sex for the next month.

When he had eventually been released by the police late on Saturday afternoon he hadn't even managed to get into his flat. Juliet wouldn't answer the door. She must have got the locks changed on the flat as his keys were no use, and she had dumped all of his stuff in black plastic rubbish bags on the apartment's landing. 'The bitch!' he thought. He'd had to phone a taxi to pick his belongings up and go round to Chloe's. He had phoned her and asked if he could stay with her for a while and, though surprised, she agreed. But when she saw the bin bags that he had brought with him he could tell she was really thinking was *what have I let myself into?* Rather reluctantly, he felt, she let him in and he knew that it was only a temporary arrangement. His life was falling apart. He had nowhere else to go though, other than a hotel, and the thought of that made his stomach turn. That was what had got him into this mess in the first place.

He knew that his job at the university was finished. He could sit it out doing nothing for a while until the investigation was complete, but the outcome was a foregone conclusion. He would lose his job. Better to quit, avoid an investigation, leave with no smear on his record. He recalled once having seen an advert looking for teachers in the Gulf States, Abu Dhabi he thought it was. That's what he needed, a fresh start, well away from anyone who knew him. He quickly searched the internet and found several websites looking for teachers in the Middle East. He spent the next couple of hours thrashing some applications together and fired them off by email. He then drafted a letter of resignation to the university.

Once the applications were emailed, he decided to go for a walk and get some fresh air. Chloe's flat was in Great George Street, halfway up a steep hill which ran from Byres Road up to the university. He didn't want to go anywhere near his work so headed downhill to Byres Road and instinctively into a pub, thinking that he should actually celebrate his new-found freedom. He bought himself a pint, then another, and soon felt the combination of the cannabis and the alcohol pleasantly erasing his worries. The idea of a pub crawl down Byres Road suddenly appealed to him. He hadn't done anything like that in years. He finished the drink and stepped outside. The cold air sharpened his senses and he felt invigorated, alive. Maybe what had happened was all for the best. In years to come, he might look back and be glad that his life had taken a different turning.

He needed to replenish his cash. He stopped at an ATM, keyed in his PIN, then requested fifty pounds. He would buy Chloe some wine and some flowers from the seller in Byres Road on the way back to the flat. It was the least he could do to thank her. But there was a problem. The machine was telling him that there were insufficient funds in the account. He tried asking for thirty instead. He got the same message. This was unbelievable. Only a few days ago he knew that there was a balance of nearly two thousand in the account. He crossed the road to the bank, which was his branch. There was an enormous queue and it took him twenty minutes before he managed to get to the counter and speak to a teller, a young woman. She asked him to key in his PIN and checked her computer.

'I'm sorry, the balance is zero in that account,' she said.

'That can't be right, please check again,' Christie said.

The teller tapped into her computer again. 'The balance in the account was transferred this morning to another account.'

There was only one explanation. Juliet must have cleaned everything out of the account. It meant that he was stony broke.

He went back to the flat and sat pondering what to do. He could remonstrate with Juliet but legally he thought there was nothing to stop her moving everything from that joint account to one of her own. He had always been useless with money, spending it as soon as he got it, so he had no other bank accounts, no savings of his own. He had let her deal with all of that and their savings were all in her name. The flat was in both their names but how long would it take to force a sale? Even then, he was the one who had ruined the marriage. Adultery. She would likely get to keep most of the assets. And he now thought about the plan to start a new life abroad. It was most likely a pipedream. Any educational institution would demand references from his past employer and what kind of reference would he get from the university? One that would guarantee he didn't even get asked for an interview, most probably.

No, he had to come up with another plan. An idea suddenly came to him. It was risky. It was crazy. But, he thought, it was his last chance.

30

Shona arrived home from work that evening with the adulation of her colleagues still buzzing about her head and feeling a bit tipsy from the glasses of wine that they had drunk after work in a bar in George Square. Jamie said, 'Your friend is here.'

She saw Alex sitting on the sofa, nursing a large glass of wine. 'Alex, God, I forgot. Hey, you're tanned! And you've got a beard.' She came over and gave him a hug.

'That's what a year down under does for you!' he said.

'I really thought you were dead. You just vanished. It must be nearly more than a year since you disappeared, you bastard and not a word. I honestly thought those Orangemen had thrown you off a cliff!'

Alex laughed. 'No chance. Listen, get yourself a drink and I'll explain. I brought wine.'

'This better be good,' she said shaking her head at Alex.

'So, let me get this right,' said Shona a while later, nursing a large glass of Sauvignon Blanc, her second since she returned to the flat. 'You just decided to take off without telling anyone where you were going?'

Alex said, 'There was no way I was sticking around after the death threats and the messages I was getting on social media. There was a bounty on my head so I had to get away for a while until it calmed down. The fewer that knew what I was doing the better.'

'How did you end up in Australia?' Shona asked.

'First down to London. I stayed in a B and B in Camden, then applied for a visa to Australia. Ended up in the fucking middle of nowhere, which suited me perfectly. Aussie-land. Back of beyond. A little one-horse town where nobody knew or cared who you were. I needed to get as far away as possible from Scotland, in case whoever wanted to kill me found out I was still alive. Australia seemed as far away as anywhere, especially the Outback. I thought if I moved fast, I could find somewhere quiet, which I did. The rest, as they say, is history.'

'And now you're back!' she said. 'I still can't believe it!'

'I got here an hour ago. It's been great chatting with Jamie. We have a lot in common. Of course, he didn't know me from Adam but I guess he'd heard you talk about me.'

'I nearly didn't let him in,' said Jamie. 'Thought he was a bible basher or going to try to sell me something.'

'Ha! Very security conscious though, so he is. Made me show him my passport to convince him I was who I said I was!' Alex said, laughing.

'Shit, I meant to phone you, Jamie, and tell you I invited him round.'

'Listen, Shona, I'm sorry I didn't get in touch but I had to just vanish. I read those articles you wrote on what Fergus found out about those Russians. I gather you got to know him?'

'Yes. Briefly.'

'He was a great guy. We worked together for a while at the Courier after I left the Gazette. Real shame what happened.'

Shona sighed. 'Those bastards who killed him, I hate them. Fucking Russian mafia or the SVR or the FSB or whatever they call themselves. I don't know who it was but I hate them all. It might even have been our so-called allies, the fucking Americans, for all I know.'

'I know. But he died trying to get to the truth. That's what we all try to do.'

'Wait a minute,' said Shona. 'What happens now? Aren't you worried that once the loyalists know you are back, they will go after you?'

Alex shrugged. 'In Australia I kept thinking someone might recognise me or recall my name from the press but it never happened. I made sure I looked a bit different growing this beard too; that helped. Maybe I was just being paranoid, though. Would the loyalists have colleagues down under? Probably. I didn't want to take the chance.'

'The beard is cool!' said Shona. 'I hardly recognised you!'

'Thanks,' said Alex, raising his glass in a toast to the compliment. 'And I didn't use the name Alex Mancini in Australia either. Obviously.'

'So, who were you?' asked Shona.

Alex laughed. 'I went through all sorts of names for who I would be when I was on the plane. I settled on John Maclean after John Maclean, of Red Clydeside fame. Of course, I didn't have any ID to prove that was who I was, but I never needed to show any. Everyone down under is pretty laid back about everything. The bar I worked in was cash in hand. If you told people your name, no one questioned it. I only had a twelve-month visitor visa but nobody bothered about that.'

Shona said, 'So now you've come back. Why? Presumably you think you will be safe? What's changed?'

'I've changed. I'm not the same person I was. I'm not scared any more. I don't know. I realised I needed to see Emily more than anything, I suppose. Plus, I can't live the rest of my life on the run, in hiding, in fear. I'm reckoning enough time has gone past, too. It's amazing how quickly you can be forgotten. I don't think they care about me now. I hope not anyway! But, you know, if they really want to kill me, I don't give a fuck! Let's celebrate being alive while we are still here!'

Jamie groaned. 'Sounds like a good idea but some of us have to work tomorrow. Unfortunately. I'm meeting a client who is a suspect in the Henderson murder case, you may have heard about it.'

'Yes, read about that. Political assassinations in Scotland. Who'd have thought it? None happen for hundreds of years then suddenly, two come along in the space of a year. What's the country coming to, eh? And Shona, by the way, well done for that excellent piece on Britain United and their links to that shit Forsyth. Brilliant stuff!' He raised his glass in a toast. I'd like to help out with your investigations into those bastards if I can. I can't believe I had to pretend to be a Rangers fan when I was undercover doing a story on them. If they'd only known I was really a Celtic fan!'

'Believe it or not, I supported Rangers when I was younger,' said Jamie. 'There are actually some decent Rangers fans. They're not all bigots. Mind you, what about some Celtic fans – supporting the IRA and all that?'

'Hmm. I was brought up as a Catholic in a Scottish-Italian family in Dumfries but everyone in my family, except me, supported Queen of the South. Instead, I wanted to support Celtic. I thought my dad would never speak to me again once I stopped going to Palmerston Park with him, but he came round to accepting it. I think you will find, though, that the Provos weren't actually sectarian. They saw themselves as fighting the authorities: the British government, the police, the Army, and all the security forces.'

'Yes, but they also bombed and killed civilians. What about the Guildford and Birmingham pub bombings?'

'Terrible stuff, yeah. I'm not going to defend that. But they weren't sectarian, that's my point. The UDA, and the UVF, on the other hand, specifically targeted Catholics. They were defending a system which discriminated against Catholics in Northern Ireland for years. They also had links to the security forces and loyalist politicians. So, when people talk about sectarian violence whether it's in Belfast or Glasgow and they make out as if it's on both sides, is that really true? I don't think so.'

'I was brought up supporting Rangers, going to games with my dad, and it sickened me when I heard those fans singing songs about being up to their knees in Fenian blood and the Billy Boys. I went to games because I loved football and I loved Rangers, but I hated all that sectarian shit.'

'Catholics were discriminated against for so long. If you had a Proddy name and had gone to a Proddy school, never mind being in the actual Orange Order, you could practically walk into a job in those days. But if you were a Catholic, forget it!'

Shona looked up from her iPad. 'Hey listen you two, while you have been debating the history of sectarianism in the west of Scotland, I've been reading up on Cameron Forsyth's background. He used to be a member of the Orange Order, did you know that? He keeps that quiet. And he went to the same school as Charles Henderson and they were supposedly friends?'

'Really? That's interesting, I didn't know that,' said Jamie.

'Yes. Fettes College,' Shona said, 'There's plenty of pictures on the internet of the two of them together at various functions over the years. Seems they were quite close. Forsyth chose to go into the Army, went to Sandhurst, and became an officer in the Marines, reaching the rank of Colonel. He left the military after he was wounded by a sniper in Afghanistan and took over the family business when his father died a year later. Henderson, on the other hand, went from a successful law career into politics.'

Jamie said, 'This guy I'm acting for, Stephen Christie, he was staying in the same hotel where Henderson was killed. Turns out Henderson was actually his biological father but he never had anything to do with him as a child. Christie was alone with him in his hotel room at some point, he admits that, and the police aren't ruling out the idea that he could have been acting out of some revenge motive. But Christie says he had nothing to do with it and I believe him.'

'Why do you think he didn't do it?' asked Shona.

'I don't know, you just can tell if they are lying by looking them in the eyes. I just can't see him murdering someone. He's a university lecturer. He teaches poetry and drama, for fuck's sake. He was only in the hotel as he was shagging one of his students. He may be a bit dodgy, but he's no Charles Manson.'

'I think you'll find that Manson didn't actually do the killings himself,' said Shona. 'Maybe this guy Christie just snapped! Perhaps he was just out of his head on drink or drugs at the time? He's clever. He's worked out how he can get away with it. Maybe he's fooled you?'

'I had a lecturer who was a bit weird when I was at university,' said Alex. 'On the one hand he was this religious freak, member of the church and all that. But you should have seen the way he lusted after all the females in tutorials. The women couldn't stand him, thought he was a complete creep. One complained after he pawed her when she was on her own with him once. He suddenly was all over her and she had to physically fight him off. I reckon he was a bit of a Jekyll and Hyde figure. I could definitely see him killing someone. No problem. I can't remember his name. It can't be him, though, he'll be retired by now. He must have been in his fifties when I was a student.'

'No, this guy is only about thirty, but he was sleeping with one of his students on the night, so he probably scores highly on the perv stakes. Right, anyway, I'm starving. You take it easy while Shona and I fix up some grub.' He and Shona disappeared into the kitchen and Alex stretched out on the sofa.

Half an hour later when Jamie returned to tell him dinner was ready, he found his friend fast asleep. 'Guess, the jet-lag has finally taken its toll,' he said to Shona, throwing a duvet over Alex's snoring hulk.

31

Shazia spotted some bruises on her daughter's arm that morning when she looked in Yasmeen's room to give her a goodbye kiss before she left for work. 'What are these?' she asked.

'Nothing,' said Yasmeen, quickly covering them up.

'Have you been hitting yourself, Yasmeen?'

'No.'

Yasmeen was no good at lying. The truth was written all over her face. Shazia thought it must have had something to do with the Barcelona trip. No doubt Yasmeen would be anxious. But when she spoke to her daughter about the marks on her arm, it turned out to be something else.

'I'm not like those beautiful girls. I'm fat. I'm ugly.'

'No, you're not, you're beautiful,' said Shazia putting an arm around her daughter. 'What do you mean, other girls?

Yasmeen opened up her laptop and logged onto Instagram. 'Look,' she said, showing her mum picture after picture of young, white, attractive girls. They were laughing and smiling. They looked carefree. They were everything that Yasmeen felt she wasn't. Yasmeen began striking herself in the face, shouting, 'Ugly! Ugly! Ugly…' until Shazia gripped her arms and held them tightly until she calmed down.

Shazia resisted the temptation to scold her daughter for going back onto social media. It had been inevitable. 'This isn't real life, Yasmeen. People select these images because they want to show off, to impress. Listen, you are every bit as beautiful as them.' She kissed her daughter and held her head close to her breast. 'Oh, Yasmeen, darling, don't ever think that you are ugly or not as good as anyone else. You are!'

Shazia went off to work that day feeling more depressed than ever. The Henderson case was a week old and they hadn't charged anyone. Yasmeen was going downhill again. And Omar had sounded unhappy when she had told him that she was too busy to see him this week. Life sucks, she thought.

On the way to work, she got a text from McLaughlin which raised her mood. His wife had gone into labour during the night and he was now the proud father of a baby girl. No name yet. He apologised for not being at work but was sure she would understand if he took emergency special leave for the rest of the week. She sent him a reply with congratulations and wishing him, Catriona and the baby all the best.

In Edinburgh, Joseph parked in the car park beside the science centre, and he and Mitchell walked over to the Holyrood parliament building.

'Bit more modern than Westminster,' said Joseph as they stood outside. 'Though that wouldn't be difficult.' It looked very European and he remembered that it had been an architect from Barcelona who had designed it, supposedly modelling the structure on the surrounding landscape; it faced onto Arthur's Seat and the swooping geometry of the hill was somehow echoed in the building's curves. There was a trace of Barcelona in there too, though. He'd been there on holiday and been amazed by the Sagrada Familia. A definite reference to Gaudi in its windows, maybe even Dali in the way the windows seemed to be melting. It was probably the least practical parliament building in the world, he thought, and probably the craziest.

'Personally, I hated it when it was first built,' said Mitchell. 'I thought, has the architect taken the piss? It didn't look Scottish enough. But it has grown on me! Now I think it's OK.'

'Think about that monstrosity in Westminster. It's gloomy and dark. This is fresh and vibrant. I quite like it, even though it's bit weird though. I like things that shock you. The shock of the new, isn't that what they say about modern art?'

'Is it? It was my partner, Grace, who got me into looking at art. Before I met her, I knew the Mona Lisa and that was about all. Didn't know anything about modern stuff really, apart from what you see in Kelvingrove. Grace paints large abstracts. Sells them too! You wouldn't believe how much she sells them for!'

'Does she really? I should have stuck in at art at school, eh? Maybe be rich by now!'

'OK. Listen to us talking all arty like a pair of pretentious posers. Shall we go in and find out what anyone has to tell us?'

The security checks to enter the building were thorough, but eventually they were inside the building and shown to a room which they could use for the day. They had asked to speak to as many Conservative MSPs as possible, including the party's leader. In turn, each of the MSPs came to the interview room at the appointed time. All were punctual and all said very little that they didn't know already. Henderson was painted in glowing terms: he appeared to have no vices, as far as his fellow MSPs knew. They were all profoundly shocked by the manner of his death and the rumours and revelations surrounding it. True, he had been accused by an assistant of harassment, but nothing had been proved against him. Politically, he was seen as loyal and hard-working. No one seemed to have a bad word to say against him. Enemies? No. Disputes within the Party? Not at all. The sense of closing ranks was claustrophobic, from the party leader downwards.

'I don't know how I can help you,' said Angus McLennan, the last to be interviewed. 'Charles's death is a sad loss. He was a dear colleague.' McLennan was a tall lanky figure, in his early fifties. He had a long thin horse-like face with a sweep of thinning light brown hair combed and gelled back, a face that Joseph thought gave him a look of being either a consular official in the days of the Empire, or a book-keeper for gangsters during prohibition. He was wearing a dark blue pin-striped suit, a light blue shirt with a white collar, and a navy-blue tie with pink polka dots.

'We understand that you and he were quite close,' said Joseph.

McLennan nodded. 'He was my closest colleague in this place. It's true that Charles and I didn't always see eye to eye but that is the nature of politics. We have robust debates, we like to challenge each other, exchange views, it's healthy. At the end of the day, though, we are all members of the same party. We must stick together.' His comments reminded Joseph of what Forsyth had said.

'Would you know of anyone who might have wanted to harm Mr Henderson?'

McLennan shook his head. 'The idea is preposterous, but Charles did tell me that he had received some unpleasant messages. We politicians do put our heads above the parapet, so to speak. There are always going to be people out there who strongly disagree with what we have to say. I expect it could have been some lunatic with a hatred of something that he had once said in a speech or something.'

'What did the messages say?'

'The usual abuse. I didn't see them but he did say they wouldn't shut him up or stop him. I admired him for that. But it may have cost him his life.'

'Why didn't he report them?'

'He said it would just give these people publicity. He thought it was best to just ignore them. He didn't take them seriously. I do the same.'

'Did he say who they were from?'

McLennan shook his head. 'No. Some lunatics, probably. There are some who are never happy with you, whatever you do. You can't please everyone, that's a fact.'

'But what about within Holyrood here? Did he have any political enemies? Either outside or inside the Party?'

'Political enemies? Adversaries, yes, but enemies, no. Politics can get dirty but I don't think anyone in here had Charles killed, if that is what you mean. Though who knows what connections some of those on the hard left have to extremists?'

'What about inside the Party?'

McLennan shook his head and laughed. 'As I said, we all don't always see eye to eye, but we are a broad church and we don't assassinate each other! Now, if that is all, I do have some urgent matters to attend to. I'm meant to be in a committee meeting about now. I'm sorry I couldn't help you more.'

'One more thing, sir,' said Joseph. 'Could you please tell us where you were last Monday night? We are asking everyone this, sir, it's just procedure.'

'Now I am thinking I really should have my lawyer with me. But just to clarify this and finish it I can tell you that I was at the opera in Edinburgh, then went home.'

'Where's that?'

'Bridge of Allan. I was with several others at the opera who can confirm this. But I live alone. I am a widow. My wife died two years ago.'

Joseph was thinking about the rumour that McLennan was having an affair with Henderson's wife, but as it *was* rumour he felt he couldn't confront the MSP with this, and there was absolutely nothing to put him anywhere near the scene of the crime.

'I am sorry to hear that, sir. Is there anything else that you can think of which would be relevant to the investigation?'

McLennan pointed his finger and wagged it at Joseph. 'Listen, if I were you, I would want to speak to that crazy boyfriend of Charles's assistant. The one who made up that allegation against him. Charles told me the bloke threatened to kill him. Now, if you don't mind, I really do have several things to do.' He stood up. 'If that is all, officers, I really need to get back to the committee meeting I was in. The government want to introduce minimum alcohol pricing, would you believe it! Talk about a nanny state!'

On the car journey back along the M8, Joseph said, 'McLennan lives alone so he really has no alibi for the night of the murder. Shagging the victim's wife would be the archetypal motive, wouldn't it? He could have driven through to Glasgow but could he have really broken into the hotel and got into Henderson's room?'

'Hmm. Or he hired someone else to do it. These tweets and messages McLennan mentioned. We did go through them, though, and there wasn't anything that stood out. So, what now?'

'Let's speak to Peter Boyle. That's the first we've heard that he threatened to kill Henderson. Let's drop in on the hotel on the way back.'

Joseph parked the car in a street a block away from the hotel. It was the nearest spot he could find and he didn't fancy getting a ticket, remembering what had happened to Shazia the first time. He and Mitchell walked into the hotel and asked at reception to speak to the manager but, instead of Jan Van Dijk or Lenna Ivanova, it was a young Polish woman with long blonde hair in a ponytail who came out to greet them. She introduced herself as Julia Nowak and said she was the Assistant Manager.

'We'd like to speak to Peter Boyle, he's one of your chefs,' said Joseph.

'I will go and see if he is on duty,' Nowak said.

A couple of minutes later Nowak returned. 'I am sorry. Peter has phoned in sick today.'

'In that case, I'd like to speak to the head chef.'

Nowak took them through the restaurant and into the kitchen, a dazzlingly bright area at the back of the building. It was incredibly hot, and flames and steam were rising from several hobs, pots and pans were crashing around, and chefs were constantly shouting across the kitchen. Some waiters stood at a counter, evidently waiting on plates of food to take out to the diners. Nowak raised her own voice. 'Louis,' she shouted. The din was so great that she had to repeat it twice, until a large man in his forties, sporting a dark goatee beard but otherwise indistinguishable from the other white-clad individuals, came over.

'Yes, what is it, Julia?' he said in a heavy French accent, 'Can you not see that we are busy. And we are a man down.'

'These people are police officers,' said Nowak. 'They would like a word with you.'

Joseph said,' I will be very quick, sir. I just wanted to ask you about your chef Peter Boyle.'

The chef looked as if he might erupt at the mention of the name. 'That little shit? He is the reason why we are struggling today. Sick? Most likely a hangover!'

Joseph nodded. 'Can you remember if you saw him on Monday evening?'

'Monday was his day off. I mean, his regular day off, not the ones where he phones in pretending to be sick! But, yes, I saw him when I was leaving. It was his night off but he was in the street outside. I wondered why? He was talking to Amy. That's her over there.' He pointed to a chef who was chopping up vegetables. 'Wait until I get my hands on him. There will be another murder in this hotel!' He turned

232

and went back to shouting at the kitchen staff, directing operations like a general in the thick of battle.

Amy was called over to speak to them by Nowak. She said that she had met Boyle on Monday night when she had finished her shift and she was leaving the hotel.

'When was this?' asked Joseph.

'About ten o'clock. He had been drinking. He asked if I would go home with him.'

'What did you do?' asked Mitchell.

'Told him to get lost.' She shook her head at the memory. 'I said I was tired and was going home and anyway he was pissed.'

'Do you two have a relationship then?' asked Mitchell.

Amy smiled. 'Sort of. Nothing serious. He's got a girlfriend. I don't like being just part of a couple anyway. We just spend the odd night together.'

'But not that night?'

She shook her head. 'Not that night.'

'Does his girlfriend know?' asked Joseph.

She shrugged. 'You should ask him.'

'So, what happened after you saw him?'

'He borrowed some money. He wanted enough to get a taxi home. Said he was skint. I gave him a tenner. That reminds me, he hasn't paid me back. He's not exactly popular in here today!'

'What's he like?' asked Mitchell.

'Peter? He's a good laugh. But he drinks too much. That's probably why he's not in today.'

Mitchell said to Amy, 'So, after you gave him the money, he went home?'

'Well, I assumed he went home, I didn't see where he went. I went off to get my bus home,' she said.

'Where do you live?'

'Dennistoun'

'Thanks, Amy. Can you give me a contact number for you in case I need to speak to you again?'

'Sure,' she said.

After she had given Mitchell her contact details, Amy went back to the chopping board.

Nowak said, 'I will be speaking to Peter when he comes back into work tomorrow. We cannot keep him on. His sickness record is very bad. We will need to let him go. Do you need to know his address?'

Mitchell wrote down the address in her notebook. They thanked Nowak for her assistance and they headed back out to the car.

Boyle didn't answer the door of his Partick tenement flat until Joseph started pounding it with his fists and the neighbour from across the landing came out, having given up ringing the bell for several minutes. Joseph waved his warrant card and the neighbour shut the door sharply. Boyle finally answered the door looking dishevelled and smelling even worse. It clearly wasn't so much a hangover he had as just plain drunk. He was wearing grey tracksuit bottoms and a Metallica T-shirt, both of which looked like they hadn't seen the inside of a washing machine for a long time.

'What do you want?' he said through half-closed eyes.

Joseph said, 'We need some proper answers from you. And no lies this time.'

'You better come in,' he said.

He took them into his living room and they sat down on the couch. Loud music was blasting from the speakers, if you could call it music. Joseph would have described it as some sort of heavy metal which made him think of the kind of noise which prisoners in Guantanamo were subjected to as a form of torture. He was relieved when Boyle switched it off. The place smelt disgusting, even worse than Boyle's breath, a combination of cigarette smoke and stale booze. Boyle sat in an armchair facing them through the fog. On the coffee table was an ashtray full of cigarette ends, several empty cans of coke, and a near-empty bottle of Smirnoff. It looked like Boyle had been engaged in a battle of strength with the bottle and the bottle was winning hands down. Boyle took a cigarette out of a packet and lit it. He picked up a tumbler of dark liquid, presumably coke and vodka, and raised it to his lips but Joseph grabbed hold of the glass. 'Don't you think you've had enough?' Joseph said.

'My girlfriend dumped me,' he said. 'I'm drowning my sorrows. Isn't that what it's called?'

'Lorna?' said Mitchell.

'Aye,' said Boyle.

'That's not good,' said Joseph, 'But why we're here concerns the pair of you. You two claimed that you were together on Monday night. At the cinema, then loving it up back here.'

Boyle looked at Joseph with half-shut eyes and took a sip of his drink, but said nothing.

'The thing is,' said Joseph, 'We know that is a pack of lies. You were seen outside the hotel late on Monday night. Apparently, you had been drinking, just as you are now, and you were not with Lorna.'

Mitchell said, 'Lorna told me that she came through to Glasgow to see you on Monday and she stayed the night here. What really happened, Peter?'

Boyle sighed and inhaled his cigarette then slowly exhaled. Mitchell began to cough. 'Sorry, is that bothering you?' he asked.

'Yes, I don't like cigarette smoke,' she said. 'And I've got asthma.'

Boyle stubbed out the cigarette. 'Sorry. You're right. I've had enough. I'll make some coffee. Do you want some?' Boyle tried to stand up, but stumbled and fell over. He pulled himself back up onto his chair.

'I think coffee is what's needed. I'll put the kettle on,' said Mitchell, 'if you show me where things are.' She helped Boyle get to his feet and he took her through to the kitchen. Joseph picked up the vodka bottle and the tumbler and followed them into the kitchen and poured the contents of the glass down the sink.

Once some coffee was made and the three of them were seated around the kitchen table, Boyle opened up. 'This is what happened, right. Lorna phoned me the day after this Henderson bloke died and asked me if I'd had anything to do with it. As if! I told her I'd been out with pals, then went home.'

Mitchell said, 'Why did Lorna make up a story saying you went to the pictures if she hadn't been with you?'

'She was worried that you lot might think I had something to do with that guy's death 'cos me and him had a bit of an argument that time. She phoned me after it happened. I didn't even know he was staying in the hotel. Mind you, the state I was in, if I had run into him, I might have swung for him after how he treated Lorna. But I wouldn't have killed him. Anyway, she said she thought it would be best if I had an alibi so we made up a story about her coming through here and staying the night.'

'OK,' said Joseph. 'Tell us what really happened that night. And no more fairy tales!'

'I ended up going past the hotel. I'd been out with some friends, we'd been in Sloans all day. I was broke and I was walking home along Argyle Street. I was walking past the hotel when Amy came out. I asked her if she would lend me enough for a taxi ride home.'

'That's not exactly what Amy says. She says you wanted her to come back here with you.'

Boyle nodded. 'Aye, that's probably true. I was fucking pissed, though, I can't remember everything that happened.'

'And did you get one?'

'One what?'

'A taxi.'

He shook his head. The buggers wouldn't stop for me. Probably thought I was too pissed. So, I had to walk home.'

'So, you have no proof that you actually came home when you said.'

'I suppose I don't, but I'm telling you the truth.'

'Did you threaten to kill Henderson?' asked Joseph.

'No, he's a liar whoever said that.'

Joseph said, 'It's never a good idea to invent a story. You have wasted our time, Peter. I'll be having words with Lorna about it too. You do realise that now you no longer have an alibi for the night Henderson was killed?'

'I didn't kill anyone. Honest. Amy just got a bit freaked out when she heard that he'd been murdered in the place where I work. We put together a story. I guess it was a mistake.'

Joseph said, 'Well as far as we are concerned, you're still a suspect. Don't disappear. We might need to get hold of you.'

Mitchell said, 'Why have you two broken up anyway?'

Boyle rubbed his face and scratched his beard. 'Lorna checked my phone when I was in the shower. I'd slept with Amy after work one night and we'd texted about it. When I came out of the shower she'd gone. I'm a fucking idiot! I told her it didn't mean anything, that we'd both just got pissed and it was just a one-night stand but she told me I was dumped. Fucking brilliant isn't it!'

'Have you considered, Peter,' said Joseph as they left Boyles's flat, 'that you might have a bit of an issue with alcohol?'

32

Alex woke up on Shona's couch when he heard a door slam and, for a second, couldn't remember where he was. All that he knew was that he was very uncomfortable and he half-expected to open his eyes and find himself still on a plane somewhere over the Indian Ocean. His back ached and his neck felt as if he couldn't straighten it out. Then he realised where he was. Glasgow. Shona's flat. He heard a door slam and got up. He looked at his watch. It was twenty past eight.

'Hi, sleep well?' said Shona. She was in her red and white pyjamas and dressing gown, seated on a high stool in the kitchen, munching a bowl of cereal while flicking through pages on an iPad. The kitchen had a black marble-topped island in the centre of the room and a matching worktop around the sides with white cupboards, gleaming stainless-steel taps and designer ovens. Everything looked modern and clean. It was very different to the more basic rustic kitchen he was used to in Australia.

'Sure,' Alex said. 'Has Jamie gone out?'

'Yes, he's off to work early. He's got a court case in Dumbarton Sheriff Court. Do you want a cup of tea?'

'Thanks.'

She poured him a cup from the teapot. 'I'm working from home for a while this morning, then I'm going into the office. What are your plans?'

Alex sipped the tea. It tasted good. 'I'm seeing Emily after school at three. I phoned Paula yesterday to tell her I was back.'

'How did that go?'

'OK. She said it would be good for Emily to see me again. I was a bit of a dick when Paula and I were together. I was drinking too much and when I wasn't drinking, I was working too much. I don't blame her for leaving me. So that's at three. First off, I'm going to try and find a room to rent. I don't really want to stay in the hotel I've booked into for longer than necessary and I can't sleep on your sofa every night. For one thing, if I kept sleeping there, I'd have to pay a fortune to a chiropractor to fix my spine.' He rubbed his back and groaned.

Shona laughed. 'I don't mind, but I don't think Jamie would be too keen on you living here!' She smiled.

'Exactly! Then I might pop into the Courier office. See what's up.'

'Sounds a good plan.'

'Listen, I meant what I said last night, about helping you with your story about Britain United and Scottish Action. You don't mind, do you?'

'Of course not.'

'Do you think I could speak to your source? I'd like to see if there is anything else we could get on the links between the two groups.'

'I don't know. I will have to make a phone call. Hang on, I'll do it now, it's probably a good time.' Shona disappeared into her bedroom clutching her phone and came back a few minutes later. 'It's cool,' she said. 'My source is happy to meet you. In fact, she says you know her. Aileen Buchan.'

'Aileen? Really? Good for Aileen. I got to know her during the referendum campaign. She's a brave woman. That was shocking what happened to her, but these guys are evil bastards. Good for her for helping you out. It's a shame not all politicians are like her!'

'I told her she could trust you. She said she remembers you and is happy to speak to you. She just told me that she received the stuff anonymously, though. Let me know if you come up with anything else. Here's her number.' She looked at her phone, then scribbled a number down on a scrap of paper and handed it to Alex.

'Sure. Thanks.'

After he finished his tea, Alex had a shower, got dressed, and logged on to the web on his phone after Shona gave him the password for the Wi-Fi. He googled *Room to rent in Glasgow West End* and scanned the results. There was a room in a flat in Hillhead that he liked the look of, and at nine he phoned the letting agents and was told he could view it that morning. It was five hundred a month. His savings would cover it for a few months but he would have to find work after that. He said goodbye to Shona.

'Don't you want any breakfast?' she said.

'I'll get something when I'm out, thanks. See you later.'

She gave him a peck on the cheek. 'Take care, see you later,' she said.

As he left, he noticed a black van parked outside. There were two men sitting inside it flicking through the tabloids. They were wearing boiler suits and looked like workmen. He thought one of them looked familiar, but he couldn't place him.

In a cafe in Cresswell Street, he had a coffee and a bacon roll and phoned the number for Aileen Buchan that Shona had given him. It went through to her office and he spoke to her secretary. She was, predictably, busy, in meetings all day. But the secretary said she would give her a message with his number. He recalled the last time that he had talked to Aileen, in a noisy pub during the Yes campaign. They seemed to hit it off and he found her very attractive. It would be good to see her again. Then he wandered round to view the room to let. The room looked OK and, frankly, he couldn't be arsed seeing any more flats. It was clean, had a decent-sized kitchen, a double bed, a desk and chair, a chest of drawers, and a wardrobe. As well as the kitchen there was a living room to share with the two other tenants. The bathroom had a shower over the bath and it looked like it had at least been cleaned a few times in the past couple of months. He paid the agent a deposit in cash and signed the lease. He agreed to move in from Saturday.

He caught the underground from Hillhead into town. Everyone in the carriage was glued to their smartphones, a sight he somehow found depressing. Whatever happened to people talking to each other or reading books or newspapers, he thought? He looked up from his seat at the adverts in the carriage. The advert opposite him asked: *Do you want to learn Gaelic?* He answered, silently to himself, *No*. He got off at St Enoch and popped into his hotel, showered and got changed and picked up his present for Emily. Then he strolled up Buchanan Street for a bit, turned right and crossed over George Square. He had a pint in Babbity Bowster in the Merchant City. It felt good to be back in Glasgow. He had missed it, he realised. Australia had been lovely. It had been great to be with Suzanne but it had all felt too nice, too safe. He needed to feel a bit of an edge in his life. Otherwise, it was like living in a dream life rather than life itself.

He sauntered down towards the river and found himself on the Broomielaw and wandered along by the Clyde until he came to the Scottish Courier building. A fierce cold wind was blowing off the river and cutting through him like an icy blade, but at least it was dry. Probably not for long though. There were some heavy dark clouds coming in from the west, covering the sky in an iron-grey sheet. He felt a long way away from the endless blue skies of Australia and quickened his pace.

When he appeared in the newsroom, he practically gave the news editor a heart attack. The entire news team stopped what they were doing and he felt overwhelmed by the attention. For half an hour all attention was fixed on him as he told his tale of where he had been for the past year but then they couldn't ignore ringing phones and deadlines so had to get back to working. He hung around the office for a while after that catching up with former colleagues and promising to meet up soon for drinks. The news editor said she would speak to the editor about taking him back on in some capacity. When he left the newspaper building, he headed towards the station to catch a train to Bearsden. Suddenly he had the feeling that he was being followed. When he stopped and glanced backwards just outside the station, he noticed a figure on the street opposite also stop at the same time. He was wearing a black jacket, dark jeans and a black baseball cap. He couldn't see his face as he appeared to be looking at the ground, bending down to tie a shoe lace. The train arrived and Alex got on. He didn't see the man in the baseball cap on the train but there had been something about the way he had stopped at the same time as him that had unnerved him. But maybe he was just being paranoid, he thought.

Alex was waiting for Emily outside the gates of the school in Bearsden at three o' clock as the school bell rang. It was an old-fashioned Victorian sandstone building situated right on the cross. He felt nervous about seeing her. Would she even remember him at all? It had been over a year. That was a long time in a nine-year-old's life. So much would have happened. Paula probably mentioned him as little as possible and there may be another surrogate dad anyway now, whoever Paula was seeing. She was an attractive woman. Men would be queuing up to date her, he was sure.

When Emily skipped out across the playground to the gates it was obvious there wasn't a trace of recognition of the man standing beside her mum. Paula had to tell her who he was. 'Emily, this is your dad. Remember I said he would be here today?'

The girl looked closely up at Alex as if examining a strange alien object that she wasn't too sure of. 'Dad?' she said.

'Hi, Emily,' said Alex. 'It's great to see you. You've grown a lot. I like your hair.'

'You've got a beard,' Emily said putting her hand out to feel it. 'You look different. Your skin is darker.'

'That's what the sun does to you. How about we go to a café and get something to eat. I'll tell you where I've been.' Emily smiled at this and nodded. 'Right,' said Alex,' I think there's a café just round the corner. Do you want to come with me?' She nodded.

Paula said, 'I'll leave you two together for an hour and then come back and get you. OK, Emily?' The girl nodded again and clutched her dad's hand hard.

He had brought her a koala bear soft toy which he had bought at the airport in Melbourne before he boarded the flight.

'Did you see any kangaroos?' asked Emily.

'See any? Hundreds of those rascals! I nearly crashed the car once when a big red suddenly bounced out in front of me in the dark!'

Emily laughed. Alex said, 'I tell you, I wasn't laughing at the time!' Emily laughed even more and so did he.

Alex loved the hour he spent with Emily, telling her all about Australia and all the different animals he had seen before his ex-girlfriend came and took her home. He had been showing Emily some photos of koalas he had spotted in a forest when Aileen phoned back. 'Alex. Shona told me you were helping her with the story. What happened to you? You disappeared.'

'It's a bit of a long story. Maybe I can tell you when I see you. I've been speaking to Shona and I'm interested in finding out more on what she has been reporting on. Can we talk?'

'I'd rather not talk on the phone. I'm in meetings until about seven-thirty. And busy all day tomorrow, too. Do you want to come through to Edinburgh this evening and we can meet later for something to eat? I could be there for eight.' She suggested a restaurant on Rose Street.

After he left Emily and Paula outside the cafe, he caught a train and found himself on Princes Street just after six. Two hours to spare. It was bitterly cold and there were tiny flakes of snow every now and again. He zipped up his leather jacket, wished he had a warmer jumper underneath, and walked more briskly into the freezing wind blowing from the east, straight off the North Sea. This is why I prefer Glasgow, he thought. It may not be called Rain Town for nothing but it doesn't freeze your balls off like this place. He walked across St Andrew's Square, around Princes Street gardens, up the Mound and down the Royal Mile, until he reached the parliament building at Holyrood. Then he saw him again. The man with the baseball cap. He was standing at a bus stop on the opposite side of the road looking at his phone. Or pretending to look at his phone. It was definitely the same guy. The cap had a New York Yankees logo on it. This time he could see the man's face. He looked to be in his twenties, powerfully built and about the same height as Alex. Definitely a fit type. He didn't take his eyes off his phone.

He must have followed him. Maybe some informer in the newspaper office had alerted his enemies that he was back and this guy had been sent to tail him. He would have seen him with Paula and Emily. Who was he? He would have to find out. He looked up at Arthur's seat and the Salisbury Crags. Would the guy follow him up there? Then he saw a bus approaching on his side heading for Leith. That would do. He got on, bought a ticket to Leith, and found a seat at the back. The guy in the cap ran across the road and got on too. He sat near the front looking out of the window. There were only two other passengers on the bus, two young women with large suitcases. They looked like they were returning from holiday, having caught the bus from the airport as the bus ran all the way from there to Leith. Alex remembered that there had been plans for the tram to do that but it had run out of money and stopped in the city centre.

Ten minutes later Alex got off the bus and walked towards the quayside at the Water of Leith. All around were offices, now closed for the night, their lights extinguished. The place was deserted and dark. He could hear footsteps behind him. He knew the big guy in the baseball cap was following him. He would be waiting for a chance to jump him. Alex had to get in there first.

At the quayside, he walked by the water's edge until he came to the back of an office block. There was no one there and he dived into the entrance to a fire exit and hugged the side of the wall, waiting for him to come past. As he did so, Alex leaped out and grabbed him round the neck, bringing him down, the baseball cap flying off. The man struggled and elbowed Alex in the guts, momentarily winding him enough for Alex to loosen his grip, and the man managed to stand up and slug him with a punch to the jaw. Alex fell backwards and felt his head hit the wall but he pulled himself together and launched himself at the man, aiming a punch which struck him on the side of the head. He grabbed the man by his jacket collar and shouted at him. 'What the fuck do you want?' But the man just smiled, then head-butted Alex between his eyes, then kicked his legs away so that he crashed to the ground, blood gushing from his nose. Now he could clearly see the big man's pale face, his menacing dark eyes peering down at him with a stare like a blast of icy wind.

Suddenly Alex was being pulled by the legs towards the water. They were only a few feet away from the dockside. He kicked his legs wildly, thrashing from side to side, and in return got a kick in the balls but the man let go of his legs and pulled a knife out of his inside jacket pocket and fell on him, aiming to stab him in the chest. Alex grabbed the guy's hand with both hands and shook it as hard as he could. The knife fell to the cobbles with a clatter, bouncing off the ground and landed a few feet away. The man stretched over to reach the knife and Alex saw his chance. He kicked the guy, sending him flying, his head striking the edge of a concrete bollard before his body disappeared over the edge. He heard a splash and looked down at the water, but the guy had disappeared into the depths. He waited and looked around. No one in sight. The only sound was the sound of the water lapping at the walls of the quay. He looked down at the surface of the water. It was still. The guy wasn't going to come back up. He thought about diving in to attempt a rescue but then there was a sudden explosion of water and the man resurfaced. 'Who the fuck are you?' shouted Alex.

'You are dead, pal!' the man spluttered, swimming towards the quayside.

'I have to disagree with you there. I wouldn't describe us as pals. But enjoy your swim anyway!' Alex picked up the knife and threw it as far as he could into the water and then jogged off as fast as he could.

She was already waiting in the restaurant. He had forgotten how beautiful her eyes were; they captivated him with their sparkling greenness. Her red hair was now a different colour but still looked great and she still looked like the woman he had fancied when he first met her a few years back.

'Sorry I'm late,' he said.

'Are you alright?' she asked.

He nodded. 'I need a drink.'

'You have blood on your lip,' she said. She leaned over and wiped his face with a tissue. 'Just a smear. It looks swollen. What happened?'

'I tripped and fell.'

She raised her eyebrows and gave him a look as if to tell him this was the feeblest excuse she had ever heard.

'I was being followed, but don't worry, I lost him. No one saw me come here.'

'Who was it?'

'He didn't introduce himself. He decided to go for a swim instead.'

She laughed. 'OK. Here, have a drink.' She poured him a large glass of red wine. 'It's good to see you again, Alex. I see you haven't lost your sense of adventure then. Who was your swimmer friend?'

'He was probably one of our loyalist chums who aren't overjoyed to see me in Scotland again. We don't seem to be very popular with them, you and I. I'm glad that right-wing bastard didn't kill you,' Alex said.

'He came pretty close,' she said. 'A few inches, in fact,' she said holding up her thumb and index finger to show the gap.

'But now you've managed to get some revenge.'

'What do you mean?'

'That stuff you gave Shona. That's going to cut off their funding stream, isn't it?'

She shook her head. 'I wish that was the case. Unfortunately, there are plenty of wealthy nutcases out there who want to pump money into the hands of those crazies. The group have been around for a long time under various names. I think Forsyth has only been funding them in the past few years, according to the information I got.'

'Maybe it will slow them down for a bit anyway.'

'I don't know about that, but let's hope so. Security has been really tightened up since Charles Henderson got murdered. He was a notorious lecher and some cuckold of a husband has probably done him in! But we had to evacuate the parliament building this morning when a suspicious package was found in the mailroom. It was addressed to Kelly McFarlane, the Scottish Labour leader. The word is that it contained some sort of white powder. Of course, everyone immediately thought it might be some sort of hazardous chemical like anthrax or a nerve agent or something, so the police and firefighters were called in. It was taken away for forensic examination and the building re-opened later and we got back in. Sounds like the sort of thing Scottish Action would do. They hate the prospect of a left-wing government at any time in the future.'

'Let's hope we will get that sort of government.'

'We need it. These right-wing nutters are one thing, but it's not just them that's the problem, the so-called mainstream right stoke the flames with talk of immigration controls and their dog-whistle racism. There are a good few other Tories like Forsyth who are determined to move the party to the right as far as they can take it, and they have friends in the media who are only too happy to give them publicity and come up with fake news to bolster their cause.'

'Fair point.'

'I think it's worth your while taking a close look at some of the links between other Tory funders and their overseas backers. There will be more skeletons in their closets, I'm sure of it.'

'I'll do that, Aileen, but first I've got a favour to ask. Do you have any idea who might have sent you that information?'

'No, it just appeared one day in my personal email inbox. The message looked innocuous and there was an attachment. The email address it was sent from looked like it was from Greenpeace, but it wasn't. Usually, I am suspicious about opening spam in case it's a virus or something, but whoever sent it clearly knows how to disguise things.'

'I thought maybe you just told Shona that and you had a secret hacker friend who could get into their system and see if we can uncover anything else about the organisation.'

'Afraid not. I would love to know more too. Since that day that I got shot, I'm a different person. I can't go anywhere without worrying what might happen, who might be waiting for me. It's been a nightmare.'

Alex leaned across and took her hand. 'Same with me. That's why I had to get away. I thought of myself as tough but those guys scared me shitless. I didn't really know what real fear was like until I realised that they wanted to kill me and wouldn't stop until they succeeded.'

Aileen squeezed his hand. 'So, we are alike, you and I. We both hate those bastards for what they have done to our lives. But we can't let them win.'

'Exactly. That's what I think now. I don't want to live in fear anymore.'

'We need to show them that we also will never stop in opposing everything that they stand for. I get hate mail every day but, you know what? I'm never going to let them beat me. They hate everything that I stand for, especially when I call the royal family a bunch of spongers who contribute nothing.' She let go of his hand and raised her glass. 'To life and pleasure and all that is good. Let's not waste time talking about those bastards any more tonight. Tell me your story. I want to know everything you've done since you mysteriously disappeared.' She took a large gulp of wine and stared at him.

He told her about living in the small town in Australia, population at last census of 622 plus another couple of hundred in the surrounding area. He had wondered at the time if it was a bit too big. Fortunately, they all drank like fish so there was a pub. She laughed. In relating his account, he realised that it sounded more exciting than it had seemed at the time. Adventurous, even. He probably made it seem so. He knew he was trying to impress her. For some reason, he omitted telling her about Suzanne. That was finished. He really needed to phone her and tell her that although she probably knew it anyway. She had said as much to him before he left, he recalled.

They drank two bottles of Shiraz and he had a sense of being alive more than ever, especially after the incident in Leith. He asked her if she was seeing anyone.

'No, how about you?' she asked.

He shook his head. 'There was someone Down Under but it's over.' There was a moment's awkwardness, then they both laughed. He was aware of a mutual attraction between them. Something was pulling them together; he could feel it. They had both been victims of extremists and now valued life more than ever.

When the meal was finished and the bill paid, he said he had better head for the last train, but she said, 'Why don't you come back for coffee?' He knew what she meant and she knew that he understood. They got a taxi back to her Stockbridge flat and tore each other's clothes off as soon as they were inside. The idea of coffee was forgotten.

They both stood in the middle of her living room in their underwear, she in her red bra and panties, and he in his ridiculous Homer Simpson boxer shorts. She looked at them and laughed. He kissed her mouth and it tasted of the wine they had drunk. Soon they were making love.

Later that night, as he lay awake listening to her breathing, he found it hard to believe he was lying naked next to Aileen instead of in the Water of Leith. But it had been a close thing.

33

Stephen Christie was waiting at the spot he had been told to go to. It was midnight in the car park of the Riverside Museum and it was beginning to rain. The place was deserted. Not where he would have chosen to meet, but Valerie Farquharson had insisted that they meet somewhere where no one would see them together. Glancing around, he realised there were no CCTV cameras and began to wonder if this had been a good idea after all.

On Monday, after realising that he was in serious financial difficulties and that his future prospects as any kind of teacher were unlikely, Christie had decided that the one thing he was good at which could save him from penury, writing, would be his future. Now he would have the time to devote himself to being an author. He already had written several drafts of a screenplay, about a serial killer in Victorian Glasgow, which he had worked at on and off over the years. This could be the start of a whole new career. The university could go fuck themselves! He had plenty of ideas and, he thought, skill. There was now nothing to stop him from realising what had always, in fact been his ambition. Well, one thing. Lack of money. He would have to live and couldn't ask Chloe for money, she was a student, for God's sake, already running up an overdraft. Yes, he could try and find some kind of casual work, he supposed, but how easy was it to find even a job like that these days? No, he realised that he a needed some capital to kick-start his new life, so that he didn't have to worry about money and could concentrate on getting the script polished up and finished. He was sure it would be a success. Then he wouldn't be broke; he would be rolling in the stuff like a pig in shit.

He had looked up Valerie Farquharson's name on the website of the paper she wrote a column for, and found her email address. The email he sent her was brief and to the point. He had added his mobile number and on Tuesday morning he had received a text telling him to be waiting at the entrance to the car park at midnight that night.

He had a meeting with his lawyer, Jamie McEwan, to discuss the Henderson case, then spent the rest of the day feeling restless and agitated. He didn't say anything to Chloe about where he was going, just that he was going out to meet someone and would be back late. He got there at five minutes to twelve. It was freezing and he paced up and down trying to keep warm. He had visited the museum once or twice, but during the day when it was open and busy. Now it seemed a desolate corner of Glasgow, isolated and devoid of people or movement. The steel zig-zag roof of the Zaha Hadid structure stood out against the sky like a giant set of teeth. Beyond the building he could just make out faint ripples on the Clyde.

Suddenly he saw a pair of car headlights. He waved so it would see him and stop. It was coming towards him. He tried to get out of the way, but he realised in terror that the car was going too fast.

34

For the second time in as many days, Alex woke up feeling unsure of where he was. Aileen had already gone, but she had left him a note. *Last night was fun. Let's do it again soon. Help yourself to coffee etc. Aileen x.* Images of the previous night replayed in his head, which were all very pleasant. What was less pleasant was the thumping headache he had. He searched around the flat and eventually located some paracetamol and washed them down with orange juice he found in the fridge. He stood under the shower, letting the hot water bring him back to life. As he was getting dressed, Aileen's landline rang and he answered it.

'Who is this?' asked the caller. 'Where's Aileen?'

Alex thought he recognised the voice. 'Is that you, Jamie?'

'Yes, who's that?'

'Alex.'

'Alex? What the fuck are you doing in Aileen's flat?'

'Eh…'

'Never mind, I can guess. I don't suppose Aileen is there?'

'No, she's gone out. Why don't you try her mobile?'

'I have. It just goes to voicemail. I wanted to ask her if she had heard from Shona as I know the two of them have been in touch recently.'

'Why, what's happened?' Alex could tell from Jamie's tone that everything was far from normal.

'Shona has disappeared. She didn't come home last night and I can't get hold of her. It's not like her, I'm really worried.'

'When did you last see her?' asked Alex, buttoning his shirt with one hand.

'Yesterday morning when I left for work. I had to go out early for a meeting and she was still in the flat then with you. Did she say anything?'

'No. Just that she was going into work later on.'

'When she didn't come home yesterday, I tried calling her. This morning I phoned her office and spoke to her boss. He said she didn't come into work yesterday, didn't turn up at a meeting, and he hasn't heard from her since. He says he also has been trying to call her. Her Facebook page hasn't been updated since yesterday morning either.'

'Shit!' said Alex. He remembered those two guys in the van outside the flat. One of them had seemed familiar. He now realised where he had seen him before. At a loyalist social club meeting. He was sure of it. They had watched him leaving the flat. That explained the tail on him later. There might have been a third man in the back of the van who was sent to follow him. Or they phoned someone else the minute he had been spotted, recognising him, despite the beard. He could hear their words. 'Guess who we have just seen?' Then one of them staked out his old newspaper office, guessing he would drop by. They were right.

'Do you think this has something to do with that story she's been working on? About Scottish Action?'

Alex didn't want to tell Jamie about the guys in the van. He didn't want to panic him further. It was important to keep calm. Maybe he was wrong but he knew he wasn't. 'I hope not. She was in the flat when I left at ten. She said she was going out about eleven. Have you tried phoning the hospitals in case she has been in an accident or something?'

'Yes, I've phoned them all. She's not there.'

'What about the police?'

'I called them. Spoke to an officer. He said he'd note it down but to be honest I don't think they are interested.

When I told him I last saw her yesterday morning, he told me she may have just gone off somewhere by herself for a few days. If she didn't get in touch in the next forty-eight hours, I was to contact them again. The cop I spoke to said in most cases like this the person turns up. He seemed to be implying that she was off on a binge or having some sordid affair with someone. But that's not Shona! Her car is still here so she hasn't gone anywhere. I did get a message on my phone from a detective but it's about that guy Christie I am defending. I should call her back but my mind just isn't in it.'

'I know, I know. But let's not panic. Where are you?'

'I'm at home. I've phoned into the office and told them I won't be in today and cancelled all my appointments.'

'OK, I'll come round when I get back to Glasgow and we'll put our heads together and come up with a plan. I'll be there as soon as I can.'

Alex was sure that Shona had probably been targeted by the same people who had tried to kill him the night before. Scottish Action. There was no doubt about it.

When Alex arrived at Jamie's flat a couple of hours later, he found Jamie nervously pacing up and down the living room, anxiously checking his phone to see if there were any messages. 'Nothing. I've phoned all her friends that I can get hold of, and even her parents. I didn't want to tell them as they will worry, but I had to. Nobody has heard from her.'

Alex sat down on the sofa. 'Jamie, listen, there's something I've got to tell you.'

Jamie looked shocked. 'What is it? Do you know something? Tell me!'

'Yesterday, when I was leaving the flat, there was a black van parked outside with two guys inside. They looked like workmen. They were reading newspapers and I didn't think anything of them. But one looked familiar. Then I thought I was being followed when I left the Courier building. I saw the same guy in Edinburgh and realised that I had a tail.'

'You think there's a connection to the blokes in the van?'

'Yes. This morning, when you told me that Shona was missing, I thought about the men in the van and remembered where I'd seen one of them before. It was in a social club when I was working undercover. A loyalist event.'

'Shit. So, they were waiting for Shona.'

'I'm sorry I didn't make the connection yesterday.'

Jamie shook his head. 'Doesn't matter. What about the guy following you? Did you lose him?'

Alex nodded. 'Yes, after a brief struggle. He went for a dive in the Water of Leith. A wild swimming enthusiast, apparently!'

'Did you find out who he was?'

'I tried to get him to tell me why he was following me. He tried to kill me. There was a struggle. He hit his head on the quayside as he fell in the water. I thought he had drowned but then he surfaced and I didn't hang about to become better acquainted.'

'Jesus Christ, Alex.'

'I think they wanted to follow me to see who I was meeting in Edinburgh. That's why I was being followed.'

'Where were you going?'

'To see Aileen. Shona put me onto her as her source. It's good I didn't lead them to her. But the point is, they have taken Shona. I know it. After she wrote that article. They want to know where she got the leak from.'

'Bastards! It must be that shit Forsyth that's behind it. I know it! Shona destroyed his reputation and he wouldn't take that lying down. He's ex-Army, he's not going to mess around, either.'

'Phone that police inspector you mentioned. Tell her what we know,' said Alex.

Jamie shook his head. 'I already told you the police aren't interested.'

'You could just say that you have good reason to believe that Scottish Action have abducted your girlfriend and you suspect Cameron Forsyth is involved. Mention Shona's article. It's worth a try. '

'OK.' He dialled Shazia's number.

'Mr McEwan, thanks for calling back. Stephen Christie was killed in a hit and run last night. I wanted to ask if you have any idea who might want to kill him? Did he confide anything to you?'

'I'm sorry, Inspector, I don't. It's come as a complete surprise to me. I saw him yesterday and he didn't tell me anything that might help you, I'm afraid. But that's not why I am calling you.'

'No? Why, then?'

'It's about my girlfriend, Shona Williamson. She has disappeared. She is a journalist and wrote a story for the Gazette this week. You might have seen it. She exposed Cameron Forsyth's links to a far-right group, Scottish Action. I think he or his men have kidnapped her.' There was silence on the line. He thought for a moment that he had been cut off. 'Are you still there?' he said.

'You will need to report this to Missing Persons, Mr McEwan. I'm dealing with a murder inquiry here.'

'I've done that already, Inspector. They're not interested.'

'I understand your anxiety, but I am afraid there's not a lot I can do. Why do you think Mr Forsyth has your girlfriend? That's quite an allegation.'

'A witness saw a van parked outside the flat yesterday with two men in it. It looked odd. Suspicious. I think she's been abducted.'

'I'm sorry. Perhaps there is another explanation why your girlfriend has not let you know where she is. Hopefully she will turn up. In the meantime, if there is anything that occurs to you about Mr Christie's death, please get in touch with me, will you?' She hung up.

'I knew it! Not interested. Let's find Forsyth ourselves and ask him what he knows!'

'I'll ring his office and see if he is there.' He went into the kitchen, his phone clutched to his ear.

Jamie sat down at the table in front of the bay window and started searching for information online on his laptop.

Alex said, 'OK, I phoned Forsyth's office. I said I represented a group of overseas investors and asked if Mr Forsyth was available to discuss some potential investments in his company. His PA said he is not in the office and is unavailable. So, then I found a landline number for his home in Helensburgh and phoned his wife. I gave her the same spiel. She said he wasn't at home, that he was away for a few days and didn't want to be disturbed. What do we know about Forsyth? Does he have a holiday house somewhere remote where he might take her? Can we find out?'

Jamie nodded. 'The property register. If Forsyth owns property in Scotland it will have to be registered on that. Let's see.' He typed on his laptop keyboard. 'That's one advantage of being a lawyer. I can access this site with a password, otherwise for the general public you would have to wait a couple of days. OK. Here we are. Cameron Forsyth. Bingo! He has two properties registered in his name, a house in Helensburgh, his family home. But he's also got a cottage in Arran, a few miles outside Lamlash. That will be his holiday home. It's remote alright.'

'I bet that's where he has taken Shona. Right, we are going to have to try and find her. We'll take my car and head to Arran.'

'What? Do we just ring the bell and say "Is Shona in?"'

'No. We're just going to have to go inside and see if she is there. There's no time to lose. If she is, we get her out. But just in case….' He pulled a gun from the inside pocket of his jacket.

'What the fuck, Alex! Where did you get that thing?'

'Dropped by Jim Kelly's on my way from the station to your flat. He's no longer in the business but I thought he'd still keep a few weapons, just in case.'

'Kelly? How do you know him?'

'It's a long story. If we get through this night in one piece, maybe I'll tell it to you sometime. Let's get going.'

Jamie pointed at the gun. 'Do you even know how to use that thing?'

Alex nodded and tried to give Jamie the impression that he knew what he was doing, as if he was Billy the Kid, but the truth was actually something else entirely. The only guns he had fired were at the funfair. 'I hope I don't have to use it but if someone is shooting at me, I'd rather be able to shoot back than just stand there like a target on a firing range.'

Earlier, Alex had phoned Kelly saying he needed help and was told to come straight over. He had got to know Kelly through his former colleague on the Courier, Fergus Mulrein, who had told him that he had taught the gangster's sons when he had been a teacher. Alex had been working on a story about rival East End minicab firms and their links to gangsters, and Fergus had arranged a meeting with Kelly. The gangster had never involved himself in the taxi trade and was all too ready to tell some stories of his rivals which exposed their criminal connections.

Alex took a taxi from Queen Street station to Kelly's house in the East End of the city, territory which had been his patch for decades but which he was now relinquishing. A 'For Sale' sign sat at the front gate of his house.

Kelly, short and stout, held out his thick hand for a handshake at the front door, his other hand holding back the Rottweiler which sniffed at Alex's legs. 'Go and lie down, Yogi!' The dog turned around and slunk over to lie down in a basket in the hall. 'You did a good job wi' that story you wrote that time. But I thought you were fuckin' pan breed, big man! Heard the Orangemen were after you. I've no' seen anything else by you in the paper since. Thought you might huv ended up like yer pal Fergus, poor bastard!' said Kelly. He was wearing a grey cashmere V-neck jumper and jeans. His bald head shone in the bright light from the hallway.

Alex sat in an armchair and explained what had happened, that a friend of his, a female journalist who had written an article about far-right unionists, had suddenly gone missing, and he and a friend were going to try and find her. 'The thing is I don't want to go looking for her without something to protect myself, if you know what I mean?'

Kelly nodded and listened to Alex's story, sitting back into the folds of his soft leather sofa. When Alex had finished, he stood up without saying anything and left the room. He returned a few minutes later and handed Alex a heavy object wrapped in thick brown cloth. 'I've wiped it doon so as ma prints are nae on it,' said Kelly.

Alex unwrapped it and saw what it was. He had never handled a real gun before but Kelly showed him how to operate it. 'It's a Walther PPQ, a semi-automatic,' said Kelly. 'That means that the cartridges are in the magazine and once a round is fired, another one automatically goes into the chamber ready to go.' He showed Alex how the cartridge fitted into the gun. 'Don't release the safety until you are ready to fire.'

Alex paid close attention and nodded. 'Thanks, Jim. I owe you big time! How much do you want for it?'

'Dinnae mention it, son. Jist get rid o' this piece when you've finished wi' it. OK? Drap it in the sea or something. And if you get caught wi' it, whatever the fuck you say, don't say I gave you it, mind!'

'As if I would, Jim!'

'Aye well, ye better. Cos if ye dae you *will* be fuckin' pan breed, son!' Kelly said, laughing.

As Jamie drove out of Glasgow, heading westwards in his Audi A3, Alex wondered if Shona had been taken abroad or was already dead. She could have been dismembered and be lying in several pieces at the bottom of a loch somewhere. Alex thought of Aileen. If Shona had told Forsyth that Aileen was the source, then Aileen too would be in danger. He should warn her. He tried ringing her mobile number but it also was going to voicemail. He left a message asking her to phone him back as soon as she could. Then he thought of Shona again. What unspeakable acts would these insane terrorists put her through to try to make her talk?

35

One of the last things Shona remembered was a shaven-headed man asking her the time as she walked down the steps at the entrance to her apartment block just after eleven on Tuesday morning. It was just a short walk to Hillhead underground station and she hadn't needed her car, so planned to take the subway. She looked at her watch and then remembered being grabbed and bundled into a black VW van parked directly outside the flat. Inside the van, a pair of strong hands had firmly taped over her mouth and someone else had injected her with something which sent her into unconsciousness. Next thing she knew she was waking up in this hell-hole. She was evidently in a basement of some sort, with a concrete floor and bare walls. Two long strips of fluorescent lighting on the ceiling illuminated the room constantly, and apart from the mattress on the floor, the only furniture was a wooden table and chair. In one corner a bucket and a roll of toilet paper had been provided. She hadn't wanted to use it, but so great was the need to pee that it was use the bucket or piss herself. Two men had come in and ordered her to strip to her underwear. They took away her clothes and they had left her alone for a while but then later the interrogations started when Forsyth seemingly had arrived on the scene. The two thugs dragged her over to the chair and tied her to it with thick rope. Always the same questions, over and over, about the source of the leaked data, punctuated with punches to the face. She repeated the same answers. 'I don't know. I don't know. Someone sent it to me. It was anonymous.' They had taken her iPhone and laptop which she had been carrying, forcing her to give them her PIN and password. She knew they would have gone through her emails and messages, trying to find any clue to the source, then probably taken the battery out of the phone in case anyone tried to track where she was. It was just as well that Aileen hadn't emailed her the file. She couldn't give them Aileen's name as her source. It would only ensure that Aileen suffered the same fate as herself.

Finally, they had stopped and untied her. She felt cold, sick and dizzy. She had had nothing to eat. They had given up asking the questions and left her for the night and she had huddled on the mattress with only a thin blanket for any warmth. It was freezing and the light was constantly on. She felt completely disorientated, managed to fall asleep only fleetingly and had a strange, terrifying dream, waking up in a cold sweat to realise that the reality of being awake was even worse than the nightmare.

She had no idea of time but thought that it must be the next day now, Wednesday, but she didn't have a clue whether it was day or night. She felt that her brain had ceased to function and she was having all kinds of crazy thoughts. She couldn't hear any noises from outside. She could be anywhere. It felt strange to know that she was condemned, like a prisoner on death row. During the night when she couldn't sleep, she tried to think of the good people whom she had known in her life, to take her mind off the gruesome reality of the here and now. There were her parents, of course, and her sister Elizabeth. She recalled all the happy times from her childhood. Christmases, family holidays, birthdays. Then there were boyfriends. None of them had meant much until she had met Jamie. She had imagined that they would have a family themselves one day. The realisation that this would never now happen depressed her so, instead, she tried to blank out all thoughts entirely. That didn't work and she was left with the single inescapable truth: she was about to die.

The door opened and they came back in again, Forsyth and his two accomplices, both armed this time. Forsyth was carrying a large canvas bag which he put on the table.

'I've told you. I don't know who sent me it,' she said. 'Why won't you believe me?'

He slapped her across the face. 'That won't work. If you don't tell me, you will die very painfully. You have a choice.'

Tears were running down her cheeks and she imagined her eyes were the colour of a sunset. 'You're going to kill me anyway.'

'True. You're not so stupid after all. The difference is, if you tell me what I want to know, I will make it quick and painless. One gunshot to your head. However, if you continue to be uncooperative, I am afraid that your death will be long, slow and very painful. You know, before I joined the army, I once considered becoming a doctor. Of course, doctors always gave their patients an anaesthetic before surgery. I am afraid you will not have such a luxury.' He nodded his head at one of the thugs, the taller one, who put down his weapon, opened the bag and produced the rope and a variety of tools, laying them on the table: a hammer, a chisel, two sets of pliers, a Stanley knife and a pair of secateurs. 'You see Andy isn't so considerate. He would like to really make you suffer. He didn't take too well to having his name splashed all over the paper, either.' Shona had realised that the thug was Andrew Campbell, the supposed boss of the shell company she'd mentioned in her article. 'He'll start with a few amputations first. A lot of pain. Then I don't think you will be quite so stubborn. Now, this is your last chance before the real pain starts. I want to know where you got that information from.' Campbell advanced towards her.

36

In police HQ, Shazia was trying to process the fact that the dead body of Stephen Christie had been found in the car park of the Riverside Museum, apparently the victim of a hit and run. As yet there were no witnesses, but she had been emailed photos of the crime scene and the body. From the images and ID found on the body, it appeared to be Christie, though his wife would have to formally identify the body. This was no accident, she was sure. By all accounts, the approximate time of death had been around midnight. What was he doing there then? It was another gruesome and disturbing twist to the case. When she phoned the number she had for McEwan, it went to his voicemail and she left a message asking him to contact her urgently. McEwan was one of the more likeable defence lawyers, she thought, but when he phoned back, he had nothing to offer regarding Christie's death and had sounded as if he was in a panic about his missing girlfriend. Bizarrely, he seemed to think Cameron Forsyth had abducted her because she had written a newspaper story about his business interests being associated with far-right politics. It did sound far-fetched. She didn't have much time for the racist figure of Forsyth but could he really be a kidnapper? Anyway, she couldn't afford to get side-tracked from the Henderson investigation and dismissed the idea. She needed to concentrate on this case. It had just become more complicated. It looked like someone had deliberately killed Christie. Why would someone want him dead? Did he know more about Henderson's murder than he was letting on? If so, why hadn't he said anything when interviewed? She drove over to the museum car park to examine the scene. She wanted to see for herself what it looked like. Yet another night-time killing. It was turning into a hell of a couple of weeks and she had been right in thinking the killings hadn't finished.

Forensics had taped off the area and were scouring the scene for clues. The body had been removed but she was told that fortunately the ground had been wet and the tyre tracks on the ground and on the body would be analysed. That could help identify the vehicle if they had a lead. She would make sure that some officers examined the CCTV on the roads nearby but unfortunately the museum's cameras were at the entrance and wouldn't have picked up anything in the car park itself, so there would be no actual footage of the incident. This was no accident, she was sure. Not only had someone knocked him down, they had then run him over for good measure. Why was he here in such an isolated spot in the middle of the night? Was he waiting to meet someone? Someone who wanted him dead? Who? His wife? She'd need to be treated as a suspect and questioned. She might have decided she'd had enough of her cheating, lying husband and, in a fit of anger and jealousy, wanted rid of him permanently.

At the investigation team meeting that afternoon, they discussed Christie's death, but there was no obvious connection to the case. There may be no connection at all. He could have been meeting a drug dealer. Or it could have been another sexual encounter leading to death. Mitchell would interview Christie's wife, Juliet. They switched to talking about Peter Boyle. Joseph had phoned Shazia after he and Mitchell had left Boyle's flat to tell her that his alibi was in shreds. 'Maybe someone tipped him off that Henderson was going to be staying there,' said Joseph. 'He could have broken into the hotel and gone up to Henderson's room, said he was from reception, and Henderson let him in just as we speculated before.'

Shazia stood up and paced around the table like a cat. All eyes followed her. 'Could be. Here is another thought. Robert Jackson killed Scobie for some reason, ripping off the supplier, whoever that is, perhaps Murray – or non-payment of money owed, whatever. But why would Jackson

266

kill Henderson? And what's the connection between the two murders, if there is one? Then the boss of the escort business is found with a bullet through his brain. Maybe to shut him up in case he felt persuaded to talk? It's all got to have something to do with Murray. Scobie had Murray's number tucked away. What if Murray is behind the escort agency connected to Henderson's death? Robertson was just a front man, in other words.'

Mitchell said, 'Scobie might have been ripping off Murray. Diluting the drugs, making more profit for himself. He had to be made an example of to any other dealers thinking of going off the script. Could Murray have wanted Henderson dead too? Maybe Henderson borrowed money from Murray?'

Shazia nodded and said, 'You wouldn't normally expect someone like Henderson to be mixed up with a gangster like Murray, but then again, we know he had contact with sex workers and liked gambling. The Murray brothers don't like it if someone falls behind with paying their debts. It sets a bad example.'

'Jackson has previous for violence after all,' said Joseph. 'Someone hired him to carry out the hit on Henderson.'

Shazia said, 'There's no sign of Jackson's car in the city centre later on at any time that night after he picked her up again and took her home. He claims he drove to his girlfriend's after taking Katarina home and his car is spotted on a camera going through Govan and through the tunnel and up Balshagray Avenue towards Knightswood. So that all fits the story he is telling us.'

Mitchell looked at her notebook. 'His girlfriend, Nicola Miller, manages a tanning salon in Anniesland owned by Murray. Her story corroborates what Jackson told us about his movements, saying he spent all night with her. As you would expect. Same as she said about the night of Scobie's murder.'

'Yes, all very convenient. But, on the other hand, we have nothing to put him back at the hotel. There's no sign of his girlfriend's car on city centre CCTV that night either.'

Mitchell said, 'If Jackson had the keycard he could get into Henderson's bedroom in the middle of the night and kill him and leave without anyone seeing him. Maybe Christie witnessed Jackson in the hotel that night when he was leaving Henderson's room. The fact that he has now been killed makes me think that someone knows he could identify Jackson.'

'You could be right. Everything points at Jackson as the killer. But a defence lawyer would take a sledgehammer to a prosecution case based on the testimony of someone like Katarina, a sex worker and drug addict who has a grievance against him, accusing him of forcing her to do something against her will to get herself off the hook. There's no evidence to back up her statement that she gave him the room key, and Jackson will continue to say she is lying. He will deny that he asked her to drug him and say she supplied the ketamine and Henderson took the drug willingly. It's her word against his. We're going round in circles speculating,' said Shazia. 'OK, everyone, take a break, then back to work. Put everything you've got into this and see if you can turn anything else up to nail the killer. We're making progress, but I'll have the DCI on my back again soon, which is the last thing I want.'

Two hours later, Shazia hurriedly assembled the team again. She said, 'We've got a possible lead. Joseph just got a call.'

Joseph nodded. 'Someone just called me from the vice team. I'd asked them to ask around and find out if any other escorts had dealings at the Moray Hotel. Seems that a sex worker has reported that she once had a client during the night in the hotel. She says she was let in to the hotel during the night and had sex with a client in the jacuzzi in the health suite.'

Mitchell raised her eyebrows. 'Sex in a jacuzzi, how unhygienic!'

'Yes, especially as she says the client was the night porter. Plus, she got the job from the Discreet agency.'

Shazia was suddenly reminded her of the first time she had met the night porter, Callum Grant, that first day in the hotel, and the odd look she had seen in his eyes. 'OK, I think I am beginning to understand what has been going on. We need to speak to Callum Grant.' An instinct had told her then what that look was, but she had dismissed it at the time. That had been a big mistake.

37

Callum Grant and a young duty solicitor acting for him, Mark Stevenson, were seated in an interview room in Police HQ. Shazia and Joseph entered and went through the preliminaries. Shazia was carrying a folder. She said, 'Callum, we have discovered some important information relating to the investigation which concerns you. You have been arrested on suspicion of conspiracy to commit murder.'

'What?' Grant looked as if he was about be sick.

'Grant, you were on duty the night Charles Henderson was killed. We believe you had a part to play in the events of that night.'

Grant said nothing.

'You are in the habit of letting prostitutes into the hotel at night, aren't you?'

'I don't know what you are talking about!' said Grant, twitching and turning to look at his solicitor.

'There is no point in denying it as we have a witness stating that you let her in and had sex with her in the jacuzzi. Only, on that night you didn't just let in a prostitute, you let in a killer. Or killers. That makes you guilty of murder.' Grant said nothing, but his face changed. His brow suddenly creased. The night porter's hands started to shake. He was clearly in a state of shock. 'You haven't been honest with us,' said Shazia. 'That is serious, Callum. You have misled a murder investigation. We know you have had a sex worker in the hotel at night when you were working. I know this is connected to what happened on the night of 6th February. If you assist us now, it will help you. Maybe you didn't know there was going to be a murder that night. If you play ball, you could face a lesser charge and maybe get a couple of years behind bars. But if you don't cooperate, it will count against you and you will be facing a murder charge, looking at a life sentence. I am afraid that the net is closing in on you,

Callum. This is your chance to open up and tell us what really happened that Monday night.'

Grant seemed to stare into space, lost in his thoughts. Shazia had been bluffing about the net closing in on him, but her instinct this time had not let her down. And her instinct was telling her that Grant was lying now. 'Callum. If a jury is convinced that you were complicit in the murder, you are looking at a life sentence. That is what the prosecution will be saying. On the other hand, if you didn't know what was going to happen, you are looking at a lesser sentence. I really need you to be honest with me. Tell me the whole truth this time.'

Grant said nothing at first. Shazia could see that he was clearly weighing up the options: say no more and face the consequences, or get everything off his chest. At last, he opted for the latter course and she could see the relief on his face as he finally told her what had happened. 'One day, I think it was the Friday before the guy got killed, I had a phone call on my mobile from a woman who said her name was Katherine. She said she had got my number from the escort agency and she wanted to speak to me privately, saying she knew about my arrangements with escorts in the hotel. I told her I didn't know what she was talking about. Then she said, "Do your employers want to know how you have had sex in your hotel when you were working?" I asked her what she wanted. She wanted to meet me in a pub in the city centre.'

'So, you agreed to meet her?'
'Yes.'
'What happened?'

'She took out her phone and played me a video clip. It was of me having sex with a girl in one of the treatment rooms. I had booked two girls one night. It was ages ago. I guess one of them had filmed it on her phone when I was with the other girl.'

'What did she want?'

'A key which would open any hotel room.'

'What did you say to this?'

'I refused. I told her I didn't want anything to do with it. Then she asked me if I wanted my employers to see what she had on her phone? I said I couldn't give her a keycard. They were tightly controlled. The bosses would find out I'd given it to her.'

'So, what did she say?'

'She said there was going to be a break-in in the hotel on the following Monday night, sometime in the early hours. She told me that if I heard anything, I was to ignore it.'

'You knew they were going to commit a crime in your hotel and you did nothing about it.'

He nodded. 'I had no choice. She said that someone who was going to be staying in the hotel had something valuable which belonged to her and she wanted it back. She was sending some men in to get it. She said they would make it look like a burglary. She told me no one would get hurt. I didn't know someone was going to be killed. I just thought they were going to steal something. I didn't even know which room it was they were wanting to get into.'

'Did you see who it was?'

'No. I stayed in reception. She told me that if I was seen that night the video went online.'

'Anything else you can tell us?' she asked.

'No. That's it. I'm sorry the guy died. I honestly didn't know that's what they were going to do.'

Shazia had been right about the strange look in his eyes that Tuesday morning when she had first met Grant in the hotel. She should have listened to the voice inside her head signalling what it was. The look of guilt.

'Describe this woman, Katherine, who came to see you on Friday night. What did she look like?'

'I couldn't really see much of her face. She was wearing dark glasses and had a scarf tied around her hair but there were some blonde strands.   Oh yes, I noticed something as she lifted her drink.'

Shazia immediately recognised who "Katherine" was when Grant told her something he had noticed about her: a tattoo of a butterfly on the inside of her wrist. Jennifer Gibson, Forsyth's mistress. After Grant was taken into custody, they went straight to Forsyth's offices with two squad cars and asked to speak to Gibson. When Gibson saw Shazia from the other end of the corridor, she turned and disappeared through a side door.

'Go after her,' said Shazia. Joseph sprinted down the corridor along with a uniformed officer and Shazia sat down on a soft leather sofa in a spacious bright room with floor-to- ceiling windows. The furnishings were expensive looking, gleaming chrome and polished leather. The modern art on the walls looked original, but cold and devoid of expression. To Shazia the signs of corporate wealth were a thin veneer of culture trying to mask the real purpose of the place: profit. A few minutes later, Joseph returned with Gibson in handcuffs. 'We need to talk to you,' said Shazia. 'Even if you don't seem to want to talk to us. And we want to know where your boss is.'

38

Jamie drove at high speed towards the Ardrossan ferry while Alex stared out of the window. Neither of them said much, lost in their own dark thoughts, wondering what was happening – or had already happened – to Shona. Jamie didn't seem in the mood for chatting. Alex found a War Against Drugs CD in the glove compartment, slotted it into the CD player, and looked out of the window. There wasn't much to see in the darkness. Rain was pelting the windows. Bad weather was sweeping in from the Atlantic and Jamie, driving like a maniac, expressed concern that the ferries might be cancelled. Alex checked the Calmac website on his phone but they were in luck, there were no cancellations so far.

When they got to Ardrossan, a ferry was about to leave so they were able to drive straight on board. They bought coffee and sandwiches from the cafeteria and grabbed seats in the lounge. Then there was the sound of the engines starting up and the ferry moved off and out of the harbour. As soon as they were into the open water of the Firth of Clyde the ship began to rock up and down as the swelling waves tossed it around like a piece of flotsam. Alex said, 'Just nipping out for some fresh air.'

'You're mad, it's freezing out there,' said Jamie.

Alex smiled and zipped up his jacket, heading for the door to the open deck. He needed to escape from the claustrophobic atmosphere of the ferry's lounge. Everything had happened so quickly; they had been spurred on with adrenaline. But now, sailing off into the darkness, with no time to pause, he felt suddenly anxious and didn't want to let Jamie see it. That's why he had to get out and collect his thoughts. The truth was that he felt scared of what might happen when they got to Forsyth's house. Perhaps Shona wouldn't be there, but they were walking into an unknown and dangerous situation. After the events of last year when his life was in danger, he had wanted to live a quiet life and for a while had succeeded. However, the violent world seemed to shadow his every move and here again he was on the brink of encountering a menacing situation, and he felt partly to blame. If only he had remembered where he had seen that guy in the van before, then none of this would have happened. He could have warned Shona.

Outside, the air tasted salty and the icy wind bit into his skin like razor blades. The rain lashed down and he realised that there was no point being out here for long as he would turn into a drowned rat, but he stood for a few seconds watching the waves crash against the hull and looking out towards Arran. It was just possible to make out the distinctive silhouette of the mountain of Goatfell against the moonlight in the night sky and ahead he could see the lights of Brodick in the distance gradually getting closer.

When they got off the ferry, Jamie took the road to Lamlash at lightning speed and they left the car half a mile from Forsyth's Arran house and walked up the steep incline, Alex feeling the weight of the gun in his jacket and Jamie carrying a tyre wrench from his car. The detached house sat in a secluded spot on a hillside overlooking the bay to the front, with dense wood behind and overgrown rhododendron bushes at the sides. The rain had ceased and there was an eerie stillness. Suddenly, there was a break in the clouds and a full moon shone down on the house like a searchlight. They could see a dark blue Bentley Continental GT and a black VW van parked on the gravel driveway in front of the house. Alex nodded towards them. 'That's the van that was parked outside the flat on Tuesday morning.'

Jamie said, 'I'm going to try the police again. Now we have some proof. I'll tell them the van is here.' But he stared at his phone hopelessly. 'Shit!' he said. 'No signal.' Somewhere behind them in the woods an owl hooted. Other than that, everything was silent and still.

Alex was standing with one arm propped against a tree as he urinated against it. Clouds rolled back over the moon and blanketed it, leaving the house in darkness again. Alex said, 'That's better, I needed that slash. We don't have time to get the police. We need to go in. Let's try the back door.'

They crossed the road towards the house and moved stealthily round the side garden to the back of the house, using the flashlights on their phones to see in the dark. There was a small conservatory at the back with a glass-panelled door. Alex held the revolver pointed at the door while Jamie tried the handle. 'It's locked,' said Jamie.

'We'll have to smash a window,' said Alex. 'Give me that wrench.' He handed Jamie the gun, took off his leather jacket, wrapped it around the wrench, and swiftly punched a panel of the glass in the door. There was a tinkle of broken glass that Alex thought anyone in the house would surely hear and they both froze and listened for a few seconds. But there wasn't a sound. He put his jacket back on and reached in and turned the key that was on the inside of the door. They were inside. Jamie was glad to exchange the gun for the wrench as Alex took the lead, inching forward, the gun pointing into the darkness in front of them.

They made their way through the ground floor as quietly as possible, Alex feeling his way along the wall in the darkness. They found their way into the kitchen and Jamie put down the wrench and picked up a carving knife from a knife block. They inched cautiously and slowly further into the darkened house towards a sliver of light coming from a gap in a doorway halfway along the passageway. Alex peeked through the gap, saw that it led to a set of stairs down to a basement. Suddenly a voice said, 'Put the gun down, arsehole! And the knife ya bawbag!'. Alex turned and saw a man standing in the shadows with a gun pointed at them. Alex slowly bent down and put the gun on the floor. At the same time, Jamie dropped the knife, but then suddenly threw a punch at the man's head. 'Aaagh,' he screamed. A gunshot went off. Alex picked up his own gun and aimed at the man and fired.

'Aaaaargh! Fuck!' screamed the man again, holding his leg this time.

Jamie was prising the gun from his fingers when another voice shouted. 'Freeze, motherfuckers! Drop your weapons. Hands in the air!' They looked up to see a tall man standing over them holding what looked like a submachine gun. Alex felt something heavy hit him on the head. He slumped to his knees and a kick to his back sent him falling down the staircase.

39

Alex felt as if his skull had been crushed from all sides, which is roughly what had happened when he had been thrown down the stairs. He realised he couldn't move his arms or his legs, looked to his left and saw Jamie beside him, his hands and feet similarly bound together tightly with gaffer tape and his face covered in blood. There were four other people in the room, two of them the men who had surprised them upstairs. One of those, the one he'd shot, was lying on the floor, sweating and swigging from a bottle of whisky with one hand, while shakily holding his revolver in the other. He was the one in the van outside Shona's flat, the one he'd later remembered from a loyalist meeting, too much later. The other, the taller of the two, was pointing his submachine gun at them; he now realised that he had been the other occupant of the van. They were both shaven-headed, muscular and in their forties, with tattoos on their bulging arms, identical black T-shirts and combat trousers. Ex-Army, he thought, wondering if the man who he had fought with in Leith had also been an ex-squaddie.

There was also another man, an older man, in his fifties, dressed in an open-necked white shirt and jeans. Alex recognised him immediately as Cameron Forsyth. The fourth person was Shona. She was tied to a chair and her face was bloody and bruised. She was wearing only a black bra and panties and she was shivering, whether with fear or cold he didn't know, but she looked scared to death. A pool of blood lay on the concrete floor from where, evidently, a finger had been removed from Shona's right hand. The stump had been bandaged up. They evidently didn't want her to bleed to death. She stared at Alex with a look of terror.

'Welcome to Arran,' said Forsyth, walking over to Alex and standing over him with his legs on either side of Alex's prostrated body. 'It's a shame you can't appreciate the view from down here. The house really does have a terrific prospect. I'm sorry not to be more hospitable but we weren't expecting visitors, you see.' He gave Alex a kick in the balls. 'Andy, search them!'

The tall one handed his weapon to Forsyth and went through their pockets, pulling out phones, wallets and driving licences. He handed them over to Forsyth and took back the gun.

'So, you are the lawyer boyfriend,' Forsyth said to McEwan. 'Which one had the gun?' he asked.

Campbell pointed to Alex. 'This one, boss.'

'Forsyth picked up Kelly's Walther from the table. approached Alex and held its barrel to his forehead. Alex felt the cold steel and took a deep breath, thinking that it might be his last. 'Alex Mancini. The journalist who wrote that newspaper article about our boys. Another fucking left-wing journalist. Think you're clever, don't you? One of our lads followed you through to Edinburgh yesterday, but says you lost him.'

Alex thought that his pursuer wouldn't have wanted to admit he got the better of him and he ended up in the sea.

Forsyth swung his hand and hit Alex in the mouth with the gun. 'Not so clever now!'

'Fuck you!' said Alex, spitting out blood and a broken tooth.

Forsyth laughed. 'So, you are full of the old fighting spirit, are you? Mancini. Italian name. A Catholic of course. Are you an IRA sympathiser? Is that where you got the gun, eh? It's not a bad piece. Get it from your friends in the Provos, or is it the Real IRA these days?' Forsyth was waving Kelly's gun around as he spoke and Alex was seriously worried that it might accidentally go off. On the other hand, if it did go off there was an outside chance that the bullet might ricochet off the walls and hit Forsyth in the skull. Equally, it could hit any one of them. 'What's up?' said Forsyth. 'Cat got your tongue? Don't worry, soon you won't need it. Just like this other journalist here. She thought she was being very clever telling her story, but look where it got her.'

Jamie said, 'You're finished, Forsyth.'

'No. That's where you are wrong. That story of your girlfriend's will all blow over very quickly, it will soon be yesterday's news. But I want to make sure you don't get your hands on anything else so I want to know her source. Someone hacked into a server and uncovered my accounts. I don't like that and I have business partners who are not so keen on being exposed either. Would it surprise you if I told you there are some powerful businessmen in the States putting money into our operation, and at least one Russian close to the Kremlin? Did you really think that the Russians would just turn and go away? Of course not, they are not stupid.'

Alex said, 'It doesn't matter. You really think that whatever a small bunch of crackpots and homophobic racist bigots do will make the slightest bit of difference?'

'That's where you are also wrong. You see, emotion is much more powerful than reason, so when you strike at people's fears, you tap into their subconscious anxieties. Even if there is nothing of substance to fear, people can imagine the threat if you conjure it up as a spectre. Then they will turn to those who offer solutions. Look at what happened after the Buchanan Street bombing. There was an upsurge of support for law and order when people feel afraid, feel threatened. Who will they trust to deliver that? The SNP? The socialists? I don't think so.'

'So, you just use your terrorists to provoke other terrorists!'

'Our terrorists? Do you think the public see attacks on mosques in the same way as a bomb on the Glasgow Underground or at Glasgow Airport? No, they see that as us defending our country. We are the real patriots. These Muslims are a scourge. I know, I fought the bastards in

Afghanistan. I didn't see good men dying and losing limbs over there just to have a bunch of mad Muslims planting bombs on the streets of Glasgow!'

'You're no patriot, you're nothing but a racist!' screamed Shona.

'No. I just believe that we should put Britons first. When people are afraid, they ask questions about why this is happening and look for answers. Immigration is the problem behind stopping Islamic terrorism but as long as we are a member of the EU, we must have freedom of movement so we can't control our own borders. More of our MSPs are beginning to see that this is the issue and the public will do too. The nationalists are in decline, their day is over, and soon the country will be tired of them. The socialists' economic policies are pie in the sky and will soon prove to be illusory. Re-nationalisation? It's a joke. How much would it cost? Taxes would have to rise to levels the country had never seen before and we would have national debt that makes what Greece had look like pocket money. Anyway, people are essentially selfish. They are only interested in bettering themselves. Let me tell you something else, you journalists. You may already know that many wealthy Russians have donated money to the Scottish Conservatives. It's not a secret. Over a million pounds last year. And they help us in other ways too. That Kalashnikov that Andy is holding, where do you think that came from? Did you think that it was just my money that was going into Mercat Partners?' He shook his head. 'You don't know the half of it.'

Alex thought about rumours that Russia had influenced the independence referendum. And in Westminster, there had been a sharp increase in the number of Tory MPs suddenly backing the idea of leaving the EU, including some of those at the highest levels of leadership in the party who had previously been supportive of being in Europe. Vast sums had been donated to the Tory Party in

England from Russian oligarchs with penthouses in the capital city.

'I've had enough of talking. I don't like people who break into my house. You thought you were being very clever but in fact we heard you breaking in. Idiots! You wouldn't last two seconds in the military, you pussies!' He turned away and spoke to the other men. 'When we have finished with her, we will dispose of them all. Put all three bodies in the van and drive round to the boat, take them out to sea, put some weights on them and dump them.'

He turned and looked at Shona. 'So, little miss journalist, now that you realise that your friends are not going to rescue you, maybe you will realise that you have no hope and cooperate. Either tell me what I want to know or have an hour or two of incalculable suffering. And, unlike the heroine of Fifty Shades of Grey, I don't think you will enjoy the pain that we will administer to you.'

Shona screamed.

'I've told you, there is no point in screaming. We are in a basement, a mile from the nearest house. No one will hear you. Andy will take a finger from the other hand this time. Unless you tell me where that leak came from.'

40

Adele Forsyth stared mystified at the two detectives. She was a very attractive woman, with long brown hair and a stunning figure, at least twenty years younger than her husband. She took them into the front room. 'I have no idea where Cameron is.' Her French accent sounded as exotic as her appearance, but her ignorance sounded suspicious. Gibson had said the same and there was no answer from Forsyth's mobile number when Shazia tried calling it.

'I have to warn you, Adele,' said Shazia.' That you are in danger of obstructing a police enquiry, a criminal offence. If you know anything about Cameron's whereabouts it is essential that you tell us. If you don't, then you will have to face the consequences, which potentially could be serious for you. '

Adele Forsyth paused and bit her lip. 'He is at the holiday house but he asked me not to tell anyone where he was.'

'Where is that?' asked Joseph.

'Near Lamlash, in Arran,' she said. 'He sometimes goes there when he needs to work on something important. It's quite isolated. He says there are too many distractions here.' She smiled.

'We've tried phoning your husband, but he's not picking up.'

'There's hardly any mobile signal in the cottage and no landline. You have to go down to the village, which is where he phoned me from earlier.'

'When did he go to Arran?'

'Yesterday. He said he wanted to get away for a couple of days and gather his thoughts. He said he would be back tomorrow. I know that the business is going through a difficult time and he said he needed to have some time away to work on a recovery plan. I think he might be there with a couple of advisers but I don't know their names.'

Shazia said, 'I need to ask you for the address of the house. It's very important that we find your husband as soon as possible.' She recalled McEwan's earlier phone call, which at the time she had dismissed; his distressed tone and his panic that Forsyth had abducted his girlfriend. Suddenly it wasn't so far-fetched after all. She remembered him saying that the journalist who wrote the report linking Forsyth to the far right was Shona Williamson. McEwan must be convinced Forsyth had taken her and, if the newspaper story was accurate about his links to extremists, she was in serious danger. These were serious paramilitaries and there was a good chance that whoever had abducted her was armed.

She tried ringing McEwan back but couldn't get through. Maybe it was the signal? As Forsyth's wife had said, on Arran, if that was where he had gone looking for Forsyth, a signal was unpredictable.

'We need to get to Arran fast,' she said to the rest of the team as they stood outside Forsyth's Helensburgh house, having left an officer to supervise Adele Forsyth and make sure she didn't attempt to contact her husband. 'I'm calling HQ and requesting a helicopter flies us to Arran immediately with an armed response team.'

On Arran a fleet of vehicles had been assembled to meet them. Detective Superintendent Hamilton and DCI Cooper had taken a helicopter from Glasgow and picked Shazia and Joseph up from a school football pitch on the edge of Helensburgh. An armed response team met them on the island, arriving by speedboat from the mainland. Everything had been quickly approved at Assistant Chief Constable level once Shazia explained that there was evidence that Forsyth was now the chief suspect in a murder investigation and also suspected of kidnapping. Within minutes of the helicopter arriving in a field in Whiting Bay, the fleet of vehicles was tearing round the coastal road towards Lamlash. When they arrived outside the house the Swat team took up their positions. Shazia, Cooper and Hamilton put on flak jackets and stood well back. The building was shrouded in darkness but the two vehicles parked on the driveway signalled that it was occupied.

Shazia was informed that a local dog-walker had reported hearing gunshots from the building. A loudhailer was brought from a vehicle and the Detective Superintendent spoke into it. 'This is the police. Come out with your hands up!'

They waited. There was no response. Hamilton issued a further identical message, adding, 'If you do not answer, we are coming in!'

There was silence from inside the house. Hamilton gave the command for the armed response team to go in. The first thing to do was to break down the front door, and one of the biggest officers stepped forward and lunged at the door with a heavy weighted steel tube. The oak door splintered. He hit it a second time and the lock gave way and the door flew open. Several armoured and helmeted officers wielding submachine guns and wearing masks charged into the house, shouting, 'Police! Put your hands in the air!' There was an indecipherable shout from the house and a sudden burst of gunfire. One of the armed officers returned fire with a blast of bullets from his automatic weapon and threw a stun grenade downstairs; the gunfire suddenly ceased and then there was only one sound: a woman's scream pierced the night air.

After the armed team had gone into the building the officers outside could only stand and wait to see what the outcome was going to be. Then one of the armed officers came over to Hamilton. 'Active shooter incapacitated with force. One fatality, sir. No injuries on our side.'

A short time later the armed officers emerged, leading out the familiar limping figure of Forsyth in shirt sleeves, his hands handcuffed behind him. Then another man emerged, a younger man dressed in black, also handcuffed, stumbling as if wounded, his trousers blood-stained. Following them, two men were helped out, and then a young woman dressed only in her underwear was carried from the building and placed on a stretcher. All were coughing from the after-effects of the percussive grenade. Shazia recognised one of the men as McEwan, Christie's lawyer; the other one, tall and bearded, she didn't recognise. The woman she didn't know either but guessed she was the journalist, Shona Williamson. As she was carried to the ambulance a foil blanket was hurriedly thrown over her as a flash went off: a local photographer who had been alerted to the speeding convoy had evidently arrived on the scene. Shazia watched the ambulance speed off and the two men go into a second ambulance along with a couple of police officers. Forsyth and the wounded man were whisked away under armed guard in secure police vans. There would be time to conduct interviews later, she thought.

The basement had been thick with smoke from the percussive devices and it took a while for this to clear enough for them to enter the building. Shazia went in with Hamilton and Cooper and descended the steps into the basement. A body lay sprawled across the bottom of the staircase, spread-eagled on its back, the force of the gunshot having blown him backwards apparently. One more corpse. How many had she seen in the past couple of weeks? Too many. But they still had the power to shock. This one's head had been blown apart; brains and blood had spilled everywhere. What had once been a face now was just a mass of bloody pulp. He had evidently taken the gunshot face-on. Another vehicle took him to the local mortuary to await a post-mortem the next day. There would have to be an investigation into the fatal shooting, but Shazia felt confident that the circumstances supported the decision for the course of action.

The rest of the night was a blur of activity, conversations, and statements being taken in the local police station and then the journey back to Glasgow with the two prisoners. The dead man was identified as Andrew Campbell and the wounded one as Iain Thompson. Both, she found out later, were former soldiers.

41

As they headed down the Clyde coast once again, the rain was being blown in from the sea by a gale. Clouds raced across the sky. The river looked dark and turbulent. In the Helensburgh house, Shazia and Joseph, along with several uniformed officers and a forensic team of SOCOs, began a thorough search of the property. Forsyth's wife, Adele, seemed genuinely shocked by what had happened, though Shazia left room for doubt. She could just be a very good actress as well as an interior designer; good with putting an artificial gloss on things. 'I had no idea that Cameron was involved in these kinds of things. He never spoke about it. It wasn't until that story appeared in the newspaper that I knew anything about it. I can't believe that he would want to have anything to do with violence!'

Shazia said, 'Your husband has been arrested on suspicion of the murder of Charles Henderson, as well as abduction, false imprisonment and attempted murder of a young woman. The men he was with were armed and dangerous. It appears that he was threatening the life of a young woman. He inflicted some very serious injuries on her and she is in intensive care after surgery. She is lucky to be alive. If you know anything about this, now is the time to tell us.'

'Murder? No, of course not. He never spoke to me about any of this. I am sure there is some explanation for this. Cameron could never have murdered Charles. They were friends. Can I see him?'

'Not at the moment,' said Shazia.

Shazia explored the house, awestruck by the extravagance on view in every room: a gigantic Bang and

Olufsen TV on one wall, several Persian rugs, paintings –
what looked like an original LS Lowry painting hung in one
room – and everywhere, designer furniture: a Barcelona
chair caught her eye. She put on a pair of blue latex gloves
and searched through drawers in a desk in a study which
Forsyth seemingly used for work; it was littered with papers
relating to his businesses. She sat down at his desk and
started up his computer, having been given the password by
his wife. She went to his emails and began to trawl through
them, looking at the senders. She was about to give up on
finding anything of interest when she found something.
There was one email with an odd sender's address. There
was no clue as to who sent it but it explained a lot. Suddenly
everything fell into place.

42

Shona lay in a bed in the Intensive Care Unit, a drip sending fluid into her arm. Wires attached to parts of her anatomy led to various monitors which, at regular intervals, made a reassuring beeping noise. Her right hand was bandaged where she had had an operation to surgically reattach her severed finger. She was propped up and could see out of the window, but her head was fuzzy with morphine and she wasn't in the mood to appreciate it. She was on the second top floor of the hospital and the window faced west. It was a clear day and she could just make out the shape of Arran's hills in the far distance. She looked away. She didn't wish to be reminded of that place and would be quite happy never to visit that island again.

She closed her eyes. Despite the drugs that were continuously being pumped into her veins, she still felt pain, or was that just her imagination? She had been convinced that she was going to die and had been resigned to it, knowing that she could only hang out for so long. The thought of telling Forsyth that Aileen Buchan was her source just to stop the torture went through her mind but she stopped herself. One part of her brain just wanted it all to stop, a bullet to her head would have been quick and then it would all be over with. It seemed appealing. If she just told them Aileen was the one who gave her the information, then they would stop hurting her and kill her quickly. But she couldn't do it. She couldn't let them do to Aileen what they were doing to her, or worse. And so it would go on. They wouldn't stop torturing and killing until they had discovered the source of the hack. Aileen had told her it had arrived anonymously but maybe she was just being secretive, maybe she really knew who was behind it?

When Alex and Jamie had been brought down and tied up, everything had felt even more hopeless. Up until then she had thought at least that Jamie wasn't there and there was a chance he might manage to alert the police and they would find her. She hadn't thought there was any chance that he or Alex would themselves be captured. Then all hell broke loose. The police were seemingly outside. There was confusion inside the basement. Forsyth and the wounded man said they were going to have to surrender but one of the men, Campbell, argued. 'I'm not giving myself up. I'm going to shoot my way out,' he said. He launched himself up the staircase just as the door upstairs crashed in. There was gunfire and more shots, and the man who had launched himself upstairs came tumbling back down and lay dead in a heap. There was a sudden flash and an explosion. She surprised herself by vomiting. She hadn't thought that there was anything left inside her to throw up. Then police in body armour, masks and machine guns appeared and Forsyth, with his henchmen dead or wounded, found himself trapped with nowhere to go, and quickly surrendered, throwing his hands in the air.

She remembered being released from the chair and lifted out of the smoky basement and placed on a stretcher, covered in foil like a chicken about to go into an oven, then transferred into an ambulance and driven off at high speed. Fortunately, before going off in the ambulance, someone had noticed the bloody stump on her hand and found her severed finger. At some point she had been given a pain-killing injection. Then she remembered being outside in the darkness again and being taken off the island by helicopter. Next thing, they landed on the roof of this hospital in the dark and she was whisked into the operating theatre as soon as she arrived. It would be one hell of a story, her editor had told her when he had phoned her that morning. But she was in no mood for telling it at the moment. It might be months before she could put down in words what had happened to her.

Her parents had been with her for an hour and had just left when she saw someone approaching her bed. Jamie stood there smiling with a bunch of grapes in one hand and a copy of the Gazette in the other. 'Congratulations! You've made the front page of your own newspaper,' he said holding up the paper. A photograph of Shona on a stretcher being carried from the Arran house to an ambulance by paramedics occupied a quarter of the page under the headline 'ONE DEAD IN ARMED RAID.'

Shona looked at the picture and tried to smile. 'Just as well my mum always told me to wear decent underwear. "You never know what might happen to you", she'd say. By God, was she right!'

43

At 9:30 pm, Angus McLennan answered the door of his Bridge of Allan house, a large two-storey Victorian villa with a view over the River Forth. A white Range Rover with a personalised number-plate which Shazia recognised, sat in the driveway beside a black Mercedes SLK 200. Rain, turning to sleet, was hammering on the windows and the wind was battering the front of the house. McLennan was holding a crystal glass containing a couple of fingers of whisky. He was surprised to see two detectives. Shazia had brought DC Mitchell along and there were uniformed officers behind them.

'This is a surprise, especially at this time,' said McLennan. 'Come in out of this deplorable weather. What can I do for you, Inspector? I could offer you a drink but I don't suppose you drink alcohol, but I can give you a soft drink. Some mineral water perhaps?'

Shazia and the others came inside. 'You are correct, I don't touch alcohol. No, thanks. This is not a social call.'

McLennan laughed. 'Not sure I like the sound of that!' He invited them into a large living room where Valerie Farquharson was sitting on the leather sofa clutching a large glass of red wine, her two dogs lying at her feet. Oil paintings of landscapes were hung around the walls and the dark oak furniture gave the room a gloomy atmosphere. The room was dimly lit, the heavy velvet curtains drawn tightly. 'You know Valerie, of course.'

Shazia gave Farquharson a smile and nodded. 'Good evening.'

Farquharson said, 'Angus has been very good to me since Charles passed away. He invited me over for supper.'

'I see,' said Shazia. 'Though, actually, I hoped I would find you here. You weren't at home. It's actually you who we want to speak to, Valerie.'

Farquharson looked flustered. 'I don't understand, Inspector. What do you want to speak to me about? Have you found out who killed Charles?'

'I can't comment on that, that's not why we are here. Mr McLennan, would you leave us alone with Valerie, please.'

The MSP looked puzzled but nodded and began to make his way out of the room.

'No, please stay, Angus,' said Farquharson.

McLennan turned back. 'What the hell is all this about?' he said.

'This concerns the death of Stephen Christie,' said Shazia.

'Who? I don't even know who you are talking about, Inspector,' said Farquharson.

'Where were you on Tuesday night this week at around midnight?'

'Midnight on Tuesday? Why, I would be at home in bed, of course?'

'Is there anyone who could vouch for that?' asked Shazia, looking towards McLennan.

She looked at McLennan. 'Yes,' he said. 'She was with me that night. What is this about?'

Farquharson remained tight-lipped, but her face appeared to have sunk to a shell.

Shazia said, 'We examined Christie's laptop once Forensics managed to unlock it. There was an email he sent you on Monday. Shall I read it out?' She pulled out a piece of paper from her pocket.

Farquharson was silent. She stared at the floor.

Shazia said, 'It reads: *My name is Stephen Christie. My mother was Fiona Christie, your husband's secretary and lover. Yes, I am your husband's son. Before he died your husband told me that it was you who wanted my mother to have an abortion. Not sure how that squares with your so-called "family values"? If I am family, then I deserve a share of my father's estate. I could write my story and sell it to the tabloids. Or, for a fee, I am prepared to say nothing about it or make any legal claim on the estate of my deceased father. I would like to meet you to discuss.* There is also a text on his phone sent to him from an unknown phone the next day telling him to meet outside the Riverside Museum at midnight on Tuesday where he died after apparently being hit by a car. I am arresting you on suspicion of murder. Do you have any comment?'

Farquharson shook her head but she looked lost in thought.

44

When Shazia arrived in HQ, Mitchell greeted her with some news. 'I've been researching Forsyth's background. Seems he used to be a member of the Orange Order. And guess who else is?' She indicated the screen of her computer. 'This is the Orange Order's website. I found this photo in its archives. It's a group photo taken some years ago at a charity function in Cumbernauld. Look at all these orange sashes! Recognise anyone?'

Shazia looked at the photograph. There was a group of about twelve middle-aged men. 'There's Forsyth.'

'That's right. He was a member of the Order at the time. And the two standing next to him? Recognise anyone?'

'Oh, yes. Greg and Paul Murray. That's interesting. You know, this is beginning to make more and more sense, especially after what I found on Forsyth's computer yesterday. I've got a report from Forensics which is very interesting. Let's see what the man himself has to say.'

The businessman seemed to have aged several years. His eyes were bloodshot and his skin, normally healthy and tanned, now looked as tired and wrinkled as a walnut. Forsyth's lawyer was Emily Douglas, a blonde-haired woman in her early forties, immaculately turned out in a two-piece black suit and a crisp white blouse. She contrasted with her dishevelled, unshaven client, and greeted the two detectives with a brisk nod and a handshake. Joseph switched on the recording equipment and Shazia ran through the preliminaries. Forsyth refused to answer any question put to him about the abduction of Shona but, anyway, that was a clear-cut case. She had been found tied up and mutilated in the basement of his property. Then she came to questions about the death of Charles Henderson.

'Did you have Charles Henderson killed?' asked Shazia, deciding that the best strategy was to immediately confront him with the direct question.

Forsyth laughed. 'No. Of course not. Why would I do that?'

'How close a friendship did the two of you really have? On the surface you appeared to be good friends. Maybe you once were, but what drove you to kill him was blackmail.'

'Blackmail? This is ridiculous.'

'Someone had threatened to expose your links to extremists unless you paid up. You believed it was Charles.'

A slight smile crossed Forsyth's lips and he shook his head from side to side. 'This is nonsense.'

'I phoned the restaurant in Edinburgh where you had dinner together. None of the waiters actually heard what you were talking about, but one of them remembered hearing raised voices at your table. I think that Henderson was drunk and the alcohol loosened his tongue. A couple of bottles of expensive claret were drunk that night, but you probably only had one glass as you were driving. I think that Charles probably needed money, he found himself in some serious financial trouble and he appealed to you for help but you refused, is that correct?'

Forsyth said nothing, preferring to stare at the ceiling.

'Is that what you argued about in the restaurant that night?'

Forsyth continued to remain silent.

'Of course, before your lawyer jumps in, I admit that this is speculation, we don't know what you argued about. But what is not speculation is this.'

She produced a clear plastic wallet containing a piece of A4 paper. 'Do you recognise this? This is a print-out of an anonymous email which you were sent on 30th January which recovered from the inbox on your computer. The email arrived not long after that dinner. I'll read it to you. It says, *'**Do you want the public to know about your links to the far-right and your dodgy offshore company based in a tax haven? I want £1million in cash or else the information in the attachment I have sent with this email goes to the press. You have just over a week to get the cash. I will contact you at 9.00 a.m. on Wednesday 8th February to arrange the drop-off at a time later that day. If you follow the instructions your secret is safe. If not, it will go online immediately.***

'Here's what I think happened next. When you received that email and the attached file which showed the links between your company in the Caribbean and a shell company Mercat, linked to a known extremist, you assumed for some reason that it came from Charles. Why, I don't know? Maybe you would care to enlighten us?'

Forsyth simply said, 'No comment.'

'OK. I think that you probably confronted him about it and he denied it. That's when you decided to kill him. The question was, how were you going to do it? Then, when your old friend from the Orange Lodge, Greg Murray, tipped you off that Charles was going to be staying in the Moray Hotel and had booked a prostitute for the evening through his escort agency, you came up with a plan. You considered threatening to expose Charles's predilection for prostitutes to silence him as a counter-threat and you could have arranged to have photographs or even a video taken of the encounter, but instead you decided to have him killed. That would give you more satisfaction and fully terminate the blackmail attempt.'

Forsyth shook his head. 'OK, you've found an email on my computer. It's true I received a threat in an email. That doesn't mean that I thought it was from Charles or that I had him killed. I don't know what you're talking about.' Forsyth smiled. 'I am enjoying this fairy story, Inspector.

You really should think of writing detective fiction and give up the day job.'

'This is certainly mere conjecture now, Inspector,' said his lawyer. 'Pure supposition. My client doesn't need to answer any of these allegations.'

Shazia stared at Forsyth, ignoring his lawyer's remarks. 'Murray had told you that the night porter in that hotel was in the habit of having sex with prostitutes in the hotel during the night. This gave you an idea. A mysterious woman met with the porter and threatened to tell his bosses about this; she had some evidence to prove it, a film. She threatened to reveal what he had been up to if he didn't cooperate. What do you have to say about that?'

Forsyth shrugged his shoulders and looked at his lawyer, then back again at Shazia. 'What's that got to do with me?'

'The night porter identified this mysterious woman. What it has to do with you is that it was your PA, Jennifer Gibson, who was the one who persuaded him to cooperate that night. We found a copy of the film on her phone. There's also a copy on your computer.'

Forsyth was silent. He stared at the wall above Shazia's head.

'I think that you asked her to do this. Then you hired a hit man to carry out the killing of Henderson. The killer got in and out of the hotel through a window on the first floor, the night porter having been threatened to ignore any intrusion and remain silent. You then kidnapped and tortured a reporter to try to get her to tell you who sent her the material when it leaked out after his death. You thought that Charles must have given the material to some lawyer friend of his to release to the press in the event of his death. You wanted to find out who it was. But she didn't tell you, did she? She's a brave woman.'

'No comment,' said Forsyth, leaning back and folding his arms.

45

Shazia still had some unanswered questions. Such as, how did Charles Henderson obtain the information about Cameron Forsyth to use as blackmail against him? Had Henderson employed some kind of private investigator? But not long after she got back to her desk after interviewing Forsyth, she got a phone call telling her that there had been an unexpected development in the Christie case and she instructed a couple of officers to arrest a suspect and bring him through to HQ.

A couple of hours later, Shazia examined the face of Euan Henderson as she entered the interview room and saw him sitting at the table. She was struck by his resemblance to his mother. He was wearing a pale blue rugby shirt with an upturned collar and navy-blue jogging bottoms. His fair hair was dishevelled, but still looked fashionably cut. Beside him sat his solicitor, an overweight middle-aged man with glasses as thick as beer bottles, no doubt from one of Edinburgh's finest family firms and a friend of the family. Shazia introduced herself. 'Euan, we have checked the cameras on the Clyde Expressway on Tuesday night and a white Porsche 911 with your registration was spotted twice, once heading west just before midnight and again a short time later heading back east. What were you doing there that night?'

'No comment,' Euan replied.

Shazia gave him a cold look. 'We were puzzled when the text message sent to Stephen Christie asking him to meet at the Riverside car park turned out not to be from your mother's phone. We haven't been able to trace the phone that it came from yet but I am working on the assumption that it was a Pay as you Go phone bought on the day the text was sent. No doubt it's been disposed of since. What do you know about that?'

Predictably, Euan answered with the customary no comment reply. 'The thing is, we might be able to trace your purchase of a phone through your credit cards. Maybe you paid cash but we could still find out where the message was sent from, though. Might it have been from the vicinity of your flat?' Shazia looked away from Euan's unresponsive face, looked up at the ceiling and sighed. It was obvious that he was taking a vow of silence. She sat back in her chair and looked at him again. 'This is what I think. You mother told you about the email that Stephen Christie sent her. Maybe she wanted to pick your legal brains? I don't know, we'll let the court decide that. But you offered to sort it out for her. Maybe you told her what you did. Or maybe you didn't. You sent Christie a message using a burner phone. That way no one would know it had come from you. And you simply mowed him down as he stood waiting in that car park. Then drove over his body just to make sure he was dead.'

'No comment.'

'We'll see what the forensic examination of your car tells us. You may have had it cleaned but it's amazing what can be missed. Then there are the tyre marks. They were quite clear at the crime scene. Did you know that forensic science can match tyres to tyre marks? No two are the same when you look at their wear and tear. Do you have anything to add to your comments today before I arrest you on suspicion of murder?'

'No comment.'

46

Joseph decided to attend Sammy Scobie's funeral when he heard about it. He felt sorry for the young man, even if he had ruined a lot of lives dispensing drugs around the city. If things had worked out differently, he realised he might have turned out a drug dealer himself on his south London estate. It was a miserable affair, with just a dozen or so mourners gathered in the crematorium in Lambhill on a cold clear day. There had been frost on the ground that morning but Joseph noticed that snowdrops had appeared on the grass at the edge of the crematorium car park. It was a good sign, a harbinger of spring, he thought, new life returning. A minister said a few words about Sammy, how he had enjoyed football and had once been a promising footballer himself, his love of Rangers FC and music. His favourite track, *Movin' on Up* by Primal Scream was played, rather movingly, thought Joseph, at the end of the brief service.

Joseph sat at the back of the building and was the last to leave, shaking hands with Scobie's grandparents and offering his commiserations and condolences. Outside, he was walking towards his car when he felt a tap on the shoulder. He turned round to face a young man wearing a black coat and black shirt. 'Glad you came,' said the young man. Joseph recognised the voice but not the face, then realised it was the mysterious young man from Glasgow Green. He was a pale-skinned man in his early twenties, with cropped dark hair and brown eyes.

'Do you need a lift anywhere?' said Joseph.

'That would be great. Can you drop me off anywhere near the Royal Infirmary? Everyone here is heading to a pub in Maryhill but I don't feel like going.'

Inside the car the young man introduced himself. 'I'm Tommy.' Joseph nodded, remembering the story that Angela had told about Sammy and Tommy "up the toon".

'I'm Joseph,' said Joseph, extending his hand.

The young man shook his hand, 'Tommy Murphy. Have you caught the bastard that killed Sammy?'

'No', said Joseph. 'We've got someone in custody who is a suspect. But we need some more evidence to be sure of a conviction. What can you tell us, Tommy?'

'Sorry about all that cloak and dagger stuff on the Green, and scarpering when I saw those cops in uniform. I got spooked.'

'They didn't have anything to do with me. It was just a coincidence they appeared.'

'OK, I believe you. But I didn't want picked up as I knew my prints would be all over Sammy's flat. I hadn't been there for a week but I knew he wasn't great on cleaning and I would then be in the frame for his murder. But it wasn't me. I'm a nurse in the Royal Infirmary and I do shifts. I'm working tonight actually and I was supposed to be on night shift that night, but I phoned in sick so spent the night on my own and had no alibi. I heard about it in the morning.' Tommy took a deep breath and sighed, turning to stare out of the window, then round to look behind. When he was ready, he opened up. 'Sammy had been in gangs all his life, you know, ducking and diving. And he got involved with a gang when he was last in jail. He told me he met this guy Jack there who was involved with some loyalist outfit. So, Jack offered him protection inside prison and for Sammy it was like finding a family, people who cared about him. He'd never had much of that with what happened to his mum and that. Then, when he got out of prison, Jack lent him money to get on his feet. Sammy wanted to go straight but Jack wanted him to deal, cannabis and heroin in the local scheme and cocaine in the city centre. Jack gave him a phone to use, a burner. He said delivering a line became like delivering a pizza – someone sent him a text and he was on his way. But he took too much of his own gear.'

'Why was he killed, Tommy?' asked Joseph. 'Did he owe money?'

Murphy shook his head. 'No. He'd more than paid back what he had been loaned. But Jack told him he wanted him to do some stuff for this Scottish Action mob. He was told it was payback for protection and security in jail. Sammy said he didn't want to do it but didn't have a choice. He said they forced him to help them in some attacks on immigrants, asylum seekers and that, stealing cars and driving.' Murphy hesitated for a moment. 'But, see, Sammy had a secret. He was gay, like me, but he had to keep it secret 'cos of these loyalists he had got involved with; they would go fucking mental if they found out, he said. Bunch of homophobes! We met in a club in town one night and I went home with him. He said it was different from anything he'd felt before and he didn't care that I had been brought up a Catholic. We started seeing each other a lot. He told me it was the first time he had ever been in love. Anyway, apparently Jack saw us together, I don't know how. Sammy said this guy Jack drove a cab, so maybe he spotted us in the street one night. I guess we were careless. Maybe we were holding hands or kissing.

'So, a couple of weeks ago, when Jack asked Sammy to do another job, Sammy refused, said he wanted out. Jack told Sammy he knew he was gay, said he had guessed as much when they were inside together. Jack offered him a deal. He told him no one else in Scottish Action would know he was gay if he did what he wanted him to do, this one last job. If he didn't, then Jack told him his life wouldn't be worth living, and he knew it. Most of that mob are bigots and they all hate gays as much as Catholics or Muslims. Sammy knew they would turn on him.'

'And what did they want him to do?'

'To help him and some other guy called Andy break in to a hotel on the Monday night,' Murphy said. 'He wanted Sammy to steal a car and be the getaway driver. But Sammy phoned me that night and told me he'd said he wouldn't do it; he'd had enough, he didn't want to be involved. He talked about running away, heading down south, somewhere like Brighton, where they wouldn't find him. The next thing I knew it was Sunday morning and he was dead. I was scared stiff they would be after me next if I went public with what I knew. I still am, but now, being at Sammy's funeral and everything, what happened has sunk in. I just feel so fucking angry with the bastard that killed him.'

Joseph stopped the car on Castle Street. A woman was walking past with a small dog on a lead. A French bulldog. Joseph thought it was the ugliest dog he had ever seen. For some reason, probably to do with digital celebrity culture. he had noticed the popularity of these dogs. They seemed to be appearing everywhere. He turned to Murphy. 'I can drop you here, Tommy, but what you have to say is really important. It's vital that it's used as evidence against the man who killed Sammy. Can you come to the station and provide a statement?'

Murphy gazed out of the windscreen and Joseph thought he was just going to open the car door and disappear again as he had done before but he then nodded. 'I'm going to see my mum. She's in hospital, here. But I'll come to the station later. OK?' He opened the car door and walked off up Castle Street.

Suddenly a blue BMW swerved around Joseph's car and stopped in front, next to Murphy. A sawn-off shotgun emerged from the passenger side and fired a shot, then the car drove off at high speed through a red light. Joseph saw that Murphy had collapsed to the pavement, and rushed out.

He knelt beside him, getting out his phone and calling for an ambulance, and police to chase the car, giving the registration of the BMW. He then threw his jacket over his chest and pressed down to try and stop the bleeding.

'Tommy, Tommy, listen to me, you're going to be OK. You're going to be OK.'

47

Alex arrived at Police HQ. Shazia had phoned him and asked him to come to the station at three o'clock. He was accompanied by Catriona Sellars, Jamie McEwan's partner in his legal firm. Shazia had phoned Alex and asked to meet him to answer some questions. 'You may wish to have legal representation,' she added mysteriously. Why did the inspector advise him to have a solicitor with him, he wondered?

Alex couldn't erase the mental images of that night from his brain. He had thought he was going to die until he heard those noises and then the deafening blast of gunfire. The gunman in the basement, who he now knew was Campbell but hadn't recognised, had tried to shoot his way up the stairs but was heavily outgunned and Alex remembered seeing him tumble backwards down the stairs like a skittle knocked over in a bowling alley, and the gaping bloody hole in his skull which a bullet had opened up as if it was a piece of ripe fruit struck with a hammer. The police who then stormed down the stairs amongst the clouds of choking smoke from the explosion made him think of storm troopers from an episode of Star Wars, in their full body armour and helmets with visors. The officers stepped over the victim's bleeding body with guns raised and Forsyth and Thompson raised their arms meekly in surrender.

He got to the police station by train after going into the city centre in the morning to do some shopping. He needed warmer clothes. After buying a few things, he nipped into the Horseshoe for a pint and some lunch. He had spent the last couple of nights at Shona and Jamie's flat, sleeping on the couch as he realised that Jamie needed the company, and he did too. The room in the West End he'd rented was now ready for immediate entry, but he wasn't in any rush to move in and be on his own. Shona was due to be let out of hospital sometime, so it could probably wait until then. He and Jamie had bonded during the last few days after what they had both been through together, but as soon as Shona came home, he would leave them in peace.

He sat in the pub watching the other customers while scanning news websites on his phone. Reports of the raid on the house in Arran and the arrest of Forsyth were still dominating the media. There were photographs of Shona, Jamie and himself, as well as Forsyth, Campbell and Thompson in the reports. The pub was busy with shoppers and Alex felt conspicuous. A few customers were giving him looks that showed that they recognised him. One woman holding a newspaper was talking to a man and pointing at him. He suddenly realised, guiltily, that he should contact Suzanne in Australia. She would probably have recognised his face from the news and he owed her an explanation at the very least. He tapped her number into his phone, realising that it would be late evening over there.

'John?' she said sounding surprised. 'Or should I say, Alex, you lying Pommy bastard! Just seen your ugly mug on the telly.' She sounded like she had been drinking; she might even still be in the pub.

'I can explain…,' he started to say but she cut him off with some choice Aussie expletives and then hung up.

Joseph had arrived at the station earlier, after following the ambulance the short distance to Accident and Emergency only to discover that Murphy had died on the way. His heart had gone into cardiac arrest and he was unable to be resuscitated. The shotgun blast had destroyed his chest and lungs. When Joseph told Shazia about the shooting, she couldn't believe it. 'This city is turning into the wild west,' she said. The vehicle with the shooter had disappeared but she had sent a team of officers out to the scene to interview potential witnesses. It was now four o' clock and she realised that she had forgotten about Mancini and his solicitor. She went through to reception and apologised for the delay, then guided them towards an interview room.

'So, Alex, you and Jamie were trying to be heroes, eh?' asked Shazia. 'Have you watched too many action movies?'

Alex laughed. Sellars remained tight-lipped. She sat with a pen poised above a notepad. Alex nodded. 'I guess so. Lucky you were there to rescue me. Thanks.'

'How did you know Shona was definitely in that house?'

'I remembered seeing the van when I left the flat the day before.'

'OK. Then, though, there is the matter of the gun.'

'The gun? What gun?'

Shazia grinned. 'Yes. Mr Forsyth alleges that when you and Mr McEwan arrived in his house after breaking in through the conservatory, you were in possession of a gun. This gun in fact.' Shazia produced a photograph of the gun from the papers on the table. 'A Walther PPQ.'

'Well, he is clearly lying, Inspector. He and his friends were the ones who were armed as you well know from the shoot-out that night.'

'I don't dispute that, Alex. But he denies all knowledge of this gun and says you brought it there. What I want to know is, where did it come from?'

'I have no idea. You will need to ask him again, Inspector.'

'I'm going to have to take your fingerprints. So, if your fingerprints are on the gun, what would you say?'

'I'd say that I found it when we came into the house and picked it up for protection. Look, that night was crazy, I might have picked it up, I don't know.'

'This gun was fired that night. A bullet fired from it wounded one of the men in the house. What do you know about that?'

Alex smiled. 'There were a lot of bullets flying around that night, Inspector. The night is a complete blur.'

'What you did going in there was extremely foolish. You could have got yourself killed! You know that. But I'd like to know where you got the gun from?'

'As I said before, Inspector. I don't know where it came from. It wasn't mine.'

After the interview was concluded, Alex declined Sellars's offer of a lift and got the train back into the city centre. He needed time on his own to think. He found himself in Buchanan Street. It was only early evening but already some rough sleepers were settling down into sleeping bags outside the luxury goods and designer shops that ran the length of the street, their windows packed with designer clothes, shoes and handbags. One man was propped up with his hand out begging and muttering something incoherently to himself. Alex went over to him and placed a ten-pound note in his hand. The man stared at it and then up at Alex, his mouth wide open in disbelief before muttering, 'Thanks, mister.'

He thought of the disparity between the ostentatious wealth displayed in the windows of these designer stores, and the despair and misfortune etched on the faces of the poor unfortunates camping for the night outside their premises. He remembered that Buchanan Street was named after an eighteenth-century tobacco merchant and slave owner, Andrew Buchanan. Glasgow's wealthy elite had grown rich on the backs of slaves. It was a history of shame and there was a long way to go before this newly independent Scotland was a fair and equal country. Maybe they had all been naïve thinking that independence would lead to a brave new world. Forsyth was just one of those who wanted to push an ideology of hatred and fear to further their self-interest; there were others out there, both within Scotland and outside it, who had vested interests to defend, and they would not give them up easily. They had rich and powerful allies across the globe, hiding their wealth in tax-free locations; they had control of multinational corporations, and they held the levers of modern technology to manipulate public opinion. It was so easy to despair.

But Alex recalled the sentiment of the bard of Ayrshire, as he strode up the street: that we were all brothers together. He realised he was an idealist. Time had told him that about himself. But he would rather be like that than a cynic or a reactionary. He walked on and reflected on his meeting with the police detective. Would she continue to investigate him, question him about the gun? Would they do forensic firing tests on it and link it with an unsolved crime, a murder even? God knows what Kelly had previously used the weapon for. If he mentioned that he got it from Kelly, then Kelly would go after him as a grass. Or was he just being paranoid? The conversation with Shazia had unsettled him. He needed a drink. He headed up Buchanan Street in the direction of the subway station. A tube train from there would see him at Hillhead in no time. He sent Jamie a text: *'Fancy a pint?'* A reply came back instantly: *'The Chip in half an hour. Your round, ya bawbag!'*

48

Shazia was standing facing Mitchell and Joseph in front of a board displaying photos of the six who had died: Scobie, Henderson, Robertson, Christie, Campbell and Murphy. The BMW, from which the shot was fired at Murphy, was found later in a cemetery in the East End, abandoned and burnt-out. Predictably it had been stolen the previous evening. The killers had clearly been keeping an eye on Murphy, knowing he would attend the funeral, and seeing him with Joseph was his death sentence. 'Forensics have positively identified blood found in the back of the black VW van recovered outside Forsyth's house in Arran as belonging to David Robertson,' she said. 'The van was registered to Campbell and had both his and Thompson's fingerprints all over it. A Glock 40, found in the house on Arran, could have been the weapon used to shoot Robertson. Of course, it's unregistered, but my guess is it belonged to either Campbell or Thompson. We'll interview Thompson today but he's likely to say nothing. Chances are it was the two of them who abducted and killed Robertson, just the same as they abducted Shona. Except she was lucky and survived, unlike Robertson who ended up in the canal with a bullet through his head.'

'Campbell and Thompson were obviously ordered to kill Robertson. Who by?' asked Mitchell.

'Thompson worked for Murray. I'm still convinced he is behind the escort agency, though proving it is another thing. But he would have wanted to have Robertson silenced in case he grassed and revealed him as the true owner. He's most likely behind the murder of Murphy too. Have we got any leads on who the driver and the shooter were?'

'No ma'am,' said Joseph. 'Forensics on the BMW looks like being a non-starter seeing it was practically destroyed.'

'OK. Anyway, something else interesting has come up.'

'What?' he said.

'Our IT technical team have located the IP address where the blackmail email came from that Forsyth was sent.'

'Oh really?' said Joseph. 'Was it from Henderson then?'

Shazia smiled. 'It was *a* Henderson. Not Charles, though. Euan.'

'Euan?' said Mitchell and Joseph in one voice.

'Yes. So, I've sent round some officers to Euan Henderson's flat to get hold of his laptop. Let's see what comes of it. Meanwhile, who wants to come with me to speak to Jackson? I've arranged to have a word with him.'

Robert Jackson was seated in an interview room in Barlinnie. He sauntered into the room looking relaxed and at ease, along with two prison guards. 'Why do you keep questioning me?' he said, staring at Shazia and Joseph. 'I've told you lot everything. I'm only a taxi driver, that's all.'

'The murders of Scobie and Henderson are linked,' said Shazia 'And you were involved in both of them. With Andrew Campbell. We now have more information linking you to the death of Scobie. You wanted him to be the getaway driver for the night of the attack on Henderson and he refused and you killed him, that's what happened, isn't it?'

Jackson shook his head. 'No comment,' he said. He thought back to that night. When he last saw Scobie, he had been out of his head, smashed on a combination of what he had been snorting and smoking. Scobie had even told him to fuck off, saying he wouldn't do the hotel job. Jackson had managed to contain himself but after he had come back down from Scobie's flat, he had phoned Campbell and told him everything he knew about Scobie, how he wanted out, how he didn't want to be involved in the job on the hotel and, crucially, that he was gay. That last fact was, he knew, Scobie's death sentence, and Campbell, who professed to hate all gays, had gone mental, as Jackson knew he would, and gone round to Scobie's flat in the early hours, kicked the door in and sent the young guy flying through the air to his death. Campbell had taken great delight in telling him all about it on the night of the attack on Henderson. 'No witnesses,' Campbell had said, laughing. 'There wasn't a soul in sight. I'm sure someone heard me kick the door in but they were all probably shitting themselves.'

'We also have the confession from Katarina Marková that she stole the room's keycard and gave it to you. Unfortunately for you, there is more evidence linking you to Henderson's murder. We recovered a phone in the possession of Andrew Campbell. It's shown us that there was contact between him and Forsyth. That's not surprising, but it also shows contact with your number on the nights of both murders. Coincidence? I don't think so. There's also a WhatsApp message sent by Campbell to you on Sunday 5th February which you must have deleted on your phone but which was still on his. It reads: *Need to be at hotel between 3 and 4.* You replied *OK.'*

Jackson looked uncomfortable all of a sudden, a vein throbbing in his forehead and sweat appearing on his upper lip. He scratched his neck and turned to look at his solicitor.

'Also, your alibi, Robert, was that you stayed the night with Nicola, that's right, isn't it?' said Shazia. So, we had a look at her credit card records and the CCTV that night. Do you want to know what we found? The card records led us to a car hire company in South Street where she hired a black Ford Focus on Monday 6th February. The car is captured on CCTV heading into the Clyde Tunnel at 02.19 on the morning of 7th February. It is spotted again heading northbound from the tunnel just after 04:23. Interestingly, Campbell lived in Govan, on the other side of the tunnel. I suspect that you went to pick up Campbell at his flat and then dropped him off again later. Am I right?'

Jackson no longer resembled the cocky, arrogant figure he had been at the start of the interview. Even his responses were now mumbled. 'No comment.'

Shazia continued: 'Here is what I think happened. I think Nicola parked the car at the bottom of one of the lanes running down from the hotel. You and Campbell approached the hotel by the rear lanes on foot, avoiding any CCTV cameras in the area, a pair of shadows, and broke in through the first-floor window at the side of the hotel. The two of you entered the room using the stolen keycard and killed Henderson, one of you holding him down while the other suffocated him. You then replaced Henderson's own keycard on the coffee table from where Katarina had picked it up earlier. Afterwards, you both left the building the same way you entered and retraced your route through the lanes to be picked up by your girlfriend, who drove back to Govan and then onto Knightswood. You were sure that you had got away with it, weren't you? Until now.'

'You've got it all wrong,' said Jackson.

'I expected you to say that,' said Shazia.

'I mean, it wasn't Nicky who was driving.'

'What?'

'It wasn't Nicky. It was me. I was the driver. I made her hire the car in her name. I drove the car that night but I didn't kill Henderson. It was just Andy who went into the hotel. He told me it was just a break-in, a robbery. I didn't know he was planning to kill someone. I just drove him there and waited outside.'

Shazia laughed. 'You expect me to believe that? All you've done is tell us lies. First, you said you had nothing to do with it, now you blame the dead guy and say you thought it was a robbery. It's just a pack of lies from start to finish, isn't it?'

'I'm not saying anything else, just leave Nicky out of it. She had nothing to do with it.' Jackson sat back, sighed, and thought back to that night. After they had failed to persuade Scobie to steal a car, he had asked Nicky to hire a car. That was his mistake and he cursed himself for it. If only he'd gone out and nicked a car himself. He'd driven the hire car to Andy's flat where he'd picked him up, then driven to a lane at the back of the hotel. Andy had put on his gloves and gone into the hotel while he waited in the car. There had to be someone in the car in case it was spotted and had to be moved. That was what they had wanted Scobie for. That and the fact he was good at nicking cars. Iain would have joined them but he was in Spain with his girlfriend. Andy told him to get Nicky to drive but there was no way he would have let Nicky be the driver so Andy had said he would do the job on his own if he drove.

'Next thing, you will be telling us that Campbell killed Scobie too,' said Shazia.

49

Forensics eventually managed to unlock Euan Henderson's laptop. They found access to an email account and recovered some documents buried in the system which were forwarded to Shazia. She handed Joseph a copy of the email. Joseph read it while Shazia looked out of the window. She was watching a fox sauntering across the street in broad daylight, looking as if it hadn't a care in the world. What would it be like to be a fox, she thought? Hungry, scavenging for food. Joseph suddenly spoke, disturbing her reverie. 'It's the same email. So, it *was* Euan who hacked into Forsyth's accounts and blackmailed him,' he said.

Shazia turned around and looked at Joseph. 'Yes. They were identical to those found on Forsyth's computer. What Forsyth got wrong was thinking that when he had Charles killed, he had killed the blackmailer. Euan must have used his computer skills to hack into Forsyth's computer and found the connection to a law firm in the Caribbean and hacked that too. He evidently decided to use what he had found out about Forsyth to extort money out of him. Euan emailed it on the 30th January using his own laptop, hence the IP address. He figured out a way to use the dark web to get a fake email account which made it virtually untraceable. Henderson was found dead on the 7th of February, the day before the supposed drop-off. Remember, Euan was going skiing for a week from the 31st to the 7th, that's why he gave him a week before he wanted to collect the money on the 8th.'

Joseph nodded. 'Then Forsyth would have thought that the blackmailer, Charles, was dead and so wouldn't have done anything.'

'Exactly. And when Charles was killed, Euan would have known that Forsyth was behind it but he couldn't say anything without revealing his own blackmail scheme. Then that information about Forsyth's links to the far-right appeared in the press.'

'Did he release that to the newspaper, do you think?' asked Mitchell.

Shazia nodded. 'Most likely. One way or another. Euan got cold feet about continuing to blackmail Forsyth after what happened to his father. He didn't want to end up dead as well. But he did want revenge.'

'So, do you think the two of them were in on the blackmail together, father and son?'

'I don't know. If they were, Euan may have given his father a copy of what he had found out but we didn't find anything like that when we searched his home. But remember that Euan had already been there the previous day to visit his mother and he'd also been in his father's flat. I'll phone his solicitor and tell him what we've found, though I don't think we'll get much out of Mr No Comment!'

But she was wrong. The message from Euan Henderson's solicitor that afternoon was that the young man wanted to cooperate. In the interview room, Euan Henderson rubbed his face with his hands and sighed. The young man looked pale and nervous. 'Dad had made an overseas investment that went wrong. He invested in a scheme in the Brazilian rainforest, but it turned out to be an absolute scam, and he lost a million that he had stashed away in an offshore account in my name. He blamed Cameron as he had introduced him to the investment manager who persuaded him to make the investment. Anyway, dad thought Cameron had ripped him off and he wanted him to refund him. When Cameron made it clear he wouldn't be giving him any money back, dad asked me if I could find any dirt on Cameron. He promised me fifty percent of the money. Then, when I had found out proof that he was funding a right-wing mob, we sent him an email. I didn't think it would lead to dad's death.'

'And several other deaths. What about Stephen Christie?' asked Shazia.

Henderson bit his lip. 'Mum showed me the email she got. I just got so angry. Dad had died and here was this shit trying to extort money out of us. I just felt our family was under attack. I told mum I would deal with it. She didn't know anything about what I did. But I only drove through to speak to him and warn him off – not to kill him. When I turned into the car park, he suddenly just stepped right out in front of me. I couldn't stop. It was an accident.'

Shazia shook her head. 'No, I don't buy that, Euan. Not only did you knock him down, you drove over him. The tyre marks on his body match your car's. The jury might still give you the benefit of the doubt that it was an accident, were it not for the fact that CCTV picked up your car on the Expressway the night before, no doubt on your way to find a suitably isolated spot for the meeting with him. Try to talk your way out of that coincidence!'

*

They had unravelled the mystery behind the murder of Charles Henderson and Jackson had made a partial confession of his involvement and, if what Jackson said was true, Henderson's actual killer, Campbell, was dead. All the evidence led to Forsyth being behind it, with Gibson as an accomplice. But Shazia was still left with a feeling of frustration: as far as finding Scobie's killer went, all they really had was the word of a dead witness that Jackson had threatened him. A successful prosecution against Jackson for Scobie's death was not a foregone conclusion. And tying Greg Murray into any of this seemed like a long way off. She knew that life was very different from fiction. Not every case got solved the way that the TV detectives managed it.

50

It was a month after the raid on the house in Arran. For the first few days after the events, when she was in hospital, post-surgery, Shona felt dazed and bewildered, a combination of what she had been through and the medication. There was still a fair amount of adrenaline, too, surging through her every time she recalled what had happened. At first, she felt high, as if she was floating somewhere in space. Everything seemed unreal. Then she crashed to earth like an asteroid and sank into a hole. Depression.

When the doctors decided that she had recovered enough to be allowed to leave the hospital, Jamie had brought her home as a passenger in her own little red Mini. She knew that he had brought it to the hospital to try to cheer her up, but her smile when she saw it was forced and she knew that he knew it. She had been ordered to rest. Four weeks later she was still resting. Rest. Rest. Rest. She felt like she had turned into a zombie and was gripped by a fear that she might spend the rest of her life like that. There was no way out, it seemed. There was a knot constantly in her stomach and she didn't want to eat, had lost all sense of taste. She hardly slept. Maybe it was the SSRIs her doctor had put her on. 'Depression and anxiety caused by post-traumatic stress disorder,' he said, writing out the prescription. Her libido had disappeared and she didn't find anything that interested her enough to pay it more than a couple of minutes of attention: not books, not magazines, not TV.

Then, when she did sleep, there were the dreams. Or, rather, nightmares. In one, she was locked in a basement.

That basement. Except this time the floor was covered in water. And it was rising. It rose and rose until she was standing on tiptoe on a chair with her nose to the ceiling, trying to inhale the last drop of air before the rising water swallowed her. She would wake up, sweating. Shaking. She was a wreck. God knows when she would ever get her life back. The future seemed like a long endless white corridor stretching in front of her, leading nowhere.

She snuggled back under the duvet and closed her eyes. But she didn't want to sleep. She tried to think of something nice. But her thoughts were nowhere to be found. Her mind was like a vacuum. Christ, what will become of me, she thought? She heard the front door open and close. That would be Jamie home. It must be evening already, she thought. Where had the day gone? It was Friday, the start of the weekend but for her that meant nothing. She used to so look forward to a Friday evening. But now it was like every other one. Pointless.

The bedroom door opened. She looked up as Jamie walked into the room. He smiled. 'Hi,' he said. She didn't feel like smiling back. She felt stupid and selfish. She hated herself. He was carrying a large box. 'I've brought you something. Close your eyes.' There was some sort of strange noise coming from inside the box. She shut her eyes. 'Hold out your hand,' he said. She held out her left hand. The finger on the right hand was healing well but there was still a bandage covering it. She felt him take her hand very gently. Then she felt something soft and smooth moving below her fingertips. She opened her eyes and looked up. The small face of a little puppy stared at her excitedly, trying to lick her fingers. Its tail wagged furiously as she stroked its soft dark fur, and she felt something change inside herself. 'He's a cockapoo,' he said. 'I thought we'd call him Fergus.'

She felt herself smile for the first time in weeks. It was as if a block of ice in her stomach had finally started to melt. 'He's beautiful,' she said.

ACKNOWLEDGEMENTS

Thanks to Maureen as always who took the time to read various drafts and for all her support and advice. Thanks to my son Jonny for some great political ideas. Thanks also to Matthew Harding who gave me helpful feedback on a draft. Thanks to my eagle-eyed editor Karen Ankers for all her amazing editing skills. Any errors are entirely my own.

Printed in Great Britain
by Amazon